QUEEN OF STATIC

PRAISE FOR *KING OF SHARDS*

"A robustly imagined fantasy world... pleasingly unpredictable. His skill at extrapolating traditional religious lore into the stuff of fantasy bodes well for future books in the series."

—*Publishers Weekly*

"In this prismatic tale of demons, righteous warriors, and multiple universes, Kressel plumbs the depths of Kabbalistic lore to create a unique fantasy cosmos... [An] engaging new epic fantasy."

—*The Huffington Post*

"With surprising twists and a deep and detailed universe, *King of Shards*, the first in a trilogy, is likely to be remembered."

—*Barnes & Noble, Sci-Fi and Fantasy Blog*

"A gripping trek across a unique desert world rich with Kabbalah-inspired magic and vivid demons builds to a whirlwind climax."

—Scott H. Andrews, seven-time World Fantasy Award-nominated editor of

—*Beneath Ceaseless Skies Magazine*

"Kressel's rich landscapes sing with ancient resonance by the light of modern flair. He weaves compelling tradition with innovative high Fantasy; culture and creativity become foundations for new myths featuring heroes built to shine."

—Leanna Renee Hieber, award-winning author of the *Strangely Beautiful* saga

"With *King of Shards*, Kressel threads portal adventure through ancient mythos. His demons and demi-gods and his very human (or mostly human) characters have to work their way through the terrifying, violent, and often beautiful alternate planes he's built using his incredible imagination and traditional and Apocryphal knowledge as a tableau. You will emerge transformed."

—Fran Wilde, Nebula Award-winning author of *Updraft*

"[A] fascinating first novel...King of Shards is the first entry of the Worldmender Trilogy, and its use of Hebrew culture and legend to build a complex, dynamic setting serves to imbue every page with an epic mythos. Kressel presents a compelling alternate reality that readers can escape to while also pondering the nature of what is real."

—*Shelf Awareness*

QUEEN OF STATIC

BOOK TWO OF THE **WORLDMENDER** TRILOGY

MATTHEW KRESSEL

SENSES FIVE

Also by Matthew Kressel
King of Shards

"The Sounds of Old Earth"
2013 Short Story Nebula Award Finalist

"The Meeker and the All-Seeing Eye"
2014 Short Story Nebula Award Finalist

"The Last Novelist (Or a Dead Lizard in the Yard)"
2017 Short Story Nebula Award Finalist

And dozens more short stories. For more, visit: WWW.MATTHEWKRESSEL.NET

This is QOS1, and it has an ISBN of 978-0-9796246-3-6.

Published by:
Senses Five Press
Ridgewood, NY, USA
www.sensesfive.com

Cover Art: Leon Tukker
Edited by: Darrin Bradley

Es per-shemp Bedu.

SENSES FIVE

For Christine
My Rock, My Sun

QUEEN OF STATIC

"Pastorello, sei soggetto
Facilmente a t'ingannare.
Bella rosa porporina
Oggi Silvia sceglierà,
Con la scusa della spina
Doman poi la sprezzerà.
Ma degli uomini il consiglio
Io per me non seguirò.
Non perchè mi piace il giglio
Gli altri fiori sprezzerò."

"Little shepherd, you are subject
Easily to deceive yourself.
The beautiful purple rose
Will Silvia choose today;
With the excuse of its thorns,
Tomorrow, then, will she despise it.
But the council of men
I will not follow.
Just because the lily pleases me,
I'll not despise the other flowers."

—"Se Tu M'ami" – Paolo Antonio Rolli

"Ours is not the first universe. There were others that came before. But they were imperfect, so God destroyed them. Their shattered husks lay scattered about the realms of darkness like potsherds in a field. Our sins cling to them and give them power, and these husks are the root of all evil in this world."

—Isaac Luria, 16th century rabbi and founder of modern Kabbalah, as recounted by a disciple

"Those shattered universes? They were *not* empty. Creatures lived on them, beings with bodies and minds and hearts and souls. I was born on the very first world to be, and I was there when the Creator smashed our world and cast us into the Abyss. Only a few of us survived the Shattering. We clung to this tumbling fragment and built ourselves a home here. We called it Sheol, and we vowed one day to reclaim that which was stolen from us, our birthright, the only thing we have ever sought: *Life.*"

—Abbadon, first king of demonkind, from his text,
Great Abbadon's Promise

CHAPTER ONE

THE HALF-DEAD MAN WAITED FOR THE LAST RAYS OF SUN TO fall beneath the jungle canopy before he set out for the monastery. The one-eyed villager had told him the way over bitter tea and proud stories of his children. And the half-dead man had understood his dialect of Thai as easily as he understood Igbo and Uzbek, Swedish and Uyghur, Portuguese and English and all the myriad languages of humanity and its seven billion personal variants. Night fell quickly in the jungle, and the mesh and tangle of leaves blocked all but the most tireless stars, which shone as bright as polished diamonds. He saw by their feeble light, his eyes attuned to the darkness like the deadliest of nocturnal predators. Hunger stirred in his stomach, a lingering chronic disease, reminding him of the flesh he hadn't eaten. No beef nor deer nor lamb nor bison nor any animal could ever satisfy this craving, only the flesh of a dead person. But despite this ever-present craving, which often rose to fever pitch, the half-dead man had never tasted human flesh. He had sworn he never would.

Big cats that feared no creature caught scent of him and scampered away; he heard the patter of their stealthy retreat. Mosquitoes buzzed his ears, caught a whiff of his sweat, and darted off for less-toxic blood. Only jungle water touched him, dripping from ten thousand leaves, soaked and laden from recent rain. Mud covered him to his knees, and he stank of sweat, mildew, and earth.

He'd lost the trail hours ago. Weeks of heavy rain had washed it away. The one-eyed villager had said few came this far, especially at night, and the monks who lived at the monastery preferred the remote solitude. Without a trail to guide him, the half-dead man followed the scent of incense drifting on the wind, like a predator stalking his prey.

At last he saw it. The monastery's halo glowed ghost-like beyond the tangle of leaves. A few scattered lanterns around the well-tended gardens tossed flickering light onto a row of golden Buddhas and ornate temples. The smell of incense and sweat was thick in the humid air, magnified by the curse seething in his blood.

The Milky Way tore a white strip across the sky above as he emerged from the jungle. A bespectacled monk in a tight-wrapped orange robe approached him. "Are you lost?" the monk said in English.

"I hope not," the half-dead man replied in perfect Thai. "I'm looking for someone. A monk named Pandate."

The monk studied him calmly for a moment. "You're not the first to come for him."

"But hopefully the last. Can you take me to him?"

The monk swiveled on his heel and walked toward one of the gilded temples, and Daniel followed. The temple's steeply sloped roof glinted in the lantern light, its facade a masterwork of intricate design. In the unsteady light the walls seemed to squirm.

"First," the monk said, "remove your shoes. This is a holy place."

The half-dead man slipped off his muddy shoes and rolled up his pants. Barefoot, he followed the monk inside. The interior was small, its walls covered in gold and crimson filigree. Monks sat cross-legged on the floor, hands in laps, palms upturned. Eyes closed, they didn't stir as the two walked across the groaning wooden floor. A giant jade and bronze Buddha, bedecked in crimson and gold, gleamed at the far end, the centerpiece of a shrine. Sticks of burning incense perfumed the air. The monk approached the statue, pressed his palms together and said, "May all sentient beings be free from suffering."

The half-dead man repeated the monk's words and mirrored the Namaste gesture.

"First, give," the monk said. "Then I'll take you to Pandate." He gestured to a wooden bowl beneath the statue.

"I'm sorry. All of my belongings were stolen back in Phuket. I have no money."

"Money is delusion. What else can you give?"

"I have only what I'm wearing. And my shoes I just took off."

The monk stared. "What use do we have for old shirts and muddy shoes, when all is samsara? What can you give to help free humanity from the cycle of birth and death?"

"I'm here to save a person's life," the half-dead man said. "Is that not enough?"

The monk's brown eyes, fixed on the half-dead man, were bright and steady. He suddenly turned on his heel and slipped through a narrow door at the rear of the temple.

The half-dead man followed. "Wait!" he said. "Will you take me to Pandate or not?"

The monk sped onto a narrow path that wound into the thick jungle. Wet leaves slapped his face as the half-dead man chased after the surprisingly spry monk. A bright lantern shone ahead in the tangle of leaves and sent sharp yellow beams into the mist. The man chased the monk, spiraling around the lamp, closing in on the light with each revolution as if he were a comet on a decaying orbit, spraying off water as he went. When at last he reached the lamp, he was out of breath.

A small natural pool lay in the center of a clearing, and the still waters reflected countless stars. The monk faced him, his shadow a black monolith reaching deep into the jungle. "I am the one you seek," the monk said. "I am Pandate Romsaitong. And you are not the first to come for me."

"How did you know I was coming? I told no one."

"I had a dream a *preta* came from the underworld to fetch me. There was no moon, and the stars of the Milky Way reflected brightly in this pool as I stood talking to the hungry ghost, as we are now."

"I've been to *one* underworld, a place called Gehinnom. But I'm from Earth. And I'm always hungry, but I'm no ghost."

"But not quite a man, either."

The half-dead man paused. On the Shard called Gehinnom he had been force fed the tongue of a Mikulal, a Cursed Man, and now that curse seethed in his blood too. He would have to eat the flesh of a dead person for the curse to quicken and become permanent, which he had not – *would not* ever do. But as his hunger grew so did his doubts. "My name's Daniel Fisher," he said, "and I've come to save you."

"To save *me*?" Pandate said. "From what? From whom? There is no self that needs saving."

"There is no time, Pandate, so I'll just get right to it. Demons are coming. They want to use you to destroy the earth and strengthen the realms of hell."

"And what about you? This *preta*, who emerges from the shadows like a hungry cat."

"I'm here to help you."

"And yet you don't know a damned thing about me."

"I know you're a Buddhist monk who used to work for a multinational investment bank in Bangkok. I know you grew disillusioned with that life and devoted yourself to the practice of Buddhism. When not meditating on the nature of mind you deliver food to rural villages, or work long hours in the fields. You arrange delivery of medicines and medical care. You've set up a dozen schools for local children. Twice a month you volunteer your time teaching math, science, and English. Some say you don't sleep, ever."

Pandate blinked. "You know a lot about me," he said. "And I know little of you. Who is Daniel Fisher?"

"Mostly, like you said, I'm a hungry ghost."

"Who's not really a ghost."

"But always hungry." Even now the urge for dead human flesh gnawed at his belly. "Have you heard of the story of the Thirty-Six Hidden Righteous?" he said.

Pandate shook his head.

"It's an ancient Jewish legend. According to it there are thirty-six anonymous saints who sustain the world. If any were to cease being righteous, the Earth would be destroyed. God abides our corrupted world on account of them. Anyone could be such a person. The Dalai Lama, the quiet man selling fruit from his cart, even *me*." Daniel paused. Water dripped from leaves. A distant animal cried out. "You could be one too, Pandate."

The monk stared at him, his eyes twinkling like the stars. "In Buddhism we have no need for concepts like good or evil, nor an omnipresent god. All the varied phenomena of the world are the play of Maya, of illusion. Good and evil are merely the winds of karma."

"Good and evil are mutable concepts, true," Daniel said. "And God? I haven't found him – or her – yet. But these thirty-six saints – they're *real*, Pandate. They're hidden among us, doing righteous acts while the world ignores them. They are known as the Lamed Vav, the Thirty Six, and they're so hidden that anyone might be one. *Anyone.*"

Pandate took three slow steps around the pool, his silhouette reflecting in the clear waters. "You speak of the bodhisattvas," he said, "those who refuse to enter Nirvana until every sentient being has gained freedom from suffering."

"Does it matter what we call them? Demons are abducting these Lamed Vav, Pandate. They've already brought four to Sheol, a realm of hell, and almost destroyed Earth and a million other worlds. As Sheol grows, Earth weakens. It teeters on collapse."

"Earth has always teetered," Pandate said. "The wheel of samsara never stops."

Daniel glanced at his reflection in the pool. The face that gazed back at him was not the one he remembered. He had been a young man with scruffy hair, pale skin, brown eyes, an Ashkenazi nose. Now, his cheeks were gaunt, his hair had become long and greasy, and his eyes glowed with the cold flame of a candle in an empty room.

"Tell me, Daniel," Pandate said, "what do you see when you stare at your reflection?"

"A stranger," Daniel said. "Pandate, if you want to help people, to continue your selfless work, then come with me. Stay here, and demons will come to harm you. Together, you and I can save the Earth."

Pandate laughed uproariously. Animals skittered in the brush and birds cawed.

"What's so funny?" Daniel said.

"I've met your kind before," Pandate said. "Well-meaning, but deluded. You flail in the world like drunk monkeys, hoping to elicit change." He reached down and smacked the water with his hand. It splashed onto both of them, and the pool shuddered. "Go ahead," Pandate said. "Quell the ripples with your actions. Show me how to calm the waters with your hands and I will bow down and worship you."

Daniel looked into the turbulent waters, a flurry of stars and shadows. "I can't."

"No," Pandate said. "You cannot. Your flailing in the world only adds to the disturbance. The only way to calm the waters is to leave them be. Meanwhile–" he took a deep breath "–I remain here in tranquility."

"And hide from the world."

"Hide?" Pandate looked up. "Half-naked under the stars? I've been in the world, Daniel. I've climbed skyscrapers of New York and Dubai. I've flown on private jets across Europe drinking forty-year old scotch. I've had a private viewing of a satellite launch in India. I can write computer code in twelve different programming languages. It may surprise you, but we have internet access at the monastery. I read the news every day. One must be cognizant of the tumult of the world. But these are all disturbances in the pool of consciousness. Once humanity realizes this, once we learn that we are the ones who agitate the world, and not the world that agitates us, all wars will cease. All strife will end."

Daniel felt his bile rise. "No." He shook his head. "No, there are demons, Pandate, whose *essence* is agitation. They have spent eons wreaking havoc. And they are coming for you, to use you to power their faltering hells. You may want to rest and be tranquil, but they have other plans."

"Your demons have come and gone," Pandate said, waving his hand as if swatting away a mosquito. "A beautiful woman adorned in gold visited me and offered me sensual delights. I refused her advances. A man came after – my preference when I still desired human touch – and teased me with his smile and otherworldly charms."

"Seduction is their first step."

"All cleaving leads to delusion."

Daniel grit his teeth. "So you won't help me at all?"

Pandate smiled. "I came here to meet you tonight, Daniel Fisher – hungry ghost not from hell – to tell you that I won't be going with you."

Daniel shook his head. "I know you mean well, Pandate. But have you considered it's you who is deluded?"

"Impossible."

Daniel was exhausted. He wanted to go home to Gram, to curl up in his old bed and sleep for an age. But he couldn't do that, not with a trillion lives at stake. If Pandate wouldn't come, then he'd just have to go on alone. He sighed. "I don't agree with your decision, Pandate, but I respect your determination."

"I don't need your respect."

"Well, you have it anyway. When I was given similar news, I didn't handle it as well."

"So," Pandate said, "what waves will Daniel Fisher make in the world now?"

The jungle seemed to wrap its tendrils around him. "I'm seeking a doorway to Sheol, one of many hells."

"The quickest path to hell," Pandate said, "is through our own minds."

"If only it were so easy," Daniel said. "Tell me, Pandate, what do *you* see when you look into the pool?"

The monk stared into the slowly calming waters. "Stars. Only stars."

CHAPTER TWO

THE DEMON LAY SUPINE ON THE FLOOR OF HIS CAGE, NAKED, emaciated, spent. He would have long reverted to his mongrel form by now if not for layers of dark magic locking him into this his human shape. His white hair had grown long, its tangled braids lying across his bare chest. His toenails and fingernails had grown lengthy and sharp. He could not remember when last he had eaten, when he had done anything but swing, back and forth, in this dreadful cage.

The ever-burning bars sent shifting palettes of red and orange across his body, and he let himself become hypnotized by their rhythm, until he was elsewhere, his old bedchamber, minutes before the twin suns of Adar and Ora rose above the black cliffs of Abbadon. The burning bars of his cage became the filigreed columns that had lined his private room. The intense heat and ashen smell were not from the rivers of lava below his cage, but a fire in his hearth throwing waves of warm light onto the walls. The steady creak and groan was not from the mammoth chains from which his cage swung, but the soft moans of his wife as he caressed her. Curse her that even after all she had done, he still lusted for her!

"You look like hell."

The voice echoed throughout the gargantuan cavern. He blinked and roused himself from the fantasy. The bedchamber still floated before his eyes as he leaned toward the sound. Had he imagined the voice?

"How the great Ashmedai has fallen."

Across a bleak gap a narrow ledge connected to adjoining tunnels, and here a young demoness draped in a brown robe stood wavering in the heat. A hood hung low over her head, but in the ruddy light her face glowed cinder-like. She had black hair, cut short, and eyes on the white side of gray, striking against her dark hair.

With great effort, he sat up. He would not allow this stranger to see him so helpless. "Another wretch, come to mock me?" he said hoarsely.

She stared back at him, breathing slowly, taking him in.

"Cowards grow bold when their foe is encaged," he said. "Open these bars, and *then* speak your curses. Will you be so brave when we're on equal footing?"

"I've not come to curse you."

"Then to what do I owe this unfathomable pleasure?"

She scowled. "You don't recognize me?"

He considered her human form. Not a First One; he would have sensed that. Then who was she? "I see a young, wretched thing," he said, "come to gloat over her fallen king. Did you serve in my kingdom? Did I speak ill of you once? Did I scold you or have you whipped? Do you desire to tear my heart from my chest? *Get in line.*"

The rocking of his cage made him ever dizzy, and he put his hand on the floor to steady himself.

"I came to see what has befallen the great king Ashmedai," she said, "since our queen has imprisoned him."

"Look closely," he said. He drew himself toward the burning bars until the skin of his face smoked and sizzled, and the air reeked of his burnt flesh. He ignored the pain and stared at her until she let slip a small but perceptible wince. He smiled; the young ones were always so fragile.

"What is it?" he said. "Do you not wish to see what the queen has wrought? Take a good look! This is the face you earn when your wife betrays you, when your children turn their backs, when your people believe lies and turn away. You come here day after day to mock and curse me. But I'm no different from you. This face you cringe at? This is *your* face, reflected. All of you did this to me."

"Queen Mashit wishes to bring new life and abundance to Sheol," she said. "But you have abandoned us."

He laughed. "What hubris! Your beloved queen nearly destroyed the Cosmos! Do you know what would've happened if Daniel and Rana had not returned to Earth to mend the cracks that your queen had left?"

"Earth would have shattered and the waters of life would have spilled upon the Shards, giving us the life we have always been denied."

"Yes," he said. "Untold fecundity, for an *instant*." He smacked the bars of his cage, and they sparked and flared, flashing light onto her face, and she winced again. "The barren Shards would have bloomed! A flowering beyond imagination! And all the sentient beings clinging to their dismal lives upon the myriad husks would, for a time, know abundance. Gehinnom had a small taste of this when Earth's universe cracked open. But once Earth was gone, then what? What happens after the waters dry up? The Shards would have dried too, withering away eon after painful eon. Do you think you suffer now on this husk we call Sheol? Our pain is but a mustard seed in the canyon of suffering she would have brought on us all." He shook his head. "And this the one whom you call queen."

"She has brought the four Pillars here," she said. "They will sustain Sheol as they have sustained Earth. Life will come, in time. We will grow."

"Sheol is a cinder in a long-dead fire. You cannot build a new fire with ash. But I almost succeeded in the greatest act since the Creator, cursed be her name, fashioned the worlds. I would have built a *new* world, one without suffering! And every creature dwelling there would have been free of pain, able to pursue their dreams as they saw fit. It would have been paradise. And despite your treachery, I would have invited you all, every last being, to dwell with me. But your queen ruined that. Rana is gone – the greatest architect the Cosmos has ever known – vanished like smoke. And Daniel–"

"The Pillar Daniel Fisher wanders the Earth."

"He is no Pillar anymore. He has been infected with the Mikulalim curse and become something else. Meanwhile, I, the greatest king demonkind has ever known, the only visionary among you, rot in this cage above this river of fire. Daily you come to mock and curse me. Curse *me*! Imagine! The one who could have saved you all! How deluded you are, how wretched." He spat at her, but it hadn't much force. It arced into the lava below and turned to steam.

The demoness clapped, a human gesture, and all the more insulting. "Bravo! Is the child done with his tantrum yet? I'd heard you liked to bluster, but I had forgotten how true the rumors were. You truly are great in one thing, at least."

Ashmedai considered her, this demoness bolder than most. "Who are you," he said, "who comes to pester me?"

She smirked. "It is you who pester yourself, though you are blind to it. I knew you once, ages ago, but it seems you have forgotten."

"Did we share a bed?"

"The thought repulses me."

"We have that in common, at least. Were you my servant?"

"How could I serve when you never asked for my service?"

"Were you in my court? A Shield of the king?"

She shook her head and grimaced. "You honestly don't remember?"

"Tell me, then. Who are you?"

She turned on her heel, and the tarnished buckles of her boots shimmered in the flickering light. "Perhaps one day soon your memories will return. Until then, Goodbye, *Ashmedai*." She said his name like a curse, then vanished into the tunnel, her footfalls fading behind her.

"Wait!" he shouted after her, his voice echoing. "I must know! Who are you?"

But there came no reply.

"Damn you!" he screamed. He smacked the bars and they flared again. Then all fell quiet but for the creak of his cage's chains and the lava flowing below.

Time passed; he fell into a stupor. He might have slept. After a while, a cadre of Legion soldiers came to visit him. The Legion, Sheol's army, the greatest army in the Cosmos, undefeated in five millennia, once were his to command. Now, they obeyed the queen. Their leader today was Rethuel, pig-faced with mottled green and pink skin. Fat white tusks arced upward from his mouth. More soldiers, amalgamations of half-formed animals, hauled a heavy iron ramp toward his cage. When the ramp touched the base, the swinging stopped at once.

What relief! Though he felt as if he were still swinging. Tusk-faced Rethuel lifted a fat golden key from a chain around his neck, and it glowed as he placed it inside the magic lock. He drew ancient sigils on the iron plate with leviathan blood. The bars ceased their flames, but still glowed red.

"Has it been a month already?" Ashmedai said. "It seems only yesterday you came for me."

"If only we could play with you every day," Rethuel said as he opened the door. He struck Ashmedai's thigh with his sword hard enough to draw blood. Ashmedai winced, but would not give them the satisfaction of a scream.

Rethuel and the others dragged him across the iron ramp. He would have pushed them to their deaths, but unseen magic bonds deprived him of strength. The demons toyed with him, jostling him near the edge, pulling him back a moment before he would have plunged into the fires. Few things could kill a First One more quickly than the ever-seething fires of Sheol.

But they were not here to destroy him. They shoved him into the smaller cage, its bars cold and dark. The demons punched, kicked, and stabbed him as he crouched inside.

He spat up blood and said, "I know all of your names. Rethuel, Jurgo, Umisban, Algas, Thimok, Humisk, Danes."

Surprised, they glanced at each other.

"Yes, I remember each of you. And when I return to my throne all of you will die, but not before you suffer an eon's torment."

"After all that you have endured," Rethuel said, "how can you still believe you'll be king again?"

"Because I am Abbadon's promise. One day, all of you will wake up to this fact."

"Maybe," Rethuel said. "But not today, for today is Stoning Day." Rethuel stuck his blade between the bars and slashed at Ashmedai's hand. Ashmedai grimaced as blood dribbled down his arm.

The soldiers laughed as they wheeled his cage through bleak stone corridors barely wide enough to fit two demons side-by-side. Torches and hanging lamps threw flickering light onto the walls as they turned through dark passages. Behind sealed doors, in chambers dark and reeking, demons lay imprisoned, forgotten or dead. A few moans echoed down the long tunnels, but most were as silent as death.

He memorized the route as they went, noting every fork, ramp and turn. Each month they wheeled him a different way to confuse him. But while his body was weak, his memory was sharp, and he knew in advance when Rethuel and his companions would open the fluted gate. The light of day smacked him in the face as they exited the dungeons. It had been a month since he'd last seen the twin suns, but it felt like a lifetime. He inhaled air that didn't reek of ash and death, but of the briny Lake Hali. And the sky, how glorious were the scarlet skies of Sheol!

They wheeled him through a private alley crowded with debris, broken boxes, animal bones, chamber pots buzzing with flies in the stale air. He'd never have allowed these streets, even this private alley, to become so filthy, but the queen apparently had better concerns. The palace rose beyond the alley wall, a few narrow windows from its menacing facade peering down upon them. But their frames were empty, their residents gone elsewhere for a better view of his torment.

They wheeled him past bulls and oxen, mute golems tethered to carts, creatures all sullen as they watched, as if regretting their distance from the coming show. Rethuel and the soldiers wheeled his cage through a narrow postern out of the palace proper and down a ramp onto Suffering's End, a street crowded with spectators.

Hanging from a cracked terrace a quadrupedal skeleton was the first to see. The skeleton, vaguely horse-like, stood on his hind-legs when Ashmedai approached, and jabbered in a high-pitched whine, "Here comes the traitor king! Cursed be his ignominy!"

Shouts rose from the throng, waves of hate.

"Cursed be the traitor king!"

"May he die a thousand deaths!"

The buildings of Sheol, ancient and imperious, built of gargantuan blocks of basalt and granite, loomed over Suffering's End, a dark, narrow canyon. Demons hung from crooked windows and slanted balconies, but the street gave the best views.

A pus-yellow frog the size of a bull leaped from a high ledge to the street, crushing three demons so she could spit green mucus at him. It splattered in his face. He tried to wipe it away, but it was as sticky as tar.

Three hobgoblin children and their fire-haired mother pounded their oversized fists in the air as they shouted, "May he drift in the Abyss forever!"

A bat the color of dead seas swooped low over his cage and flung a stone that struck him in the head. He toppled against the bars, his head ringing.

A thousand demons cursed him as they wheeled him down Suffering's End.

How tall they grow, he thought, trying to straighten himself, fighting off waves of nausea, *how loud they curse when their foe sits helpless.*

"I shit on the traitor king!"

"Cursed be his ignominy!"

"May he rot in the Abyss!"

Stones and piss and shit pelted him. He could have covered his face to avoid their blows, but he would not cower to them.

They turned onto Final Despair, where more demons waited, then onto Last Gasp of Desperation to greet yet more, and then onto Cessation of Agony, each street more crowded than the last. The briny smell of the lake was thick in the air as they emerged onto Abbadon's Peace. The plaza overflowed with demons, shoulder to shoulder, wing to wing, claw to claw, all here to catch a glimpse of the traitor king, and it seemed as if every demon in the Cosmos had come to mock him. In the center of the plaza, the iron statue of Abbadon, first king of demonkind, loomed over all.

Great Abbadon had liked to sit beside the lake and ponder his kingdom, and for this, they named this plaza Abbadon's Peace. But it was also because the dead king had promised to bring a lasting peace to demonkind.

Great Abbadon, Ashmedai thought, *you'd weep if you were to see us now. I was so close to fulfilling your promise. And for this, they curse me!*

The plaza bordered the sandy shores of Lake Hali, and the crowd pressed up to its black waters but dared not wade into it. Even the denizens of Sheol feared the unseen creatures that stirred in its depths. The twin suns shone onto the masses, reflecting off of flesh, leather, metal, fur and hair. But the lake was as black as night.

On the other side of the plaza, the palace rose sharply behind a tangle of buildings, a black, many-fingered talon grasping for the sky. Through a veil of blood and shit, he gazed up at it. A gilded parapet jutted from one spire, and from there he had once watched ten-thousand soldiers march through Abbadon's Peace as all Sheol had praised his name.

"Look at the ugly wretch!" they shouted now. "So weak and foul!"

Memories, like everything in the Shards, were short-lived.

Objects struck him with numbing regularity. Blood and shit dribbled down his face, over his eyes, but he kept his head up. In the crimson sky, gloom vultures circled the palace, waiting to scavenge the refuse. From the palace's spired heights, walls sloped down in concentric spirals, expanding into innumerable windows and balconies, a thousand lanes and walks, each concealing ancient mysteries. He had lived in the palace for near five thousand years and still he had not explored every corridor.

The palace teased him, and he vowed, as another stone struck below his eye, that he'd stand there again, powerful and free. His entourage wheeled his cage beneath the statue of Great Abbadon, and the shadow of the dead king fell across his face. Rethuel and his soldiers pushed the crowd back, forming a wide circle as all eyes turned to the palace, to the gilded parapet high above.

He struggled to keep himself upright as he wiped the filth from his eyes and steeled himself. Rethuel lifted a ram's horn from a chain at his belt and blew one long, sustained blast. Silence spread over the crowd, and even the gloom vultures paused. Queen Mashit pushed aside a crimson curtain and stepped onto the parapet. Though she was far from the crowd, magic threads weaved into the air magnified her image so she appeared as if she stood right before each of them. She wore a flowing white robe, belted below her breasts with a band of reflective silver. Her black hair long and wavy, shimmered in the twin suns. A second figure stepped from behind the curtain, a young demoness. She wore a green gown bedecked with angled golden plates. They flashed and winked in the suns.

He squinted, trying to identify her, but there was too much

blood in his eyes. The queen raised her hand, and if there had been whispers, none dared speak now.

"Behold," Mashit said. "Before you cowers the disgraced king, who betrayed the Shards for his own selfish ends." The city shook with her voice. Her words, lofted by magic, spoke directly into his ears, curling around his mind so that there was no escaping it, as if her thoughts were his. For a moment, he even agreed with her. "Look at him, my children, and glimpse failure. His hubris nearly destroyed us.

"But I, your queen, am here to serve you. My beloveds, I have grand designs for Sheol and for all the Shards. I have brought four Pillars here so that you shall know peace. This is the promise of Great Abbadon that I will fulfill."

She paused and the air grew tense. A brave demon said, "Hail Queen Mashit!" And a hundred others joined him.

She raised her hand. Their silence was swift and absolute.

"Soon," she said, her voice curling around his ears, "you will see the fruits of my labor. You will know why you have chosen me as your queen, why I shall be remembered for all time as the one who repaired the Cosmos."

At this they were so ebullient he thought for a moment they would riot. She let them cheer, and he was glad for the respite. He wiped gunk from his eyes so he might better glimpse the figure in the gold-plated robe next to Mashit. Her face was pale and striking. Like Mashit, her short-cropped black hair shone in the light. Side by side, their faces were nearly identical, and he gasped as he realized the truth. She was same demoness who had visited his cage this morning.

How am I so daft? he thought. *Have my senses grown so dull I can no longer recognize the face of my own daughter?*

Daphna was her name, and she stared down at him. Mashit turned and vanished behind the curtain as the cheers continued. But Daphna lingered, still staring, her white eyes brimming with life. She appeared before him just as she had before, and he wondered if she could see him just as clearly as he saw her.

"Daphna," he said, "my daughter. Forgive me."

Abruptly, she turned and followed her mother inside, and the crowd let out a collective sigh; the festival over, they had to return to their execrable lives.

Ages ago he had cradled Daphna in his arms in that same lofty room, and there Mashit had remarked, "Her eyes are so like her father's, as bright and white as moons."

"But she has her mother's face and skin," he'd said.

"A sign," Mashit said, "that someday our daughter will be great."

"No," he said. "Daphna is *already* great."

He heart ached. Ages ago he and Mashit had sired a new child almost every year, and the laughter of their children had filled the palace halls. Sheol had always been a place of suffering, but for those all-too-brief decades he had believed happiness was possible.

He swallowed. Were those moments gone forever? No. He would not allow it. Happiness was *still* possible. For him and for everyone. All other thoughts led to madness.

He was staring up at the palace when a stone pelted him in the head.

"Cursed be the Traitor King!"

CHAPTER THREE

BEYOND THE CRIMSON CURTAIN THE MAD ROAR OF THE CROWD was slowly fading as the soldiers wheeled Ashmedai back to his cell above Sheol's fires. Daphna felt no pity for the self-righteous creature who could not remember the face of his daughter. She and her mother sat on a luxurious rosewood couch of sinuous curves and delicate lines, its large panels curving up behind them like wings. It was one of many masterpieces in the opulent Emerald Drawing Room, a large and well-decorated chamber. They each held a crystal goblet of black wine, fermented from the fungus that grew in the caverns where the slaves mined gold. Daphna had only taken two sips and already felt dizzy from its mild hallucinogenic effects.

"They liked you," Mashit said.

"They barely noticed me, Mother."

Mashit sat with legs crossed, one arm draped over the rear of the couch. With her silken white gown, belted below her breasts with a gleaming silver band, and her fingers glittering with precious jewels, Daphna thought her mother looked more like a caricature than a queen. "Oh, come now," Mashit said. "You stood beside me as I told my people their redemption is near. *Everyone* noticed you, my child. You *shimmered*."

Daphna brushed a speck of lint from her velvet green dress. Its plated gold facets glinted in the rays of ruddy sunlight shining through the curtains, and their hard metal stiffness made the dress thoroughly uncomfortable. She wished to be rid of it as soon as possible. "These clothes don't suit me, mother," she said. "I feel like a clown."

"Don't be silly," Mashit said. "This dress suits you beautifully. You shine like a gem. Besides, I couldn't have you stand beside me in those rags you wear."

Mashit leaned over and lifted the snaking pipe from the hookah. With a wave of her hand she ignited the pungent leaf and mold mixture in the bowl. She took a puff, and the hookah gurgled like a hungry belly. Mashit inhaled deeply, then let out a long stream of blue smoke from her lips, lighting sunbeams.

Her mother offered her the hookah pipe, but Daphna declined. "You sure?" Mashit asked. "It's quite excellent."

"No, mother. Not today."

Daphna wished only to strip off her uncomfortable dress and return to her chambers. There, in a secret room, she'd hoarded a small collection of human books. Trips to and from Earth were horribly rare and energetically difficult, so she treasured each book as if it were her child. *The Story of Hong Gildong, The Palm Wine Drinkard, The Little Prince, Alice in Wonderland.* A few dozen others. Years ago she had taught herself the most popular Earth languages so she might read their literature, what little Sheol had. And while her palace tutors had taught her to loathe humanity, their frailty, their conforming mediocrity, she secretly envied them. Humans, as repugnant as they were, had great dreams.

Mashit's hazel eyes glazed and her pupils dilated as the drug took effect. How could Mother rule, Daphna wondered, when she was so inebriated? In this world where demons slew each other on a whim, Daphna had always felt keeping her senses sharp was necessary for survival. Perhaps Mother knew something she didn't.

Mashit stared at the tapestry on the wall. Woven from human hair, it depicted the Shattering, when the Creator, cursed be her name, smashed the universes she had created. Demons tumbled into the Abyss from a shattered egg. A sharp black fragment lay at the bottom, where a many-spired palace rose from the ashes. Great Abbadon stood at the palace peak, fists upraised, challenging the Creator, a halo of fire burning behind him.

Mashit was a First One, there when the Creator smashed her world. And while countless demons had perished, a few others survived. They had settled on this barren husk and named it Sheol. They were forlorn and despairing, but Abbadon raised them up. He built a kingdom here and promised demonkind a future.

Mashit said, "We've a hundred thousand works of art in the palace, but this is my favorite. Look carefully. Do you see the fire behind Great Abbadon?"

"I do."

"And beyond?"

Daphna squinted through smoke-lit sunbeams. "Another halo, but fainter. I'd never noticed that before."

"Look even further."

Daphna traced a rising path on the tapestry. "The haloes go all the way to the edge."

"And beyond. Millennia ago, Great Abbadon lit the fire. And it is we who keep it burning. Soon, my dear, that fire will tear through the Cosmos. It is our destiny."

Daphna stifled a yawn; perhaps it was the second-hand smoke. More likely it was that she'd heard this a thousand times from her palace tutors, how demonkind would take its rightful place in the Cosmos. How Sheol would rule all. It was all so dreadfully boring.

She much preferred the bright worlds of human books to the dreary proclamations of Sheol. Years ago, she had written and staged elaborate plays, poorly disguised retellings of the books she'd read. She'd taught herself to play the gut-stringed harp, the clavichord, and violin and composed baroque melodies to accompany her plays. But whenever she had invited her parents to see her perform, neither deigned to attend. So after a time Daphna stopped vying for their attention. She hunkered down in her chambers, whiling away the years in solitude, briefly venturing out of her cocoon to watch Mother usurp the throne.

But Daphna hadn't the stomach for fanfare. It didn't matter who ruled Sheol, as long as she had her books and a sunny nook to read in. Nor did she miss Ashmedai's rule. How could she miss that which she had no part of? And as for Mother, Daphna had seen her only once since she had taken the throne, and then only at her coronation. From Daphna's point of view, nothing had changed.

Then last night a page had knocked on her door. The queen, the gelatinous, foul-smelling creature had said, required Daphna's presence in the Emerald Drawing Room at dawn. A dress would be delivered along with an aid to help her into it. Daphna had never needed help dressing before.

"Mother," Daphna said now, "this is all so sudden. I see you only at the feasts of the Swap of Suns, and then only from across the huge banquet table. Now you have me stand beside you before all of Sheol? I don't understand. Why am I here?"

Mashit beamed. "My child, I've always admired how you jump right into the heart of things. Come, there's something I need to show you." Her silken robe swished and fell into shape as she stood, and Daphna rose with her.

They pushed open the creaking iron door to exit the Emerald Drawing Room, where nine Shields of the Queen waited. The heavily armed soldiers escorted them down the enormous hallway, where fluted columns framed the distant mountains. Clouds dusted the crimson skies, and a warm breeze blew across the corridor, tousling her hair. A bolt of lightning struck the cliffs, and thunder rumbled through the city below. High on the bleak mountainside a tuft of bright green shone gem-like.

Are those trees? Daphna wondered. *Here, on Sheol?*

A few struggling plants in the palace gardens could barely produce a new leaf in a year, even when coerced by powerful magic. No – trees were impossible; she'd inhaled too much of Mother's second-hand smoke.

Halfway down the corridor, they descended a grand staircase. Their armed escorts made a heavy racket as their boots and hoofs and claws clapped down the marble steps. They reeked, these Shields of the Queen, and Daphna wrinkled her nose.

On each landing, basalt, granite, and iron statues of dead demons loomed over them. The most famous was Great Abbadon. He held his flaming sword over his head, which even after all these eons, swirled with vortices of blue flame. Abbadon was the only male Mother had allowed to remain on these stairs. She had all the other male statues melted into weapons and jewelry, or smashed and tossed into the fires below Sheol.

A marble Eisheth, naked except for a veil, guarded the next landing holding two suckling cherubim to her breasts, her long, branching horns a full story tall. Lilith waited on the next, hands on her wide-belted hips, foot on the neck of Adam, eyes skyward.

They descended, and light from the twin suns shone through tall stained-glass windows that spilled colored light onto all. It was only after they had descended several stories that Daphna recognized Mother's face in the glass. Many stories tall, the visage depicted the queen in elaborate royal attire. At the bottom of her likeness, sweating glaziers and metalworkers toiled before small furnaces, melting glass. The workers kneeled before Mashit as a hot breeze blew in through the open frame of the wall.

"My queen, you honor us with your presence," said one of the glaziers.

"Visiol, your work is beyond compare," Mashit said.

"Your divine visage makes our work easy."

Mashit smiled, and down they went. Then down again. They crossed a corridor decorated with busts and paintings and tasseled curtains, then down yet another stair, across another corridor, and down again and again, until Daphna wasn't sure if she could find her way back alone.

They paused at the end of a windowless hallway as gloomy as a cave. Ten hulking Legion soldiers stood at attention before an enormous iron door. Beside the door was a spacious and undecorated room, dimly lit, but not dark enough to hide the fifty soldiers arrayed inside. At the sight of the queen, they snapped to attention, their boots clapping on the marble floor.

"Welcome, Queen Mashit!" said a frog-faced demon with four sets of eyes, standing before the huge door. His swollen figure seemed ready to burst from his leather armor, and Daphna stifled a laugh. A cracked iron egg pinned to his breast identified him as a high-ranking general of the Legion.

Daphna had no love for soldiers, Legion or Shield. They were stupid creatures who thought all problems could be solved with violence, when words would usually suffice. This she had gleaned from her human books and found by patient experiment to be quite true. These Legion stank too, worse than the Shields, and eyed her as if she were a soft piece of meat to fuck. She despised them all.

"General Joil," Mashit said, "how are our guests?"

"Well enough, my queen," said Joil. "Though they have not eaten any of the provisions you've sent to them."

"Such a waste. Joil, open the door."

The general snapped an order, and the soldiers took two steps forward. The clap of their boots echoed down the hallway. Joil whispered in ancient Demonsbreath, and Daphna shuddered at the great power in his spell. He lifted a rusted key from his belt and inserted it into the lock. The bolt slid away and the door creaked open.

"Close the door behind us."

"Yes, my queen."

Daphna hesitantly followed her mother inside. By palace standards, the chamber was small, barely thirty paces wide. Saffron curtains hung over the walls, disguising the fact that this room, deep inside the palace, had no windows. Columns adorned with looping arabesques framed the corners. Poster-beds butted against the walls. English translations of famous demon books lay on one table. Thumiel's *Vengeful Garden*, Egrieth's *The Hypocrisy of Humanity*, and Yom Yim's classic, *Great Abbadon's Promise*.

A huge plate of food sat on another table. Shamir worms fried in leviathan tallow. Stymphalian drumsticks. Baked greyel mushrooms. Daphna salivated at the sight of them. All delicacies, seldom seen even at the palace feasts, and all the more shocking that not a single item had been eaten or touched.

A magic-lit chandelier swung gently above their heads, making everything in the room squirm, so that when Daphna finally set her eyes on the four humans sitting on the couches and chairs, she recoiled in horror.

The only flesh-and-blood human she had ever met had been a prisoner, cursed with a mental disease they called schizophrenia. Palace mages had stoked his fear to a fever pitch, and because emotions were energy, they used his fear to power their spells. And this human had been especially good at being afraid. When Daphna had peered into his ghastly eyes, when she had smelled the shit and piss and sweat that had stained his clothes, she knew she would never willingly meet one again; books would be the closest she ever got.

"Behold," Mother said. "The Pillars of the Cosmos. The Lamed Vav."

There were three human women and a man, all eyes on her. But she thought only of that hideous human creature in the dungeons, and could not meet their eyes. She felt sick just to be near them. How, she wondered, did *these* wretched creatures sustain the Cosmos? The Creator truly was demented.

"This is Daphna, my daughter," Mashit said in English. Daphna had learned English centuries ago, but it felt strange to hear the human words come from her mother's mouth. "Daphna, may I introduce you to Paula Baumgarten, Baaba Lankandia, Sunil Pranadchandr, and Maya Dorje."

Maya, a squat woman, rose from her seat. She wore a loose and sleeveless crimson robe. She pressed her hands, palm to palm, before her chest and stuck out her tongue.

"That's how they say hello in Tibet," Mother said. "Maya is a practitioner of Tibetan Buddhism. She's been teaching me all about their customs and practices."

Maya's round face framed brown and steady eyes. Her black hair was tied into a tail. Maya held out her hand and Daphna stared at it in frozen revulsion. She knew the gesture from her books, a shake of hands established trust. But she would not trust this human any more than she could trust a Legion soldier. Daphna stared daggers at her mother and growled in Demonsbreath, "*I will not touch that.*"

"Now, now," Mashit said. "Play nice, or I won't give you your gift."

Daphna grumbled. What was Mother playing at? She took a step toward Maya. The human was a full head shorter than her, and there was an assuredness in her gaze that calmed Daphna unexpectedly. She took Maya's hand and tried not to gag. It was warm and calloused, as if she'd worked for years at hard labors.

"You resemble your mother," Maya said.

"I assure you we are quite different," Daphna said as she yanked her hand away.

"No," said Maya, "I see much of her in you."

The other Lamed Vav had not risen from their seats, a grave insult to the queen. But Mashit did not seem to care. Daphna was thankful she wouldn't have to touch another.

Paula Baumgarten, suddenly stood. She was middle-aged, had

a pale face, short brown hair, and bright green eyes, and she wore black pants and a navy blouse. "Allow me to get a message to my children," Paula said, "and then we'll consider helping you."

"Soon enough," Mashit said. Then to Daphna she whispered in Demonsbreath, "Paula is a school teacher from Atlanta, but she previously worked in covert operations for the U.S. government. This message is almost certainly *not* for her children."

Mashit's gaze scanned the room, over uneaten delicacies, unread books and the unsmoked hookah, and lingered on the unopened bottles of greyel wine. "You haven't touched anything," Mashit said. "In Sheol, it's considered a privilege to have such luxuries. It's a great shame to let it go to waste."

"Then why not give it to the starving in your slums?" Sunil said. Sunil Pranadchandr stared at Daphna, his eyes dark and luminous. Even from his sitting position, he seemed taller than her. His skin was the color of tanned leather, and he wore a collared blue shirt and belted slacks.

"Sunil is from Hyderabad, India," Mashit said in Demonsbreath. "A programmer. Do you know what that is, Daphna?"

She shook her head.

"Someone who writes instructions for calculating machines. Sunil was a heroin addict – a powerfully addictive and destructive human drug – and was close to death. But like Great Abbadon he picked himself up from the ashes. He programmed what humans call an *application*, which has revolutionized medicine in India."

Baaba Lankandia, large-bodied, skin as dark as basalt cliffs, watched Daphna and Mashit converse. Baaba wore a gown and headscarf with a matching orange, yellow, and black pattern. A leather patch covered her left eye, a scar cut across her cheek, and her left arm was cut short just beyond her elbow. "We don't want your vile food, your stupefying drugs, your brainwashing books," Baaba said.

Daphna was shocked at Baaba's tone, but Mashit just smiled and said to her in Demonsbreath, "Baaba ran a school for girls in Nigeria, and all her students were murdered by religious zealots who believe women should remain ignorant and subservient to men. She lost her eye and part of her arm defending them, and was left for dead."

"Speak so we can understand!" Baaba said. "Or don't speak at all."

Daphna gasped, but Mashit raised her hand and said in English, "My friends-"

"We are not your friends," Baaba said.

"My *friends*," Mashit said again, "For a plant to grow, it needs air, water, soil, and sun. Deprive it of any, and it withers. Sheol is a plant, and you are its air, water, soil, and sun. On Earth, through your selfless acts, you sustained the world, and countless others. And what was your reward? To fester in anonymity."

"Do you think we do what we do to be famous?" Baaba said. "To be praised? You don't know us at all."

"I know you better than you know yourselves," Mashit said. "For it was I who told you what you truly are, Pillars of the Cosmos. You selflessly gave of yourselves to alleviate the suffering of others. But humans don't suffer alone. We on the Shards drink the rare drops of life that dribble down from the Earth. Without them, we would wither like a corpse in the desert. You have sustained us without knowing it. But we are malnourished, stunted, unable to reach our potential. My friends, I have brought the four of you here so that you can help us grow."

Maya played with her ponytail. "You wish to help your people," Maya said, "and that is commendable. But you've tricked us and brought us here against our will. Do you understand why this makes us unwilling to trust you?"

"Would you have come," Mashit said, "if I'd simply asked?"

"I might have," Maya said. "Yes."

"Demons come in many shapes," Baaba said, shaking her head. "I've known your kind on Earth, most often in the guise of *holy* men. They tell me what they do is for the greater good just before they murder children." She spat on the floor. "No, I will not help you. You can kill me first."

Maya sighed and drooped. "What Baaba means," Maya said, "is that we have no reason to trust you."

"Don't speak for me!" Baaba said. "I mean *exactly* what I said. I'd rather die than abet evil."

"I'm sorry," Maya said. "I meant no disres-"

"Don't speak for me," Baaba said. "Don't fucking speak for any of us."

"Please," Mashit said, raising her hand. "Do not fight amongst yourselves. All I want is that you consider the possibility that you might do some good here. Read the books, ask us questions. Get to know *our* point of view. I want to help you understand that demons are not who you presume, that we suffer greatly too." She turned to Daphna. "Come now, my child, let us depart."

Daphna followed Mashit to the door as if in a trance. These humans were not what she had presumed. They were nothing like what her tutors had taught her, neither frail nor cowardly. She turned to gaze at them, and all four stared at her, but Mashit pulled her out the door. Outside, General Joil bolted and sealed the heavy door.

"I have one more thing to show you," Mashit said. "This, I'm certain you will enjoy."

Daphna's gold plated dress itched from sweat and from the fabric, but she dutifully followed her mother along another labyrinthine path through the palace, until they emerged onto a domed parapet. The city's jumbled agglomeration of basalt and granite blocks spread beneath them. Towers rose above the chaotic tangle like mammoth tombstones. The base of the mountains and the windswept wastes of the Dissipation spread beyond the city gates.

Mashit pressed a finger to her silver belt. A circle of light appeared, then slid out like a drawer, extending half an arm's length. Inside the drawer was a bronze spyglass. Mother took the object from its enclosure and handed it Daphna. When Mashit pressed the circle again the drawer slid closed, sealing with a soft click.

"What else do you have in there, Mother?"

"More than you should care to know." She pointed to the mountains. "Use the spyglass and gaze at The Ogre's southwestern side."

Daphna felt as if she were playing a children's game as she lifted the spyglass. Its bronze was warm against her eye. She adjusted the tubes until The Ogre, Sheol's second tallest mountain, came into focus. It took her a moment to see them. Trees. Real trees, growing on the mountain, leaves a brilliant green against the dark cliffs.

"I saw them before," Daphna said, "but thought I'd imagined

them. Since when are there trees in Sheol, Mother?"

"Not just any trees, but apple trees."

"How?" Daphna said, her eyes fixed on the grove, the bright leaves and dun branches. Only the most vicious plants in the Cosmos could grow in the barren soils of Sheol, and even then were found only in the most remote places, cleaving to life.

"The four whom you just met are responsible."

"The Pillars planted them?"

"No. The trees arose on their own."

"Without seeds?"

"It seems so, yes."

Daphna lowered the spyglass. "So your plan is working! That's wonderful, Mother!"

"Yes," Mashit said. "Life has come to Sheol. But it's been months since the Pillars have arrived, and only a few trees have sprung to life. Here and there, a shrub or weed appears. My advisors tell me at this rate it will take a thousand years for Sheol to bloom as I have hoped. We don't have such time, Daphna. This is why I've called on you."

"To plant a forest?"

"Of a kind. My child, I want you to go to Earth."

Daphna nearly dropped Mother's spyglass. "To *Earth*? Why?"

"Like Abbadon's tapestry, you will bring Sheol's fire to Earth, like a spark blazing across the Cosmos. You will help shift the cosmic balance. You will diminish Earth's power, and you will help raise the Shards. I need someone on Earth to speak for me, to be my proxy there."

"Me? Up until this morning, Mother, you had all but forgotten about me."

"I remembered those plays you performed. Those lovely songs you wrote."

"You never came to my plays. You never heard my songs. You and father were always too busy."

"And I regret that more than you will ever know. I never told you, but I sent servants to listen on my behalf. They always came back mesmerized, singing your praises."

"And yet you did not see fit to ever come?"

"A grave mistake, one that I seek to now rectify. I hope to make up for my remission. I'm giving you a chance to be great, as I always knew you were."

"But *Earth*?" Daphna shuddered. To dwell among those alien creatures? The thought terrified her. But it excited her too. "But what will I do there?"

Mashit stared at Daphna. "My child, you will lead them."

"Lead?" Her head spun. "Like a queen?"

Mashit smiled. "You will rule them, but not as a queen. Humans of this age loathe kings and queens, and those who wear such masks. No, you will be what the humans call a *celebrity*." Mother used the English word. There was none in Demonsbreath.

"A *celebrity*?"

"You once loved to perform. Now you sit locked in your room reading your dusty human books. Yes, I know about your habit, Daphna. That's why I picked you. You know human culture better than any of your siblings. This will be your chance to perform not just for a few palace sycophants, but for millions. You will enthrall with your stupendous talent. They will adore you. They will wish to emulate you. *This* is how you will lead. Not by royal edict, nor force, but through music. Your songs will teach them new ways and bring about a change in their consciousness."

"My songs?"

"They will make the humans more compliant and easier to rule."

Mashit placed her hands on Daphna's shoulders. "I may have been absent, but I've never forgotten you, Daphna. You were always on my mind. The duties of a queen are long and taxing, and I have ignored you for too long. But now an unbreakable bond will link you and me. You will be my right hand on Earth. And you will show humanity what true art is, why abundance is our birthright. So, my child, what do you say?"

Daphna looked across the city, where huge spikes of iron marked the city gates. Without the spyglass, the grove of apples was a fuzzy green speck. This had always been her home. She had never considered leaving.

"I'm flattered, Mother. I truly am. But are you sure I'm the right one? What of my sister, Neta? She has a voice like the sparrows of Gehinnom. And, Olem, my brother, who writes such epic poems? Surely they are more qualified than me!"

"Daphna, my child. *You* are the one. Accept this."

Daphna felt as if she were falling; this was all so sudden.

"Well? I need your answer, Daphna. Now."

A gloom vulture circled above their heads and let slip a sharp cry. The sound echoed through the folds of the city, over its dark lanes and barren corners. She took a deep breath and lifted her shoulders. To help bring life here, to this dusty, harsh world, that would be beyond wonderful.

"I will go, Mother," Daphna said, "on one condition." She pointed to Mashit's waist. "I want a belt like yours with secret drawers."

Mashit chuckled and kissed Daphna on the forehead. "Funny you should mention it. I have just the thing. Daphna, my child, we're going to do such great things together!"

Daphna's heart warmed at her words; finally Mother appreciated her.

"Go now," Mashit said. "Ready yourself. You'll leave in the morning."

"*Tomorrow* morning?"

"Sheol cannot wait, Daphna. Mages have been preparing the portal to Earth for seventy-one days. I've been waiting to tell you for a long time."

CHAPTER FOUR

THE PINK AND PURPLE SUNSET RIBBONED THE SKY AS DANIEL slunk from the freighter's humid hold. He hoped for relief from the rank smells and heat of the shipping container where he had hidden for more than a week with little food and water. But the semi-tropical Indian air was no less sweltering. A waxing gibbous moon floated above the Bay of Bengal, shimmering on the waters. Its ghostly silver light spread over the port city of Visakhapatnam, twinkling in the twilight. The air smelled of diesel and sea, and a steady wind blew from the south. Most of the crew had left the ship, and the bulk of the dock workers had fled. But scattered voices, switching effortlessly between Hindi and Arabic, echoed through the maze of shipping containers and cranes crowding the docks.

He kept to the shadows, sensing cameras and smelling humans before he saw them. It was easy to slip past them all, and he tried not to enjoy his new powers too much. This curse was temporary, he reminded himself.

He snuck past a texting guard and headed into a forest preserve, the plants weedy and overgrown. He turned west and walked down dozens of branching roads, each smaller than the last, and pavement devolved to gravel, to dirt, to sand. He steeled himself for the long journey.

He had learned the names of only six Lamed Vav, himself included. The other thirty would remain forever anonymous. With four on Sheol and his own ability to sustain the world highly suspect, the Earth teetered dangerously close to collapse. Like a house built on thirty-six pillars, the more you removed, the more unstable the house. Until...

He shuddered as he thought of what had almost happened. If Rana, the girl from Gehinnom, hadn't sacrificed herself to save Earth – a world not hers – trillions would have died. He mourned her as he walked. But just because she had saved the Earth didn't mean it was out of danger. Demons were single-minded creatures. In order to secure the safety of Earth, Daniel had to bring the four Lamed Vav home. Except he had no idea how to get to Sheol. Getting to hell, despite Pandate's proverb, was neither quick nor easy.

In Bangkok, Daniel had met Hanuman, a lapsed Hindu, in the private section of a brothel. Over homemade liquor that tasted like turpentine, Hanuman, his face gnarled from too many bitter days, told Daniel, "Outside a small village in India lives a guru who nightly travels to hell. He'll take you with him for the price of your sanity." Hanuman grimaced as he downed his liquor.

Daniel replied in perfect Thai, "How do I know you won't just give me some random name and take my cash?"

"Look at me," Hanuman said. "I'm forty-six, but I look twice that. Twenty years ago, I wished to conquer my fear of death. The man you seek took me to hell, and since then I've spent the bulk of my days trying to forget."

"What's his name?" Daniel said.

"I'm old and bereft," said Hanuman. "What is his name worth to you?"

Twelve hundred baht, apparently. Hanuman nodded as he counted the bills, but he never smiled. He said, "My friend, I want your money. But why go to hell?" A topless dancer swayed before them, and Hanuman stuffed a small bill into her panties that bulged with cash and possibly a penis. "There are plenty of hells on Earth. Some are better than others."

"I don't *want* to go there," Daniel said. "I have to."

"No one has to do anything."

"That's where you and I differ."

"So you're still a believer?"

"A believer?" Daniel said.

"I sensed it the moment you walked in. A man on a holy mission. You walk the Brahmin's path."

Daniel took a deep breath. "If I don't help the world, who will?"

"Why help at all? Life is meaningless." Hanuman placed his hand on the dancer's crotch, but when he didn't flash another bill, she sauntered off to another table.

Hanuman frowned as he watched her go. "We float down the Ganges like flotsam," he said. "If we pass a million devotees in the season of Descent, we say, 'Look how the world bows and worships us! Our lives are full of blessings!' But if we pass the same shores in a quiet season when the banks are bare, we say, 'Woe is us! The Infinite One has forsaken us!' Yet both lives end the same. All flotsam floats out to sea. Death, my friend, lies at the end of all paths."

"You don't believe in rebirth or liberation?"

"Rebirth, yes. But liberation?" He snorted. "How many humans have achieved the perfected state? A few hundred? Even if it's ten thousand, this is still a drop compared to the bulk of humanity. I could spend my life locked in a monastery meditating, or wandering the world seeking wisdom, or I could end my suffering right here, right now, in the arms of a warm body."

Hanuman waved another bill, this one larger, at the dancer, then he turned to Daniel and said, "Why not enjoy ourselves while we're here? It seems foolish to do otherwise."

Hanuman rose and whispered into the dancer's ear, and together they entered a private room. Another dancer sidled up to Daniel and pointed to a different room, but Daniel politely declined. He downed his liquor – it burned as it went down – then he left the brothel for the neon-bright Bangkok streets. That night, he got so drunk he passed out in the gutter, awakened only when the rising sun nearly killed him.

And now, more than a week later, as he walked the dusty Indian road under a spray of bright stars, he thought, *Why, old man, should we let life sweep us out to sea? Did it never occur to you that we can swim to shore?*

A curtain of clouds slowly rolled in from the west. With a clap of thunder there came a torrential downpour. He shivered and pulled his hood tighter over his face.

It would be a long journey.

—

He reached the village of Marishamehadi, the town Hanuman had given him, three days later. In that time the rain had never ceased. He was always cold and wet, but it made movement easier, because under a cloudy sky he could walk outside during the day without fear of burning to death in the sun. But it was dusk now, and the rain had finally tapered and stopped. The world had become an enormous lake, knees deep, infinitely wide. And over hours, like the receding waters of Noah's flood, the earth appeared again. Birds sang and took to the sky. Leaves dripped and whispered in the wind. He was covered in mud and hadn't eaten for days, but he had hunger only for the flesh of the dead.

Shivering, he walked under the pale light of a rising moon. A tangle of mangrove trees dipped their crooked roots into a rushing river, and he followed them to the village. Pale yellow light lit the insides of the two dozen concrete and wooden homes of Marishamehadi. Wild jasmine beside the road perfumed the air, and Daniel longed for home, for Gram's summer garden, for her voice. He hadn't spoken to her in weeks.

Outside a house a woman was hanging clothing on a line to dry. A battery-powered lantern on the ground encircled her in a sphere of yellow light. As she draped a sun-bleached dress over the line she noticed Daniel and froze. Her eyes were neither menacing nor friendly, but indifferent, as if he were a bird, come for a moment before flitting off. An emaciated cow beside her stared at him with huge, twinkling black eyes.

He said in Hindi, "Namaste. I'm looking for Shyama Lahiri. Do you know where I might find him?"

Her indifference turned to scorn. She spat, grabbed her basket of clothes, and fled into her house. The screen door slammed behind her, and he heard a snick as the latch slid into place.

"Yeah," he said. "Nice to meet you too."

As he walked further down the road, snatches of Hindi radio escaped from windows. The scent of cigarettes and evening meals filled his nose, and his belly grumbled, but not for any sane food.

He paused at a large, empty corral. A bare-chested man with long hair and a full beard sat on the grass smoking a pipe of marijuana. Its sweet and pungent smell filled the air. "Namaste," Daniel said.

The man gazed up at him.

"Could you please tell me if a man named Shyama Lahiri lives in this village?"

The man blinked several times. "Shyama is no *man*."

"But Shyama *does* live here?"

The man shuddered. "Why do you want to see *him*?"

"Because he has something I need."

"Answers?" He shook his head. "He has only madness."

"So he is here?"

The man pointed up the road. "The Breaker of Minds lives a few minutes walk past the village. Look for a trail to the right."

Daniel felt a weight lift from his chest. Bitter old Hanuman had not lied. "Thank you."

"You shouldn't thank me," the man said. "The one who ventures to The Breaker of Minds is not the one who returns. Death lies up that road, the worst kind. The one where you go on living."

"I've been told as much."

"Then why go?"

"Because I have to."

The man nodded. "It is your dharma."

"Yes, it is."

Daniel continued down the road. Trees and brush in riotous bloom replaced the homes of Marishamehadi. While he had loathed the incessant rain, the plants had loved it. They grew giant leaves, bloomed fragrant flowers, and were so densely packed they formed thick vegetative walls. Twenty minutes down the road he found a narrow path in the trees, and when he stepped onto it the moonlight vanished behind the thick verdure. He weaved a crooked course through the dense forest, following the looping trail.

Its turns made no sense, turning randomly, and he was beginning to think he was the butt of some local joke when he finally slipped from the thicket into a moonlit clearing. There was a primitive hut of wood here made of metal and fabric, less a house than a tent. The air reeked of an unwashed person – and worse. To his sensitive nose most people smelled as if they hadn't bathed in days, even after a shower. Those odors were unpleasant, but not a tenth as offensive as the smell that assaulted his nose now. It was shit, human and animal, left to fester, topped with rotting fish and a touch of lavender.

He retched as he approached the hut. Beyond it was an overgrown meadow, where the moon shone down through an opening in the trees and spread its silver light onto the grass. Here, sitting on a large rock, was a man.

Half his body lay in shadow. The other half was as gray as the moon. He was naked, save for beaded bracelets on his wrists and a necklace of dark stones. He had long, flowing white hair that did not flutter in the hot breeze whispering through the leaves. His ribs poked sharply against his taut skin. He might have been dead for how little he moved. Was this a cursed one, a Mikulal, like him?

"The dog-man cometh," the man said. His voice was the croaking of frogs and the trickling of water over stone, and its cadence temporarily froze him, as if from a spell.

"Shyama Lahiri?" Daniel said. With great effort he stepped closer to the man.

"Stop!" the man said. "Do not approach."

Daniel stopped.

"You reek of ghoul," the man said, "yet you are not a dead-eater. Explain."

"*I* reek?" Daniel said. "That's a little pot-kettle, don't you think?" The reference didn't quite translate into Hindi.

"Answer the question. Why do you reek of dead-eaters?"

"I was force-fed the tongue of a Mikulal against my will."

"And have you eaten of the flesh of the dead?"

"No, and I never will."

"When men die we bury them in the earth, where they rot and turn to soil. The soil feeds the plants, which we eat. Even if you eat only plants, you are eating death."

"I've never eaten meat from a human body, dead or alive."

"All is Anant, neither born nor dead. You are not liberated, and therefore not a master of your will. You *will* eat."

Daniel shuddered. "No, I won't."

Shyama turned into the moonlight to reveal his face, round

and surprisingly childlike. His eyes looked entirely black, with no whites at all. "I cannot cure your condition. I don't think ghoulism can be cured."

"I'm not here to be cured."

Shyama tilted his head. "Then why have you come?"

"I was told you can open doors to hell. I need to visit a hell called Sheol."

Shyama adeptly leaped to his feet. He chuckled – a gurgling sound, like an animal's last gasp as its throat was cut. "There are millions of hells. Few are asked for by name. What do you seek in Sheol?"

"To bring my brothers and sisters home."

"Other dog-men?"

"No. Siblings of a different kind."

"Demons?"

"Human."

Shyama approached, his steps careful and measured, then he leaned toward Daniel and sniffed. "No, you haven't eaten the dead." Shyama nodded and put a hand to his chin. "Neither ghoul nor man, with a strong will, and carrying a taste of something...else. Something exceedingly rare. What are you?"

"I'm not quite sure anymore."

Shyama inhaled sharply, then he slapped Daniel's shoulders. "You interest me! I will help you!"

Shyama leaped toward his hut like a child rushing to open a gift. It didn't inspire confidence. Daniel followed him inside. The hut was small and amplified the man's foul smell. There wasn't much here. A natty rug. A portable gas stove and kettle. A dozen small jars filled with various powders and herbs. Shyama lit a lamp, and from a box removed three glass bottles, one with brown powder, one with black, and one with white.

Using a large leaf Shyama scooped out measures of powder from each bottle and placed them in a stone mortar. He ground them with a pestle, then spilled the ingredients into the kettle, adding water and tea leaves.

"What are you brewing?"

"You cannot open certain doors without a key."

The air grew thick with a new smell, like boiling tar and sewage, and Daniel feared he might vomit. "How does this work? Will you cast a spell?"

"Of a kind. The mind is the most magical instrument of all." One moment, Shyama was staring into Daniel's eyes. The next, Shyama had become a skeleton, all his flesh removed. He laughed maniacally, his jaw chattering as it bounced up and down.

Daniel winced and leaped back, only to blink and see Shyama as he was before, with all his flesh, what little of it he had. "Mind is the only truth. All is Brahma. Are you ready to die and be reborn?"

Shaken, Daniel nodded as Shyama poured the reeking brew into two small cups. "The key works quickly. Envision the hell you wish to see as vividly as you can. As the Upanishads say, 'When the food is pure the mind becomes pure.' Drink all of the liquid in one gulp. If you don't, I will have to drag your corpse into the woods for the animals to eat."

Daniel took a deep breath and nodded.

"Now repeat my words," Shyama said. "This tea is Shiva, the Lord of the Dance, who destroys the universe so Brahma may create the world anew. May Shiva bless our journey into the abyss. May we safely ride his waves of flame into the netherworlds and return unto the light."

Daniel repeated the words.

"Now close your eyes. Focus. Make this hell bright in your mind."

He imagined Sheol – he had only a brief glimpse – its twin red suns, its black mountains, its gargantuan palace that grasped at the sky.

"Now drink. All of it."

No amount of precaution could have prepared him for its horrid taste. It was liquid dread, a billion holocausts, lifetimes of pain, a child's terror as he wakes from a nightmare into a dark room where every imagined monster has always been real.

Cackling laughter. A wail. A siren. The sounds grew in pitch until they became a deafening roar. Shyama's face shone like a star. Around him spun a million-colored mandala. Daniel fell into Shyama's eye, his pupil a black hole sun.

Daniel tumbled into a cathedral of light, of colors that did not exist on Earth, kaleidoscopic and mesmerizing. The cathedral's ceilings stretched to the end of the universe, but if he'd had hands, he might have caressed their infinite arabesques. His body was gone; only his mind remained.

The angles were wrong. New space unfolded from extra unseen dimensions. A dozen spheres floated down from the ceiling, mirror-bright, reflecting the cathedral's walls. They giggled and whispered unintelligible words. When he tried to speak, they turned black and reflectionless. But after a moment they became mirror-bright again.

The spheres imparted profound secrets, a million thoughts per second, and Daniel struggled to understand. Shyama sat beside him, cross legged, smiling, as rays of purple light streamed from his body out into the universe. One of the rays pierced the floor, opening a chasm that widened into a pit. The spheres laughed as Daniel and Shyama tumbled into the darkness.

Daniel screamed. He knew this place. This was the Abyss, the ineffable void, which he had tried so hard to forget. In the impossible darkness a trillion sharp fragments tumbled. There were beings on them, tempest-tossed, clinging like survivors of a shipwreck to debris, to the scrap of world they'd found. These were the Shards, the fragments of shattered universes.

Powerful currents tugged at his mind-body, and he was nearly swept away, but Shyama grabbed him – how, Daniel did not know – and yanked him deeper into the Abyss. They sped toward a tumbling fragment, a Shard, and entered its broken realm.

He floated above a rocky desert under a gray-orange sky. A steady wind blew across the landscape, stirring the ubiquitous yellow dust into a storm. A few large stones peeked up from the ground, and here and there menacing plants like black metal spiders dotted the wastes. He and Shyama sped over this barren, rocky world until they reached a small city. Its stone buildings had been poorly constructed. Many had collapsed ages ago. The yellow sand covered everything and had worried away at the stone walls. There were no sharp corners here, only dull edges.

A group of scaly creatures, like upright iguanas, left the city gates carrying tall spears. Their narrow eyes were the same color as the dust. Inside the city, black smoke coughed from a narrow building, and Shyama and Daniel entered it. Two gaunt men and women – humans, Daniel was shocked to see – shared a table with two demons, a many-toothed beast with a flurry of limbs and claws, and a similar but smaller one beside it. On the table was a tiny creature much like the many-toothed demons.

A baby, unmoving.

They were silent as they stared down at the creature. Shyama shoved Daniel inside the larger demon's head, and suddenly they were one being, sharing thoughts and emotions. Sadness. Emptiness. Despair. Hunger. So much hunger.

This was his child. Dead before her third nameday.

The demon took a rusty cleaver from the wall and held it above the child. All four placed their hands upon it. Then the demon chopped his baby into pieces. Daniel wanted to look away, but he was in the demon's eyes and saw all. The four shoved metal spikes through each piece of the demon and hung these above the coal fire in the corner, where they sizzled and smoked. For minutes they watched the flesh burn, then the larger demon retrieved the spit from the fire and took the first bite.

The others joined him.

Shyama pulled Daniel from the demon's mind, from this personal hell. They flew out the building and into the wastes beyond the city. Where were the twin suns? Where were the black cliffs? This was not Sheol. The sky was thick with gray cloud, but every now and then a glimmer of a dim orange sun peeked through. They flew toward an enormous crater in the distance. Yellow dust blew over the edges to plunge into the depths. Five demons, a different species from before, hovered on the crater's edge. One by one, they leapt off the cliff, splattering onto the rocks below until all were dead.

Shyama pulled Daniel toward the horizon. They flew for many miles, faster than birds, until they reached a small enclave, tucked in the shadow of rocks.

A black and cylindrical obelisk rose several stories tall. It had been inscribed with complex symbols. Eleven humans in heavy robes, powdered yellow from the dust, faced the obelisk and chanted in an alien tongue. Shyama pushed Daniel into one of their minds.

"Ichsoom, save us. Ichsoom, protect us. Ichsoom, watch over us. See that my unborn child flies to the never-dying sun that shines beyond the horizon of death."

Thirty small obelisks rose from the ground near the great one, all wind-worn and smooth. But one had been newly carved and set. Daniel shared the human's thoughts.

My child whom I will never meet, I spare you a name and thus spare you existence. You were wise to close your eyes in the womb.

Shyama yanked Daniel out again, and they hurtled back into the Abyss, away from this wind-shorn Shard, and into the cathedral of light. The bouncing mirrored spheres giggled one last secret to him, then they zipped into hyperspace, vanishing through a crack in the universe.

Daniel blinked. He was back in the hut, the empty cup on the floor where he had dropped it. Shyama stared into his eyes. It was gray outside. It would be dawn soon. Daniel collapsed to his side, utterly exhausted. Weakly, he whispered, "That wasn't where I wanted to go....It wasn't Sheol..."

"I took you not where you wanted to go," Shyama said, "but where you needed to."

"There is too much suffering....Too much despair..."

"To exist is to suffer. The only escape is the realization of the Absolute, achieved through devotion to the Thinker of all Thought, who is ever present and unchanging."

Morning light spilled through the opening onto the floor, and Daniel used the last of his strength to slide away from the creeping sun beam. Shuddering, sick with horror, he curled into a fetal position.

"It's always the same," Shyama said. "They wish to see truth, and when they glimpse it, they wish only to forget." He sighed and the whole Cosmos seemed to sigh with him. "But forgetting would be a mistake, because if you calm your disturbed mind enough, if you are patient, one day you might remember one of the many great secrets those laughing mirrored spheres have told you."

CHAPTER FIVE

THE BRUISES FROM HIS STONING HEALED AS SLOWLY AS stalagmites grew, so that mostly pain and tortured sleep filled Ashmedai's days. And his cage's damned incessant swinging, suspended by chain above the flowing lava. Back and forth, back and forth, it whined like a crone. When he had been king, he had designed this cage to drive its captives mad. He was mildly pleased that it was working.

Why, he thought during brief moments of lucidity, had Daphna come to see him? Why did she step onto the parapet beside Mashit for all to see? His daughter, unknown to most, had stood before all as if she were Princess of Sheol. Mashit was using her, but for what? Last he'd heard, Daphna had become a recluse, locking herself in her chambers. Still, he loved her, as he loved all of his children, even if they had abandoned him. He wished he could warn Daphna how treacherous her mother was. She deserved that, at least.

"You look like hell."

The voice echoed throughout the gargantuan cavern as Ashmedai sat up. On the ledge across the gap was a giraffe-shaped demon covered in white fur. The demon had a rat's face and was so tall he crouched so as not to scrape his curving horns on the ceiling.

"Kokabiel," Ashmedai said. "I thought I smelled shit."

Kokabiel laughed, and the echo filled the cavern. "Captivity has not softened your wit, I see," he said. His voice was deep and silken, rekindling memories of the pair delighting each other's bodies under fur sheets.

"No," Ashmedai said. "Hovering above these fires has only tempered my spirit. To what do I owe the pleasure of your presence, Koko?"

"If you weren't so full of venom. I might actually believe you were happy to see me."

"Are you serious? Happy? Here? After what you did to me?"

"I made a strategic choice."

"Rethink your strategies, *Second* General. You were *First* General under me."

"My strategies are long-term."

"And proprietary. I was never privy to any of them."

"What would you have me do? Side with the Traitor King and be killed or exiled with you? What good could I have done then?"

"It's called loyalty! But I shouldn't have expected it from you. Daniel, Marul, and Rana – they loathed me, but still they showed more loyalty than you, my right hand."

"I can do more inside the kingdom than out."

"More of what?" Ashmedai moved closer to the bars to get better look at his old lover. "Eat? You've grown fat, Koko."

"And you thin."

"I'm on the prisoner's diet."

"How would you like to be on a king's?"

Ashmedai perked up. "You're a master on the battlefield. And even more skillful in bed. And I'm just another foe to conquer. Don't pretend you have a key to my cage unless you actually do."

"I wield a key of a kind. Ashey, my treasure–"

"Don't call me that. You cannot call me that anymore."

"Lord Ashmedai – you believe that your people have abandoned you, that your friends have turned their backs. But this is not entirely true." Kokabiel peered down the corridors. "I sent the guards away and cast spells to shield our words. Ashey, my tre– my *lord*, there are some in Mashit's court who preferred your rule."

"And you are, of course, one of them."

"I am."

Ashmedai grimaced as he shifted his bruised body. "You've a curious way of showing it."

"It was safer to keep quiet. There was too much turmoil, too much hunger for change. But now that we've seen what she's capable of, some of us have grown restless."

"Pity you and your horrid *restlessness*. You're an opportunist. You always were."

Kokabiel's face contorted into a scowl. "And not you? People say you would have abandoned Sheol forever."

"The bastards threw me out!"

"They say you tried to build a kingdom on another Shard."

"How little they know! No, Koko, I was trying to build a new universe. One free of this unremitting suffering. But they were too stupid to see the use in that."

"There are four Lamed Vav in Sheol," Kokabiel said. "Trees are growing on the mountains – *apple* trees! There are algal blooms in the lake. And even more subtle changes. The oldest buildings have ceased crumbling. Some cracks have even healed. Mashit believes the Lamed Vav are helping Sheol grow."

"She is right."

"Ashey, in this new world, I'd rather have you as my lord than her."

"I'm flattered. But, as you can see, I'm occupied."

"There are others who share my views."

"Who? Name them."

Kokabiel's face wavered in the rising heat, but the demon said nothing. Ashmedai breathed in deeply and felt more awake than he had in days. "I'm beginning to see now. The Second General plots a coup."

"It's too early for revolution," Kokabiel said. "People still hope Mashit will bring abundance. But many grow impatient. She does things so...differently. I think their restlessness can be directed, focused, but only if the people have a cause to rally around."

"The return of their deposed king to his throne."

Kokabiel stuck his long neck out over the pit of lava so that he was but an arm's reach from Ashmedai's face. "Yes."

"This sounds wonderful, Koko, and I'd love to help. Can you get me out of here?"

Kokabiel withdrew his head from the expanse. "First I need information. You shared a bed with Mashit for millennia. She was your wife."

"And look where marriage has led me."

"You know her deepest secrets."

"Are you seeking bedroom advice?"

"I want to smash her smug face with a mallet. I want to tear open her flesh with my bare hands and pull out her frigid heart."

"Ah." Ashmedai leaned back. "The story becomes clear. You've betrayed me, Koko, and now you seek my place in bed beside my wife. Did she promise you great things if you sided with her? Did she tease you with sex, with promises of love and power, only to spurn you just as you thought you had arrived at the prize? You don't care a shred for my rule. You only seek revenge against her."

Kokabiel wilted, and the fire went out of his eyes. "Does it matter my reason if it frees you?"

Ashmedai sighed. "No, it doesn't. I can't tell you how many times I wished to tear her throat out too."

"So why didn't you?"

"Because I loved her."

"And now?"

Ashmedai stared at Kokabiel. He said nothing.

Kokabiel kneeled before the ledge, bowed his head, then looked up at Ashmedai. "My king, I've betrayed you." He pulled a bone blade from his hip and raised his left arm. He held the sharp knife above his palm. "Allow me to avenge both of us. Show me how to kill Mashit. Show me her weaknesses, and I swear by Great Abbadon and the Fires of Sheol I will never betray you again." He sliced the knife across his palm, and a stream of dark blood dripped to the fires below, turning to steam long before it touched lava. The air filled with the burnt smell of it.

"Impressive," Ashmedai said. "The only problem is, she's a First One. And as you can see, we're very hard to kill." The truth was that to kill a First One all one had to do was cast them into the fires of Sheol, the same fires churning beneath his cage. But spreading such information around wasn't good for his long-term health. Kokabiel had betrayed him once. There was no reason to think he wouldn't again.

"You don't know how to kill her?" Kokabiel said. "Or won't tell me?"

"Go," Ashmedai said. "Foment this rebellion. Prepare your

army, and let me regain my strength. Perhaps, with rest, I might remember a secret or two she whispered in the dark, as we lay in each other's arms."

Kokabiel rose. "You were a better lover than she ever was."

"And you a worse liar."

"I don't lie to you now."

"I'm tired, Koko. I need sleep. Rethink your plan. You're in a good station. Why risk losing it all?"

"Don't you want to be free? Don't you want to be king again?"

"I do, but not just because you can't fuck my wife."

"I'll speak to my friends and tell them you'll help us," Kokabiel said. "They'll be happy to know their king will rule again soon. Rest, Ashey. And get over your silly pride. You never think clearly when you're tired."

"And you when you're horny."

"I do this for the realm."

"You do this for your cock."

"Goodbye, Ashey. I'll return soon."

Kokabiel had turned to leave when Ashmedai said, "Koko?"

The tall demon paused.

"You were right," Ashmedai said.

"About what?"

"I *am* happy to see you."

"You've an odd way of showing it." Kokabiel vanished down the corridor.

For months, countless demonfolk had bribed the guards so they might have an audience with him, the Traitor King, to curse and scorn him. But they were from low stations in his court or mere palace servants whom he had once offended. Yet now, in quick succession, his daughter and Kokabiel? Something was stirring in Abbadon, a nervous energy, and he sensed it even down here, swinging in the dark.

Though Kokabiel was not a First One like Ashmedai, but of the subsequent inbred generations, Kokabiel had sworn upon Great Abbadon, and the blood vow was not to be taken lightly. Perhaps the furry demon believed his own lies. Maybe he did want to return Ashmedai to the throne.

But Ashmedai would be a fool to tell Kokabiel how to kill a

First One. His old lover could easily have his chains cut and cast him into the fires below. But there was another reason why he had remained coy. Even after Mashit had exiled him, after she'd had him stoned and humiliated, after she had locked him in this dreadful cage, he still loved her. And he knew she still loved him too. Hers was a twisted, spiteful love, but love nonetheless. It was the only reason why he was still alive. He floated away on a dream of her pale beauty as his cage swung, remembering ancient days and the laughter of their many children.

The air still stank of Kokabiel's vaporized blood.

CHAPTER SIX

IT WAS JUST AFTER DAWN AND MASHIT AND DAPHNA MARCHED through the gleaming palace corridors, down endless marble steps, escorted by fifty soldiers of her Shield.

Everyone must see the face of my daughter, Mashit thought, *my emissary on Earth.*

Scribes walked with them, one to record the procession via memory crystal, two to write on their leather scrolls everything that happened. They would ensure this day would be remembered for eternity.

Mashit smiled as they entered the octagonal Hall of Broken Mirrors. The twin suns shone through narrow slits high in the walls, and blood-red sunbeams girded the air above. Thirteen black candles were mounted on iron poles around the periphery, their crimson flames steady and bright. Arched doorways framed the adjacent chambers, but the light did not penetrate their black thresholds.

Sorcerers in ashen robes, twice again as tall as the tallest in the room, stood beside each candle, faces hidden under hoods. On the floor, complex sigils and signs had been inscribed in blood, and an oval full-length mirror mounted on ornate wooden braces waited in the center, faintly wavering.

One of the sorcerers threw back his hood to reveal a tall and narrow head covered in a moving mass of eyes and lips. "My queen, welcome," he said with most but not all of the lips, their voices barely above a whisper. "We are ready to open the pathway."

Mashit gestured to Daphna to wait, then she approached the mirror alone. Minute whorls of emerald fire leaped from its oval frame. Its energy, built up over months, seethed and pulsed, making the hair on her neck rise. She stared at her reflection, her flowing white gown, the band of silver at her waist, hair black and straight, face pale as chalk, eyes brown with flecks of green. She was a fragment, becoming whole. She was Sheol herself.

In the mirror Daphna was staring at her. Her daughter wore human attire: a sleeveless black dress cut above the knee, black pumps, a thin belt. Her hair was tied back, and her lipstick was the same ruddy shade as the sunbeams girding the space above.

It pleased Mashit to see how much her daughter resembled her. Only their eyes were different. Daphna's were gray-white, like her father's. And like her father, she was sharp and clever, but also stubborn. This was why she would not be going to Earth alone.

"My beloved child," Mashit said to Daphna's reflection. "You will venture across the Great Deep to a new world. But I will be with you, always."

Mashit approached her daughter and grabbed her hands. "You are so beautiful," Mashit said. "So clever and smart. Go to Earth and show them what true artistry is."

"I do this for my queen," Daphna said, "for Sheol, and for all the Shards." Mashit smiled at her practiced words, uttered perfectly, and the scribes marked this moment in their records, when the queen's daughter departed to conquer the Cosmos.

"May Great Abbadon's fire guide you through the dark," Mashit said.

"And may our light burn eternally outward."

"Go, go, my child. Spread the fires of Sheol to the far corners of Creation." Daphna's hands were steady and firm in hers. "You have such poise, my daughter. Such dignity. It will serve you well, on your journey."

"All I am I owe to you, Mother."

"I know."

Hand in hand, they approached the mirror. Mashit nodded to the lead sorcerer, and nine figures emerged from the shadows. They looked human at first blush. They wore human jeans, collared shirts, blouses, suits, but all were demon, heavily disguised with spells so powerful only Mashit could undo them. Each carried many overstuffed bags and satchels, and four hefted a massive metal trunk.

The nine paused beside Mashit and Daphna, and the lead sorcerer raised a fist. With his fingers he made gestures that the other sorcerers repeated. The candles flared up, yellow flames long and bright as swords flashing in the sun. In ancient Demonsbreath the sorcerers chanted, "The light is bent over the sky, and the way is shortened. The greater the death, the greater the path. The light is bent over the sky..."

Three more figures emerged from the shadows. Two were thick-armed and bull-faced, wearing leather and metal armor. Drops of yellow sweat spilled down their cheeks. They dragged a hooded creature between them, a frail, emaciated thing. Its bare feet slid across the stone floor, leaving trails of blood.

They threw the creature to the floor, then one of the soldiers yanked off its hood. A human woman of perhaps twenty Earth years gasped and blinked as she hurriedly gazed around. Her skin was pale and sickly, and her sand-colored hair was streaked with white. Bleeding tattoos – sigils and seals carved into her flesh – covered her naked body. Like the mirror, her tattoos swirled with miniscule flames.

"Please" she whimpered in French. "Stop.... Stop..."

The lead sorcerer emerged from the circle holding a clear crystal orb. He lowered it before the woman, but she turned away. He grabbed her chin and held the orb before her face, but she squeezed her eyes shut.

"Open your eyes," he said in French.

"Please...make it stop! Kill me!"

"Soon. If you open your eyes." He squatted before her, and in a voice that sounded like a middle-aged human woman he said, "This is all a bad dream, my little cabbage."

"Mama?" The woman gasped and opened her eyes, hopeful, but when she saw the demon's quivering face she wailed. The crystal orb flashed, and her eyes dilated into colorless holes. Her mouth fell open and drool spilled onto the floor.

Mashit looked at her daughter, expecting her to be pleased at how easily humans were manipulated. Instead Daphna had a look of revulsion on her face.

Mashit felt her ire rise. *Do you think it easy to travel between worlds?* she thought. *The foods you eat, the luxuries you know – all come through suffering like this!*

Earth lay across the gargantuan void of the Great Deep. To cross such a chasm, one needed immense power, and there was immense power in terror. These sorcerers were adept at finding a human's greatest fear and feeding it back to them in nightmare after nightmare, while inscribing their bodies with amplifying spells, for months and months, sometimes years, until their fear became a tangible thing. This young woman was, essentially, fuel. Mashit's world was shattered to make room for these human wretches. Now, she shattered them to make room for hers. She found it poetic. So why didn't Daphna?

The other sorcerers closed in on the woman, who watched the orb, transfixed.

"Give me the orb," Mashit said to the lead sorcerer.

A scowl crossed his face. He would have been recorded in history as the one who opened the door. But Mashit would not give him that honor. Sense finally got the better of him, and he handed over the orb, bowed, and said, "The honor is yours, my queen."

Mashit stepped closer to the woman and held the orb before her eyes. "Escape is coming," she said in French. "All you have to do is look, and the pain ends."

The woman trembled, a flash of hope crossing her face.

"That's it. The nightmare ends as soon as you look into the glass."

Sparks like diamond dust floated from the woman's eyes into the sphere. She wretched, and the sparks stopped. Tears fell from her cheeks into the sphere.

"It's over," Mashit said. "You can let go. Nothing lasts forever. Not even you. Think of the relief when the pain finally stops."

The woman resisted. But Mashit would have her power.

"Your life was not void of meaning," Mashit said. "Your death will serve a purpose. Others will suffer less."

A spark drifted from her eyes. Psychological walls were finally crumbling. "That's it," Mashit said. "Give up."

More sparks flowed from her eyes, increasing until they were a scintillating beam.

"That's it," Mashit said. "Let go. And, by the way, this *will* hurt. It will be the most painful thing you've ever felt."

The woman shrieked. The sound swirled within the hall. Light leaped from her body into the orb, and she collapsed into a pile, a sack of skin and hair, all viscera gone. Mashit grinned as she held aloft the glowing orb, bright as a sun. The woman's terror floated inside, the product of months of labor. An enormous amount of power.

Mashit held it aloft for all to see, so it might burn into their minds that it was she alone who wielded such power. And when she was sure all had seen, that the scribes had recorded this moment, she turned and threw the sphere into the mirror with all her strength. The glass shattered, and a howling wind erupted. All the candles blew out. The mirror had vanished, but its oval contour remained.

Smoky at first, a vision appeared on the opposite side. Instead of her reflection, there was a capacious room. A yellow sun shone through tall windows onto an empty floor. Beyond the windows rose a city of steel and glass.

"Hurry, my queen!" the sorcerer shouted above the winds. "The portal will only stay open a minute!"

"Go!" Mashit ordered, and the nine demons in human clothing stepped through the oval doorway with their supplies. As they crossed the threshold, their aspects changed, like a straw bending in a glass of water. Their bodies steamed as bits of ice on their clothing boiled off. Once through, they gazed back through the portal.

Daphna stood beside Mashit, staring down at the remains of the dead human woman. With the point of her shoe, Daphna tapped the deflated heap of skin and hair.

"Leave that mess," Mashit said, "and go!"

Daphna frowned as she looked up at her mother, disappointment in her eyes, as if to say, *Was this really necessary, Mother?*

"You must leave now!" Mashit shouted over the rushing wind; she made a mental note to have the scribes erase any records of her daughter's hesitation.

Daphna stared at the portal, then back at Mashit. Slowly, she climbed over the dead woman and stepped across the gargantuan dimensions onto Earth. Once through, she looked back. They faced each other – mother and child – and Mashit felt as if the mirror were still there, and she was looking at her younger self.

With a clap of thunder, the portal closed. The mirror's fragments vanished. Only the wooden braces remained. The dead woman's skin had turned to powder, which slowly blew away in the remnant gusts still swirling in the chamber.

CHAPTER SEVEN

IT HAD TAKEN DANIEL A WEEK TO RECOVER FROM THE BREAKER of Minds, and he had spent most of that time running out of the washerwoman's house where he had taken shelter to vomit in the humid woods when it was dark, or into an old plastic slop bucket when the sun was high. Her name was Prabha, and she did not ask questions; she just stared and nodded, as if she knew all that ailed him, and made him recite the prayer of Karaagre Vasate every morning with her, her voice high and haunting like the evening birds. And after prayers, they meditated together, taking deep pranayamic breaths that calmed his panic and the nagging feeling that all was meaningless, that he was a bit of debris tossed about in the Great Deep, and would spin there, in its pointless eddies, in emptiness, forever. Slowly, his acute panic ebbed, replaced by a constant underlying fear, a lurking predator threatening to devour his sanity – the Breaker of Minds indeed; the world was not the same as it had been. The world never had been that way. He had believed in lies, that the world was, even though parts needed repair, ultimately beneficent. But the Buddhists had it right. He saw now that the Cosmos was mostly suffering. It took him a week to stop shivering.

He tried to remember what secrets those giggling mirrored spheres had told him, but this only brought about more bouts of panic. But once, as he was meditating beside Prabha, he remembered something they had whispered to him. A name and a city – Dvoyre Gottlieb, Ternivka, Ukraine. Only later did he understand what they had told him. Dvoyre Gottlieb might have a door to hell.

He had offered Prabha money, but she refused. It was her dharma to help, she said. Still, he left two thousand rupees on her table before he fled Marishamehadi in newly washed clothes. He hadn't much cash, and all the money he had wouldn't be enough to repay her; money could never repair anything, not really, but it was all he had to give besides his gratitude. And as he left, he knew there were far more than thirty-six people upholding the world.

He went north. He crossed into Nepal, and was astonished by its breathtaking beauty. He paused to admire the temples of Kathmandu blazing like gods in the orange sunset before he moved on. He climbed the mountains of Tibet and, because he spoke Lhasa Tibetan, he received a warm welcome and was invited to participate in a private sky burial, where vultures, called forth by smoke, swooped down to devour the wrapped corpse of a respected elder. He should have refused their invitation and ventured on, but instead he quietly salivated as raptors pecked at the body, envying their easy feast, hating himself for coming here, like an addict to watch others shoot up. He fled before the ceremony ended; that night he gorged on raw lamb.

In Kyrgyzstan, he joined a small horse caravan – his fluency in Kyrgyz made him a wonder and a friend – and they crossed the sprawling plains and climbed the snow-capped mountains together. The days were long and peaceful, the nights quiet and contemplative. He hid under bundles of burlap when the sun was high. At night he stared up at the heavens, as if the stars were slowly fading sparks from an ancient fire. How long, he wondered, until everything winked out?

In each country, he felt like an impostor. He had no connection to their cultures, nor had he studied their languages. Fluency had been foisted upon him; he had not earned their warmth. Still, the people bestowed their friendship easily, which surprised him. They loved this foreign-faced stranger who knew the local slang for "fart" and "curmudgeon" and "the emerald hue of the grasses at sunset after rain."

Each time he moved on, even if he had been with these people only a short while, he felt as if he were abandoning old friends.

Once, a famished young boy offered him bread as a departing gift, and Daniel wept long and openly while the mother watched; Daniel didn't take the bread. How could he?

He crossed Kazakhstan by train, staring out the window as a thousand yurts zipped by, tent-like dwellings dotting the plains like giant seeds. Here and there grazed wild yak, while chain-smoking passengers beside him effortlessly switched between Kazakh, German, Russian, Korean and so many other languages he wasn't sure what they spoke, but still he understood every word.

Across the plains, grasses grew wild, natty, tall, and after a rain glowed with a fluorescence that left spots in his vision. When not on trains, he sought out stinking-alleys, where windswept garbage and rodents found homes, and there he made shelter during the day. Sometimes he slept in abandoned cars, and when he could not find shelter, covered himself under dirty blankets beneath the open sky, lying awake for hours, wondering if this was the day he'd burn alive.

One evening, while stuffed in the back of a crowded and coughing German van filled with soil-stained Chinese farm workers, the elderly driver said to Daniel, "My grandmother in Huangnan spoke those same words you do, and she died fifty years ago. No one speaks those words anymore. How do you know them?" His tone was accusatory, as if Daniel had awakened old ghosts.

"I've studied languages," he said, forcing a laugh. "I must have learned it in school."

The man pursed his lips and stared at Daniel in the crooked rear-view mirror. "You couldn't have heard it before. No one spoke those words except in our village. When Mao made us all learn Mandarin, we spoke our language only at home, with the windows shut. No outsider came to study our language, and if he had, we would not have spoken it in front of him for fear he was a spy."

Daniel shrugged. "I must have overheard you earlier," he said. "I'm good at picking up things."

The man slowed the car, and the others inside grumbled and cursed. "Devil, get out!" the man said.

"What?"

"Get out, demon! Get out, before you regret it!" He reached over the passenger's lap to open the glove box and pulled out a silver pistol. The shocked passengers shouted, but Daniel would not let this escalate further. "All right," he said, holding up his hands. "I'm leaving."

They left him in a cloud of dust on the side of the road. Nothing around but an empty plain and growing darkness. He was twenty miles from town, from shelter, from anything except wild grass. The hunger gnawed deep into his psyche, twisting pain into anger.

"Fuuuuuck!" he screamed.

He was tired of searching, tired of traveling. He could go eat the dead and live for centuries. Sheol would grow powerful, but who cared? Earth could fend for itself. But then he remembered the boy, and his bread offering, and Prabha, the washerwoman who had asked for nothing, and he hated himself for letting his heart grow cold.

He caught scent of a carcass on the wind, and he grew excited. But as he sniffed more deeply he recognized the mildew smell of dead dog. He sagged, disappointed, and this disgusted him even further, because he had wished this dead thing was human.

CHAPTER EIGHT

EARTH'S YELLOW SUN WAS STRANGE AND INTENSE. DAPHNA had hung blackout curtains over the tall windows of her apartment to make it more like her shadowed palace chamber. These Earth days were so incessant, so bright. But her work had been imperfect, and slivers of sun slipped through the cracks onto the floor, laddering across her large studio like the vertebrae of some light-born beast. For the first few days, as furniture and ornaments were hauled in by small hordes of servants, demon and human, she kept looking over her shoulder at the light, expecting some great conflagration, only to remember that Earth's sun burned hotter and warmer than anywhere she had ever been.

She walked crooked lines across her apartment, avoiding the shining vertebrae, as if this new sun had the power to illuminate well-kept secrets. She hadn't been here long enough to miss home, but she began to wonder why she had agreed to help Mother. She was flattered Mashit had asked her, of all her siblings, to be her emissary here. But during Earth's long days, she wondered if she was ill-suited for this burning world.

She longed for night, when in the comfortable darkness, under a shaded electric lamp throwing dim light onto the walls, she would sit upon the plush blue cushions of her new rococo couch and read one of her recently purchased paperbacks. There was so much she wished to read, and the Earth had an abundance of books.

But not tonight. Now, as she sat upright on the same couch,

Duile and Khein drilled her on her new identity. Her other escorts had left two hours ago for a nearby hotel, but Duile and Khein lingered. They were experts on Earth culture, and had been here twice before, studying, preparing. They wore black suits, white shirts, and black ties. Duile's skin was as dark as the mahogany bar that had been installed this morning, darker even than the demons of Fintas Miel. His tuft of curly black hair was almost invisible on his head. His eyes were dark and deep-set. Khein was his physical opposite. He had skin as pink as a baby piglet, wavy blond-white hair that never seemed to move from its windswept style, and blue eyes that seemed to shine with their own light. But these human forms were mere clothing, a spell wrapped around their hidden demonic shapes. Yet despite their differences, both were cut from the same bland mold. They frowned often, said little unless it was to order her around, and were suspicious of everyone and everything, even the escorts who had come with them. When she wasn't looking, Daphna had trouble telling their voices apart.

"And before you were famous," Duile asked her in English, "what was your name?" He spoke in a curious flattened voice he had said mimicked an American TV presenter. She had never watched TV – such things did not exist on Sheol – but she had learned of this human magic which allowed them to share images across great distances. Her tutors had told her television robbed the mind of imagination, replacing one's long-held thoughts with perverted distortions. And perhaps, Daphna thought, this was why humanity in this current age had ceased to dream; their dreams weren't theirs any more.

"My name is Carina," she answered.

"Carina what?"

"Just Carina," she said. "What came before doesn't matter." She rolled a cigarette and lit it, savoring the buzz as she exhaled a stream of smoke. She had wanted to take up tobacco smoking ever since reading about it in *All Quiet on the Western Front*. It was the first human thing she had tried since she arrived.

"You can't smoke in public," Khein said. "You definitely can't smoke on TV."

"We're not *on* TV," said Daphna. "Are we? Besides, this place stinks of paint and human fabric. I'm just trying to deaden the grotesque smells. And why does my home have to be so human-like?" On the freshly painted red walls hung prints from artists she had only just learned about. Edward Hopper, Jules Breton, and Marc Chagall. One from Martin Lewis. The last was her favorite: a nighttime underground train entrance; a young woman on a metal balcony staring up at a giant building taller than Abbadon's palace, its top obscured by fog, lines of hanging clothing in the foreground. Something lonely about it all. Humans could be so creative, when they wished to be. But she had learned that all too often they chose mediocrity and cliché. Still, even these impressive works made this place feel alien. "No human will ever visit here," she said, "so why can't I decorate it my own way?"

"Because," said Duile. "You must *become* Carina. You must live and breathe her."

Daphna exhaled in his direction. "And by association," she said, "so must you breathe me." She smiled wickedly.

"This is no joke," said Khein. He blinked. The smoke irritated his eyes, but to his credit he did not wince. "The humans will question you until you grow weary, then they will probe you even deeper. If there's a flaw in your story, they'll find it and tear you down. In this age humans love nothing more than to destroy their heroes. It makes them feel as if they are powerful."

"Now tell me," said Duile, assuming the TV-presenter voice, "where are you from?"

"Sheol," she said, then after a long puff of smoke, she tamped her cigarette out. "I mean, I'm from the Ukraine."

Duile frowned. "Do not use the article."

"Which article?"

"Drop the 'the.'"

"I'm from *Ukraine*."

"Where in Ukraine?" he said.

"A small town outside of Lviv."

"No, it's pronounced *L-View*," said Khein.

"And your accent," said Duile. "You must never forget your accent, or they'll know you're lying."

Daphna affected what she had been taught was a Slavic accent. "Is *vis* better?"

Duile frowned. "Don't overdo it. And remember to occasionally drop articles from your sentences. Use less 'the's and 'a's."

"Pass tobacco pouch, will you?" she said.

"Better," Khein said. "But only drop your articles once or twice in a conversation, so it won't seem affected. It will influence the humans on a subconscious level."

"Why can't we use magic?" she said. "Everything I've been taught said humans are such malleable creatures."

"In a short time," Duile said, "you'll appear before millions. It's not yet possible to use magic on so many people at once. That takes more power than we presently have. Such times will come. But for now, we must uphold the ruse and do it this way."

She was still stuck on *You will appear before millions.* Excited, terrified, her heart thumped. She dreamed of performing a song she had written for the harpsichord when Khein woke her from her reverie.

"Carina?"

"Yes?"

"Please tell us your life story," he said.

She cleared her throat. "At thirteen, I was sold into sexual slavery. At fourteen, I–"

"No!" said Duile. "Your previous life was horrid and bleak. Humans are never so forthcoming about their suffering. It hurts to speak of your past. You are troubled by it. Again."

"At thirteen," she began, "I...I left home. A man took me in, promised me...money. He used me for his clients. Got me high."

"Better. Who was he? How did he use you?"

"It was a difficult time," she said. "I'd rather not talk about it."

"No, be more forceful."

"It was a difficult time! I don't want to talk about it."

"But, Ms. Carina, your fans wish to know more."

"Carina! It's just Carina. And that is all I wish to say about that."

Duile looked at Khein, and both men nodded. "Can you tell us anything about your past, Carina?" Duile said. "Anything at all about your life before music?"

"Only that I came to United States to escape the horror that was my life. The past is over. I came here to start again, to begin anew, and I will not look back."

"Very good," said Klein. "Very, very good."

Daphna rolled herself another cigarette. She offered one to them, but they declined. The window was open, letting in warm air from the streets below. At times it smelled like Sheol, spent fires and ash. But there were many new and interesting smells here, things she hadn't yet identified. Laughter drifted through the open window, and she went to it and drew back the shade.

This area of Manhattan was called SoHo, South of Houston, and was, she had read, one of the most expensive. Ornate buildings with masterful stonework glowed yellow-orange in the streetlamps. Below, five humans reveled across the cobblestone street and vanished around a corner.

They have so much, she thought, *yet they intoxicate themselves to oblivion.* They reminded her, she was loath to admit, like her mother. "I'm tired," she said, sighing. "Let's stop for tonight."

"You don't have time for tired," one of them said. She wasn't looking and couldn't tell who. "When you are the most exhausted you have ever felt, when you have given all your energy to your performance and just want to lie down to sleep, that's when the human media machine will shine their brightest light on your face. If you err, if you say something wrong, you could jeopardize–"

"Did you fucking hear me? I'm tired! We're done."

"Daphna, you don't understand–"

"Shut your maggoty mouth," she said. "I'm the daughter of the queen, and you answer to me. When I say we're done, we're done."

Khein and Duile glanced at each other. "Very well, *princess*" Duile said with a trace of scorn. The men rose together. "But this is the last time we will call you that. We return at 8 a.m. tomorrow to take you to the recording studio. Your time as the daughter of the queen has ended. From now on, you will be Carina. In public, we'll address you as such."

She waved her hand at them as if swatting away flies. They let themselves out, and she bolted the heavy metal door behind them. At last, freedom! She let out a scream of relief. She flopped herself onto the couch and savored the peace and silence.

Now, all she had to do was figure out when 8 a.m. was. She'd come across human clocks in books, but their notions of time always seemed so rigid and inflexible, unlike the fluid arcs of time and space on the Shards. At any rate, there were no clocks in her apartment. She would have to get herself a watch. She'd always wanted one.

She rolled herself a cigarette, forming it lovingly, a work of art, and lit it as she moved to a soft chair and opened one of the books she had purchased. *1984*.

She exhaled smoke as she read the first line. "It was a bright day in April, and the clocks were striking thirteen." She scratched her chin with her cigaretted hand. Thirteen o'clock? All the clocks she had ever seen had only twelve hours. This human notion of time would be harder to grasp than she'd thought. She read a few pages, when the sounds of automobiles and people outside drew her to the window again. Manhattan thrummed. The city was alive, a vibrant beast, unlike the cold and dead palace of Abbadon with its thousand empty halls, unlike the mournful and windswept streets of Sheol. How could she stay locked up here when this living city breathed outside?

She fled her apartment in a flash, pressed the elevator button, but impatient, she leaped down the stairs. The cobbled street was slippery from recent rain, and the air smelled deliciously of moisture. The clouds had parted, and a few stray but bright stars glimmered above the skyline. The stars here were small and faint, little twinkling diamonds in a black-blue sea. The street was a wide chasm bordered by the lovely and ornate buildings. Up close they seemed to breathe. She wondered what their lives were like, the humans who lived inside them. Iron latticework clung to their sides, knots of ladders and stairs, so elegant it took her a moment to recognize them as escape routes; demons seldom had such safety concerns. She smiled and understood why so many human artists chose this city as their muse. There were endless fascinating corners and ornate edifices for light to fall and make parades of shadows. It was a city of extremes.

A young man and woman walked down the street, laughing. They paused to take a photo of themselves with a smartphone, technology Duile and Khein had only just taught her. There was bright flash that startled her. The two carried many bags, each branded with the name of a different store. When the couple saw Daphna, their giggling ceased, and they whispered to each other. Smiling, they sauntered over. The man puffed from a black tube, and as he inhaled a small green light glowed. He exhaled a cloud of white smoke that smelled faintly like Mother's hookah. They reeked of alcohol.

"Howdy!" the woman said, and the man giggled. "Wow. Great eyes!"

"Hello," Daphna said, shivering. These were the first humans she had encountered alone, without Duile and Khein or Mashit by her side, and she didn't know what to expect. She feared them, yes, but she also found herself intensely curious about these creatures who had spent their entire lives on Earth.

"Lose your shoes?" the man said. His voice was deep, in an accent she had never heard before, and he took twice as long to speak his words as he needed to.

Her feet were bare. Theirs were covered in shiny, well-cut leather. How she wanted shoes like them! "Do you wear shoes like that often?" she said.

"It helps," he said, smirking.

"Helps what?"

"You know, walking." The woman chuckled.

It had not occurred to her as she had fled her apartment that she might need footwear. A demon could walk on cut glass and it would not cut her soles. "I like to feel this Earth under my toes," she said. "The stones feel so nice and cold."

The two looked at each other and laughed, as if Daphna had made some obscure joke. Faint footprints across the cobblestones – not human, but clawed like a hen – led back to her apartment. She made a note to remember to wear shoes outside. At any rate, these humans didn't notice her footprints.

"Well," the woman said. She pointed her index finger toward Daphna, her thumb to the sky, and made a clicking sound with her mouth. "Catch ya later."

The man snorted and they turned to go.

"Wait," she said. "Tell me, can you recommend a good book?"

"Huh?" he said, turning.

"Do you have a favorite book?"

He grimaced, and the woman shrugged. "What for?" he said.

"Because I love to read."

"Uhhhhh," he said, as if the very act of thinking was painful. "I don't know."

"What was the last novel you read?" she said.

"Shit, I don't remember."

"Me neither!" the woman proudly exclaimed.

"Are you joking?" Daphna said. "You really don't remember?"

"No," the man said. "I really don't."

Daphna shook her head. "Did you know there are more books published on Earth today than in the entire history of your . . . of Earth. Almost all the works of humanity are available to you through that thing you have in your pocket, and you don't read any of it?"

The man let go of the woman and puffed himself up before Daphna. She steeled herself. "Who the fuck are you to judge us?" he said, his breath foul.

"C'mon," the woman said. "Leave the bitch. Can't you tell? She can't even remember to wear shoes. She's broken." They turned and began walking away.

"I'm not broken!" Daphna shouted. Why did this small barb from a stranger – a human at that – hurt so much? "You know what broken is?" she screamed. "It's having the greatest works of literature at your fingertips and choosing to ignore them all!"

"Loser!" the woman shouted. She put her thumb and index finger to her head as she and the man disappeared around the corner.

Humans were so full of hubris, so proud of their ignorance! Perhaps few exceptional ones had understood the rare bounty they had been given. But the bulk of their execrable lot did not deserve this fertile Earth. She would be all too happy to snatch it from them when the time came.

She wanted a cigarette but had forgotten the tobacco in her apartment. She was about to return home when she decided she needed to walk. At the end of the block she turned left onto Canal Street. The noise of automobiles and light from streetlamps assaulted her, and she squinted. Even at night, humans preferred things bright, as if they were still children hiding from monsters lurking in the dark. She walked along the sidewalk until she found a small store. Its awning said, "Fast Yummy Deli," and signs boasted of cold drinks, beer, newspapers, and cigarettes.

She nodded to the small, elderly man behind the counter, who was casually reading a Chinese newspaper. He acknowledged her presence long enough to notice her bare feet, frowned, and went back to his paper. Along the wall, refrigerators were fully stocked with thousands of beverages. Whatever she might imagine was here: juice, soda, water, milk, tea, coffee, beer, wine, cider. A metal island dominated the center of the store. Windows of clear glass hung over neatly arranged trays of hot and cold foods. She walked around the island, reading each tag aloud, "Chicken wings, beef lo mein, papaya, pork short ribs, cantaloupe, yellow rice, hard boiled eggs."

Such rich smells! Such colorful variety!

On another wall was a long, glass-enclosed container filled with sandwiches, whole-wheat wraps, egg and tuna salads, turkey, salami, roast beef, paninis, Swiss, muenster, provolone, mozzarella cheeses. Crowding the checkout counter were nut bars, potato chips, chocolate bars, candy, apples, bran muffins, sugar-free gum, brownies. Behind the man were rows of cigarette boxes, in assorted flavors, sizes, and brands. In fact there was no space inside this Fast Yummy Deli that did not satisfy one craving or another.

She grew heated, and she felt as if her heart might tear from beating so hard. She wanted to scream or break something. For her entire life, century after moribund century, she and her fellow demons had lived in squalor and scarcity. On Sheol, they struggled to grow food, animals were small and frail, plants rare. The occasional thing of substance was hidden deep in the palace, visited only by a select few. And Sheol, she knew, had it easier than most. Upon the myriad Shards, where life tenaciously clung, misery was rife. And yet here, a minute's walk from her apartment, in a small store run by an aging man, was more abundance than she had ever seen.

"Is it like this every day?" she said.

He looked up from his paper. "Huh?" His glasses hung on the edge of his nose reflecting the lights.

"This store. Is it always like this?"

"We open twenty four hours," he said.

"Every day?"

He nodded. "Always open."

She reached deep into her pocket and pulled out a fat roll of human currency that Duile had given her. More than a thousand dollars. She carefully placed the roll down on the counter. "How much will this buy me?"

He stared at the money for a moment before he looked nervously back at her. "What you want?" he said.

She stared deeply into his eyes. "Everything."

—

Skittles. Why had she never heard of such astoundingly delicious things before? When all this was over, she would import a million bags of these sacred little candies and spread them freely over Sheol like confetti so that all demons could taste their absurdly pleasurable sweetness. She had four bags of assorted flavors open on the table in the recording room, less a room than a closet. Its walls were covered with soundproofing yellow foam, and she liked to run her fingers over its sinuous curves. A large black microphone attached to a swivel arm rose from the table. In the corner was an overgrown plant, its heart-shaped leaves green and vibrant. A large window peered into the engineering room, but didn't alleviate her nagging claustrophobia.

"I know you love your Skittles, my dear," said Richard, the sound engineer, through her headphones. "I love me some Skittles too. But your lips are smacking like crazy, darling. Mind taking a little break from noshing so we can do another take?"

Richard was a fifty-something human, adept at modern sound recording and editing, Duile had said. Richard had mastered songs for famous artists and cost an absurd sum. A dark beard with salted gray streaks wrapped his round face, and headphones cupped his ears. His voice was gentle, deep and soft, accented with what she came to learn was a trace of Georgia drawl. A decade ago, he might have been handsome. But time had sagged his brown eyes and cheeks. He was what humans called "stocky," and his overall aspect hinted at a great sadness come and gone, but still festering. And even though he wore no wedding ring, Daphna sensed its former presence like the afterimage of a smartphone's bright flash.

Duile and Khein, in identical black suits, stood on opposite sides of Richard, arms crossed, reflections of each other. Sweat dripped down their faces, but they refused to take off their jackets. The three hovered over the sound console, a wondrous piece of technology with a thousand knobs and levers and lights. Off to the side, a news magazine lay open to an article about the earthquakes and unexplained dimming of the sun that had rocked the Earth five months ago. Daphna had read their theories, which posited everything from the wrath of God to an invisible celestial object that had passed outside the solar system, causing ripples in gravitational fields that temporarily reduced the sun's nuclear fusion. The truth, she thought, lay somewhere in the middle.

She threw a handful of Skittles in her mouth and pushed the bag to the far side of the table, out of reach, opposite a patch of green mold. "Last one," she said, chewing.

"Sorry about the mold, darling," he said, sighing, his voice velvety in her ears. By Abbadon, she could listen to him all day.

In the corner where table met wall, mold reached sticky green fingers toward the ceiling. Nothing like this ever grew in Sheol, and its presence filled her with pleasure. "The green is beautiful!" she said, and Duile and Khein shook their heads at her.

"Beautiful?" Richard said. "Huh. Anyway, I wash that damn table with bleach every morning and the cursed mold grows back each night. Thought it was a moisture problem, so I put that philodendron in there to help. And you know what, that plant's been growing crazy too! You ever read *The Secret Life of Plants*? I think the plants dig the music!"

"Can we fucking get back to work?" Khein said so loudly that Daphna heard him through Richard's headset. "We're paying you by the hour." His voice was grit in her ears, and she winced.

"Excuse me," Richard said. "Of course, gentleman. Apologies. Carina, doll, you ready?"

She glanced at the sheet music. She had learned to sight read when she was still a girl, pestering Igriel, the palace composer under Ashmedai, when she couldn't suss the musical notation on her own. One read-through an hour ago, and she had memorized the notes. The lyrics took longer. They were strange and nonsensical.

"After this song," she said, "I have several of my own I'd like to record."

Khein looked at Duile, then bent to press the "talk" button so

Daphna could hear them. "We'll get to those later, Carina. We need to finish this first."

"These lyrics," Daphna said, "they're idiotic. The song wants to be happy. It's in E major, but the words, they're–"

"Just sing the words," said Duile. He let go of the button and whispered something to Khein, cupping his mouth so she couldn't see. A moment later, both men nodded.

Khein took out a small plastic rectangle with a metal tip from his pocket, and he handed it to Richard as if it were a key to a long-locked door. Richard stared at it, nodded, then placed the rectangle into the console, metal tip first. What strange human magic was this? The three were talking, but she couldn't hear what they were saying.

"What's going on?" she said.

Richard flicked the talk button. "They're changing the back-track, doll. They think it'll inspire you." He looked over his shoulder and smiled at Duile, then turned to his computer screen, his face bright in its blue glow. "Holy smoke, there are hundreds of tracks here. You sure you want this in her ears? It's...whoa. It's complex. Binaural beats. Huh. Well, I like to minimize the phoned tracks when recording. Helps the artist stay in key."

"Play it for her," Duile said.

"Okay, boss. I can always adjust pitch problems in post."

Duile leaned over and flicked the talk button off, and the three spoke some more. Daphna grew impatient and ate more Skittles. She vowed to get a message to her mother about these two escorts. They had the manners of the wretches who lived in Sheol's slums and ate the insects that fed on shit.

Richard frowned. He nodded and said, "Okay, we're going again with these new backing tracks. You ready, doll?"

"At this point," she said, "I just want a fucking cigarette."

Richard counted down from three with his fingers, and the music began in her ears. Before, the track had been a simple, boring melody, a keyboard "synth" that sounded vaguely harp-like. But the music that rushed into her ears now overflowed with tonal complexity. It was too much. She felt as if she were drowning, as if more than sound was flooding into her. Emotions, feelings, thoughts were pouring in too, overwhelming her body. The music wasn't so much an aural pattern but a physical gestalt.

The initial panic was quickly subsumed by an intense and all-consuming pleasure, comfy, womb-like, as if she were floating in a bath of warm water. She felt good, ecstatic even, but there was a sinister side to it, as if some part of her had to drown in exchange for this pleasure. She wanted to stop listening, but the music promised a greater ecstasy and infinite release if she continued. And as she did the pleasure grew.

She was so overcome by the feelings that she almost missed her cue to begin the first verse.

"Good day, good day, goodbye to day

"I've nothing to love except my reflection

"The days are dead, I hide in your shadows

"My greatest moments are when I

"Give up, give up, give up

"Days are so much easier when you don't

"When you don't do anything at all..."

The music assaulted her. Something odd was happening. Years studying under the finest sorcerers in the palace had taught her to recognize this exchange of power, when someone was using magic to drain her. This multi-layered song was infused with spells.

As a child of First Ones, she was a powerful demon, and yet she felt herself falling under its sway. Humans, who had few defenses against such magic, would be absolutely wrecked by it.

Swept up in the current, she sang the remaining verses, and when she looked up, Duile and Khein seemed pleased, if such an emotion could register on their stoic faces. But Richard looked altogether different. There was something odd in his gaze. His eyes were deadened, devoid of the luster that had shone a moment before. Richard stared at her, his mouth parted an inch, as if in a trance.

The song ended. Silence descended. It was a full minute before anyone spoke.

"Well, that was fucking intense," she said, shivering.

Richard swallowed, blinked. He rubbed his face as if he'd just nearly been killed and could not believe he was still alive. He pressed the talk button. "I've...that...I'm..."

"We need a radio edit by Friday," Duile said. "It's in our contract that if we don't receive it by then, you refund our deposit and you get nothing."

Richard nodded, slowly at first, then faster. "Yes...yes. Of course. Sooner! I'll push some of my other clients aside. I swear, in my whole career I've never..."

"We'll call you tomorrow," said Khein. Then to Daphna he said, "We're done for today. The afternoon is yours. Your driver is waiting outside. Try to stay out of trouble." Khein and Duile left the control room, leaving Richard alone. He stared at her before slowly reaching for the "talk" switch. "Carina, that was.... That was.... Hang on."

He fled the control room as if he suddenly had to go to the bathroom. A moment later there was a knock on the door. Richard peeked his head in timidly at first, a circle of beard hovering by the door. Then he fully entered, as if unable to stop himself. "I just wanted to say," he said, "I've been doing this for thirty-five years. I've recorded some of the most famous artists in the world. And I've never...." He seemed terrified. "I've never heard anything like you before. Your voice, it...it filled me."

"You liked it?" she said. Besides a few palace sycophants, who were probably just seeking her favor to get closer to her parents, none had ever praised her art before.

"Oh, I truly *loved* it, Carina." He stepped closer. "I hope this isn't too forward of me. I'm not good at these types of things, but I was hoping you might, well, sign me on, on a more permanent basis. I could be your resident sound engineer. I have to be honest, when you first walked in this morning, I thought you were just another wannabe pop-star. I had no idea how talented you are!"

His eyes were dilated, black abysses, and he didn't blink. He seemed to be daydreaming with his eyes open. His hand shook as he shifted his stocky body from one foot to the other.

"Richard," she said, "you're a little intense."

He blinked and looked down at his feet. "Oh gosh, oh gosh, I'm sorry," he said, retreating. "I'm being way too forward. Shit. This isn't like me. Shit, I don't even curse! Fuck!" He laughed nervously. "Sorry. Let me get back to work. Real, sorry."

He reached for the door, but she put a hand on his shoulder. "Richard, wait."

He flinched, and his hand froze on the doorknob. She spun him around. He was a large man, almost bear-like, but he was so terrified and in awe of her that in aspect he was more like a puppy. "I'm new to this world," she said.

"The music industry can be intimidating at first."

"Right, the, uh, *industry*. Duile and Khein, they're so stiff. And they're not from here. I could use someone local, a guide, to help me find my way around. Richard, would you be that person for me?"

A smile grew on his face, until he seemed to shine as bright as the spotlights above them. "Oh, I'd be honored, Carina. Honored."

"You really liked my song?"

"Oh my gosh! I want to hear you sing again as soon as possible."

"Come here," she said, pulling him closer.

"Ms. Carina, I, um, I..."

"It's Carina," she said. "Just Carina."

She pressed him down onto his knees, and he obeyed. He stared up at her, eyes wide and waiting. "You want to hear me sing again?" she said. She unfastened her belt and unzipped her skirt. They fell away. She wore nothing underneath.

"Oh my," he said. "Oh my."

She grabbed the back of his head. "Tell me how much you loved my song."

"More than anything. You're going to go so far, Carina. You're going to be famous. People are going to adore you."

She pressed his head deep into her crotch and he licked her. She moaned and fell back onto the table as he continued to taste her. He went at her like an animal. Just one song, for one person, and look at how he worshipped her. How she would rule them! How she would be adored! Moaning, she fell back against the table and knocked the plant beside her to the floor. The pot shattered. Its leaves had wilted and turned brown, and the green mold had turned black as cigarette ash. Such power!

She screamed as she came, a violent shudder like a universe cracking. Richard continued to happily lick away as he stared up at her. In his eyes was nothing but worship.

CHAPTER NINE

Adar, the Daughter Star, dipped beneath the western mountain peaks as Kokabiel slunk from the palace to venture down into Abbadon's darkening streets. A tattered robe, acquired from a large and recently dead prisoner, hung over his tall shoulders. Its wide hood draped over his horns and face. The patchwork fabric swept over the debris-strewn streets, stirring up dust and dung so that he sneezed as he went. It was usually beneficial to have an ultrasensitive nose like his, but this was not such a time. He had shrunk his long neck, tucked his chin deep into his chest, and had taken off his iron cracked-egg pin that identified him as a general. With a series of spells he had shrunk his horns to nubs, collapsed his frame, and changed the color of his fur to brown. If one didn't peer too closely – and few would outside the palace – none would recognize Kokabiel, Second General of the Legion, traipsing through the city's slums like vermin.

When he was First General under Ashmedai, he had ordered regular sweeps of these streets. The oldest and frailest demons, those who could not flee from his approaching army, were killed, their bodies burned in heaping pyres that sent up columns of black smoke. Or they were carried to the dungeons to be used as test subjects for the palace sorcerers. He had loved those days, the powerful sense of release at having purged the city of its most loathsome. But like the midden spiders and other vermin, the slum dwellers always came back.

In some ways, all the streets of Abbadon, all its grotesque and convoluted corners, were slums. But among these sordid avenues and reeking lanes a few districts rose to rarefied heights of loathsomeness, so that even the lowliest avoided venturing into them if they could. And while the days in Sheol were hot and sun-blasted, its nights were frigid and wind-swept. Fat red stars glowed above like coals, but gave no warmth, and the winds could blast the skin off of a poor soul caught without shelter, scattering the dust of their flesh across Sheol. Perhaps it was such dust that made him sneeze now.

He made his way into Last Chance, where huge stones bent at fierce angles, where high precipices looked down upon shadowed pits and gray towers like pinnacled dung rose from unseen depths. Here Sheol's most pitiful demons swarmed around impromptu fires, lit by makeshift spells to keep warm for the coming night. The spellcraft fires sent flickering shadows onto the walls and made their number seem greater than it was.

If only they were to pool their magic, Kokabiel thought, *they could build a great conflagration. Instead, they remain apart, shuddering through these frigid nights.*

He shook his head and spat. This was why they lived in squalor. They were the cause of their own low station, yet they blamed others for their lot. What hypocrisy!

He listened to snatches of conversations as he walked through stinking tunnels and under teetering ledges formed from long-collapsed buildings. The rising wind stirred up ash and shit as the suns fully set and the pregnant red stars burned through the gray haze.

A cracked stone block from a building collapsed ages ago formed a windbreak, and several creatures huddled around a hovering ball of green fire. Their voices, echoing through the folds of stone, were loud and argumentative. Kokabiel paused to listen.

"Midden crawlers? Blech!" hissed a mantis-faced creature. "We'll soon have a *new* food supply." The ball of green fire hovered in the air, agglomerated by fragile magic, flickering and dropping sparks that vanished before they hit the ground.

"I heard that too," said an amorphous leathery black mass of mouths. Some mouths squirmed and shifted, and Kokabiel realized each was a child, suckling off their mother's flesh. "We'll soon have a new food source," she said, "imported from Earth!"

"Not from Earth, imbecile," said the mantis. "From *Sheol*. Here! Haven't you heard? The mountains are blooming!"

"Abbadon's ass," said a glistening white worm covered in crystalline purple fur.

"But I've seen the trees!" said the mantis.

"Have you, now?" said the worm.

"You can see them too! Climb the thousand stairs up Lilith's Wish. From there you can see the whole city, the mountains, and the Dissipation beyond. Things are growing on the cliffs. *Green* things. Apple trees!"

"You've never seen a tree," the demoness said from several of her mouths. "Nor an apple. How do you know what a tree even looks like?"

"Because I've heard of them," said the mantis. "And besides, it *looks* like a tree."

"Tommyrot," said the worm. He spat a viscous yellow substance into the green orb, and it sizzled and evaporated. "You speak tommyrot."

"Not so," the mantis said. "It's all the certain true."

"Dust has addled your brain," said the worm. He bit into the well-chewed and rotten abdomen of a large gray midden spider, common in these slums. Dark juices dribbled from his chin. "Last month you said you saw Abbadon's ghost floating over the lake tell you his ancient vision would soon be fulfilled."

"I wasn't the only one who saw him!"

The mass of mouths rocked on her four short legs. "And there was also that palace cook," she said. "Pheth, who built an aviary of birds without anyone knowing."

"It goes on," the worm spat. "You're a golem's golem if you believe any of that."

The mantis fell back on his triple-jointed legs, defeated. "But it's all the certain true."

Is this all it takes to defeat them? Kokabiel thought, disgusted. *Mere words? No wonder they are out here, freezing, while others sleep warmly indoors.*

The mantis slumped. "But it's all the certain true. I swear it."

"Swear by whom?" said the worm. "Your word is worth less than

Sheol's unsettled dust. Your words are like the dung that flows from the queen's lips."

The mass of mouths twitched at the worm's words, and several of the smaller mouths clinging to her shifted. "Mashit's spies lurk in all corners," she said. "You should watch your tongue."

"And you, your mouths," said the worm. "Besides, I don't care. Let them hear! They know the truth as well as we do. Queen Mashit has been spreading lies. She promises abundance. But what has she given us? We *still* shiver by this pathetic fire. We *still* eat vermin that crawl over the midden heaps."

"But not forever!" said the mantis. "Soon we'll–"

"Soon, we'll die. That, at least, will be relief."

"My children," said the mass of mouths. "What of them?"

"What of them?" said the worm. "Don't you see? No one cares for us. No one is going to save us." He inhaled sharply. "And, by the way," he said, turning to Kokabiel, "who the fuck are you?"

Kokabiel put a hand on his concealed sword. Had this been any other situation, Kokabiel would have quickly disemboweled him. But this insolent wretch did not recognize him in his disguise. He released his hand from the hilt and took a calming breath, then stepped forward. "I came to see if I could find warmth," he said, "but it seems I have found none."

"What warmth we have," the worm said, "is not for sharing."

"All the more reason," said Kokabiel, "why your fires remain small."

"If you've a problem with our fire, build your own!"

"I plan to," Kokabiel said. "A rather large one."

As he turned to leave, the mantis said, "Wait! Before you go, answer me one question. Do you think the queen will bring abundance to Sheol, as she has promised?"

Kokabiel studied these demons. The mantis, frail, spotted and scabbed, but hopeful. The grimacing worm, old, ringlets gray and dull, exhausted, skeptical. The mass of mouths, her clinging children, desperate, lost. He pitied them, for they could not see how they exacerbated their own suffering. "Do you think the Cosmos cares a whit what we think? *Actions* define us, not thoughts or feelings. Mashit makes promises, but what has she done? Behind her grand elocutions, I see a drunk stumbling about in a dark cavern and only her hubris to light her way. She will fail miserably."

"Careful!" said the mass of mouths, all of them quivering. "You'll get us killed!"

Kokabiel laughed. "Do you think words are poisonous barbs? That the queen cares what a few shit-covered slum dwellers think of her? Of course she doesn't. But raise an army a thousand-strong against her, then she will listen. But, yes, stay huddled around your stuttering fire, hoping for change. That will surely save you."

"This is what I've been trying to say!" the worm said. "We're nothing and will remain nothing. And all her promises are empty. We might as well throw ourselves off a ledge. Anyway, who are you, stranger? Don't think I've seen you around before."

Kokabiel paused. "I am one who also grows tired of Mashit's promises." Their woeful fire flickered and faded, and he allowed himself a moment of sympathy. "Did it ever occur to you that your warmth might increase if you combine your fires with others?"

"Who?" said the mantis. "Righulem and his soul-killing breath? Mimrim and her endless cackling? I'd rather freeze than sit with any of them."

"And this is why you suffer." With a quick wave of his hand he boosted the energy of their fire, and it flared up, bright and warm.

As they gawped at the flame, he slipped into the shadows, where unseen insects skittered into the dark. He headed down ever bleaker streets, and the air grew pungent with foul-smelling gas spluttering up through cracks in the street. He walked through dark tunnels girded with iron and stone, over balustraded lanes that rose above the knotted subterranean city. The suns had set, but their light rimmed the sky, turning the streets a shadowed scarlet. But their light quickly faded, so that by the time Kokabiel reached the effluvium tower a thousand fat stars crowded the sky like spatters of blood.

The cylindrical effluvium tower exhaled gas from the rivers of dung flowing underground. He put his back against its exterior and gazed up at the sky. Exhalation cavities spiraled up its granite facade, pointing a twisting path to the stars.

He was born here, on Sheol, the first generation to rise from the ashes. They had called his generation the Fulcrum, for they were the pivot upon which demonkind would shift from scarcity to abundance. The Fulcrum were heralded as hope for the future. They were groomed to lead. But as his generation developed, the First Ones clung to power with a dead-man's grip. They would not cede even a fraction of their dominion, and though they spoke often of bringing abundance here, Kokabiel had watched time and again as they acted only for their personal ends. In fact, it seemed as if their every breath was designed to further Sheol's demise, their every step imbecilic, short-sighted, and solely in the interest of a select few. How could his generation be the fulcrum upon which the world shifted when the First Ones refused even to bend? They proclaimed their hatred for humanity, yet Abbadon, Ashmedai, Mashit, and nearly all the First Ones, took human form, believing it superior to the animal amalgamations of the subsequent generations. Their hypocrisy knew no bounds. He loathed them all.

He had never seen the Creator's face, had never known the horror of being thrust into the Great Deep, yet that didn't stop First Ones from telling him over and over again how much *they* had suffered, how cruel the Creator had been to *them*. It was as if Kokabiel and his generation were inferior because they had not suffered enough.

But the First Ones were old and growing stupider by the day. Great Abbadon had fallen, Ashmedai wasted away, and Mashit bumbled aimlessly about her throne. Soon she'd fall, and it would be his generation's turn.

He didn't want to be king for long. He would pass the throne to someone else from his generation. Perhaps Thalum, the orator, or Opshnai the philosopher. They had temperaments more suited to rule. It would be enough to know that he had lived to pass the reign, to be written down in history as a true fulcrum, fulfilling the promise that had been denied his generation.

A distant laugh rose and died, as if mocking his ambitions. He shuddered as he slipped into the vaulted antechamber of the effluvium tower, and its reek assaulted his sensitive nose. A diamond of red fire zipped out from a tall passageway, tumbled up to him, and paused above his head, its light shimmering across the walls. "By the queen's decree, this tower is closed under punishment of death." Its voice was like grinding crystals, high-pitched, whiny, and he sensed powerful magic holding it together. This was no slum demon's spell; an expert had crafted this.

"Take me to the tunnels," he commanded.

It did a somersault and drifted closer, its light intensifying. "By the queen's decree, this tower is closed under punishment of death."

Then he remembered: he'd been given a password. After a moment of concentration it came to him, and in ancient Demonsbreath he said, "*Adar, the lesser sun, shall rise.*"

The diamond's red fires turned cyan. "Splendid! Follow me!"

It darted into a narrow corridor, and he chased after it. He followed it down a twisting flight of stairs, and the offensive smells grew bolder. He stifled a sneeze, careful not to stir whatever lay waiting for him in the dark. The walls were roughly hewn, not meant for habitation, but only to safely exhale the plumes of noxious gas fermenting below before they rose to explosive concentrations. He wondered how well it was doing its job. Would a wayward spark from this diamond be the last thing he saw before he exploded?

The diamond's cyan light reached a mere ten paces before the shadows consumed it, as if the air itself ate the light. Down they went, story after story, through ever narrower tunnels, and he worried he was being led astray.

A faint throbbing grew louder, and the floor began to rumble under his feet. The diamond led him down a narrow passage, and with every step the sound increased, until it pummeled his chest, stealing his breath, and the ground thrummed. He stepped into an enormous chamber where a great roaring assaulted his ears.

The diamond arced up into the vaulted space, its cyan light unable to reach the furthest corners. But the light was enough for Kokabiel to get a sense of the chamber's size, immense even by Sheol's standards. Pillars ten paces on a side, square-cut and rough-edged, rose to meet the curved ceiling more than hundred-paces above. Their shadows spoked radially away from the diamond's light. A chasm, forty paces across, tore through the space, the source of the mad roar. A putrid brown sludge poured from an upstream tunnel into its basin. Bone fragments, offal, and sundry unwholesome bits tumbled in the waters, the tangled mass of foul energy at the heart of Sheol, which some said was the liquefied wrath of the Creator herself.

The diamond turned the scarlet shade of the twin suns, and the rushing water now seemed like a river of blood, as if he were inside the body of a great beast.

"I was beginning to think you'd forgotten," said a voice, barely audible above the roar. A squat figure stepped out from behind the closest pillar. He carried a hefty tome in two of his six hands. Short and round, he had a mushroom-gray face like a crocodile's, and a much-foreshortened nose. His nostrils were nearly as large and round as his eyes. Fiery red hair grew in a thick tuft on his head, tied into a pony tail that hung down to his waist and was tucked into the front of his leather belt.

"How could I forget *you*, Gedeon," Kokabiel said. "Your ugly visage is seared into my memory."

Gedeon snorted and took two steps closer. "You look shorter. Have you shrunk, *Second* General Kokabiel?"

"My change in stature is temporary, Gedeon. But you've grown fat."

Gedeon smiled. "It's true, I've been eating well. One thing about being the Chief of Sewers is the pay is far better than it was as Master Archivist. Still, I miss the library."

"The queen has more regard for shit than literature," Kokabiel said.

Gedeon nodded and put a finger to his lip. "Both can flow and stink, but only one makes good company."

"Never short on wit," Kokabiel said.

"Or what passes for it, now. Times are strange. Among the effluvium of Sheol, things go unnoticed. Like cleverness, for instance."

"And our rendezvous," Kokabiel said.

"One hopes." Gedeon looked him up and down. "This disguise of yours. This is the best you can do?"

"You don't approve?"

"Your magic is, if I may say, amateur. There are many spies about who might have seen you."

"Half of them are probably your skittering spiders."

Gedeon squinted. "It's the other half I'm concerned with. I could teach you a better concealing spell."

"That must wait." He gestured toward the book Gedeon held. "Is this what I've come to this giant toilet for?"

"Alas, no, but it will be of interest, I think." Gedeon burped, and Kokabiel caught of whiff of meat and cheese even above the putrid smell of the river.

Kokabiel took the book from him and paged through it. It had tables of numbers and place names he recognized. "What am I looking at?"

"Work orders, from the queen."

"The whole book?"

Gedeon nodded. "Three hundred and seventeen pages."

Kokabiel looked more closely at it. "All work orders for new sewers?"

"Astounding, isn't it?" Gedeon said. "We're expanding the city by fifteen percent, just in phase *one*."

Mashit had never mentioned any of this, and he grew angry. What else was she hiding from him? "What's phase two?"

"I haven't received those orders yet, but one of my, well, *spiders* has heard Mashit plans to double the housing of Abbadon by the next Swap of Suns. And there are plans in the works for Sheol's other cities too."

Kokabiel did a quick calculation. "The Kalanit Swap of Suns is just five weeks away."

Gedeon pulled a pouch from his pocket with one of his hands and snacked on its contents, pellets that resembled rat droppings. "As I said, I knew you'd find it interesting."

"When was the last time the city expanded?"

"Four centuries ago," Gedeon said, "and then only by two percent."

"I don't understand. Why does she need to build so quickly?"

"You're the tactician," Gedeon said, burping. "I thought you would have figured it out by now."

"She plans a rapid population increase?"

Gedeon nodded. "A massive one."

"But how? Even the slum dwellers don't reproduce that quickly. Does she think we'll all suddenly give birth to a thousand young?"

"Well, yes. She believes the birth rate will greatly increase. And my sources say she's planning to bring others here."

"Others? From where?"

"The Shards. And I heard from a different source that she also plans to bring humans from Earth. She wants Abbadon to be the great trading city of the Cosmos. A *new* New York, if you will."

Kokabiel cursed into the roaring waters. "Madness! Does she believe her own lies? Does she think that the Lamed Vav will actually bring abundance here?"

"They're not *entirely* lies," Gedeon said. "Apple trees are growing on the mountains, if you haven't heard."

"It is rumors, not seeds, that she plants!"

"It's neither seeds nor rumors. The trees have spontaneously sprouted. And I've eaten one of the apples. It was deliciously sweet."

Kokabiel grimaced. "And you think these Lamed Vav are responsible?"

"They've always been more than Pillars. They have a power that goes beyond simple support. In essence, they've an amplifying effect. Now that they're here..."

"But they've been locked in a room for months."

"How else can you account for it? Her plan is working, though much slower than she'd hoped. The queen is mad, yes, but when has Sheol ever not had a mad ruler? Abbadon, Ashmedai? Neither were what I'd call sane."

"She must be stopped."

"A few months ago, I might have agreed with you. But apple orchards in Sheol? This will change things."

Kokabiel stepped closer. Gedeon was of the Fulcrum generation too. He more than anyone would understand. "Her hubris will destroy Sheol, Gedeon. Please tell me you don't support this madness?"

"I preferred my station as Master Archivist over Chief of Sewers, true. Books over shit, as it were. But I must admit there's something romantic about her plan. That apple was delicious. I'm curious to see what else she might achieve, if given enough time."

"Romanticism is a human notion rooted in fantasy. You've read too many books."

"There's no such thing," Gedeon said. "And besides, had I not read all those books, you would not be here, seeking my help."

"So tell me, in all those many books, have you found a way to kill him?"

"*Him?*"

"Don't be coy."

Gedeon averted his eyes. "I've heard you've visited the Traitor King."

"Few things escape you, Gedeon. Ashmedai rattles the bars of his cage, thinking we tremble beneath him still. He was always pathetic, but now I see him for what he is, utterly self-deceived. I told him I would help him get his throne back, and he believed me."

"Why tell him such a thing?"

"So he might tell me how to kill a First One."

Gedeon wrung four of his six hands together. "If he knew, I doubt he would tell you. Ashmedai is not as self-deceived as you might think. I wouldn't underestimate him. That would be a grave mistake."

"The grave is what I'm seeking, Gedeon. For him. You must show me how to kill a First One."

"And what will you do for me?"

"I'll return you to your post as Master Archivist. You can curl up with your dusty books again."

"With the same food ration as I have now?"

"You can double it."

The squat demon smiled. "Do you swear it?"

"I do."

"Swear it by the blood vow."

"You still believe in that old superstition?"

"Did not you just swear before Ashmedai?" Gedeon said, with a knowing smirk. "Swear it, and I will believe *you.*"

Kokabiel frowned. "Very well." He pulled his bone blade from his hip and held it over his palm, which had not fully healed from when he had sworn to Ashmedai. "I swear by Great Abbadon and the Fires of Sheol I will return you to your station as Master Archivist and double your current food ration if you show me how to kill a First One." He sliced the blade across his palm, and the blood spilled onto the ground. The pain was sharp, but he'd cut his arm off if he knew it would give him the answer.

Gedeon nodded. "First Ones were fashioned by the Creator herself. They are made of different stuff from you and me. It may not even be possible to kill one."

"Abbadon is dead, isn't he?"

"Yes, but Great Abbadon's death was–"

"A suicide."

"Surely not!" Gedeon said.

"Believe what you wish. Abbadon was weak. He failed to bring his vision to this world and he could not live knowing this."

Gedeon looked ill. "What you say is heresy."

"And I am the heretic who will cast these vile creatures into the Abyss. The First Ones may have been great once and now they stand in the way of greatness. But they refuse to step aside, as they have promised. It's time to remove them ourselves."

"What you ask will take time."

Kokabiel squeezed his fists. "How long?"

"These things are not graffitied on Sheol's walls. The First Ones have purged such knowledge from all records, to protect themselves. But a trace of it must remain, I'm certain. If anyone can find it, I can. If I were Master Archivist, I'd plunge myself into study of ancient codices and not emerge from the stacks until I found an answer. But my access to the libraries has been rescinded. The occasional books I garner come via idiot go-betweens who don't know the difference between Azazel's *Codices* and Lilith's *Desiderata*."

"I'll get you access, Gedeon. I will do whatever it takes to stop them."

"*Them*?" Gedeon stared at him. "It wouldn't be wise to kill the queen just yet."

Kokabiel straightened. "Why do you think I want to kill her too?"

"It's written all over you, like a book."

"Would you miss your apples, Gedeon? Do you want your old station back or not?"

"I do. But perhaps I also wish to wait and see what Mashit might do. If she can truly bring abundance to Sheol, then–"

"She can't."

"But if she can, she–"

"She won't."

"Kokabiel, it's no secret you and the queen shared a bed, that you cuckolded the king of Sheol just before she usurped the throne.

Even the palace cooks gossip about it."

He lifted his chin. "Ashmedai deserved his fate. I had nothing to do with his fall."

"It's known that you also shared *his* bed from time to time too, while you were his right-hand. Rumors say you play both sides with allegiance to none. In the short term, this has favored you. But as events play out, your enemies will only grow."

Kokabiel spat. "You know nothing of my plans."

"I know you think you're manipulating them, but they play you too. Mashit used you when it was expedient. So did Ashmedai. It seems to me the true reason you wish to murder the king and queen and destroy our best chance of abundance is because you were ultimately rejected by them both."

Kokabiel had had enough. He dropped the book, threw off his patchwork robe, and unraveled the spell that disguised him. He stretched his neck to its full height and felt the delicious cracks as tension released. As his body inflated to his full size, he snatched Gedeon and held the fat creature over the rushing waters. Gedeon yelped, and his six arms squirmed like an insect. "Please! Don't!"

"You sniveling imp!" Kokabiel shouted. "I've slaughtered more creatures than any who's ever lived. I'm second in command of the strongest army in the Cosmos. You're not a First One, and I know a thousand ways to kill you. Speak that way to me again, and those will be your last words." He flipped Gedeon over and dipped his head into the putrid river. Up and down he bobbed him, and the demon spat and choked as the filth stuck to him.

"P–please for–forgive m–me!"

He lifted Gedeon above the waters again, and Gedeon coughed and whimpered. "If Mashit brings about these changes," Kokabiel said, "she will destroy Sheol. All will be lost. She does not bring abundance, only chaos."

"Oh, I agree!"

"Then do as I ask! Find a way to kill a First One, and leave the rest to me."

"Yes, yes, of course! Please! Put me down!"

"Call me your king."

"King Kokabiel, Lord of Sheol, please, I beg you, my lord, put me down!"

Kokabiel smiled. It was good to feel someone's life hanging in his grasp again. For too long, he had not engaged in battle. All he had to do was squeeze, and Gedeon would burst like a pimple. But he needed this coward. He pulled Gedeon back and threw him onto the ground.

Gedeon, covered in sticky shit that glowed faintly yellow, rolled over and sat up. His snack pellets lay scattered on the ground, and purple millipedes slunk from the shadows to snatch them and slip away.

"Now," Kokabiel said, strutting over. "Give me that spell."

"Which spell?"

"The disguise. To better hide me."

"Yes, yes, of course!"

"Of course, what?"

"Of course, *my lord*. My king!"

Kokabiel nodded. Blown by gusts of foul air from the rushing waters, the book flipped through its many pages, one after another, a thousand figures and numbers and tables, work orders for a new city that would never be built.

CHAPTER TEN

DANIEL WAITED AT A BUS-STOP IN DONETSK, UKRAINE NINE exhausting days after he'd left Prabha, the washerwoman, at Marishamehadi. It was just after sunset, and the cold rain blew in sheets down the road, curling the leaves of a row of giant elms. The bus stop bordered an overgrown lot, a jungle of tangled weeds, and a flock of soaked magpies solemnly waited out the rain. Across the street three lights glimmered from the curtained windows of mostly-dark high-rise apartments. In the twilight, everything had become gray, shorn of color, save for the odd passing car beaming yellow headlights into the gloom. He wanted only dry clothes and a bed.

The bus was late. It was supposed to have arrived an hour ago, according to the schedule. But the driver who'd dropped him off had said he was lucky the buses were even running at all, what with the economy the way it was and the latest border dispute with Russia. And because Daniel spoke Ukrainian fluently, the driver presumed Daniel shared his loathing of all things Russian, and had spent most of the car ride lamenting how his country was being destroyed by those "fascist pigs."

A streetlight flickered on, and Daniel caught his reflection in the transparent plexi of the bus stop. His body had thinned since India, his stubble was getting long, and his clothes were filthy and worn, so that he looked a lot like the homeless he had once helped. He smelled himself and winced. He wondered if they'd even let him on the bus.

The flock of magpies sulked in the weedy lot beyond the plexi, doing their best to stay dry under the leaves, when they suddenly screeched – it sounded like metal bending – and took flight, a hundred black-white-and-blue shapes spiraling off in the opposite direction Daniel needed to go.

He sagged into the plexi and wondered what his former self would think of this disheveled wreck who had traveled across Asia, following a cryptic clue some giggling mirrored sphere had given him during a particularly horrific psychedelic outer-body experience that was induced by a reeking hermit who shattered people's egos because they asked him to. Yeah, either he was onto something big or he had fucking lost it.

He collapsed onto the bench, fighting off the urge for sleep. He'd come this far and he would not miss the damned bus. Tangled weeds had clawed their way up through the metal slats of the bench, pressing against his backside. Grasses burst from the cracks in the sidewalks, buckling them slowly. This was how Sheol would destroy the Earth, he thought, rising from the cracks in the world to shatter all. Maybe Earth didn't deserve to be the apex of the cosmic hierarchy, but he wouldn't allow the Cosmos to be ruled by hell.

Time passed. The rain continued, and despite his best attempts to stay awake, he dozed. From a far-off dream of reeking corpses and ancient walls breaking, he heard whispers, footsteps, and smelled the stink of men. He opened his eyes.

Something slammed into his head and he buckled over. "Fuck you, scum!" said a man, kicking Daniel in the head. Through the pain, he dimly registered that the man had spoken Russian. He fell to the ground and stared up at the bleak clouds. Rain fell into his eyes as a boot came to crush his face. "Dirty American dog!" said another. Five men pummeled him, and one took out a pistol and pointed it at Daniel's head.

The man was young and wore a black cap on his shaved head. He had a sharp jaw and intense blue eyes, and his green army jacket dripped rain as he said in heavily accented English, "Why you here? Speak, or I kill you."

Daniel put his hands up slowly and used one to cup the back of his throbbing head. "Please," he said in Russian, praying it was the correct dialect and accent. "Don't shoot!"

"Wait!" said another. He looked nearly identical to the pistol-wielder, except he was at least a decade younger and not quite out of puberty. "He's Russian!"

"They're trained to be fluent," said the elder.

"Please," Daniel said, honing in on their accent, "take my money. My wallet's in my coat. I want no trouble!"

"If he's a spy," said the younger, "his accent's perfect. Where you from, friend?"

"Volgograd," Daniel said, spouting the first place that came to mind, a city he'd passed through.

"Yeah?" said the elder, lowering the pistol an inch. "What are you doing here?"

"My grandmother," Daniel said. "She lives in Ternivka. I'm visiting her."

"You're a fucking spy," the elder said, and the gun rose again. "I know how you sneak in and pretend to be people we don't look too closely at, like street vermin."

"I'm no spy," Daniel said, but the elder kicked him in the ribs, and Daniel groaned. The others grabbed him and yanked him to his feet.

"What's your name?" said the elder.

"Vlad," Daniel said, and it was only after he had spoken that he'd realized the elder had spoken English.

"I knew it!" the elder said. "A fucking American spy."

"No," Daniel said in Russian. "I learned English at university!"

"What school?"

He fumbled to think of a name. "The University of..."

"Your clothes are American. You can't buy those brands here. You people think you're so fucking clever, but you stand out like a rat in a field. We saw you from a kilometer away." He spat in Daniel's face and pressed the pistol against his forehead.

"Please," Daniel said. He stared into the man's eyes. "The world needs me."

The elder laughed. "No one needs you."

"Wait," said the younger brother. "You're really going to off him?"

The elder looked around. "Not here. Too many eyes. We'll do it by the van."

They kicked and punched Daniel again, and he screamed. They dragged his aching body down the sidewalk, and his shirt tore on the concrete. A city bus turned the corner a mile away, its headlights shining like beacons as it crept closer.

But they dragged him from the light, down a side street of small houses, toward a tall black van parked conspicuously at an angle. They opened its rear doors, and on the floor was a blue tarp, stained red. Daniel recognized the smell of human blood.

Heat stirred in his gut. Rage and...something else. Older, and more powerful.

"Say your prayers, fucker!" the elder said. He spun Daniel around and pushed Daniel's head into the tarp with the cold barrel of the pistol.

He couldn't die! Not yet. The world needed him, even if they didn't know it.

The sudden heat in his gut was like a match thrown into a puddle of kerosene. His belly flared, and sounds erupted from his gut, modulated by his tongue into speech: ancient, potent words that scratched the fabric of the universe, making friction with reality. He'd heard this language back on Gehinnom and had never learned its name.

"*Burn!*" he growled in the ancient tongue. "*Burn and roast and turn to ash!*"

And there was light and there was fire. Bright flames leaped from their skin as he turned to face them. They screamed, the gun went off. The bullet nicked his neck, ricocheted off the van, and tore through the chest of the younger. The kid went down, blood spurting from his stomach as the flames leaped higher from all five men.

His belly furnace-hot, Daniel watched them scream and collapse, and thought, *God, what have I done?* A scent came to his nose, deliciously enticing, the smell of grilling meat to a starving man. *No!* he thought. *I can't...I won't!*

But he remained. As they burned and screamed, he salivated. A porch light flashed on in house, and an elderly woman came running out. "Oh my god!" she shouted. She looked a bit like Gram, but without the scars, and Daniel saw himself through her eyes. What would she think if Gram saw him like this now, salivating over these burning bodies?

Ashamed, terrified, he ran.

When he reached the corner, he looked back. The men still writhed as they burned, their screams echoing down the rain-dark street. He ran for the bus as it pulled in. The doors opened, and a woman in dripping rain gear slowly climbed aboard. He kept looking back, afraid he'd see their carbonized forms sprinting around the corner. The woman was finally aboard, and he leaped on. The driver sized him up and scowled. Daniel fumbled for cash, shivering while the driver inspected each bill. Finally, the doors closed, and the bus rumbled away.

He moved to the back of the bus as they drove off, bending over to see out the windows. The fire still burned, its reflection glimmering off of the windows. It flickered as they moved away. The woman who had boarded before him was staring up at him from her seat. "You're bleeding," she said.

He touched his neck. His fingers were covered in blood.

"Here," she said, handing him a handkerchief. "Use this."

—

The bus drove through the country, stopping every few miles to exchange motley collections of passengers, none of whom seemed interested in human contact. They sat alone, rows from each other, sleeping or staring into smartphones. He slumped in the back, the woman's handkerchief pressed hard against his neck, shivering, unable to sleep. Peace would not find him.

He had burned those men alive. He had whispered words of fire into the fabric of the universe, a power he hadn't known he possessed until now. Was it self-defense or murder? They weren't innocent, he told himself, as he tried and failed to forget the image of the young boy's melting face, the sound of his screams. Did he deserve death too, or had his elder brother roped him into his schemes? Those men had killed before; there was human blood on their tarp. But Daniel would not allow himself to play both judge and executioner. That was how demons behaved, not men. But what scared him the most was how he had actually enjoyed watching those men die, that he had been thrilled with his new power of fire. The woman looked back at him from her seat and smiled wanly.

Slowly, like a receding tide, his shivers abated, and lulled by the rumble of the bus, the patter of rain, he fell into a deep sleep. He awoke when the driver tapped him on the shoulder. It was dark and quiet, and the bus was parked in a depot surrounded by evergreens. All the passengers had gone.

The streets of Ternivka were dark and empty as he exited the bus. The ticket office was closed, and a solitary white streetlight beamed into the rain. Next door was a gas station, closed. A dark grocery across the street brooded silently. Up above, the stars shivered in high-altitude winds, broken by wispy clouds. He had no idea which way to go.

He waited while the driver cleaned the bus and locked it, and there was something grounding about the mundanity of his motions, as if, despite the hells people lived, floors still needed to be swept, doors needed to be locked, common labors had to be performed. That despite all the suffering in the world, life went on.

He wanted to ask the driver if he knew Dvoyre Gottlieb, but the man was already squeezing himself into an old German car. It coughed, complained, and started up. The driver lit a cigarette, and rolled down the window a crack as Daniel came over. The little cherry danced around in the dark as the man leaned forward. The smoke reminded Daniel of the burning men's delicious-repugnant smell, and he gagged.

"You got a ride?" the man said through a half-closed window, as if Daniel might bite.

"Maybe." Daniel shrugged. "Do you know Mrs. Dvoyre Gottlieb?"

"Afraid I don't. You need to make a call? You can borrow my cell."

A generous offer, but even if he'd had her number, what would he say? "Hi, I'm Daniel Fisher, half Cursed Man, former Lamed Vav. I need you to teleport me to Sheol. Can you pick me up at the bus station?"

"Thanks," he said, "but my ride'll be here soon."

The driver shrugged. "Suit yourself. But don't think about sleeping in the bus or inside the building. I don't give a crap, but the owner will shoot you come morning if he finds you here. He's done it before." He rolled up his window and drove off, watching

Daniel as he went. The car's red taillights vanished around a bend.

Which way to go? He had no map. No address. Only a fuzzy psychedelic memory whispered in his ear. For all he knew Dvoyre might not even be real and he was just following a delusion. The Breaker of Minds had said that if he quieted his mind, he just might remember what secrets those mirrored spheres had told him.

He closed his eyes and took a breath. The wind blew and died, and he felt....nothing. If this didn't pan out, he wasn't sure what he'd do next.

He sighed and headed toward a distant halo of light, possibly the city center. All the stores were closed as he walked under the cold stars. The buildings grew sparser and older the further he went, as if he were walking back in time, toward an era when few humans walked the Earth. He wondered if he were headed in the wrong direction. The homes were plain wooden cottages, in dire need of repair, separated by wide fields, great landscapes of arrayed grain and plots of untamed grasses, all shining under the moon. The wheat basket of Europe indeed. Lights glowed inside farmhouses, and dogs barked as he passed, but otherwise all was silent but for the occasional gust of wind.

He followed the glow, and after an hour of hiking over muddy hills and cracking roads, he reached the bright lights of a gas station. Open, thank god. A large semi rig without a trailer was filling up at one of the pumps. A wiry, middle-aged man with a fuzzy beard eyed Daniel as he approached. Daniel pulled his hoodie over his head to hide the graze-wound on his neck.

He ignored the driver and walked inside the station. The clerk, middle-aged, clean shaven, with neatly combed hair, looked up from a book, a cigarette dangling from his lips. There wasn't much besides him. Motor oil, cigarettes, warm beer, vodka, dusty bales of newspapers that looked as if they would never be read.

"Hey," Daniel said. "My aunt lives near here. But I don't remember her address. Can you help?"

"What's her name?"

"Dvoyre Gottlieb."

The clerk looked Daniel up and down, breathing slowly, and murmured, "I should have guessed."

"Excuse me?"

The man took a heavy drag and tamped out his cigarette in a plastic ashtray. "You got a map?"

"No," Daniel said.

"I do."

"Great. Can I see it?"

"You want to buy something?"

Daniel sighed. He hadn't much money. "How much for a newspaper?"

"Those aren't for sale."

"What is?"

"Cigarettes. Vodka. Beer."

Dusty packs of cigarettes had been stacked on the counter in mini pyramids. One stack, partly sold, had become a ziggurat. "How much for a pack of Skif?"

"400 Hryvnia."

Likely an absurd sum, but he paid it anyway. He put the soft pack in his pocket as the man produced a sheet of paper from under the counter, its image the great-grandchild of an ancient road map, photocopied, shrunken and copied again until all its details had blurred into occult mysteries and endless dark specks that might have once been Cyrillic letters or more likely wayward dust.

"We're here," the clerk said, pointing at a spot in the southeastern quadrant. And this is where the old Jewess lives." He made an X on the map with a pencil.

"The old *Jewess*?" Daniel said.

"It's a six kilometer walk," the man said without looking up. He folded the map and handed it to Daniel. "You really her nephew?"

"Yes."

The man blinked at him.

"Is there a problem?"

The clerk sighed and lit another cigarette. "I wanted to thank you."

"Thank *me*?"

"Well, your family."

"For what?"

"During the Holodomor, the Gottliebs fed my father. He would have died if it weren't for them, and I wouldn't be here now, talking to you."

Daniel remembered reading about the Terror Famine, when the Soviet Union intentionally starved to death millions of Ukrainians. He pointed to the map. "Why not go thank her yourself?"

The clerk frowned. "That woman, she's..."

"Yes?"

"Unusual."

"How so?"

The man blinked. "Some say she's a witch." He took another drag. "Is she?"

Daniel took his map and his cigarettes. "I honestly don't know," he said, while thinking, *I really fucking hope so.*

As he stepped outside, the rig pulled away, rumbling down the road, spewing exhaust. He took out the pack of cigarettes, unwrapped the plastic, and threw one in his mouth. The smell of tobacco was strong and welcome. He hadn't smoked since he was in Gehinnom, and before that it had been years. He didn't have a match, and thought about going back inside. Then he remembered: he had the power to make fire.

He concentrated on the tip. Nothing happened. He concentrated more. The tip felt cool to the touch. He thought of those men who had tried to murder him, the moment when he thought he was going to die, and his belly grew warm. Then a word escaped from his mouth in that harsh language that scraped the fabric of the universe.

Burn.

The tip of the cigarette burst into flame. He cheered, and before the flame petered out he took a puff-

-and doubled over in excruciating pain.

It was like swallowing hot coals, like lava pouring down his throat. He screamed and fell to his knees. A strong wind gusted, and with it came a sudden squall. The rain stripped the heat from him. He threw the cigarette to the ground and it winked out. Slowly, over minutes, the pain ebbed. He stared across the street into the darkness, and it seemed blacker than before.

There was a shift in the world. Or was there? At first he thought it was the weather, a drop in air pressure. But this change came from within. He gasped when he realized the truth: his hunger was gone. He no longer craved the dead. The thought of meat – of any kind – disgusted him, as it had ever since his parents had died in the fire.

The Mikulalim – the Cursed Ones – could survive for weeks without food or sleep. They lived for centuries. But the sun could kill them. So too could fire. On Gehinnom, the Bedu had killed several Mikulalim by tossing them onto a large pyre. The Mikulalim could weave fire with words, yet their bodies shunned it, as they shunned the sun, the ultimate furnace. Did the cigarette, its small flame, destroy that part of his cursed nature? Did the smoke suppress the curse like a man with a firebrand chasing away an encroaching pack of wolves? Inhaling had been painful – awful – but not fatal, and if it afforded him freedom from that vile hunger, then he welcomed it.

He pocketed the smokes and headed down the road into the rainy darkness. Eventually, the clouds parted, and the rain ceased. The half-moon shone above the trees, and he used its pale light to read the crude map. The cigarette had deadened his hunger, but it had also weakened his senses. He could not see well in the dark now, nor smell the animals lurking in the shadows. The night was a thing to fear again.

Orion was sinking low when he reached the address, where a single-story cottage, its white paint chipped and weathered, sagged into a mild hill. Weeds and shrubs had taken over the garden, and the field beyond was a knotted tangle of branches and limbs, their tall fingers shivering in the breeze, silhouetted against the stars. The air smelled earthy, as if the soil had been tilled. Her overgrown yard was crowded with trellises, stone imps, gnomes, toads, a surfeit of garden tchotchkes, which made it hard to traverse without stepping on something. Dogs barked in the distance as he approached the door.

Curtains were drawn over the windows, but a light was on. What time was it? He had no idea. Late, for sure. What sane person would open the door for a filthy stranger at this time of night? But there was nowhere else to go.

A shadow walked across the adjacent field, and he froze. Two eyes, green and glowing, stared back at him. It was too dark to see its full shape, but the creature almost certainly walked on four legs. It paused and stared, unblinking, and Daniel stared back. Its eyes were too large to be a cat and quite possibly much larger than a dog. Its unwavering gaze unnerved him, and he retreated slowly from the house, fearing an attack.

Something creaked and Daniel's blood went cold. The light inside the house had gone off. He stepped back onto a garden ornament, and it cracked underfoot.

"*Go away*," said a voice from inside the house like the creak of an ancient tree. He had no idea what language it had spoken – if even it was language – but he understood it just the same. Its sound sent horrid shudders through him, and he knew this voice was full of magic.

With great effort he managed to say, "Mrs. Dvoyre Gottlieb? My name is–" he swallowed a knot of fear "–Daniel Fisher." The green-eyed creature staring from the shadows crept closer, and he shivered again. "I need your help." He had meant to speak Ukrainian, using the same accent and dialect he'd heard at the gas station. But his words came out solely in English.

"The best advice I can give," the voice said, and it sounded like a thousand croaking frogs, "is for you to leave." This time, it spoke English.

"Please," he said. "I've come all the way from India. I know this sounds crazy, but these, well...these mirrored spheres told me your name."

There was a sudden shift in the air, as if an invisible knot around his body had been loosened. The tension fled, and the green-eyed creature slunk back to whatever dark abode it had come from. There was the sound of chains and locks being undone. The door opened a crack and a small woman peered out. She stood less than five feet tall, stooped and insubstantial, but he knew not to judge her by her size. Her stark-white hair had been tied into a bun, and her prominent nose was striking. Even through the darkness, her brown eyes shone with intelligence.

"It's a long way from New York," she said in English, and her Slavic accent took him back to his childhood, when he had played on the linoleum floor while Gram and her friends from the Old Country chatted over endless cups of coffee.

"How do you know I'm from New York?" he said.

"Who else has such an accent? Have you eaten?"

"Actually, I'm starving."

She looked him up and down. "Take off your shoes before you enter my home."

Just like Gram, he thought. He approached the door and slipped off his shoes as she watched. "Now kiss the mezuzah." She pointed to the doorpost, where a brass mezuzah gleamed in the moonlight, the Hebrew letter Shin pointed like licks of flame. He touched it and kissed his fingers, while she watched. A proper mezuzah, he remembered, was said to keep evil spirits and malignant influences out of one's home.

"I'm no dybbuk," he said.

"No," she said. "But when strangers knock on your door in the dead of night, one can never be too sure." She eyed him and he sensed she was peering at far more than his face. "Before I let you into my home, answer me one question. *Death, remove thyself!*"

The words were not in English, but he knew them just the same. He shivered and said, "That was no question."

"To those who fear it, it is. Come in, Daniel." She stepped aside to let him pass. Her home was small and modest. The kitchenette overflowed with notebooks, candlesticks, bowls, and sundry objects. Tables, holding teetering piles of Ukrainian, Yiddish, German and English books, framed a worn couch. An old radio cabinet stood against the wall. Many silver amulets hung on the walls between prints of Frida Kahlo and Marc Chagall. Everything had a dusty, aged feel, but the amulets gleamed. In Hebrew, Aramaic, and Yiddish, the amulets warned off the demons Lilith, Dumah, Hema, and Af. But to his surprise he could not read them anymore.

She sat him at a small table in the kitchenette and brewed him some tea. She offered him oatmeal cookies, and he ate too many. He took off his soaked hoodie and she hung it on a rack to dry. "That's a nasty cut," she said, pointing to his neck.

He grimaced, not wishing to remember the burning men.

"How'd you get it?"

"I was mistaken for someone else."

"Whoever did this, are they following you?"

"No, I really don't think so."

"Are they dead?"

He broke her gaze.

She sighed. "Let me get some antiseptic." She returned with a small bottle of alcohol and some bandages. He tried not to wince as she tended to the wound.

"No one is quite whom they seem," she said, staring at him. Her brown eyes peered into his, and he had a sense she saw things in him he couldn't see in himself.

"You're very kind," he said.

"*Nishto far vos,*" she replied in Yiddish. *You're welcome.* But he only knew this from the bits of Yiddish Gram had sprinkled in her conversations, not from any true comprehension. He longed for it now, to speak Yiddish, the language of Jews for a thousand years, until the Holocaust, American assimilation, and the adoption of Hebrew as the language of Israel destroyed that in a generation. Now Yiddish was spoken only by the ultra-religious, a few secular pockets, and those from the old world, like Dvoyre. But it was gone from his mind like a forgotten dream.

"I'm sorry I've come so late," he said in English.

"Late? I don't know the meaning of the word. I'm writing a sermon for this week's Torah portion." She pointed to a scribbled-upon notepad. "I had written and erased the same sentence twenty times. Your arrival was exactly the break I needed."

"You're a rabbi?"

She nodded. "And you're Jewish."

"How do you know that?"

"You didn't bat an eye when I asked you to kiss the mezuzah."

He smiled. "Of course."

"I'm a rabbi for a small shul a short walk up the road. A crumbling house we consecrated a while back. I hold services there on shabes for a few aging Jews. Not enough left for a minyan. The Nazis, may their names be erased—" she mock-spat into the corner "—saw to that. I'm the only one left who can read Torah. The rabbinical courts of Israel frown on this old woman rabbi. But you make do with what God gives you."

He sighed. "Nine rabbis don't make a minyan, but ten shoemakers do."

She nodded. "Or six old farmers, in this case. I think God understands. Daniel, when was the last time you prayed?"

"I'm not really religious."

"All men are religious, they just worship different things."

She walked to a shelf covered in dusty books and half-burnt candles, and opened a drawer. She pulled out a wrapped ball of tefillin, the leather phylacteries pious Jewish men wrapped their arms with when they prayed.

"This was my father's," she said. "I was only four when he died. I don't remember much of him. The soldiers came and marched the Jewish women five kilometers to the train, shooting anyone who resisted. They shoved us into train cars like we were animals. The smell of human feces and urine was so thick my eyes burned. But I wasn't scared so much as angry. Why did God let this to happen? We were good, honest people, tossed into hell, for what? For what sin were we being punished?" She gestured at the books around her. "I've read these and a thousand more, and I still don't have an answer."

"How, after all that, can you still believe in God?" It sounded more accusatory than he had intended, and he regretted saying it.

"All the Jewish women were shipped to the death camps and gassed. All the Jewish men were marched into the fields, forced to dig their own graves before they were shot. Almost none of the graves are marked. My father's remains lie out there, but I will never know where." She swallowed. "I *have to* believe," she said. "Because without God, all those people died for no reason." She stared at the ball of leather tefillin.

"I'm terribly sorry," he said.

"Don't be sorry for me. Be sorry for what humanity let happen. Only fools think it can never happen again. Holocausts continue today, to Jews and gentiles alike. Always, we blame some other and seek to destroy him for our own failures. But we're all human. Most of us anyway." She held up the tefillin. "Please put these on."

"I'd rather not."

"If you want me to help, you will put these on."

He sighed. "You'll have to walk me through it. It's been ages."

"Stand up."

Not since his father was alive had Daniel wrapped himself in the leather tefillin straps. The ritual had always felt too intimate, too vulnerable, as if he were Isaac bound up by Abraham to be slaughtered for a fickle God. Dvoyre opened up a drawer and fetched a yellowed tallis and a leather yarmulke. She hung the tallis over his shoulders and put the yarmulke on his head. The linen of the tallis was musty and he stifled a sneeze.

She paused, as if waiting for something. "These come from an innocent time of my life," she said, "They're imbued with the power to repel impure things."

She unraveled the tefillin. On the end of the leather strap was a box, containing four biblical passages written on parchment. She made a loop with the strap and slid the box up his left arm so it rested beside his heart.

She opened a small prayer book and had him read, "Blessed are You, Lord our God, king of the universe, who has sanctified us with His commandments, and commanded us to put on tefillin." The words were Hebrew, but he remembered their meaning.

She wrapped the straps twice more around his bicep, seven times around his forearm, and once around his palm. Then she placed a second prayer box on his head, a loop holding it in place, and wrapped his hand with the remaining length of leather.

He read aloud the Shma, the declaration of the unity of God, and the V'ahavta, which he remembered from Hebrew school. "You shall bind the commandments as a sign upon your arm, and they shall be for a reminder between your eyes..."

When he was done, she said, "There's great power in words."

"That, I know," he said. Some of the unknown Hebrew words were beginning to make sense again. The cigarette's curse-muting effect was fading.

"A dog is afraid of a stick; a demon is afraid of *tzitzit*," she said, running her fingers through his tallis fringes.

"That was a test," he said. "To see if I was a demon."

"Congratulations, Daniel. You're human. More or less." He froze for a moment, when she laughed. "So, what can I do for a Jew?"

"I've been traveling all over the world and I met this Indian man named Shyama Lahiri. They called him The Breaker of Minds. He took me on this, well, *journey*, and–"

"He broke your mind."

"Pretty much, yeah. But there were these entities–"

"The mirrored spheres?"

"Yes! They whispered secrets to me. There were so many. I don't remember most. But they told me your name."

"I see. And what do you think I can do for you?"

"I need your help to get somewhere."

"You've traveled here all the way from India to go somewhere else?"

"Yes, because that somewhere else is *else*-where."

Her smile faded. "I see." She took off his yarmulke, his tallis and tefillin, and carefully put them away. "And this elsewhere is?"

"Sheol."

A pause. "Contrary to what you might have learned from your Bubbe, the dead don't dwell in Sheol. Sometimes they're reborn on Earth, with no memories of their past life. Mostly, however, the dead drift in the guf, the well of souls, a place not fit for the living to visit. If you're hoping to speak with a lost loved one, I'm afraid I don't do that anymore."

"I know what Sheol is, Dvoyre. A *kelipa*, a husk of a shattered universe. It's full of demons and, as of recently, four Lamed Vav."

She scratched her chin. "The *Event*," she said. "The earthquakes, the fading sun, the thinning air. It wasn't an astronomical event, as they've been saying. The foundations of the world have shifted."

His heart pounded. Finally, someone he could speak the truth with! "Yes! Four of the thirty-six Lamed Vav have been abducted from Earth and brought to Sheol. I need to bring them back before Sheol grows too powerful. You know what demons will do. They will destroy the Earth."

His stomach rumbled, and just like that, the curse was back. The revolting urge to eat a dead person surged to new heights. His senses shifted, and he smelled Dvoyre's body odor, the oatmeal cookies across the room, the wet tea leaves, the spices in the kitchen, the mildew in the bathroom, the cat spray in the yard, the wheat pollen on the wind, and under it all the subtle reek of some ancient beast lurking in the weeds – a demon, Daniel realized, enslaved to Dvoyre, here to protect her.

Dvoyre's eyes went wide. She gasped and leaped away from him, lifted an amulet from the wall and, holding it before her, chanted in Aramaic, "Out demon! I adjure you, demon, in the name of God and in the names of the angels sent after you–"

"I'm not a demon!" Daniel spat, holding his hands up. "I've been poisoned with Azazel's Curse of a Thousand Tongues!"

"You're a ghoul?"

He nodded. "Only half!"

This did not assuage her. "After the funerals of my friends, I sit in cemeteries and watch for your kind, to scare you away before you can defile the bodies. And yet you come here, to *my* house, seeking *my* help?"

"I haven't eaten the dead," he said. "And I never will."

"How can I believe you?" she said. "You've lied to me once already!" She cursed. "I should have sensed you!"

"The reason you didn't sense me is because I'm not fully a Mikulal yet. Not until I eat. Also, I think, it's because of these." He removed the soft pack from his pocket.

"Cigarettes?"

"They suppress the curse, somehow. I had one before I came, but its effect must have worn off."

Slowly she lowered the amulet, but her eyes had lost their warmth. "How did you get this curse?"

"It was forced upon me."

"Tell me everything, Daniel. But first, smoke one of your cigarettes."

He nodded. He used one of her matchbooks to light one, and the searing pain came again. He screamed and fell to the floor. But it hurt a little less this time, and he was able to take a second puff before he extinguished the butt in an empty brass candlestick. His senses dulled again as the nicotine raced through his blood.

"Amazing," she said. "You seem like a different person."

"And to think I've always been taught cigarettes were bad for you."

At this, she let slip a laugh, then they sat beside each other on the couch. "Now," she said. "Your story."

And so he told her how the former demon king Ashmedai had snatched him from his almost-marriage to his fiancé Rebekah, who was, unknown to him then, the demon Mashit. ("*The* Ashmedai and Mashit?" she said, incredulous. "Like in the tales?"). He told her how Grug, a Mikulal, gave Daniel the Curse of a Thousand Tongues in order to help him communicate with Marul Menacha, a powerful witch who had traveled to the Heavenly Orchard and stole the names of six Lamed Vav from God himself (at this, she blinked and shook her head.) He told her how Marul had been touched by the no-things in the Jeen and had turned to dust. ("What a horrid way to die," she said.) He told her of Gehinnom's sky cracking open, the light shining through, bringing life to wherever it touched, and how Ashmedai had used the Horn of Azazel to hurl him and Rana through the Great Deep back to Earth (at this point, Dvoyre's mouth hung open.) But Daniel's presence wasn't enough to sustain Earth – he wasn't a Lamed Vav anymore – so Rana gave her life to save the world.

When he finished the tale, Dvoyre was choking back tears.

"All that remains of Rana," he said, "is a single blade of grass in Central Park."

"So you," she said, shaking her head, "are a Lamed Vavnik?"

"*Was*," he said. "I've changed, as you can tell."

"And this woman, Rana, just vanished into thin air?"

"Like smoke."

Dvoyre blinked rapidly, as if in deep thought. "The Lamed Vav uphold the world through anonymous acts of kindness and justice," she said. "But what Rana did was entirely new, entirely different."

"She was a mason," he said. "I like to think she did what she always had done. She sealed the cracks with mortar, but in this case, she became the mortar herself."

Dvoyre shook her head in disbelief. "Thousands of the world's most intelligent people speculate on what happened, and none have a damned clue. But a ghoul knocks on my door in the middle of the night with the truth!"

"Half-ghoul," he corrected. "Dvoyre, I have to bring these Lamed Vav home before Sheol gets too powerful. If I don't, billions may die."

Dvoyre paced. "But I've never opened a door to Sheol!"

"Then why did those mirrored spheres tell me your name?"

"I've no idea."

"So you can't help me?"

She stared at him. "No...I can. I will!" She ran into her bedroom and emerged with a small table-top mirror in wood frame. She blew off a layer of dust and placed it on the floor. They moved the table aside and sat cross-legged before the glass.

"Grab my hands," she said. She positioned herself so that they could see each other's eyes in the mirror. Then she said, "If I ascend up into heaven, thou art there; if I make my bed in Sheol, behold, thou art there." The words were Hebrew, but he understood.

"Our minds are linked," she said, answering the question he was about to ask. "Now keep still." She repeated the Hebrew phrase over and over, and the room grew colder, as if a window were left open to a winter chill. Her hands were charged with energy, and power coursed through them. Painful shocks jolted his arms, and he wanted to let go, but couldn't.

She shouted, "By the power of the Holy Name, take us there!" With a great downward blow she smashed the mirror. Its shards tore into their flesh. But there was no blood. Instead the shards, like liquid mercury, coalesced into a whole mirror again that no longer reflected her eyes, but another world.

A row of blossoming trees leaned on a steep and dark mountain, their pink and white petals coloring an otherwise barren cliff. The sky was a deep red, like some gloomy winter's sunset. As if they were a bird, they flew over huge towers, some spired and sharp, but most just irregular agglomerations of dark stone. Black and weatherworn ziggurats jutted up from the tangled structures below. Flickering firelight hinted of hidden lanes and avenues buried under all, and the city seemed to shiver in the light.

They dove into one of those dark streets. Fluorescent molds clung in patches to the walls, bristling, thriving. Trees sprouted in the streets, breaking through the hard stone as if it were as soft as paper. Vibrant flowers sprouted from heaping rubbish piles. On window sills, tufts of wild grasses reached for the feeble ruddy light.

It was only as they approached the palace loomed behind all that he recognized Sheol. Like a clawed hand the mammoth palace reached for sky. Its hundreds of floors and walks twisted on itself, as if it were a vortex slowly swallowing everything.

On a high balcony, Mashit stood beside four humans. He hadn't known their faces until this moment, but he knew these were the Lamed Vav. He stared at them, marking their features so he could recognize them later. And the sight of Mashit's face, once

Rebekah's, brought him a moment of nostalgia for those halcyon days, when he was in love with a phantom. But he pushed those away. She was a monster.

The vision shifted. There was intense light and sound, a huge screen flashing complex patterns and colors. A music performance? A young woman danced on stage, singing into a mic. She wore an iridescent purple outfit and bright golden accessories, her necklace, bracelets, watch, belt, and even the tips of her shoes – all were shining gold. As she hopped around the stage, the lights reflected off her and she gleamed. The space outside the stage was mostly in shadow, but this was some kind of TV studio.

The screen behind the singer zoomed-in to her face, and Daniel gasped, because the resemblance was uncanny. She looked just like Mashit, but a decade younger. And her eyes were so gray they were almost white, like Ashmedai's.

She sang and danced, while her back-up musicians, a drummer, keyboardist, and guitarist, remained in shadow. The screen shifted, and the word "CARINA!" spiraled out of a dizzying geometric pattern, where a fluorescent pink heart flashed many times per second. "You can find love anywhere," she sang.

The song ended. The screens went dark. A spotlight shone on the woman's face. Her sparkling eyes gazed up and away, to another time and place, and the vision ended.

Dvoyre's mirror shattered again, and a dozen shards reflected his startled face.

"Take me back!" he said. "Take me back there!"

"That's all I know," she said. "All I can do."

He let go of her. "That singer – she looks just like Mashit. Why did we see her?"

"I think I know," Dvoyre said. She stood and walked over to the kitchenette and removed a newspaper from the trash. She flipped through the pages, and pointed to an article several pages in, but the Cyrillic letters were meaningless to him.

"I can't read that."

"It says, 'American Pop-Star Carina Says She Was Former Ukrainian Sex Slave.'"

He looked closer. A small photograph showed the same face he had just seen.

"I saw this yesterday," Dvoyre said. "I thought there was something off about her."

"Who is she?"

"She calls herself Carina. She says she was sold into sexual slavery in Ukraine when she was a girl. But the author of this article casts doubt on her story. He says it's is a fabrication she's using to get attention, that it maligns Ukraine in the international eye. I'm inclined to agree."

"She looks a lot like Mashit. I bet she's a demon too. Dvoyre, I have to find her. I'm certain she knows a way to Sheol."

Dvoyre squinted at the paper. "It says she just moved to New York City to record an album. Guess you're going home."

Home. He hadn't thought about it for too long. "Dvoyre, may I use your phone?"

"You're going to call Carina?"

"I want to call my grandmother. I can call collect, if that matters."

"You didn't tell me you had family." She fetched an old rotary phone attached to a long cord that snaked into the bedroom. After a few unsuccessful tries Daniel was able to get a call through.

"Do you accept the charges from a Mr. Daniel Fisher, calling from the Ukraine?" the operator said.

"Ukraine?" Gram said. "*Kinayn'oreh!*" His heart panged at the sound of her voice.

"Excuse me?" said the operator. "I didn't get that?"

"Yes, I accept."

"Gram..."

"Danny." Her voice was distant and full of static. "Hello."

"I'm sorry it's been so long, Gram. I've been traveling and it's not always easy to find a phone."

Dvoyre moved into her bedroom, leaving him alone.

"Nu, what have you been doing?" Gram said. "Christopher keeps calling, asking about you. He misses you. Says the shelter is falling apart without you. I told him I had no idea when you're coming back. When are you coming back, Danny?" There was despair in her voice, an emotion she almost never revealed.

He wanted to reach across the thousands of miles that separated them and pull her close. "Soon, Gram, I'm coming home soon."

"So you keep saying. What are you really up to, Danny?"

"I think you know, Gram."

"Do I?" She coughed away from the phone for almost a full minute.

"Do you have a cold?"

"No. Nu? When are you coming home?"

"As soon as I can. A few days."

"Will you come by to see me, or are you too busy?"

"Of course I'll come by!"

"Danny..."

"Yes?"

"I miss you."

"I miss you too, Gram."

"You know I love you."

"And I love you."

"Come home soon, Danny, will you?"

"Gram, what's wrong?"

"I just miss you." But he heard the quiver in her voice over the static-filled line.

"Tell me, what's going on?"

"Just come home, Danny. *Zay gezunt*. I'll be here. *Zay gezunt*."

She hung up, and the silence on the line terrified him more than his journey with The Breaker of Minds. The moon shone through a slit in Dvoyre's curtains and fell on one of the shards, reflecting cold light into his eyes.

He smelled the blood of a wild rabbit wafting in from outside, and his stomach rumbled. He reached for a cigarette.

CHAPTER ELEVEN

As HER LAST NOTE HUNG IN THE AIR DAPHNA STARED BEYOND the glare of the spotlights and dreamt of the masses of adoring fans chanting her name. Her note faded, and the director, after an extended moment of silence, said, "C–c–commercial break... back in three!" The lights came up. The black abyss around her became wheeled TV cameras and their gaping operators, PAs and pages in headsets and tool belts, executives in suits. Mechanical blinds rolled up, revealing the maddening, flashing lights of Times Square.

Kimberly Kay, the blue-eyed, blonde-haired talk-show host, had been brusque when Daphna had met her in the green room before the show. The woman had smelled strongly of cloying perfume and wore so much makeup Daphna wondered if there was any part of her face that was real. But now Kimberly Kay stood beside the stage, mouth agape, staring at Daphna as if she were the chosen one. Everyone stared at her, the PAs, the cameramen, and the executives in their thousand-dollar suits.

Someone clapped. They all joined in, and the sound rose to a deafening crescendo, until the director shouted, "Quiet in the studio! Returning in two..."

Kimberly Kay strode up to Daphna and put her palm on her shoulder. Her blue eyes were large and baby-like. "That was stunning, Carina." Kimberly said. "Just. Wow. We get a lot of hacks come through here, and I smile and pretend they're important. But with you, honey, there's no faking it. Goddamn. You can sing."

Daphna tried to forget that Duile and Khein had forced the studio to use a specific pre-amp they had prepared for her vocals, that it had harmonically enhanced her voice, and teased out frequencies designed to have the most pleasing effects on human emotional meridians. On top of that, the backing music oozed powerful magic, a spell so dense and layered that it would take an expert sorcerer years to unravel all its coercive knots. They were all being compelled to like her, she knew, but it didn't matter how she became the center of their attentions, only that she was. How they looked at her now, with such awe and devotion! Even Richard, her audio engineer, had made time to come here. He stood in the back, an ear-to-ear smile on his bearded face. He gave her a double thumbs up when she looked.

"I'm glad you liked it," Daphna said, growing warm.

"Like it?" Kimberly said. "Jesus, girl, I loved it!"

"One minute!" shouted the director. "Places..."

Kimberly escorted Daphna to two large leather chairs beside the towering windows. The studio's spotlights were warm and bright, and the flickering lights of Times Square spilled colored patterns over the studio floor. She felt dizzy as she sat.

"Thirty seconds..."

"Carina," said Kimberly, "I love your accessories. I thought they were a bit much at first, but on stage. Wow. The gold really pops! Who's your designer?"

She let slip a practiced smile. "The designs are mine."

It wasn't true, of course. Duile and Khein had provided her clothing, designed to attract the human eye. She wore an iridescent knee-length dress that flashed rainbows whenever she moved, like the frenetic video billboards outside. And she wore a glamour of golden accessories: necklace, cuffs, belt, watch, even gold-plated shoes, as if she were a character from one of her moldering science fiction pulps, a queen alien bent on conquering Earth; she smiled at the thought. As Kimberly had said, the getup had seemed overwrought before. But now, in the lights, she blazed.

"Ten...nine..." The director counted off the seconds with his fingers. He pointed at Kimberly Kay on one.

"Aaaaand...we're back, with pop-star sensation Carina! Welcome, darling! Let me be the first to say that was *amaaaaa-zing!*"

"Thank you, Kimberly," Daphna said, affecting her Ukrainian accent. "I'm flattered."

"So, Carina, we want to know, how did you get your start in music? Did you grow up in a musical home?"

"Well, Kimberly..." Duile was staring at her; they had trained her for this. "I don't like to speak too much of my childhood." Behind the camera, Duile nodded. "But, yes, music was always in my life. When things were their most painful, music was my escape."

"In an interview you did last week with *Teen Pop Idol*, you said that you were a 'child sex slave' in the Ukraine. Honey, I'm so sorry. That must have been awful. What was that like?"

Damn. She'd heard Americans could be abrupt, but even demons were seldom this forward, and she respected this Kimberly Kay quite a bit more for it.

"Horrible," she said. "And not something I wish on my worst enemy. But I don't want to be known for my past, only for what I am now, and the happiness I can bring people through music."

"I'm sure it will be a lot! Your new single, which we just had the pleasure of seeing you perform, is called 'The Night Mirror.' Can you tell us about it?"

"'The Night Mirror' is about fear. Learning to let go of the past. Sometimes letting go of pain can be the hardest thing, because pain becomes familiar."

Daphna stole a glance at Duile and Khein, who were both nodding.

"So where do you go from here? Will we see an album from you?"

"Oh, yes. I've already recorded four tracks, which are in post-production. I've got three more in the works."

"Got a release date for us?"

"Not yet, but very soon."

"All right, there you have it! New pop-star sensation Carina. Check out her new single, 'The Night Mirror,' available now at your favorite online music retailers. We'll be back in a minute with Tina Yin to show us a new salmon recipe that will not only help you lose weight, but feel full too. Back in a flash!"

The director said, "Out for three," and Kimberly got up and said, "I hope it's not too forward..." She revealed a business card from a pocket. "If you ever want to get a drink, or just talk. I know a lot of people in this town. I could help you."

Carina smiled and took the card. "Thank you, Kimberly." The make-up artists scurried over to check Kimberly's face, and a page in a black dress and heels escorted Carina across the studio toward her dressing room. Everyone was staring at her as she walked, as if she were a shining jewel. The dressing room had been stuffed with fruit and snacks, but once inside and the door closed she reached into her leather Michael Kors bag and pulled out a half-eaten packet of Skittles. She threw a dozen into her mouth and washed them down with vodka straight from the bottle as Duile and Khein burst in.

"You could fucking knock," she said. "I might have been undressed."

Duile's dark skin was unnaturally reflective in the room's fluorescent lights. Perhaps the spell concealing his demon nature was waning. "You did wonderfully," he said flatly.

"She didn't drop her articles," Khein said. "She was too fluent in English."

"I don't think anyone cares," Daphna said.

"True," said Duile. "They seemed sufficiently enamored. This might be easier than we thought."

Daphna was slipping off her bracelets, when Khein said, "No, leave them on."

"Why? The show's over."

"Haven't you been paying attention?" Duile said. "The show is *never* over."

"But why is it important I wear these uncomfortable things?" The gold reflected her iridescent dress, the room's couch and chairs, the basket of fruit and nut-bar snacks. A cosmic goddess stared back at her from the mirror, a character from one of her human books. She looked absurd, overwrought, ostentatious, but perhaps that's what being a pop-star meant. One had to exaggerate everything, be part of the constant show. Her gold accessories sparked and flashed as she turned, shining with their own subtle iridescence that vanished whenever she looked directly at them.

"Your look is just as important as your music," Duile said. "If they see you out of character, the spell will be broken."

"But why *these*?" She gestured at her accessories. "What do they mean?"

Khein and Duile exchanged glances. "It's the look our queen has chosen for you."

"Is there something you want to tell me?" she said.

"Have a drink," Khein said. "Breathe. You did well. Frix is waiting in the car to take us back to the studio. We have to record another track today to meet our schedule."

Daphna remembered how everyone in the studio had been looking at her. Soon, millions would look at her the same way. She shivered with excitement and poured the last of the Skittles into her mouth, chasing them down with a swig of vodka from the bottle. Then she grabbed her bag and headed out the door. The two men followed.

A few office workers asked her for an autograph or a quick selfie as she traversed the halls. One girl had a headshot of Carina she wanted autographed. When had Duile and Khein had time to prepare that? She didn't remember when they had taken the photo.

They went down the elevator to the side-street exit and onto a street leading away from the bustling Times Square. Two large men waited outside the doors in dark glasses and headsets. One said, "Carina at rear exit," as she came out.

At first she thought the people crowding the street were part of the tourist mob, rushing to and fro to experience the Times Square spectacle. She had only been in New York City for short time, but already she understood the allure of materialism. On Earth, limits were few, and anything could be had for the right price. But then she spotted the barricades, the tape and signs, the dark-jacketed men stationed along the perimeter. All eyes widened when they spotted her.

"CARINA!"

The screams came in a rising wave, and a wild cheer erupted from the crowd. There were at least four hundred people, teenagers mostly, lots of girls, but plenty of boys. It was a weekday, and she knew they should have been in school.

They waved and shouted and took photos of her, while off to the side four paparazzi snapped away, their photo flashes adding to the sensory assault. She squinted and held up her hand.

"Smile," Duile said. "Go be a star."

She took a steadying breath and stepped up to the crowd, while the black-jacketed men held back the most aggressive fans.

"Carina, I love you!"

"Oh my god, Carina!"

"You're so friggin' hot, girl!"

Khein gave her a Sharpie, and she signed the backs of phones and shirt sleeves and bare forearms and scraps of paper. Two had her *Teen Pop Idol* article. Their hands shook as they handed her things to sign, their eyes bright and young and over-dilated. "I love you so much," a girl said, crying, while Daphna signed a boy's forehead.

After a few minutes, Duile said they had to go. "Always leave them wanting," he said.

She blew them a kiss, and there was a collective sigh. They cheered as she was escorted to a black town car. Inside, the doors closed and locked, the stuffy silence felt strange. Duile and Khein seemed pleased.

"Go!" said Duile, and Frix hit the gas. Frix was a wiry woman with Asian features and hard, dark eyes, but underneath, a demon too.

They sped off, and Daphna swallowed her nausea. She would never get used to traveling in cars. She glanced back at the receding crowd, and all eyes watched her go. The car turned into a sea of yellow cabs on 7th Avenue.

"I don't get it," she said. "I've performed one song, had one interview, and there were hundreds of children waiting to get my autograph. How is this possible?"

Frix stared at her in the rear-view mirror as she accelerated in front of a green cab. The cab honked aggressively. "Did you think you were the first?" Frix said. Her voice was high-pitched and sharp, and Daphna thought Frix might shatter glass if she screamed. But the woman spoke slowly, enunciating each word as if she were acting out a play. "We've been conditioning humanity for decades to adore celebrities." Another car honked loudly as Frix cut it off. "If you present to them as famous, they rush to adore you. It's automatic at this point. We don't coerce that anymore. It's built into the system now."

"But what do they think I will give them?"

"A dream," Frix said. "If we present them with a fantasy, no matter how far-fetched, if they think it might happen to them, they latch onto it. Your rags to riches story is their story too. They see themselves in you."

Daphna gazed at her accessories. "Of course they do. I'm wearing only mirrors."

They passed Penn Station, a thousand people rushing to and fro, a terrifying sight compared to the stillborn silence of Abbadon's streets. She shuddered. Hanging over the throng of pedestrians was a huge video billboard. An enormous and sparkling face smiled down on everyone. Displayed underneath her face, in burning hot pink letters, was, "Carina, the hot new sensation! Saturday, April 2nd, at Webster Hall. Tickets on sale now!"

It was her own face she saw. She hadn't recognized it.

CHAPTER TWELVE

MASHIT LAY IN BED, STARING UP AT THE GREEN SILKEN CANOPY, shivering in the delicious afterglow of orgasm. In these rare moments, the weight of rule temporarily lifted, her thoughts were clear and pure. Beyond the city, the barren wastes of the Dissipation would be farmed, she knew, and soon the day would come when swaying fields of grain would stretch to the horizon like the great farms of Earth, and no demon in the Cosmos would ever go hungry again.

Ubaist lay beside her, a muscular, many-limbed young thing, decades old, just a boy. His forked red tongue lolled from his mouth as he slept, and by Abbadon he'd known how to use it. Still, while he had performed his duty, she imagined he were someone else. A human, of all creatures – a Lamed Vav, Maya – and this deeply puzzled her, for they'd spent only a short time together, and never alone. Perhaps it was Maya's eyes, which seemed to offer endless compassion.

There came a knock on her door, and she cursed. What now?

"Out!" she said to Ubaist, shoving him awake. He grabbed his clothing and fled through a hidden door in the corner, which led to a network of not-so-secret tunnels that snaked through the palace like a stone vascular system. She rose and attached a knife to her thigh with a thin leather strap. She carefully unsheathed the blade and checked its gleaming silver handle, its crystalline blade that shone like moonlight; even one small nick could kill. As she slowly turned the knife, it cast shadows about the room. The blade had been fashioned from a fragment of the first universe – her universe – that the Creator had obliterated. She had never used her Shard Knife, but rested easy knowing she had to just lift her leg to draw it and destroy any who touched its lethal point.

She carefully sheathed the knife again, then slipped into her white gown. She used the large mirror facing the bed to adjust the gown's many soft folds. She recoiled at her face in the mirror, a raw ugliness hovered about it – her true demon nature had seeped through – and she quickly cast a glamour to bring herself back to her perfected human form.

When she was finally ready, she said, "Enter."

Kokabiel stooped to fit under the doorframe, and the floor shuddered with his massive weight. "You called me, my queen?" he said.

"I didn't think you'd arrive so soon, Koko."

"My first duty is to my queen."

She raised her chin. "How have we let ourselves become so formal? Koko, my dear, have a seat." She gestured to the metal and glass table beside the window. Tall emerald curtains filtered the morning light into a thousand shades of green.

One day soon, she thought, *I'll open these curtains and the green will remain.*

The two sat, and she lifted a delicately curved wooden pipe from a tray and lit the bowl with a few words of magic. She took a long puff of the fungal mixture, exhaled slowly into the girders of sunlight, and offered the pipe to him.

"Doesn't that addle your mind?" he said, frowning.

"I seem to recall you enjoy addling your mind with me quite often, Koko."

"The situation now, my queen, calls for clarity."

"You may dispense with the formalities, Koko, when we're alone."

"Then I'll say it like it is, Mashit. There is unrest in Sheol. People grow impatient. And here you smoke your pipe and–" he sniffed the air –"get pleasure by palace slaves."

She stared at him, trying to decide if she wished to be offended, but as the smoke's effects hit her, she merely frowned. "I think I preferred your formalities. What's troubling you, Koko? All is going according to my plan." She took another puff, savored the bitter taste, then exhaled slowly. The smoke tumbled in the still air. "Even you behave exactly as I have predicted."

"Because I have come when you order me to?"

"How many eyes do I have, Koko?"

"What?"

"Answer me. How many eyes do I have?"

"You have two eyes."

"No, I have a million."

He looked at her pipe, then into her eyes. "Perhaps you've had too much smoke."

"How many ears do I have?"

"A million?"

She nodded. "And with all those eyes and ears, Koko, I see and hear everything." She waited for his reaction, but he did not betray a change of expression.

"I'd be worried if it were otherwise," he said.

"So tell me, why does the Second General of the Legion sneak into the bowels of the dungeons to speak with the Traitor King, using spells to conceal himself?"

Kokabiel turned to the window, and a sudden breeze, the first of the day, fluttered the curtains, stirring the smoke. "I'm impressed," he said. "I thought no one had seen me. You'd make a good spy."

"I make a better queen. Tell me, why were you there?"

Kokabiel took a slow breath. "I've not visited the Traitor King since you took the throne. Never alone."

"And you wished to apologize for betraying him?"

"Hardly! I loathe him for what he did. He abandoned Sheol. He abandoned me. I visited the Traitor King in the dungeons to rub the dung of failure in his face. To curse him. To spit upon him."

"This is what Stoning Day is for."

"Yes, and on those days I watch from afar as every last demon in Sheol curses and defiles him. I wanted to – no, I *needed* to face him alone, without the masses."

"In secret?"

"There are things between him and me that should not become known."

"Like how you betrayed him? And how you might one day betray me?"

Kokabiel stared at her. "I had to show him what I am, and what he's become."

"And what are you, and what is he?"

"I am a smith, and he is my metal. I hammer and fold him into shape. Is this not why you keep him alive, so the masses may vent their frustrations upon him instead of you? He is your scapegoat. Well I have my own frustrations to vent."

"Like how you are dissatisfied with my rule, and wish him to be king again."

"Never. He betrayed us all. This smoke clouds your thoughts, Mashit."

"Or clarifies them. Koko, if there are things about my rule that dissatisfy you, you must tell me. If not yours, then whose council can I trust? My ears are always open."

"All million of them."

She smiled and stood, growing dizzy from the smoke, and approached the window. She spread the curtains and looked down on the knotted streets of Abbadon. Clumps of green mold had begun to grow in twilit corners. And there were rumors of new breeds of flying insects spawning in the slums. Such life had never existed here before.

"I wanted to destroy Ashmedai," she said as her hand touched her thigh, where under her gown the Shard Knife lay concealed. "But once dead, he'd become a martyr, an immortal symbol, like Great Abbadon. Then I'd never be able to destroy his legacy. By keeping him alive, by using him to vent the people's frustrations–"

"You weaken his legacy, day by day."

She nodded. "Yes, my wise Koko. Unlike my court sycophants, you among them have a brain."

He slammed his fist on the table, startling her. "Then why make me *Second* General, and that blathering idiot Talman the First?"

"Because I owed Talman a favor."

"For helping you seize the throne?"

"Yes, and for other things."

He glanced at the ruffled bed. "And those other things continue even now. Whose sweat do I smell? Larniel the screecher? Ubaist, the long-tongued dolt?"

"That's quite a nose you have. My sense of smell is not as acute as yours, but it's strong enough to smell your jealousy."

"Maybe I will take that pipe," he said, reaching for it.

She put a hand on his forearm, stopping him. "No, keep your clarity. I prefer you angry. That's the only time you ever tell the truth." His arm shivered beneath her, and she smiled, knowing this enormous creature, who had slain more creatures than he could count, was completely under her thrall. "You may despise me for fulfilling my desires, Koko, but I'll make no apologies for them."

"Have you called me here to boast of your bedroom conquests? It's not much of a victory if your victims can't refuse your orders."

She chuckled. "And were you one of my victims, Koko?"

"That remains to be seen."

"Indeed. Koko, did you know the Vestigal Stem has bloomed?"

He stared at her. "I presumed it was a false rumor."

"No, it's no rumor," she said, and her mind drifted off, thinking about the Vestigal Stem, the only plant that had survived the Shattering. Great Abbadon had planted it in Sheol and ordained that it be tended and cared for until the end of days. On a well-guarded terrace protected from Sheol's violent weather, the gnarled thorn bush had lain dormant for millennia beside four ever-burning censers of blue fire. But on the day Daphna had left for Earth, the Vestigal Stem awoke from its eon-long sleep. "Four carmine flowers have opened," she said, "one for each Lamed Vav in Sheol. Do you know what that means? It's said that when the Vestigal Stem blooms–"

"Sheol will emerge from the ashes to resume its place in the Cosmos." He harrumphed. "I've never put my faith in prophesy."

"Neither have I. Until now. Change is happening, Koko. Apple trees grow on the cliffs. Plants have begun to spontaneously grow in the streets. And insects! Flying and crawling and swarming creatures. Think of it, Koko! If bees can survive on Sheol, they can pollinate the plants. Life will be self-sustaining. The era we've been hoping for will soon be upon us, and I, Mashit, your queen, will be the one who has heralded it."

"Can we farm the Dissipation now?"

"No, but–"

"Can we feed the people with your apple trees?"

"There are not enough apples, but–"

"Then all you offer the people is another dream, the same as Abbadon. Dreams cannot feed the hungry."

She frowned. "I've come closer than any before me. And though it may seem to you I sit idle here smoking away the hours, I have plans in motion that will expedite matters."

"Such as?"

"A plan to bring to Sheol the one thing it has always lacked."

"Life?"

"Power. To survive, we collect the life-force that spills from Earth in drips and drops, but it's barely enough to maintain us. I plan to increase the flow many-fold. The gold we mine from Sheol's mountains will be imbued with powerful magic. Soon, I will send a massive shipment of enchanted gold to Earth, where it will be fashioned into human adornments. They will drain the power of those who wear them and funnel it across the Great Deep to us."

Kokabiel shook his head. "Shemhazai and Azazel tried this three millennia ago, and they nearly destroyed Sheol. This world cannot hold so much power. If you try that, you'll crack Sheol in two."

"That may have been true before. But with the four Lamed Vav here, we are like a house with solid foundations. We *can* hold such power now, Koko."

He shook his head. "Even if you could bring such power here, humans are gullible creatures, but they will not willingly allow themselves to be drained."

"That's the beauty of my plan. The spell that drains their power also drains their will. The more they wear our charmed gold, the more compliant they become."

"And how do you plan to get these humans to wear your gold?"

"My daughter, Daphna, has gone to Earth. She will become what the humans call a *pop-star*. She's already well on her way. She will sell them our gold, and they will buy it."

Kokabiel abruptly stood, and his massive form towered over her. "It's a bold plan," he said. "But you play with fire. You could destroy Sheol."

"Or I will save it," she said. "Koko, I want you to lead the construction of new power vats. Enormous ones to hold the immense power which will soon flow our way."

"Me? A foreman? I'm a soldier, not an engineer."

127

"Thubael has already completed the designs." From a drawer she removed a scroll of blue parchment, unrolled it on the table, and Kokabiel's eyes grew wide. Upon it, drawn in luminescent yellow ink, were numbers and charts and symbols, a complex plan for new power vats. "You will spearhead the construction, Koko."

"But why me?"

"Because it must be built in absolute secrecy. No one must know of this yet. This is why I need a soldier and not an engineer. Only someone with your authority could command such fear to keep demons from talking."

"But why such a secret? Is it because you don't want the people to know your first plan has failed?"

"I have *not* failed! It has only taken more time than I anticipated."

"And if this new plan doesn't work," Kokabiel said, "you could destroy Sheol."

"It won't fail. Not with your help."

"And what will the queen do for me?"

"Since when are my orders not enough? I could have you killed for disobedience."

"You need me, Mashit. You said so yourself."

She sighed. "Very well, Koko. When you finish this project, I'll make you First General again."

"No."

"No?"

"I will do this for you, Mashit, if you promise me your hand in marriage. If you declare your marriage to me in front of the entire city."

"I will not make you king, Koko!"

"No, but you will make me your consort. By the old laws, this can be done. I won't rule Sheol. That will be your role. But I will have a place in the inner court. Now, I'm but an outside observer."

She lifted the pipe and took a long puff. "My, my, Koko, your height is only matched by your ambition. Very well, if you do as I ask, then I will make you my consort."

Kokabiel unsheathed a knife from his belt, a long curving metal blade inlaid with swirling arabesques. He turned the hilt toward her. "Swear it," he said, "by Abbadon."

"So formal?" she said.

"I'm in a formal mood, my queen."

She frowned and snatched the blade from him. She squeezed her hand around it, and the sharp edge sliced her palm. Blood dripped onto the floor. Her human form unexpectedly cracked open, and her four heads burst free, a goat, a pig, a scorpion, and a human. Kokabiel smiled as she shoved her untamed spirits back inside herself, sealing them behind her human shape, a form she and other First Ones preferred over the grotesqueries of the subsequent generations. "I swear by Great Abbadon and the Fires of Sheol I will make you my consort if you do what I ask."

"And may the ashes of your blood rise to meet him."

"There," she said. "Do you feel better?"

"Ecstatic," he said, and his cold eyes bored into hers.

She made a fist to staunch the bleeding and wiped the blade with a cloth. She gave him back the knife. "You've always been much too serious, Koko."

"These are serious times."

"Take these plans," she said, handing him the blueprints. "Start today, and report your progress to me every morning. And if anyone finds out before you've completed this task, I'll kill you in your sleep."

He stared at her.

"I'm kidding, Koko." She smiled. "You really need to lighten up."

Kokabiel towered above her in the high-ceilinged room. He opened the door, stirring the smoke. "Good day, *my queen.*"

He shut the door, and she was alone again. Her head spun, and ephemeral sparks flashed in the corner of her eyes. Perhaps she had smoked too much. She collapsed onto the bed. After a few minutes she opened a small drawer beside the bed, from which she removed a photo. She and Daniel Fisher had been walking the High Line, an old elevated train track turned nature park, in Manhattan one spring morning. They were laughing.

She ran her fingers over his face. He was no master in bed. He had little cleverness, no wit. And yet this simpleton had held up the world. She had imagined she loved him, and had chased Daniel across the Shards. But it wasn't him she sought – she knew that now – but a feeling. She put the photo down, and stared up at the ceiling. She thought of Maya, the Lamed Vavnik, as her hand slowly slid down between her legs.

CHAPTER THIRTEEEN

THERE WAS NO SUN TO MARK THE TORPID DAYS, NOR STARS TO mark Sheol's frigid nights. And even the period of his swinging cage changed subtly across the long hours, so there was no way for Ashmedai to measure the passage of time. Had it been ten hours since his stoning, or ten weeks? He lay on the floor of his cage, covered in sweat, ash from the fires below clinging to his flesh. Odd visions came and went with the rocking of his cage. Most were fragmentary things, never congealing into a complete image. All but one.

He was soaring high above the palace, where strong winds pushed him out over the black lake, over its dark and reflectionless waters, as if he were a doom vulture caught in a southern gale. Something lurked under the waters, an enormous muddy shape. Vague and indistinct, it waited, watching. Soon it would rise to stand taller than the palace, more massive than the city, greater even than the mountains. It would break free of its eons-long slumber and destroy anything that stood in its way. And Ashmedai would welcome it, if it meant an end to this incessant swinging. The vision came and fled again and again as the hours passed.

Things stirred in the fires below. Sheol's bowels gurgled and spat as a bolus of stone passed through the fiery intestines of the world where it was digested into liquid rock. A flurry of sparks rose from the fires and flew past his cage up into the darkness above. He followed them with his eyes as far as the view allowed.

They are like stars, he thought, and he was hurtling through space. *I fall through the Shards*, he thought, and he was plunging into the Abyss at the Shattering. *So much time has passed, and I've never stopped falling.*

One spark did not rise into space, but paused to hover beside his cage, like a curious insect. He inched closer to this visitor, and the visitor crept closer in return. He grimaced from the bruises and the pain as he crawled toward the spark, and a faint whisper grew in his ears just above the thrum of lava below.

Master, can you hear me?

It was not a whisper, nor even a sound. The words formed in his mind as thought pictures, as gestalts.

This is it, he thought, *the moment where I go insane.*

You are not insane, my lord! I am truly here!

A shudder of recognition passed through him. The spark spoke the Silent Tongue, the oldest language, which predated the creation of demonkind, the creation of matter itself, and was spoken by all creatures, though most had forgotten it.

You are a dream, he thought. *My mind torments me with phantoms. Go away.*

I am no dream, my lord! Nor have I come to torment you. Your brother sent me.

Ashmedai laughed, and his voice rose through the burning silence to echo in the cavern. "Go away, Mashit," he said weakly. "I will not fall for tricks."

Please, hush, my lord, lest they discover I am here! I come at the behest of your brother, Lord Azazel, our first master.

You are Mikulal? he said.

Aye. From the mines.

Ashmedai sat fully up. The ledge where he had seen visitors was empty and silent. If there were guards nearby, he had not seen one for a long time.

Who are you, spark?

I am Raigul, son of Deneb, and a seventh ring stonemaster. I offer my fealty to you, beyond the compulsion which impels me to obey you. I give myself freely to you, my lord.

And where are you, Raigul, son of Deneb? I see but a spark shivering in the hot air.

I am near, my lord. I stand beneath you on a ledge, where the lava burns too close for my liking. My skin smokes. It pains me to remain where I am. Another pace forward and I will die. A spell carries my voice to you, conveyed through this spark.

Ashmedai stuck his nose between the bars of his cage and peered toward the fiery river below. There were hundreds of stone crevices where one might hide, but in the wavering air, they were impossible to see clearly.

How is it, Raigul, that you have passed through Mashit's spell around the city that prevents your kind from entering?

This far underground, my lord, am I truly still in Abbadon? Mashit's spell wavers beside the fires. I cannot visit you up there, but from down here I can weave my thoughts into the sparks so that you may hear me.

I want to believe you, Raigul. Prove that you are real.

I hope to do so. I come with a message from your brother, Lord Azazel. He says, "Now we are both enchained."

How delightfully observant of him. Is that all?

No. He says something is wrong with Earth. Strange things are happening there.

Such as?

An overabundance of plants, for one.

He laughed. *Oh, poor Earth and its abundant plants!*

We have received a message from our brothers on Earth. They say there is an unhealthy imbalance there. They sense it in the air.

Mashit stole four Lamed Vav from Earth. When you remove the pillars that support a house, the house becomes unstable. Of course there's an imbalance.

Yes, and Lord Azazel has accounted for that. What they have sensed is not from the missing Pillars themselves, but something heretofore unseen. Rana–

What of her? What do you know of Rana the Gu? The anger came unexpectedly, and with it, a burst of energy. He approached the burning bars, readying to snatch the spark and extinguish it between his fingers.

I know Rana the Gu gave her life to save the Earth, and subsequently all the Shards.

Ashmedai trembled as a sob rose in his throat. Rana, the greatest artist the Cosmos had ever known, forever gone. *Do you know the magnitude of what we lost, Raigul? Do you know what she might have built? Paradise! Yet now, Sheol festers, and I rot in a cage. There were none like Rana in all the Shards. There will be none like her ever again.*

My lord, Rana was pregnant.

Ashmedai paused. *What did you say?*

Forgive me, my lord, but you and Rana lay together in Azazel's Lair. And you impregnated her.

Ashmedai shook his head. He remembered lying under her, the Horn of Azazel shining like a sun in her hands, as she took him. He had never felt more alive, more whole.

Rana could not have gotten pregnant so quickly! he said. *She went to Earth only minutes later.*

You are a First One and Rana was a Gu. You lay together while she held the Horn of Azazel in her hands. It carried enough power to build a new universe. You did succeed with your plans, my lord, just not the way you had hoped.

Is it true? Ashmedai thought. *Did Rana and I make a child?* He wished she were here, if only to curse him, just to hear her voice again. The air was heavy and full of ash, and he felt as if he were choking on it.

You did, my lord. And when Rana, pregnant, teeming with power, gave herself to the Earth, all her energy went with her. Something is growing on Earth, my lord. Something with purpose.

What do you mean, 'with purpose'?

It's too early to tell, but Lord Azazel thinks this growth is self-aware. The overabundance of plant life on Earth is an expression of its awakening.

Ashmedai was astonished. *What strange fetus rouses itself awake on Earth?* he thought. *And what does it want? Is this my child, or a monster?* He shuddered. *I need to be free of this cage, Raigul! Have you come here just to torment me with this?*

Schemes are in motion, my lord. But Mashit's spell makes our movement difficult. Others have tried getting close to you, and many have died trying. I am the first to succeed.

When I am free, all the dead shall be honored as heroes. But you must expedite your plans, Raigul. Even us First Ones have limits. I don't think I'll survive another stoning.

We are moving as quickly as we can, my lord. But if you have any knowledge that might help, now is the time to offer it.

Ashmedai had a ready answer. *I need you to deliver a message for me, Raigul. Can you do that?*

Say the words, my lord, and I'll deliver it to any soul in the Cosmos.

Ashmedai squeezed his fists. At last, his swinging above this fiery chasm would end. *Send a message to a demon named Gedeon. He was once the Master Archivist, but now is the Chief of Sewers. Do you know of him?*

Yes, my lord. We have seen much of him these recent days.

Then tell Gedeon only this: 'At the next stoning day, only one sun will rise."

Outside his cage, the spark tumbled in the air.

CHAPTER FOURTEEN

AFTER SO MUCH TIME AWAY, GRAM'S HOUSE SEEMED LIKE A dream. It was just after sunset when Daniel arrived, and he stood outside as the cloud-striped crimson sky spread bloody palettes over the rows of suburban houses. The homes of Gram's street had been painted new colors, sported new additions, shrubberies, walks. New cars were parked in driveways. People mulled about he didn't recognize. He had spent the bulk of his life here in Babylon. But Gram's home seemed a stranger.

The whole block was green and fecund and well trimmed. But Gram's lawn was wildly overgrown. Yellow dandelion heads bloomed riotously. Tall weeds had sprouted, blossomed, and gone to seed. She had always been so meticulous about her garden, and he wondered why she had let things go.

He took two painful drags from a cigarette. He would not let the curse defile him here, in this sacred place. He had become adept at smoking without screaming, without coughing or bowling over, and after the pain and the nicotine and the suppression of his curse, the world became a bit more familiar. At last, he was home.

He stamped out his cigarette and stepped up to the door. By habit he reached for his key, but he had lost it weeks ago in a Thai jungle. He knocked, and when no one answered, he opened the door. Despite changing times, she had, in all these years, never locked it when she was home, "An offense," she had said, "to the notion of community." The house smelled like brisket and dusty linens and bread. It smelled like home.

"Take off your shoes." His heart panged at the sound of her voice, and he slowly stepped into the living room.

She sat in her reclining chair, book in lap, reading glasses hanging off her nose. Because of her scars to most people she seemed a monster. But to him, she was always a savior. He ran to her, and they hugged.

"Where oh where do you go, Danny, that you always come back to me smelling like a homeless person?"

Shivering, he sat beside her on the couch. The thriving houseplants by the window blocked the view of her twilit backyard. "Gram, it's good to be home."

"Are you?" she said, smiling wanly. "Home?"

He sighed. "For now." He stared at her. She was really here, beside him. But her once-vibrant blue eyes had gone rheumy, and her face was gaunt. "Gram, are you okay?"

"I will be once you get your shmutsiker tuchas into the shower. Go wash up. When you come out, we'll eat."

Daniel smiled. It was great to be home.

—

He showered, shaved, and dressed in some ancient clothes he had left behind from childhood, old whitewashed Levis, a Hobie surfer tee, both loose on him. He sat across from Gram in the kitchen at the neatly set table. On the sill below the sink window, two candles burned in tall silver candlesticks, and only an inch of their melted tapers remained.

"It's Friday?" he said. "I've totally lost track of days."

"Every shabes, I waited as long as I could before lighting them, hoping you'd walk in like you did tonight." She smiled. "It was always a joy to light the shabes candles with you. I know your parents were watching us when we said the blessings together."

"I'm sorry I've been away, Gram."

"There's still the challah," she said. "And the wine."

He nodded, then performed the blessing over the wine, first in Hebrew, then in English. "Blessed art Thou, our Lord, our God, King of the Universe, who created the fruit of the vine." He took a sip of the oversweet Manischewitz, but Gram abstained. He blessed the bread, "...who brings forth bread from the Earth," while thinking of all the abundance he'd seen across the world: Thailand and its dense rainforests, Ukraine and its swaying grain, Kazakhstan and its grassy plains, even Gram's house plants – all were "bringing forth" in abundance lately. He was grateful for being born in such a place and time. He tore off a piece of challah and handed her the soft bread.

"You'll eat the brisket?" she said.

"Sure."

"You used to hate meat."

"Things have changed. A lot of things."

"I can see that. But I'm glad you haven't changed so much you've forgotten who you are." She gestured at the wine and bread.

"I thought I'd lost myself," he said. "But here, with you, I feel like myself again."

"You were in Ukraine?"

He nodded.

"And how long were you there?"

"A few days."

"Where else?"

"All in all, I visited seventeen countries."

"*Got in himel.* What in heaven for?"

He tore off a piece challah from the loaf. "I've been looking for a door."

She squinted at him. "What kind of door?"

He sighed. This place had always been a simple one, unspoiled by the outside world, even when things were at their worst. He would not pollute it now, when he needed her comfort and security more than anything else. "A door that leads to a place few people would ever want to go."

"So why do you want to go there?"

"Because I have to."

She stared at him, and after a moment, she began eating. If Gram was ever one thing, she was accepting, with the sole exception of Rebekah, and she had been right, after all.

They ate the brisket, and it was delicious, but Gram had only a few bites before she patted her belly and declared herself full. She coughed, a heavy rasping sound, and Daniel didn't need his heightened senses to glean that she was ill.

"You don't sound good," he said.

"Just getting over a cold."

"You sure that's all?"

She got up and began to clear the dishes.

"Let me," he said.

But she insisted, and when Gram had a notion, there was no stopping her. But she moved more slowly than he remembered, and there was something cautious in her motions, as if she were afraid she might break herself. He spotted a herd of orange pill bottles in one of the cabinets as she put away a glass from the drain board.

He longed to hug her. He had spoken to her from across the world, over shoddy connections and static-filled lines, and yet now as she stood beside him she seemed to float a world away. "Are you sure you're all right?" he said, terrified of the growing silence.

"Me? Sure!"

"What have you been doing?"

"I see Maureen a few times a week. I read, watch the news. Talk to my plants. That's it. Your friend Christopher doesn't call much anymore. It's been quiet."

"Gram, are you going to tell me what's wrong?"

"Don't be silly."

"I've never been more serious."

She put both hands on the sink to steady herself and stared out the window, beyond the guttering shabes candles. "We're all mortal, Danny."

He swallowed. "Gram?"

"I suppose this is punishment."

"What are you talking about?"

"I have metastatic lung cancer. There are nodules on my lymph nodes and next to my spine. Maureen's been taking me for chemotherapy three times a week. In the best case, I'll be dead in six months."

No. This wasn't happening. He had misheard. Gram wasn't dying. She wouldn't leave him. When his parents had died, she had been there. When he was hit by a car on his bike, she had taken him to the hospital. When he had been assaulted at school by two older boys, Gram stood by his side as she scolded the principal. When his first ever girlfriend dumped him on his birthday and he was disconsolate, Gram had told him to toughen up, that life was full of heartache. And though Gram had loathed Rebekah – for good reason, in retrospect – she still had come to his wedding. She was always there and always would be. She had to be. Nothing else made sense.

"Gram," he said, shivering. "Gram."

"My advice to you, Danny, is to never take up smoking."

He approached her, and the tears came.

"No," she said, moving away from him. "I'll have none of that sappy stuff. I've led a good life and raised an incredible grandson. You don't have to tell me what you're doing, hopping around the world, looking for doors." She stared at him. "I already know. You're upholding the world."

One of the candles sizzled and went out, releasing a brief puff of black smoke.

—

He helped her clean the kitchen, and though it was only 9:30 p.m. when they finished, she was ready for sleep. He set up her humidifier and helped her into bed. For a brief moment, she had forgotten to close her nightgown, and he glimpsed her scarred stomach and legs. The doctors had said she would be in pain for the rest of her life. But she had never complained, and he could not remember a time when she pitied herself or succumbed to despair. She had stood firm even when Danny, especially in his teenage years, was the most difficult.

She had given him everything. She had lived for him alone. How could he leave her again? She was dying. She was in pain. She needed him.

When he shut off the bedroom light she was already dozing. He stared at her for a moment before returning to the living room. The smell of brisket was heavy in the house, and he inhaled deeply, savoring it. How many more times would he smell this? How many more shabes dinners would he share with her? But when he sniffed again he also detected the urine of the neighbor's dog and a raccoon rummaging in the garbage and the earth, wet from this morning's rain.

And just like that, it was back, the gnawing hunger, the craving for human flesh, tearing at him. He grit his teeth and fought off the overwhelming urge to find a deceased body to feast upon. "Not here!" he growled. "Not in this house!"

He slipped out through the back door in the kitchen to the yard and lit a smoke, fully aware of the irony. Here he was puffing away while his grandmother was dying of lung cancer in the next room. But then the nicotine coursed through his body, and the fierce desire for human flesh abated. No longer could he hear the TV two houses over, or the snoring of the neighbor's dog. All faded into the sounds of crickets. He puffed and tried not to grimace or scream from the pain.

The stars were sharp and bright, and there was no moon. Somewhere, across the infinite expanse of the Great Deep, Sheol was gaining power. He knew what demons wrought, how death and destruction followed in their wake. Sheol could not succeed.

But what would happen, he wondered, if he did nothing, if he stayed here and remained with Gram until the end? Would someone else rise to take his place? Could he pick up later, where he'd left off? Surely he had done enough already.

He tamped out his cigarette and went back inside. In the living room, pictures of his parents hung on the wall. More rested atop the flat-back piano. He stood with them, aged three, five, nine. In the last photo before their death, he was ten. Everybody smiled. A stylized painting of the Tree of Life, the ten Sephirot, hung above all of the frames. Ten circles connected by twenty-two lines, the divine blueprint of reality. In one circle, Gevurah, judgment. In its opposite, Chesed, mercy. Not long ago, in the shattered universe of Gehinnom, he had stood atop a life-sized pattern just like this and cast a spell to thrust himself across the Great Deep to Earth.

He shook his head. Was any of this real?

He sat in her recliner, and even with his dulled senses he smelled Gram on everything. This was home. It could not change. He rose and walked down the hall to her room. Her light was off, her snores and the humidifier the only sounds. Her sleep mask lay over her eyes. Her lips were spread apart. He stood beside her bed, like he had when he was a boy and she lay unconscious in the hospital, delirious from pain, her skin burnt to black. He had thought she would die, and yet she had gone on living, living for him.

Now it was his turn, to go on living, living for another. Would Gram ever understand why she was not the object of his efforts, why he had to leave? Because if he didn't rise to the task of saving the Earth, who the hell would?

He wanted to leave a note, but struggled to find the words that would capture his tangled knot of feelings. Besides, what could he say that had not already been said?

"I'm sorry," he whispered as he leaned over to kiss her forehead. "I love you so much, but I have to go."

Faintly, she said, "Don't stay out too late." Then she was snoring again.

—

The late train to New York was sparsely filled, and when he arrived at Penn Station he stepped onto 7th Avenue to smoke a cigarette. His nicotine cravings came often, and in between cigarettes, the hunger grew fierce and violent; his Mikulal nature would not be so easily tamed. The streets around Penn Station had been subsumed by Times Square, and one long glare of neon-corporate light stretched from 50th down to 32nd. Though it was near midnight, people scurried about, leaped into cabs, or ran to the station. But this place of bustle and abundance left its most vulnerable to suffer. On the coldest winter nights homeless people often died. Thousands more went hungry every day, even though there was more food within ten square miles than most places on earth.

Rainbow light from a giant video billboard shone down on him, and he gazed up at the image of a smiling woman with long black hair and piercing gray-white eyes. "Carina, the hot new sensation! This Saturday, April 2nd, at Webster Hall. Tickets still available!"

She wore an iridescent dress bedecked with golden accessories and looked like some sci-fi alien goddess. As she turned, her smile widened, and lens flares filled the screen. All faded to black, replaced by a Macy's advert. "40% off Spring Sale!"

He extinguished his cigarette, ducked back into Penn Station, and took the 1 train up to Columbus Circle. He hiked up Central Park West and entered the park at 67th Street. Though the park was technically closed, people still milled about under its towering arbors and twisting paths. Runners, bikers, long-boarders, pedestrians, the homeless. A few months ago he would have stopped to ask the unfortunate if they'd had enough to eat, if they needed a bed, when they last showered or had seen a doctor. But he had other plans.

It took him the better part of an hour to reach the Great Lawn. Skyscraper lights shone down on the same riot of growth, the same absurd profusion of plant life he'd seen throughout his travels. The world seemed more alive since he'd returned to it. Trees had too many leaves, and the fragrant, blossoming bushes seemed more at home in a Thai jungle than this urban one.

He walked through the knotted grass. Usually, the city lights drowned out the cosmic spectacle above. But it had rained before, clearing the air, and the stars shone bright and steady. He stopped when he reached the spot.

The grass was dense, in dire need of a cut. And here a single blade of grass rose many times taller than the others. He remembered the phrase from the Talmud: *Beside every blade of grass is an angel who whispers, "Grow, grow."*

And it was here, on this very spot, where Rana had given herself to save the world. Rana, the mason from Gehinnom, the Gu of boundless creativity, had transformed herself into mortar and sealed the cracks of the broken Earth and all the Shards that depended on it for life, and yet hardly a soul knew her name. The silhouetted turret of Belvedere Castle and the sweep of the Delacorte Theater rose in the south, as they always had. The trees swayed in the wind, and the pigeons and hawks and sparrows and starlings laid their eggs. People watched television and wrote emails and made love. The stars survived to shine down upon the world another day.

In Thailand he had visited an ancient Buddhist temple, and one twilit evening he had paused before a large stone sculpture of a woman holding a thick braid of her hair that sprayed a fountain of water.

"Who is she?" he asked a passing monk.

"She is Phra Mae Thorani," the monk said. "The Earth Mother. The waters from her hair help the seeker reach enlightenment." The water splashed into a small pool, and the monk encouraged Daniel to drink from it. "Phra Mae Thorani is a goddess of the Earth, who was called by the Buddha himself to help him overcome Maya, the play of delusion. Without her, the Buddha would not have reached liberation."

Daniel cupped his hands and drank, and the water tasted surprisingly cool and refreshing in the oppressive heat. The monk kissed a small stone in his hand and dropped it into the pool. Hundreds of such stones covered the pool's bottom.

"Why do you do that?" Daniel said.

"Because all things have Buddha-nature. By blessing the smallest, we help all rise."

Daniel nodded at the truth. He searched and found a small stone in the jungle, dipped it into the water, and silently thanked the goddess. And now, weeks later, in Central Park, he removed the same stone from his pocket and turned it over in his hands. He placed the stone on the grass, just beside the tall blade, just like the Jewish custom to leave a stone on the grave of the deceased, so Phra Mae Thorani's blessings might find their way to Rana, wherever she might be.

And then, because he didn't know what else to do, he said the Kaddish, the Mourner's Prayer. The wind blew, and the Earth lived on another day.

—

He spent the night in the park, under a tree. It no longer felt strange to sleep outside, and lately he preferred the familiarity of the stars to strange ceilings and rooms. He smelled rats and heard squirrels, but they steered clear of his cursed scent, sensing better than people who and what he was. He thought of Gram, how she would wake in the morning to find herself alone again. It killed him that he hadn't left her a note, and he vowed to call home the first chance he had. As the stars turned their slow course through the sky, sleep eluded him.

Before the sun rose above the skyline he crept into the subway and spent the day hiding among the underground malls of Rockefeller Centre, Penn and Grand Central Stations, thumbing through magazines, reading first chapters of books, purposefully avoiding smoking so that his senses grew sharp. His desire for human flesh rose as the day wore on, and he felt himself grow feral and strong.

He was heading toward the subway escalators inside Grand Central around 5 p.m. when Susan Blackburn emerged from the throng and came walking toward him. For years they had worked side by side at the Shulman Fund, fighting for justice one philanthropic battle at a time. They had even gone on a few dates. She looked him right in the eyes, and he froze, unsure of what to say. But he didn't need to speak, because she broke eye contact and hurried past. There was no awkward change in her body language; this was not malicious. No – he was certain Susan had simply not recognized him. She vanished into the rush-hour throng, one body among thousands.

He sighed as he headed down into the subway, missing Gram terribly.

It was not quite dusk when he stepped out into the crowds of Union Square. Chess players, protesters, dancers, students, execs, weirdoes, and hawkers formed a seething mass, while the granite underbelly of the city held everything firm. The sun was hidden behind the skyline and sinking fast. He walked down 4th Avenue, then turned left onto 11th Street. Eager fans were already queuing by the doors to Webster Hall, dressed in bright fluorescent colors, tight pants and leggings, lots of make up, lots of gold. Up above, the marquis said, "CARINA TONIGHT, WITH SPECIAL GUEST DONOGHUE."

Scalpers whispered, "Tickets, tickets..."

"How much?" Daniel said to one.

"$275," said a goateed man with bloodshot eyes, a cigarette dangling from his lips.

"Jeez," Daniel said. "I'll give you $50."

"No way," the man said, and turned away. But he remained close, waiting for Daniel to make a better offer. But fuck – Daniel had traveled across the world and had visited other universes and had fought with demons. He would not be stymied by the price of a goddamned ticket.

He crossed the street and waited near the growing queue, fighting the urge to smoke, the stabs of grotesque hunger. He needed his senses sharp.

The crowd was predominantly young, baby-faced, bright-eyed, not yet soured on life. Nervous, hopeful, they giggled and danced from the rumble of DJ music spilling out from the hall, and their anticipation was contagious. They surreptitiously drank from flasks and toked weed from vaporizers. Three cops chatted with the most attractive ones, ignoring the not-so-subtle breaking of laws. Daniel scoped the building, looking for ways in.

There was the wide, main entrance and several regular-sized doors off to the side. Under a rusted copper awning a heavyset man on a stool guarded a nondescript entrance. Beside him, up a small ramp, his door was plastered with warnings about trespassing and hidden cameras. Daniel maneuvered to the side, waiting for the right moment.

They started letting people in. It was six thirty, not quite time for the opening act, but he wasn't here to see the show, only to find a way to Sheol. And he was certain this Carina knew how to get there.

The music shifted, and a sudden roar and applause came from inside the hall. A boy snarled and howled over a synth symphony, his baritone voice intentionally off-key, an auto-tuned grotesquery.

"What the hell do you kids listen to?" said a graying cop to a golden young woman. She just shrugged.

Daniel needed a distraction. Across the street, flattened boxes of cardboard had been tied up with twine and leaned against plastic garbage pails. He concentrated, but nothing happened; the words of fire would not come. So he tried to stir his anger. He thought of Gram, how he had left her alone, of Mashit, who had deceived and abducted him, of Ashmedai, who had left a trail of death in his wake. A word escaped from his lips and scraped the fabric of the world.

Burn.

Light flared at the bottom of the cardboard, and a puff of smoke rose. Someone shouted, "Hey, there's a fire!"

A cop ran over to try and stomp it out, and Daniel spoke again. *Burn!*

Flames leaped from the cardboard. The cop cursed, and some kids laughed. The bouncer on his stool got up, grabbed a bottle of water, and sped across the street to help douse the flames. As soon as the bouncer was up, Daniel leaped over the railing and slipped through the door.

He shoved the door closed behind him. It was dim inside, but he could see just fine. The place reeked of beer and sweat and ancient cigarette smoke. To the left, the bouncers scanning tickets hadn't noticed him. To his right a door was marked "Employees Only," and he darted through. Dusty boxes and stage equipment crowded a wide corridor. He crept past bathrooms, locker rooms, small offices. In one windowless space, nothing but a calendar on the wall, an older woman smoked as she whispered into her cell phone. She didn't look up as Daniel sneaked past.

He found a stair at the end of the hall and went up. Red exit signs and bleak corkscrew bulbs lit his way as he stepped on crushed cigarette butts and abandoned joints. Two flights up, a sign read, "Green Room this floor."

He quietly opened the door and tiptoed down a small hallway reeking of cigarettes and bourbon, feeling stealthy and catlike, when he heard the voices.

"But these bracelets are so damned heavy," a woman said. Her voice was soft, lilting, and very familiar, but he couldn't place it. "It's hard to dance on stage with these weights on my wrists."

"Your mother will soon send new accessories," said a man, his voice raspy as if from years of smoking.

"So you say," said the familiar voice. "But I need to speak with her myself. How can I get a message to her, Duile?"

"It's your mother's will that all communication passes through Khein and myself," said the man. "And communication home is outrageously expensive. Even the simplest messages require... complicated arrangements. Only the most important messages may go."

"This *is* important. And she's my fucking mother! I need to speak with her, soon."

Daniel slid along the wall, closing in.

"That will come," said the man. "If you do your part, communication home will soon become much less complicated. Now put on the bracelets. You're going on at nine."

"I don't like being kept in the dark," she said, and Daniel finally knew where he had heard her before. This was Rebekah's voice, as he had known Mashit, but this was not her. This was Carina, the pop star he'd seen in Dvoyre's vision and on the billboard above Penn Station, and this "mother" she spoke of was none other than Mashit herself.

"There you are, motherfucker!" said a voice from behind him, and Daniel spun. The large bouncer from the street, panting and sweaty, barreled toward him. Daniel tried to leap out of the way, but the hallway was narrow and there was nowhere to go. The bouncer slammed into him and shoved him up against the wall. He grasped Daniel's neck and squeezed. "Don't fuck with me dude!"

"Let me go!" Daniel growled. He flung the huge man off of him into the opposite wall, and the bouncer coughed and stumbled to the floor. The Green Room door swung open and two men and a woman stepped out. All three were dressed in black suits and ties. One man had ebony skin. The other was as pink as a piglet. The woman was tall and narrow, with Asian features. "What the hell's going on?" said the dark-skinned one.

The bouncer answered by charging at Daniel, head down like a bull. The blow knocked the wind out of him, and Daniel fell to the ground, gasping. "This asshole snuck in," said the bouncer. He gave Daniel another kick. "I'mma call the cops."

"No!" said the woman. "No cops."

The woman stepped closer as another person emerged from the Green Room. Dark hair, pale face, eyes as gray as the moon. A familiar face, younger than the one he'd fallen in love with. Carina wore an iridescent dress and reflective golden accessories, a walking kaleidoscope. He couldn't take his eyes from her as the other woman approached. And the last thing he remembered was the tall black-suited woman raising something large in her hand and bringing it down to crash on his head.

—

He awoke among piles of garbage in an abandoned lot on 12th street as the sun, rising over apartment buildings, singed his exposed shin. His head throbbed brutally as he hopped in the shadows across the East Village and fled into the subway at Astor Place. He jumped onto the first train that came, an uptown 6, and sat in the corner seat, nursing the wound on his head, feeling sick, stupid and defeated. He'd missed the concert, and Carina had moved on. Why did he think he could just walk up to Carina like that? Of course she'd have friends. He closed his eyes. Fuck. He just wanted a cigarette and a place to sleep. To call Gram and hear her voice. Fuck.

The uptown train had reached 86th street before he noticed the poster-sized ad behind his wounded head. "Carina, On Her First World Tour!" Her dancing figure smiled into a mike, the same glittering woman who had popped her head out of the Green Room just before the other woman knocked him out. Colored stage lights flared brightly behind her. Underneath her face, a list of dates. For the next two weeks, Carina would be in South America. After that, Asia. After that, who knew.

But he knew, as he the subway doors closed and the train rumbled uptown, that he would not be going home for a long time.

CHAPTER FIFTEEN

"As you can see, General Kokabiel," said Thelus, Chief of Mines, "we're working as quickly as we can. But we simply can't go any faster." She shouted over the tumult of hammers and chisels, and the enormous cavern shook with the sounds. They stood on a promontory before a cavern so large a hundred torches and half as many fireglobes barely lit the space. Shadows loomed beyond, wavering in the flamelight, vaguely threatening.

Chained slaves, human and demon, hacked at the stone walls with pickaxes and chisels, while Mikulalim taskmasters whipped their backs. Their plaintive wails rose from below between peals of tools against stone. The air reeked of blood, sweat, and dust.

Thelus was a grizzled demoness, a quarter of Kokabiel's height, wiry and thin, with a crooked nose, and greasy yellow hair. Watches and clockwork devices hung from many chains affixed to her leather shift. Time had not been kind to the smith who had once worked in Abbadon's forges before Mashit shuffled all. Thelus looked old and ill.

"Why don't you use magic to excavate the stone?" Kokabiel said. "Manual labor is excruciatingly slow."

Thelus was sucking on a rootstick, and she pulled the gnarled tip from her mouth, leaving a purple stain on her tongue. "I see you're new to mining, sir."

Kokabiel flared his nostrils at her.

"What I mean to say, General Kokabiel, is that this rock we stand upon, this body of Sheol, is a fragment of the first material universe

149

to ever exist. It has properties unlike all subsequent worlds. One of those properties is that the bedrock is extremely dense. The type of magic we would use to split the rock must be so powerful we might split Sheol in two. I think you can understand why we don't wish to take that risk, sir."

"And yet we split this same rock with slow raps from hammers and chisels?"

"Drops of water cannot move a mountain, but over millennia they will dig a canyon as deep as the Abyss."

"We don't have millennia, nor do we need to dig as deep."

"Why the rush?" Thelus said, shoving the rootstick into her mouth. "Why does the queen need vats so large, so quickly?"

Kokabiel peered into Thelus's beady little eyes. She was small, unthreatening, but the diminutive smith was renowned before Mashit's shuffling. Her enchanted swords and shields were highly sought after treasures, especially by Legion soldiers. And before the shuffle, she had crafted machines in her spare time, room-sized clockwork contraptions of iron that counted the orbits of the suns and predicted the precise moment Sheol would pass through a turbulent part of the galaxy and cause all the swollen stars to shift positions in the sky and send a flurry of meteorites into the atmosphere.

"You excel at calculation," Kokabiel said. "The answer should be obvious." He let his words hang between them as bait, so she might put the pieces together and think the realization was her own.

She took a deep breath before speaking. "The question I have, General, is not so much *what* the vats will be used for, but *how*. To build ones so large implies the queen expects to receive huge amounts of energy. But by my calculations, the energy currently reaching Sheol is a mere one point three *thousandths* of a percent of what these can hold. So where does all this new energy come from?"

He smiled. He was wise to choose Thelus. Not only was she a master engineer, she was keenly perceptive. *You're close*, he thought. *So close to the truth. Your analytical mind hungers for an answer, and I dangle it before you like a savory meal.* "I do only as the queen asks," he said coyly. "And that is all you should do too, Thelus." This, even though he knew she would not. "Now, continue my tour."

"Yes, sir," she said, nodding. "We will build the first vat there." She pointed to a deep half-circle in the cavern. Slaves were chipping away at the other half, one rap at a time. "Three other vats will follow, there, there, and there." She pointed further into the cavern. "Four more vats will be built elsewhere in the mountain. The caverns to house them have not yet been excavated."

"And when do you expect to complete the first vat?"

"At this speed, by the Ayalah Swap of Suns." More than twenty weeks away. "We still have to excavate tons more stone. Then we must build the superstructure, line it with gold, and cast all the powerful enchantments that go along with building a vat. This takes patience and time. The vats under the city took decades to build, you know."

"I do. And you say you're working as fast as you can?"

"We are," she said. "More hands would not help, as only so many bodies can fit side by side. More, and they get in each other's way. The slaves are already working double shifts, and we lose a half-dozen to attrition every day. I know the queen wants this sooner, General, but these are the realities."

He faked a frown, but inwardly, he smiled. Mashit's plan – draining human power and shunting it here – was madness! She put all of Sheol at risk with her idiocy. The people were already growing impatient with her, and this delay would only foment their agitation. He let out a dramatic sigh. "Well, Thelus, I will have to tell the queen this regretful news."

"Please, General, make sure she knows it's not my fault! I rather value my head."

"I'll tell her all you've told me, verbatim."

Thelus looked nervously up at him. "Should we tour the gold mines? Like all good guides, I have saved the best for last. You will see not all is bad news."

"Lead on, Thelus."

They climbed down a rugged stair and snaked through several narrow tunnels of roughly hewn walls, stirring up clouds of stone dust. Kokabiel stifled a sneeze. Suddenly the cavern shook with a tremendous earthquake. The air cracked with thunder and pebbles fell from the cracks above their heads. He crouched with his hands over his head, fearing the tunnel would collapse.

"It's just rockfall," Thelus said, standing upright beside him. She seemed disappointed with him. "They're quite common, General. Nothing to fear."

He scowled as he stood, wishing to be out of these claustrophobic passages as soon as possible.

They emerged from the cave onto a high promontory facing a space so bright he had to shield his eyes. An enormous cavern opened before them, and the air glowed yellow-white, filled with a scintillating mist. It was uncomfortably hot, and he began to sweat.

In the space below, demon and human slaves, whipped by Mikulalim taskmasters, worked to free huge chunks of gold from stone. The gold and its billion little flecks thrown into the air with each hammer blow were the source of that blinding light. No fireglobes were needed here. The slaves hauled the gold chunks onto a moving belt, which shuttled them away down a tunnel. As they worked, blue lightning forked across the space, and Kokabiel's fur rose and fell with each flash.

"It's as hot as a damned oven down here!" he said over the noise.

"It's the smelting furnaces on the other side of the tunnel," said Thelus.

"Why is there lightning?"

"Energy discharges. The gold acts as a capacitor. When you-know-who smashed the first world, some of her power entered the gold. It resides their still. When we remove the chunks from the wall, some of that power discharges."

"What do you do with the gold?"

"After it's smelted from the other minerals, we plate it onto large, flattened sheets of an alloy, then box them for shipment. Where the gold goes after that, I couldn't tell you. The whole process is highly compartmentalized. But the queen should be happy to know that we've increased gold output seventeen percent in the last week."

"Excellent, Thelus. Now, let's get away from this heat. It does hell to my mood."

They retreated into the tunnel, and after a few hundred paces, Thelus suddenly paused and turned her eyes toward him. "General Kokabiel, something has been troubling me, and I hope you will lay my suspicions to rest."

Yes, he thought. *This is where she figures it out.* "Speak, Thelus," he said.

"I gather the queen plans to bring enormous quantities of power here. But no matter how I calculate it, I always come up short. I just can't figure how we will ever receive this much power. Because even if we capture all of the energy dripping from Earth, it won't be enough. There's not that much energy in all of the Great Deep! So either I'm missing something profound, or the queen is..."

"Yes?"

"Misinformed."

Kokabiel paused before responding. The palace courtesans had a phrase, *You must have heard it in the mines.* Rumors leaked from this place like water from stone. And a well-placed rumor was a powerful tool. No demon was a Shard, drifting alone. Thelus had friends, and they had theirs, and Mashit was a fool to think she could keep such a project secret for long. She was weakening, and here was proof of her cracking facade. Her promises had not materialized, and wise ones like Thelus had begun to see.

"The queen will deliver on her promises," he said. "And you've every reason to trust her implicitly."

It was a simple reiteration of what he'd said before. But one only repeated things if facts were in doubt. Thelus stared at him, slowly nodding.

Yes, he thought. *Let the seed of doubt grow. Tell your friends. Let rumors of Mashit's ineptness spread throughout Sheol. This is the tilling of the field.*

"I see," Thelus said. "Well, General, if that's all, I must get back to work. Thank you for allowing me the pleasure to give you this tour."

"No," Kokabiel said. "The pleasure is all mine."

"I'll escort you to the surface."

"No. I'll find my own way back."

"Are you sure? The tunnels are complex and–"

"Go on, Thelus. I know my way home."

"Yes, I trust that you do. And, General, I hope it goes without saying, I have full faith in the queen. *Full* faith."

"It does, Thelus," he said. "Your faith is without question."

At this, they departed. Kokabiel weaved through the tunnels

toward a main junction. But instead of heading to the surface, he followed his nose toward a faint noxious smell he had caught earlier. Gedeon, Chief of Sewers, was waiting somewhere down these dark and reeking corridors, perhaps to convey the secret of how to kill a First One. Kokabiel smiled. Everything was coming together.

CHAPTER SIXTEEN

MASHIT WAS DISCUSSING THE CITY'S EXPANSIONARY PLANS with several skilled but argumentative engineers in the Violet Drawing Room when the knock came on the door. Three short raps, then two, then one.

Mashit raised her hand and the engineers instantly stopped their bickering. "Leave me," she said. And just like that, they all stood and fled out the door.

A sole figure remained at the door's threshold, the one who had knocked. Ulmon, wispy, like a burning bundle of reeds, more smoke than matter. What physical parts she had were adorned like a palace page, a servant of the queen. But she was much more.

"My queen," Ulmon said, pushing the heavy door shut. Her smoky formed wavered in and out.

"Ulmon, what news have you for me?"

"You asked me to observe the Lamed Vav, my queen, and inform you of anything of note. Well, my queen, the one called Maya has begun taking visitors."

"Visitors?"

"I was away this morning, and when I returned, the queue was dozens long and growing. Demons seem to think she has some kind of healing power."

"Maya has a queue?"

"Yes, my queen."

She took a deep breath. "Thank you, Ulmon. Keep up your good work." Ulmon bowed and fled, and Mashit followed her out of the

Violet Drawing Room, where her Shield waited. "We're going to see the Pillars," she said, and down they all went.

One of her advisors, a student of human psychology, had suggested she exchange the Lamed Vav's small quarters for one much larger, nearly an entire floor of the palace. This living space, the advisor had said, was much larger than most human domiciles, and therefore the humans would feel like well-treated guests and be grateful to her. But to the advisor's surprise – and hers – the Lamed Vav seemed only to resent her more. All except Maya. The Buddhist monk grew more curious of Mashit and her philosophy, asking thousands of questions. And Mashit had been all too happy to answer them all.

She glimpsed the queue before she descended the final stair, a hundred demons lined up outside the entrance to the Lamed Vav's inner chambers, gibbering excitedly. She spotted General Kokabiel beside five Legion soldiers, where Sheol's crimson skies shone through the open-aired terrace to fall upon their shoulders.

"General!" she shouted, heading straight for him. As the many demons became aware of her, their voices fell quiet. "What in Great Abbadon's name is this?"

"My queen," Kokabiel said. "I didn't expect you to arrive so soon. I just sent a soldier with a message a moment ago. It appears that Maya is taking visitors."

"So I've heard. Why?"

"From what I gather, they wish to be blessed and counseled by her."

Among the motley crowd, creatures of every form and color, high-born palace dwellers – even First Ones – waited alongside grease-stained servants. A feathered, hawk-beaked demoness barreled around the corner. When she saw Mashit her eyes went wide. She wasn't watching her step and slammed right into a snake-headed horse, twice her size. The hawk-beaked demoness bounced and fell flat on her back.

"Forgive me!" the feathered one said from the floor.

Mashit waited for the snake-headed one to squash the offender or toss her out the window, what any sane demon would have done. Instead, the snake-headed horse scooped up the feathered one and deposited her on her feet.

"There's no need for forgiveness when no slight is done," the snake-headed one said. "Are you all right, friend?"

Friend? Mashit thought.

"My ego is bruised more than my body. But we should be quiet now. We've gained the attention of our beloved queen." She gestured at Mashit, and they both fell quiet.

"What's this absurdity?" Mashit said to Kokabiel. "Demons being *polite*?"

Everyone bowed at her. She approached a small and brown beetle-like figure. "Tell me, why do you loiter here?"

"My queen, we wait for a turn to speak with Maya, the Giver of Life."

"The what?"

The demon hung his head and bashfully said, "The Giver of Life."

Mashit grew sick with rage. "Shame is a vulgar human trait!" she shouted. "It is most grotesque on a demon. You disgust me." She scanned the hall. "Where's the keymaster, Joil?" She stormed over to the towering ironwork door that led to the Lamed Vav's inner chambers, and Kokabiel, her Shield, and the Legion soldiers followed. The others parted to let them pass.

The door to the Lamed Vav's inner chambers was a great ironwork intricacy, prevented from rusting by ancient spells. Frog-faced Joil stood at attention as she approached, his four sets of eyes looking every way but at her.

"My queen," he said, bowing. General Joil had grown fatter than she remembered and seemed ready to burst from his leather armor.

"Explain this absurdity, Joil."

"My queen! The people have been requesting to visit Maya."

"And you let them in?"

"Well, no, not at first. But there were *so many* requests. And your orders were not to let the Lamed Vav *out* of their chambers without your permission."

"And I said no one shall visit them either!"

"Yes, but Maya says that–"

"*Maya* says?'"

"My queen, if you would just speak with the Giver, you'd easily see that–"

"Give me your pin."

"What?"

"Your Legion pin!" She held out her hand.

"But—my queen!"

"Kokabiel," she said, and the giraffe-necked demon withdrew his sword. He and the Legion soldiers moved closer.

"But..." Joil sagged. "I thought I was helping!"

Kokabiel snatched the iron cracked-egg pin that declared Joil a Legion General from his chest in one swift motion, tearing away leather and skin, and Joil yelped.

"You were unfit to be a soldier anyway," Kokabiel said.

"Take Joil to the dungeons below the palace," said Mashit. "Place him in a cell with no light, no food, and no water. His friends shall be midden spiders and despair, until his flesh rots and his bones become dust."

"My queen!" he screamed. But the soldiers were upon him and dragged him down the hall. The others watched, horrified, and she scanned their faces.

"When did you all become so meek?" she shouted. "You are demons, and this is Sheol! Great Abbadon is cursing you from his grave." They turned away from her, ashamed, and she grew even more enraged.

She could not face them any longer. The door to the Lamed Vav's inner chambers was unlocked, and she shoved it open. She stepped into the common area, a large space sparsely filled with furniture and decorations, and Kokabiel alone followed her. Maya sat in the center of the room in a large high-backed metal chair. A bear-like demon with a green monkey's face kneeled beside Maya, but when he saw Mashit enter, he rose and bowed to her. On the table beside Maya was a growing pile of sundry things: figurines of ancient demons fashioned of stone and glass, candles molded into the forms of Lilith and Abbadon, necklaces and earrings made of bone, mineral, and glass, even a shawl with Maya's likeness weaved into its fabric. Gifts, it seemed, left by the visitors for the Giver of Life.

Maya scanned the room. Sunil sat on a long couch, a tall hookah beside him, its snaking pipe dangling in his hand. The room smelled faintly of its smoke, and by the redness of his eyes and the slackness of his body he'd been at the pipe for some time.

Paula and Baaba sat at a table beneath the room's only window, and the translucent olive curtains above them fluttered in the afternoon breeze. When Mashit had entered Paula had been writing something on parchment while speaking with Baaba, but Paula secreted the parchment away. Mashit made a mental note to address this later.

"Wait for me outside," Mashit said in Demonsbreath to the monkey-faced demon who had been kneeling.

"My queen," he said, "I beg your forgiveness. I–"

"Outside!" she snapped.

He bowed and fled, and the door creaked closed behind him. Maya beamed at Mashit, an expression of pure joy, of total and unconditional acceptance, and Mashit's anger burned away like the morning smog in the light of the twin suns. She could bask in Maya's smile all day.

"I knew you'd come," Maya said.

"What do you think you're doing?" Mashit said.

"I was counseling that poor soul."

"Why does that creature need counsel?"

"That '*creature's*' name is Goshamael, and he wished to learn how to be kind. He works in the kitchens, and I told him that instead of throwing away the scraps of unused food, he should distribute it to the hungry in the slums."

"And who gave you this idea to counsel demons?" she said.

"It was my own."

Mashit glanced up at Kokabiel, who towered beside the door. She had to show the giraffe-necked General she was in full control of this situation. "I suspected you might do something like this, Maya."

"Did you?" Maya said. "This surprises me. When I tried to teach you about the human concepts of kindness and compassion, you scoffed and said, 'Those sentiments do not apply to demonkind. We are made of different stuff.'"

"We *are* different."

"Yes, but all sentient beings have the potential for awakening. Even you."

Mashit shook her head and glanced at Kokabiel, gauging his reaction, but he was as stoic as ever. "You've only been here a short time," Mashit said, "what makes you think you can counsel us?"

"Can't you see, Mashit? I'm fulfilling Abbadon's promise."

Now Kokabiel stirred.

"What do you know of Great Abbadon?" Mashit said.

"I know that he promised he would raise demonkind from the ashes. Your kind were nearly extinguished, and he gave you hope. This is much like the plight of my own people. I wish to help you rise, but I must teach you the ways of compassion and kindness so that as you grow you become more–"

"Human."

"Well, yes."

On a small table beside Maya several thin, hand-woven books lay in a neat stack. In a delicate Demonsbreath cursive, the cover read, *A Demon's Code of Ethics and Hygiene, by Maya Dorje.* Mashit picked one up and scanned its pages:

"A demon should bathe at least once per day. It's also important to clean one's teeth (if you have them) and the areas within and around where you urinate and defecate (if you have such organs). Your external cleanliness mirrors your spiritual health."

She skipped ahead:

"Kindness is contagious. If you act charitably toward your fellow demons, they will be more likely to act charitably in return. A trusting society is rooted in kindness."

And a different page:

"The ancient practice of killing your enemies, eating their children, and taking their possessions must end. Instead, consider discussing your differences with an independent arbiter. Let your anger go. Anger is a destructive emotion and will never bring about long-term well-being."

There were more than twenty pages in all. On last page of the book, Maya's name was written in Tibetan underneath a drawing of her likeness.

"What is this?" Mashit said.

"A primer."

"A what?"

"A kind of instruction manual. General Joil translated my words into Demonsbreath. And a talented artist called Romichaul printed all these copies. Aren't they beautiful?"

As physical objects, they were, but as a guide to living? "If a demon had written these," Mashit said, "he'd be put to death."

"For teaching hygiene and compassion?"

"Do you know what hells my people been through? How many times we barely escaped annihilation, even after our world was destroyed? Our society may look violent and grotesque to you, but our ways are how we survived." She pointed to the books. "These human ways might make sense for you, but they don't make sense for us."

"I don't believe that. Otherwise, why have you brought us here? You want a better world. So why won't you let me help you?"

Kokabiel didn't need to speak, because Mashit sensed his judging eyes. She knew exactly what the General was thinking, that she wasn't strong enough to rule, that she let this petty human offend and affront her and all of demonkind. She considered having Maya whipped, as a show of her power, but the thought of harming Maya made her physically ill.

Kokabiel strode over, ducking to avoid the chandelier. "For the sake of Sheol, my queen, we must destroy these books. This human is poisoning our minds."

Mashit stared at the stack. Maya had clearly worked hard to make them; it pained her to destroy them. But she had to show Kokabiel she was in control. "Yes," she said. "General Kokabiel, see to it all copies are destroyed."

"With pleasure," he said. He quickly grabbed the stack of hand-woven books, cast a spell, and the books vanished in a bright flash of light.

Maya abruptly stood and gave Mashit such a look of sadness that Mashit had to turn away. "What a shame," Maya said. "What a damned shame."

"Clear the hall," Mashit said to Kokabiel. "Let it be known that anyone who comes seeking advice from the Pillars shall be flayed until death at the next Stoning Day."

"It shall be done, my queen," Kokabiel said.

Maya grabbed Mashit's wrist and said "Do you want to change this world or not?"

Kokabiel put a hand on his sword.

"No," Mashit said to him. She firmly pried Maya's hand from

her wrist. "Change will come," Mashit said. "But on my terms. I'll not have my kingdom weakened by these meek human ideas."

"You are wrong. These ideas are not meek. Compassion and kindness often require great strength. Your kingdom will be stronger for it."

But Mashit would not allow Maya to humiliate her in front of Kokabiel any further. "Clear the hall, General," she said. "Now!"

Kokabiel opened the iron door and shouted, "Clear the hall! By the queen's decree, the Pillars shall take no more visitors, and any who seek her counsel shall be flayed to death at the next Stoning Day."

The startled voices outside turned to screams as the soldiers forcefully cleared the hall. Mashit stole a glance at Maya, whose joyful, accepting smile had vanished, replaced by its opposite. Scorn was unbecoming on a monk.

"And this is why," Maya said, "your suffering has endured for millennia."

CHAPTER SEVENTEEN

SUNBEAMS BLAZED THROUGH THE OPEN PATIO DOORS TO SHINE onto the grand piano and the Turkish carpet. It was the first thing Daphna had noticed about Rio de Janeiro, how the light penetrated everything, giving life even to dead things. The house was far from the city, but even last night, when she had most needed rest, the city lights trickled through the densely leaved jungle around the property to ripple delicately upon the backyard pool. The light got in, and Daphna hated it.

She accepted the truth now; she was desperately homesick. She missed Sheol's sweltering days, the torch-red Adar and cinder-orange Ora twirling about each other in the sky. And she missed Sheol's frigid nights, the sky pimpled with plump red stars. Here on Earth, the stars were faint, distant, twinkling echoes of worlds long since spun away or dead. The solitary sun was an oppressive force, best to avoid.

Just like Mother, she thought.

Daphna reclined in her divan, smoking a cigarette, savoring this rare moment of peace. Every damned instant had been planned for her. Wake, bathe, dress, meet, practice, record, makeup session, interview, more makeup, interview, makeup, lunch, bathe, dress, makeup, practice, record, perform, perform, perform.

She wondered if mother had cast a spell on her, because she felt so unlike herself. Freedom had become a thing of the past. Duile and Khein would not permit movement outside of her busy schedule, so that even here, in seclusion, on this quarter-day of rest, she was not allowed to explore Rio or leave the house. She hadn't spoken to her mother since she'd left, and yet Mashit's yoke was tight around her neck.

Richard, the sound engineer, strolled into the living room, newly adorned in white chinos, a tan and short-sleeved button-down, and a white panama hat. He had dyed his salt-and-pepper beard brown and had recently begun moisturizing. His face shone like the city. He carefully tore open a bag of Wild Berry Skittles and filled an elegant glass bowl beside her divan. He poured them one at a time, *ting – ting – ting.*

"Would you fucking stop that!" she said.

He gaped at her, then hung his head. "I'm sorry, Carina. Forgive me!"

"Stop sulking. Go do something else."

"There's nothing else to do."

"Go for a swim."

"I didn't bring my trunks."

"Then swim naked."

"I don't know how."

"To go naked?"

"To swim."

She frowned and tamped out her cigarette. "I need something to do." She rose and walked over to the large glass table and woke her sleeping laptop. Such an amazing device, this machine that connected the whole Earth in a vast web of information. The entire library of humankind, here before her. Most humans didn't believe magic was real, for fear, perhaps, of their own unrealized power. But that belief was absurd in the face of this glowing screen. If ever there were magic, this was it. She opened up her Twitter account.

Two days ago, she had nine thousand followers. Today, two hundred and twenty four thousand. Her video of "Goodbye to Day" had gone up on YouTube the previous night, and her tweet announcing the video had been retweeted thousands of times. They had shot the video last week in an empty warehouse in Williamsburg, Brooklyn, and Daphna clicked the link to watch it again.

She wore her iridescent purple outfit accessorized with gold, and she sang and danced before a dizzying and ever-changing array of psychedelic patterns. None of the patterns had existed on the set; she had danced before enormous green screens, and the patterns were added later. As she watched, she felt as if she were falling into the screen. At the chorus, when she reached the high notes, strobe lights behind her flashed in successive bright arrays. In the video description there was a disclaimer and warning that people with epilepsy should not watch.

Richard sat next to her. "Man, that video....It's so intense!" He removed a pack of Winstons from his shirt pocket and lit one. "I can't watch without getting dizzy."

From what she could discern, Duile and Khein had manipulated the angles of the set to maximize subtle magical energies. A demon who had lived on Earth for centuries had provided the digital animations that flashed behind her. The video was a carefully constructed work of art designed to make people love her. And it worked. Well.

She scrolled through a thousand tweets, tagged with "—lovecarina", "—carinamiamor", and "—goodbyetoday."

Richard exhaled a cloud of smoke into the sunbeams. "Did you notice," he said, "how all the plants are weirdly overgrown here, like they've been fed Miracle Grow on steroids?"

"No," she said, scrolling through tweet after tweet. She had desperately sought adoration, but now that it was upon her, why did it all feel so strangely empty? *I should feel wonderful receiving their outpouring of love,* she thought, *shouldn't I?*

She stopped scrolling at a photograph of a young woman, who had tattooed the lyrics of "Goodbye to Day" on her wrist.

Good day, good day, goodbye to day
I've nothing to love except my reflection
The days are dead, I hide in your shadows
My greatest moments are when I
Give up, give up, give up
Days are so much easier when you don't
When you don't do anything at all...

"Look at this," Daphna said. She spun the laptop around so Richard could see.

"Sweet!" he said. "A superfan." He put his hand on her arm. "Congratulations, you've made it, girl."

"Why are you congratulating me?"

"I've seen folks struggle for years to get the kind of following you got in weeks. You're gonna be huge, you know that? I hope you see how special you are. One in a million."

She spun the laptop around. "Those aren't my words. It isn't my music. Someone else wrote it for me."

Richard walked over to the patio, cigarette in hand, and his white clothes glowed in the light. "So what? You know how many songs weren't written by the people who got famous singing them? I can name fifty off the top of my head."

"But all these fans, they're not adoring *my* work. They're adoring someone else's."

"But it's your *voice*. I've never heard anyone sing like you. You're a siren, and we're all sailors, drunk on your voice."

"Until you all crash into the rocks."

"Gladly," he said, smiling.

But Daphna frowned. She walked over to the grand piano and sat before it, placing her fingers over the keys. Clavichord lessons flowed into her mind as she began to play.

Richard sidled up to her. "Bach," he said. "The Goldberg Variations, right?"

She nodded as she played.

"That's beautiful," he said. "I didn't know you could play!"

"I learned on the clavichord. I didn't know if it would transpose."

"The clavichord? Jesus, you're full of surprises."

She stopped. "Richard, I want to write a song. Will you be my amanuensis?"

"Your what?"

"I want you to transcribe for me. You can read much, right?"

"Since I was nine."

"Good. Take a song down for me."

He beamed. "I got a digital recorder in my suitcase. Let me just go–"

"No," she said, grabbing his arm. "Let's do this the old-fashioned way."

"Of course," he said, staring at her hand, blushing. He removed a small notepad and pencil from his pocket so smoothly it was as if he'd been waiting for this moment his entire life. "Anything for you."

"I want to write about freedom."

"Like Neil Young?"

"Who? Never mind. This song will be about total freedom, all bonds broken, all ties severed. It'll be raw and vicious. And we won't use any technology. Just you and me."

"Sounds fucking brilliant."

Suddenly Duile, Khein, and Frix barged into the room. They were followed by four young, glassy-eyed women. The women wore altered versions of Daphna's golden accessories. Their necklaces were narrower, their watches smaller, their bracelets shorter and simpler. Their golden belts were smaller and thicker. The leather straps of their heels were ribboned with tiny strips of gold. Underneath all this, they wore black jumpsuits.

When the women noticed Daphna, their eyes brightened. Frix ordered them to line up against the wall, and they obeyed.

"What's this?" Daphna said, rising from the piano.

"An upgrade," said Duile, depositing a heavy silver briefcase onto the glass table.

"A what?"

"Test groups have shown that your previous outfit, while striking, wasn't having the desired effect," Duile said.

"We've toned it down and classed it up," said Frix. "Your accessories need to be *accessible*. No one wants to look like a Venusian space queen. But as it turns out everyone wants to be a human one." Frix walked down the line of women. "These models are wearing the latest from Moda by Carina, your new line of affordable fashion accessories."

"My what?"

"Let me show you," Duile said.

He punched a code into the briefcase, pressed a lever, and the briefcase popped open. He spun it around so she could view its contents. A suite of golden accessories, like those the models wore, flashed in the sunlight.

"You'll wear these," he said. "And the paparazzi will photograph you in them."

"Your fans will want their own," Frix said.

"What's wrong with my current outfit?" Daphna said. "I *like* looking like I'm from Venus. Technically, I *am* from another planet." She scanned the women. "These girls look like the spoiled daughters of a pharaoh."

"Actually," Frix said, "they are Egyptian-inspired."

"I don't want to change."

"Sorry," Duile said. "These are orders from home."

"Mother sent you a message?" Daphna said. "When?"

"I told you," said Duile, "only the most important messages may go through."

"Carina!" one of the women said, "*Eu amo sua música!*"

Frix stepped up to the woman and lifted her palm before her face, and the woman immediately froze, as if entranced. "*Eu lhe disse para ficar calado!*" Frix said.

Daphna approached the women. They all blankly stared ahead, their pupils as wide as pitted olives.

"Do you speak English?" she said, and all three nodded. "Tell me," she said, "what is your favorite song of mine?"

"Goodbye to Day!" they all said in unison, and their instant response startled her.

"And your second favorite song of mine?"

They all shivered, and seemed to struggle to answer. "We love you," one said, and they all nodded. "We love your music," said another. They spoke sluggishly, like her mother after long hours smoking the hookah.

"Time to go," Frix said. "Follow me, girls. I have a special gift for your help." They obeyed as Frix ushered them out the door.

"There's a new black jumpsuit in your closet," Duile said. "Make sure to wear *all* of these." He pointed to the briefcase. "We leave in ninety minutes."

"So soon?" she said. "I haven't even showered!"

"I told you this morning. We have a photo shoot with three magazines before your performance. And a stylist will be here to do your hair in forty-five minutes." As he stepped toward the door, he mumbled, "I swear, sometimes you're such a damned child."

"Excuse me?" she said.

But he ignored her and left the room. Khein silently followed, closing the door.

"A fashion line?" Richard said, standing beside the piano where she had left him. Damn, you waste no time! And speaking of time, you heard Duile. I'll let you get ready." He moved toward the door.

"I was going to write a song," she said. "You were going to help me."

He shrugged. "Yeah, I know. But they'll be plenty of time for that. Right now, you have to get ready for your fans. They're the most important thing, after all." He left the room and pulled the door gently closed. Distantly she heard a muffled scream – a woman's voice – followed by urgent sounds of gurgling. More screams followed, but they ended in quick succession. A clap of thunder rocked the house, sending ripples across the pool, even though the sky was clear.

On the piano, Richard's notebook lay open to a blank page. His pencil rolled off the edge and fell to the floor.

CHAPTER EIGHTEEN

AIR TRAVEL FOR A CURSED ONE WAS ESPECIALLY DANGEROUS. Daniel could have booked a red-eye to Brazil, but flights could be delayed. An hour or two either way, and he would be a human firecracker, bursting into flames the moment some nervous flyer opened his shade to watch the sunrise. But even if he did risk flight, he couldn't afford the airfare, not if he wanted his savings to last more than a few weeks. Gram would have given him money if he'd asked, but a heavy shame prevented him from calling her – he had left her again – so the only other option was travel by land. He'd done it before and thought himself an expert.

He was wrong. For the most part, he had been able to travel across Western Asia and Eastern Europe via car, truck, and train. But Latin America was a different beast. Mexico was simple enough; his fluent Spanish allowed him to move quickly south by bus. He befriended long-haul truckers at late-night cantinas who took him further south as they smoked cheap tobacco and lamented how the narcos were destroying the country. He had few problems moving at night, when the moon was high and the stars wheeled brightly across the sky.

Guatemala, Honduras, and Nicaragua were more difficult. Though people were friendly, when he asked them for a ride, they came up with all sorts of ridiculous excuses why they couldn't bring him along, and progress south was excruciatingly slow. He hitched rides when he could. He rode on local buses, calculating his cash down to the cent. Exchange rates were hell.

Once he hung onto the waist of a young woman on a motorbike while she laughed and sped dangerously over dusty roads. Another time he traveled in the back of a wagon beside three black-bellied sheep, their human-like eyes considering him the whole way. The sheep did not approve.

He traveled by mule over a mountain pass, led by an ancient, leather-skinned farmer. He rode with a caravan of horses over rubble and scree. Always, he traveled by night, under a spray of stars and a crescent moon, or soaked in brief but torrential rain. The most important thing was to keep moving, over terrain that changed from sere, barren landscapes not too different from Gehinnom's deserts, to lush, verdant valleys so full of life he wished he could remain in them forever. The plants shone in the moonlight, exuberantly alive. And he had seen this same profusion of green everywhere, as if all earthly life, sensing how close it had come to annihilation, lived that much more fully now.

He slept where he could by day, in cheap motels, or with goats in a shed, or in abandoned huts. Any shaded place would do. He was seldom hungry, not for normal food. But the nagging hunger for human flesh pestered him daily, so he kept a fat supply of rolling tobacco and papers close. He was so good at rolling now he could do it with one hand. One night, just after sunset, a group of children in the back of a pickup truck called him *"El Dragón,"* and he couldn't tell if this was in endearment or terror.

He crossed most borders without incident, and his passport filled with stamps. But when he crossed into Nicaragua, the border guards shot at a motorcyclist who tried to drive through the checkpoint without stopping. The biker and the woman in the sidecar crashed into a barrier and exploded, and Daniel caught a whiff of their charred flesh as they were carted off in an ambulance. The smell stayed with him for days.

He reached Caracas six days after he left New York, a filthy specimen, reeking of goats, cigarettes, and sweat. He bought used clothes from a thrift store and rented a motel room for sixty bolívars, then he collapsed on the bed and slept all day with the shades drawn. He awoke in the late afternoon, showered and shaved, then sat on the edge of the bed, thinking how best to approach Carina at her concert tonight. After Webster Hall, he thought it best to do recon first and decided he would be safest in the crowd, one face among many. He dressed in white chinos and a baby-blue collared shirt. Both had faint grease stains he hadn't noticed in the store. He donned a black-ribboned panama hat and checked himself in the mirror. "What a fucking gringo," he said, and sat on the edge of the bed. He wanted a cigarette, but he needed his senses sharp tonight. He waited for the sun to go down before he went out.

Caracas's buildings were a mix of Latin and European architecture. Modern skyscrapers and condos rose next to dilapidated shanties. The sky faded from cinder orange to steel blue as he made his way to Palacete, the night club where Carina would perform. It wasn't large, nestled between a Turkish restaurant and a brand-name clothing store. Young people waited outside, dolled up for the show, but there were fewer people here than in New York; Carina's fame hadn't quite followed her to South America. The women wore black, burgundy, or chocolate dresses, heavily accessorized with gold. Their glasses, necks, wrists, waists, and shoes all gleamed. The men wore navy jackets and dark button-down shirts, and their faces shone with gold-rimmed spectacles. Their arms blinged with gold watches and rings.

They all sparkled as he approached. No scalpers here, so he visited the ticket booth, and to his surprise young woman with bright green eyes sold him a ticket without fanfare. It cost a truckload, but at least he was inside.

He sat at a small table in the back, with a clear view of the club, round tables neatly circled by stools, rows of leather couches against the walls. In the center, a dance floor, and beside it a mirrored stage. Along the opposite wall, a blue and purple neon bar.

The place filled with patrons as a DJ spun out salsa and techno dance tracks. Daniel tapped his feet as the disco lights cut colorful beams through cigarette smoke. The hunger was coming on full force now; he needed a smoke badly, but instead he ordered a vodka tonic from a waitress and nursed it as the place slowly filled. The crowd's average age was about twenty five, with a decade or two on either side. Some kids were barely out of their teens, but a few patrons were in their sixties, potbellied and sunworn.

It was easy to see who was here for Carina. As more people moved onto the dance floor, their wealth of golden accessories flashed with the strobes. It almost seemed as if they were wearing a kind of uniform. The waitress brought him two more drinks, before the growing crowd slowed her return.

By the time the DJ switched the beat to introduce Carina, he was drunk, and the crowd's roar was so loud he spilled his drink. The lights went down, and everyone turned their attention to the mirrored stage. Smartphones were swiped on and raised, their glow shining onto a hundred eager faces.

A silhouette strolled onto the stage, and the crowd howled. Green and yellow lasers fanned across the space as a tense chord rose in volume. Carina stood motionless, eyes closed, dressed in black and gold, arms spread wide. If before she was an alien queen, now she was an Egyptian goddess. Lasers reflected off her accessories into the crowd, beaming into eyes, retinas be damned. But he could not look away. The chord rose in volume until the seat rumbled beneath him. The mirrors shook, about to shatter. Everyone was spellbound.

The beat dropped. Strobes flickered madly. The walls shook. Carina hopped around stage, quick on her feet. The tune was catchy, a layered descending arpeggio in a minor key. Her voice was sublime. Almost certainly canned, but she lip-synched well. He'd heard this song on the radio on his way south and hadn't realized he'd been singing it in his head for days. He stood to get a better view. Lights flashed, and he was dancing.

Damn, he was tired. So fucking tired. But the music buoyed him, and he found himself singing the chorus with her. The whole audience sang.

"Give up, give up, give up! Days are so much easier when you don't...when you don't do anything at all!"

The music promised so much release, if only he would let go. So he did.

—

"Thank you, goodnight!"

Carina dropped the mike and fled stage left, and Daniel found himself staring at himself and the spellbound crowd reflected in the stage mirrors. He stood on the dance floor with a hundred others, unable to remember how he had gotten here. He blinked and rubbed his eyes. The audience awoke from their stupor, stumbling toward the bathrooms, the bar. He remembered songs, his heart thumping with the tempo. He remembered the intense need to listen as deeply as he could, to open himself up to the sounds, because if he didn't, he would miss something glorious.

He felt as if he were awakening from one dream into another. How many songs had she sung? Three? Five? Nine? He was exhausted. It was definitely the alcohol and the days of travel. But it was also something more. He felt as if he'd been drugged. Those around him had a curious blankness in their eyes, and he'd seen the same look in addicts who had one too many bad trips. He wondered if he had that same look now.

A few made it to the bar, but most headed for the doors. He fled with them, wanting only sleep. Outside, people lit up and mumbled softly to each other, like zombies milling about. One stupefied dude accidentally brushed the cherry of his cigarette into Daniel's elbow, and the pain jolted suddenly him awake. For the first time since the show began he remembered why he had come here.

"Fuck," Daniel said. "Holy fuck."

"Sorry, pal," the sleepy-eyed man said as he stumbled off.

The music had drained him – had drained all of them – and he fought off tidal waves of despair, the same dread feeling he'd had after his trip with the Breaker of Minds. But he forced himself awake with slow pranayamic breaths, the way Prabha, the washerwoman had taught him, and slowly the panic and despair ebbed, replaced by the vile hunger. And he welcomed it – *almost* – because with the hunger came strength.

The show had just ended. Carina couldn't have gone far. She hadn't come out the front entrance, so he walked around to the rear of the building, looking for a stage door.

Jackpot. A black coach bus with tinted windows idled in the alley, and four paparazzi waited with cameras ready. They looked up at Daniel for half a second before they went back to their phones and cigarettes. This had to be Carina's bus, and he would follow it wherever it led. Except he didn't have a car. And he doubted that even in his cursed state he could run as fast as a bus.

He had another idea. When the paparazzi were sufficiently

engrossed in their phones, he hopped onto a nearby dumpster and from there he carefully climbed onto the bus's roof, treading as quietly as he could. He lay flat on his belly and crept toward the roof vent, which was open a few inches. Air conditioned air spilled out from it.

Over a radio, a modulated voice said, "She's coming out in five. Any more show up?"

"Still only four," the driver said.

"Damn," said the radio's voice. "We called all the fucking tabloids. I guess four will have to do. Be ready."

"Copy that."

Daniel heard but did not see the rear door of Palacete open, a flurry of voices, shutter clicks, shouts for Carina to turn her head and smile, the shuffle of footsteps. Photo flashes bounced off the walls and into the starry sky. After a few moments the bus shook as people stepped aboard.

He peered through the open vent, but kept low, afraid to be seen. The two identically-suited men, the same men Daniel had encountered at Webster Hall, sat first. The woman who'd struck him sat opposite them. Carina sat alone, and the sight of her in her golden attire brought back ecstatic memories of the show, and he fought to stop himself from drifting into a waking dream. Carina opened a bag of Skittles, poured a large amount into her palm, and devoured them.

The bus started and he nearly slid off as it pulled away.

"You did well," a man said. "You had them enchanted. Literally. One more stop."

"No," Carina said, and her voice took Daniel back to the show, the laser lights, the release. "I'm exhausted."

"You need to drop in a club where wealthy Caracas kids party. They'll gossip about you and take pictures. There'll be buzz about you in tomorrow's tabloids."

"No, Duile. I'm fucking spent. Take me home." Her Ukrainian accent had vanished.

"Carina, we have to–"

"You'll have to fucking drag me into that nightclub kicking and screaming. Is that what you want in your tabloids? Take me home. I'm going to read a book and go to bed."

"Carina, your mother will be–"

"Fuck my mother! Fuck you too. I'm going home."

For a minute, no one spoke, and the bus drove on.

"Haph, drive us back to the rental house," Duile said.

"Right," said the driver.

The bus turned off the main road and struggled up a long, winding hill.

"How are we doing with scheduling, Frix?" said Duile.

"Good," said Frix. "The first deliveries have arrived in Venezuela, Brazil, Columbia and Argentina. More are on their way to a dozen other cities. Moda by Carina is already on eBay and in a few local boutiques. Preliminary figures are highly promising, with as high as forty-five percent penetration into youth markets. But there's a problem."

"Which is?"

"The amount of our...*product* is limited. If demand for Moda by Carina peaks, we'll run out in a couple of weeks. When does the new shipment arrive?"

Daniel listened more carefully.

"They're working on it," Duile said. "It depends on how quickly Carina does her job."

At this, Carina said nothing.

"What about U.S. market penetration?" said Duile. "You told me the U.S. clothing markets are tightly controlled and resistant to new players."

"Don't worry about the United States," said Frix. "We don't need to sell directly there. The U.S. mostly imports from China and Singapore, the American boutiques buy directly from Asian wholesalers, and the fashionistas from boutiques. If we saturate the Asian markets, the American boutiques will follow. So it's really just a matter of time."

"Good," said Duile. "Very good. Things are going well then."

"I'm not sure," said Frix. "I'm concerned about Carina's popularity. Palacete should have sold out within a day. But there were still tickets available when she went on stage. We need something more. Something to bring her global attention."

"We have a new video launching tomorrow. And two more are in post-production."

"I know, but videos only reach a certain market. I'm thinking of a film."

"A film?"

"A motion picture distributed all over the world. It'll reach a different demo, but we need to expand rapidly if this is to succeed."

"An excellent idea, Frix. I'll talk to some of our friends in the morning."

"There's also the human. Richard."

"What about him?" said Carina, perking up.

"He's getting too close to you, Carina. I don't trust him. Where is he now?"

"Back at the villa, sulking because you didn't let him come to the show."

"He's mixing a new track on his laptop," said Duile. "But we'll have to re-edit whatever he does."

"I like his edits," Carina said.

"These are *special* edits."

"You have to get rid of him," Frix said. "He's a liability."

"No!" Carina shouted. "You will absolutely not get rid of Richard. If you so much as harm a hair on his head, I'll kill you all. Do you understand?"

No one spoke.

"Do you fucking understand me?"

"Yes, Carina. We all understand."

"Daphna. My name is Daphna."

This, Daniel thought, *was getting more interesting by the moment.*

They pulled into the driveway of a large villa on a hill surrounded by palm trees and a dense wall of tropical plants. He lay low as they exited the bus and headed inside. But Duile said, "Khein, hang on. Let's have a smoke."

"Right," said Khein, as the others went inside.

Daniel heard doors closing, the flick of a lighter. Soon he smelled cigarette smoke. After a minute or two, Duile spoke. Or was it Khein? He had trouble telling their voices apart. "We're losing control of her."

"I know. What do you suggest? A coercion spell?"

"No, she's too powerful. She might sense or resist it. Besides, we shouldn't do it without the queen's authority."

"We could ask her permission."

"And tell her we've lost control of Daphna? The queen will replace us."

"Yeah, you're right."

They fell silent for a time.

"Any ideas?"

"One, but it's not pretty."

"Nothing worthwhile is. Tell me, Duile."

He whispered the next part: "We kill Daphna and find a lookalike to take her place. With a spell, we could make her appear just like Daphna. But she'd be our puppet."

"I thought you said Daphna is too powerful?"

"She's very powerful. But she's not a First One. We *can* kill her."

A pause. "The queen would notice an impostor."

"Would she? Everything Mashit knows of her daughter here comes through us."

"But down the line, when travel to Sheol becomes commonplace–"

"Then our puppet can have an unfortunate accident."

"Interesting. And before then, this lookalike would be–"

"She'd be entirely under our control. The Earth would be ours to rule. Behind the scenes, of course."

"I like it, but it's risky."

"Quite."

"If the queen discovers our plan–"

"It would not end well for us."

A pause. "Let's get rid of Richard too, while we're at it."

"Good. I'll start searching for lookalikes. We'll speak again soon."

The men finished their smokes and went inside. Daniel waited a few minutes, then snuck down from the bus to scope out the area. Three stuccoed buildings surrounded an verdant atrium with a pool at its center. As he crept toward the buildings, he was reminded of that night on Gehinnom – a lifetime ago now – when he first approached Rana's house. Faintly, he heard Carina's voice drifting from an open window, and he crept over and crouched down beneath the sill to listen.

"I don't understand," said a deep-voiced man with a heavy Alabama drawl. "It wasn't a good turnout?"

"It wasn't sold out," Carina said.

"And that bothers you?"

"A little. Yeah."

"You're still new. Soon you'll be selling out stadiums, I promise. Anyway, I'm sorry I couldn't come. Duile insisted I have your edit done tonight. I'll tell you, I've worked with a lot of assholes, but he might be the biggest I've ever met."

"You don't know half of it, Richard. I'm getting in the shower, then I'm going to bed."

"All right. Good night, then."

"No! Please stay."

"Stay? Um...sure. I mean, of course. Whatever you want."

A door closed, the shower turned on, and Daniel heard the sound of Richard clicking away on laptop keys. There came a knock on the door.

"Yes?" Richard said.

The door opened. "Have you finished the edit?" Duile said.

"I finished uploading the uncompressed track to your private server twenty minutes ago. The wifi's god-awful here. Took me over an hour to upload!"

"We need to discuss some things."

"Are you firing me?"

"Richard, would you come with me, please."

"Now? Carina told me to–"

"Get your fat fucking ass up and come with me, now!"

"Jesus. All right, man. No need to be rude."

Richard and Duile left the room. The shower was still running, and Carina's honeyed voice hummed through the closed door. Daniel pushed up the window screen and slipped inside her room as quietly as he could. Carina's black jumpsuit and golden accessories lay on the floor, discarded like a shed snake skin. As he looked at them, a curious desire arose in his chest. He needed to accumulate these objects, to don them as she had. Her belt lay at his feet, heavy and substantial, brighter in the room's light than it had any right to be. He reached for it and a blue spark of electricity leaped from his finger into the metal. It stung like hell, and he withdrew his hand.

He was suddenly overcome with exhaustion. He wanted to curl up on the bed and not wake for days. Was this his hotel room? He couldn't remember how he had gotten here. He sat on the bed, and his eyes drooped. He dreamed of Carina dancing, lights flashing. It felt so good to let go, to sleep.

"Who the fuck are you?"

He opened his eyes. Carina stood before him, wrapped in a bathrobe.

He blinked awake and stood. "Carina! Hello!"

"How did you get in here?" She glanced at the open window. "Where's Richard?"

He struggled to remember. He was here to find a way to...to get somewhere, wasn't he? But, Carina! She was here! Right here!

She approached him. "I saw you at the show tonight, didn't I?"

"Yeah." The show. So amazing! He had to tell everyone about it!

"Your eyes, they glowed like....What's your name?"

"Daniel."

She tilted her head. "You were at Webster Hall, weren't you?"

He struggled to remember. "Webster Hall? Yeah, I think so."

She walked around the bed, keeping her distance. She removed a pouch of tobacco and rolled herself a cigarette. "But you're more than just a fan, aren't you?" she said as she lit it. "Wake up, Daniel, you're under a powerful spell."

Wake up? A vague memory of a man bumping into him. "Can I have your cigarette?"

"Here," she said, carefully handing it to him. "Have a drag. Maybe it'll help."

Instead he pressed the cherry into his forearm. The jolt of pain woke him right up, and his memories came flooding back. He deeply inhaled the smell of burnt flesh.

"Interesting," she said.

He handed her back the extinguished butt.

"You're Daniel Fisher." She crushed the butt in her hands. "The Lamed Vav."

"Or something else. And you're Mashit's daughter."

"Or something else. Why are you stalking me, Daniel?"

He glanced at her clothing on the floor. "Your music, the gold, it's draining people, making them mindless and stupid. Easier to control."

She smiled. "How astute of you."

"I can't let you do this."

She smiled and rolled another cigarette, taking her time. "Is this the part where you play the hero who thwarts the plans of the evil one? Have you come here to kill me? Because I assure you that's not going to happen. You do realize how stupid you are for simply stepping in this room? I could kill you with a word."

"So why don't you?"

She took a slow drag. "Maybe because I find you interesting. My mother chased you across the Shards, and still you escaped her. I heard you have Azazel's Curse too."

"Yes, but it hasn't quickened. I haven't eaten dead human flesh."

"Like I said, interesting. So if you're not here to kill me, then why are you here?"

"Because I need something from you."

She laughed. "And what makes you think I'd give you anything?"

"Because I have something you need too."

"What's that?"

"Someone wants to kill you, Carina."

"My name is Daphna. Who wants to kill me?"

Daniel stepped closer. "Get me to Sheol, and I'll tell you."

She stared at him. "Are you serious?"

"Dead serious."

"Do you know how difficult it is to travel between worlds?"

"I do, actually."

"Why do you need to go to Sheol?"

He stared at her. "Will you help me, or not?"

She smiled. "You're bold, I'll give you that. Stupid, but bold." She raised her hand, and he sensed she was about to cast a spell.

"Duile and Khein are planning to kill you!" he blurted. "They're losing control of you and want to replace you with a lookalike, someone they can manipulate."

She lowered her hand. "What? That's absurd!"

"It's true. I heard them speaking outside a few minutes ago."

She shook her head. "Why should I believe anything you say?"

"I offer it as a gesture of goodwill. You can take it or leave it, at your peril."

She looked him up and down. "I see what my mother saw in you. You're fascinating, I'll give you that. Not really my type, though." She took another drag. "Daniel, even if I wanted to help you – which I don't – there's no easy way to get to Sheol."

"You came here, didn't you? So did Mashit."

"It takes enormous amounts of power that I don't have. And it's not really my area of expertise. Now, what shall I do with you? Kill you, or–"

The door swung open, and Duile, Khein, and Frix sprung in. Duile said, "Unfortunately, Carina, we had to let Richard–" He saw Daniel. "Who the fuck are you?"

"It's the man from New York," Frix said, "I told you we should have killed him!"

Frix leaped for him, but Daniel was ready. He whispered words of fire that scraped the fabric of the world. *Burn – burn to ash!*

The curtains erupted in flame; fire swept across the carpet. In seconds the room was engulfed. And suddenly he was ten years old again, trapped in the fire that had burned his parents alive. Horror consumed him. He had to flee. He leaped through the window, shattering it, and tumbled onto plants and earth. He struggled to his feet and ran, looking back as he fled. The three demons screamed and squealed as their clothes burned. But Daphna stood motionless in the flames, watching him go. She might have waved goodbye.

CHAPTER NINETEEN

Underneath the palace, not far from the animal the pens, the Legion's barracks stretched deep into stone. Kokabiel walked down a tunnel wide enough for two battalions to pass side by side unencumbered. The great iron doors to the barracks had been wheeled open before dawn, allowing him entry into ten thousand private chambers, where the myriad beasts of Sheol's army readied for war.

Kokabiel walked unseen, hidden by the concealing spell Gedeon had taught him. He passed a chamber, dark but for a glowing scroll in the clawed hands of scorpion-legged Penemue. The scroll's many symbols and glyphs shone hoary blue light onto Penemue's yellow-slit eyes and densely tattooed abdomen. Arrays of such symbols, drawn in the right order, could obliterate an attacking army. As Penemue stared at her scroll, Kokabiel dropped a hand-woven book inside her door, *A Demon's Code of Ethics and Hygiene*, by Maya Dorje.

He had made it appear to Mashit and the Pillars as if he had destroyed these books. But he had only whisked them away for later use. Only a dozen remained.

He walked on. Steam poured from another chamber, where hot springs bubbled with foul subterranean gases. The walls dripped with sweat, and the beads reflected the hearth's blazing fire. Rahab the sea dragon rose from the waters. First his horns, sharp and numerous as his teeth; then his eyes, large and green, blinking away water; last came his scaly head. He crawled from the water to don plates of shining armor. Unseen, Kokabiel deposited one of Maya's books inside his door.

Sustained, high-pitched notes echoed from the next chamber, where Naamah practiced her harp strung from the tendons of those she'd slain. Her room smelled like rust and dead flowers. Sheet music covered the floor and walls. Her songs, in a thousand different modes and keys, could enchant, enliven, and slaughter, often all at once. At the next somber pluck of string, Kokabiel deposited a book.

He dropped one in Abezethibou's quarters and one in Roeled's. One in Hemah's and one in Buldumech's. His targets were deliberate. All Legion soldiers were fierce, but these demons bore a brutality unmatched in the others. By their nature they would find its words abhorrent and vile. Concealed, he walked down corridor, depositing more books. When he had delivered the last, he returned to the main cavern, which connected the spoking corridors like the axel of a wheel. Alone, he removed his cloaking spell, and struck the Call to Readiness.

The iron bell, three stories tall, hung in the huge central chamber, bathed in the dawn's crimson light spilling down from the skylight above. He struck the bell five times with a hammer, and its ring barreled down the corridors. The echoes returned in a deeper key, resonating with the bell, and it warbled. His gut shook, stirring up delightful memories of former battles. The demons, roused to attention, stepped into the corridors, wielding weapons, armor, and spells in their hands, claws, hoofs or tentacles. The bell rang with their footfalls.

Eventually, though, the bell stilled, replaced by the Legion's heavy breathing as they waited for command. Kokabiel gazed between giant ironwork arches into each corridor, inspecting his charges. The soldiers, arrayed in neat rows, pinnacled by their battalion commanders, gazed back at him with eyes raging and aflame.

"Who are we?" he shouted.

"WE ARE LEGION," came the ten-thousand voiced reply, and the bell rang again.

"Why do we fight?"

"TO LIBERATE OURSELVES FROM TYRANNY."

"For whom do we fight?"

"FOR HER INFINITE GLORY, MASHIT, QUEEN OF DEMONKIND."

"And what is our reward?"

"TO DIE BY FIRE, SPELL, OR SWORD."

"Who are we?" he said.

This time he joined them as they said, "WE ARE ONE."

He waited for the echoes to fade, for the bell to stop thrumming. "Today, we march into the Dissipation," he said, "to practice split-field and scatter-group battle formations. We march out from the southern doors. Assemble there before your commanders, and await further orders."

They turned on their heels, wings, bellies, cilia, and marched south, and he savored the power of his command. Since he had been demoted, First General Talman seldom let him have moments like these. After a few minutes he climbed a wrought-iron stair that led into a narrow passage. It would take him directly to the southern doors, bypassing the marching soldiers. Kokabiel spotted Talman running in the middle-distance, a small grayish figure. The First General, supreme commander of the Legion, was panting and sweating profusely as he approached Kokabiel.

"Why didn't you wait for me?" Talman said. He stood less than half as tall as Kokabiel, but what he lacked in height he made up for in breadth. Talman's gray, leathered skin resembled granite, and from battle practice, Kokabiel knew it was nearly as hard. Talman's legs and arms were as thick as the emerald columns in the hall of Gabriel's Tears. His human-like face nearly vanished into the folds of skin that made up his ziggurat-like head. The First General didn't walk so much as heave, like a boulder. But in battle, Talman was quick as an arrow and just as deadly.

"The suns have been up for more than an hour," Kokabiel said. "I assumed you had overslept, again. Sir."

"Never assume, Kokabiel!" Talman turned and dragged his massive bulk southward, and Kokabiel followed. The tunnel was dark but for the distant flicker of a lamp, and the floor rumbled from ten thousand soldiers marching in the caverns below.

"Did you enjoy yourself?" Talman said.

"Sir?"

"What were my orders, Kokabiel?"

"You said, General, we would take the Legion into the Dissipation, past the sinkholes, to Bocker's Crack, a day's march from the city."

"Yes, Kokabiel. *We*! Not you, alone!"

"I'm your Second General, sir," Kokabiel said. "When you didn't arrive this morning, I merely followed your orders as you relayed them to me."

"Exactly! You are Second, and I'm the First! I'm the one who commands my army!"

"With respect, sir, they are not *your* army. The Legion of the First belongs to Sheol, and is under command of the queen."

Talman glared over his shoulder at him, his bluish-gray eyes twinkling like beads of agate. "I know you loathe me, Kokabiel. But I'm not your enemy!"

"I do not loathe you, sir," he said. *You are merely an impediment,* he thought.

Talman took a deep breath. "You think because I came from a low station that I'm a dolt. But wisdom I gleaned from my low station landed me in this position of authority."

So wise, Kokabiel thought, *that you arrive late to the very excursion you ordered*? "Indeed, sir," he said.

"It's all right," Talman said. "I forgive you your weakness."

"*Weakness,* sir?" Kokabiel said.

"Anger is a self-destructive emotion."

Kokabiel seethed; how had this babbling idiot risen to such a rank? "Anger is an energy," he said. "Channeled on the battlefield, no army can defeat us. We are masters of our rage."

"And when we're not battling?" Talman said. "When we whittle away the long days between combat, what then? Our anger has to go somewhere. Usually it gets directed at other demons. Our allies, most of all."

"My anger, sir, never leaves me."

"And thus the cycle continues. I've given up on my rage, Koko. It hasn't been easy. It's been bred into us demons. We always choose the abysmal path because that's what we've always done. But the old ways aren't working anymore."

"I disagree, sir. The old ways have kept Sheol alive. If not for the old ways, we would be husks of ash hurtling through the Great Deep."

"If not for the old ways, the mountains might have bloomed millennia ago."

"Or would have crumbled to dust."

"I am an optimist," Talman said. "I have chosen hope over despair."

"And I'm a realist," Kokabiel said. "And I have chosen reality over delusion."

They walked in silence for a time, while the floor rumbled beneath them, until Talman paused before a tunnel junction that led to the palace. "Go," Talman said. "Take the Legion to Bocker's Crack, perform the drills, and bring them back tomorrow. I'll be watching from the palace."

"You're not coming, sir?"

"No."

"Are you fucking serious?"

Talman hardened his jaw, and Kokabiel tensed. On the open battlefield, he might defeat Talman. But here in this restricted space Talman had the advantage. "You forget your place, Kokabiel," he said.

Kokabiel took a deep breath. It was not yet time for rebellion. He bowed his long neck. "Forgive me, General. I've not grown used to being second in command."

"Nor I being first. But we do what we must. I'll be watching the you from the palace heights. Do as I ask, Kokabiel."

"I will. Sir."

"And Kokabiel..."

"Yes?"

Talman checked the tunnel to make sure they were alone, then he reached inside the strap of his thick belt. His hand lingered there for a moment, and Kokabiel recognized the cover of Maya's hand-woven book. But Talman slowly removed his hand from it. "Never mind," he said. "This isn't for you."

"Sir?"

"Go. Command the Legion. Stoke their rage in the wastes as you always have. It's what you're best at. I have business elsewhere." And at this Talman fled into the passageway and vanished into shadows.

"Coward," Kokabiel said after him, not caring if the general heard. He knew this knave was off to see Maya, despite Mashit's firm orders restricting it. Kokabiel's spies had told him the First General had been secretly visiting Maya for days. But Kokabiel didn't need spies to sense this. It was written all over him. If Maya Dorje was teaching Talman how to be weak, it was working.

During one session, one of Kokabiel's spies had recounted, Talman had told Maya he regretted killing so many in his lifetime and wanted only peace from his inner torment. And Maya had sat beside him and held his head, while the highest commander of the most powerful army in the Cosmos wept like a baby in her lap.

—

Later that afternoon a fierce wind whipped the dust of the Dissipation into a gray, obscuring haze, and the air reeked of burnt wax and ash. The twin suns of Adar and Ora burned holes in the sky as Kokabiel led the Legion toward Bocker's Crack. This far from the palace, the city of Abbadon resembled a insect's graveyard: buildings lay belly up, their crooked legs pointing at the sky, and the palace menaced above all. From this distance, blurred by haze, the city seemed a fading dream. He knew Talman wasn't watching, but sitting at Maya's heels, begging advice, and Kokabiel seethed.

He walked before his five lieutenant generals as they marched across the Dissipation's wastes, the footfalls of the ten thousand Legion soldiers behind them shaking the ground. He carefully led them around regions where the earth might give way and send them plunging to their deaths.

"General Kokabiel," Ieropael said, her voice thrumming. She was made of fragments of translucent pink crystal, had a roughly bipedal shape, and walked on hundreds of sharp points. "Why are we traveling all the way to Bocker's Crack to do exercises that we could do beside the palace? We leave the city vulnerable and exposed."

Because our leader wants us to look away, Kokabiel thought, *while he defies the queen's order.* But he could not voice this; it would imply he knew of the infraction and did not act. "First General Talman wishes to test us," he said, which was partly true.

"A foolish test, General," said Nefthada, a mass of hundreds of green worms, roughly ball-shaped. "We could perform these battle formations in our sleep."

"Yes," thrummed Ieropael. "Is there some angle we're missing?"

"The only angle to concern yourselves with," Kokabiel said, "is our approach to Bocker's Crack. These are General Talman's orders." The lieutenant generals grumbled, but said no more. Silently, he praised their restlessness. When he became king, he would reward each of them with a high position.

The gray wastes spread before them, endless miles of dust and ash, surrounded by jagged black cliffs. Far off, a haze-blurred fissure tore across the Dissipation. Bocker's Crack, a remnant from the Shattering, when the first universe was torn apart, remained a half-day's march away.

He reached into the pocket of his leather cloak to make sure the stone was still there. He wrapped his fist around it, then let it drop back into his pocket.

Not yet. *But soon.*

The wind gusted, and for a moment, the dust cleared enough to reveal the mountainsides, where, nestled between crags, a grove of trees grew high on a mountain ledge. The green was stark against the bleak stone. The Legion saw it too, and many stared in shock. Kokabiel himself had never seen anything like this on Sheol before, and for a moment he entertained the thought that Mashit's plan was working. She would bring abundance after all. But the dry fog returned, and the vision was gone.

She had brought a few trees. And what else? Walls of clumping fungus and thick mold? Reports of strange vermin in the streets grew daily: hawk-sized flies planting maggots inside living creatures; swarms of dog-sized rats with three reads eating demons alive; mammoth mosquitoes bleeding demons dry with a single sting; infestations of moth and lice and fleas that no spell could remove. This was not abundance. It was madness.

He burned with rage. A fungus of change was growing on Sheol, and it would devour the world if he didn't stop it. He tapped his cloak pocket, where the stone rested against his breast. "Generals!" he shouted.

"Sir!" the five responded.

"It has come to my attention that contraband is being passed around the barracks. Reading material of an *alien* nature, toxic to any who read it. If anyone is caught possessing such vulgarity they shall be tortured and killed. Make it known among your soldiers."

"Yes, sir," they said.

"This contraband," Ieropael said, "is being spread by an unknown infiltrator. Two of my soldiers have discovered books written by the Pillar, Maya Dorje, in their quarters. Placed, they said, without their awareness. These writings preach weakness as a virtue. I burned them all."

"So you read them?" Kokabiel said.

"Only the first lines, and only because I did not know what I held. Once I discovered what it was, I destroyed them."

"Very good of you."

"Sir," Ghoful said. "You have a...*closer* relationship with the queen than us. Can you enlighten us? Why does she keep Maya Dorje alive? Even in seclusion, Maya spreads poison into the minds of Sheol. Swords and spells are strong, but ideas are what glue a people together. Maya has become, in some ways, more powerful than the queen. Her ideas are spreading like a cancer. The queen has ordered the destruction of the books, and yet bootleg copies are being made and being distributed around the city. They have even found their way to other Shards. This Maya Dorje is a danger to Sheol and demonkind. How does the queen not see this?"

He was severely pleased with Ghoful's words. When Mashit had seized power, she shuffled everyone's roles to break up long-standing networks loyal to Ashmedai. But where could she put Naamah who knew only to play her deadly harp? Or Rahab who knew only how to breathe fire and death? These soldiers were adept warriors, master tacticians. Of course they would see the flaws in Mashit's plan. Finding weaknesses to exploit was their highest skill. It was also his. He smiled. It was time. They were ready.

"The queen plans to bring abundance here," he said. "But like the Dissipation, her plan has a great crack." He reached into his breast pocket and grasped the stone. He whispered five words in ancient Demonsbreath, and the stone grew hot and turned to dust.

The air cracked with thunder behind them. The Legion turned to look at the sky. But there was a storm of a different kind. The cliffs beside the palace exploded, and enormous chunks of rock flew into the air. The soldiers raised their weapons and readied spells. Huge rocks and whirling flames erupted from the new crack in the mountain. The air roared, and the ground shook. The stones arced away from the blast to crash in the city and in the wastes. Vortices of energy, sparking prismatically, corkscrewed into the sky.

"General Kokabiel!" Ghoful shouted above the din. He drew his iron shield and placed it before him on the plain. A boulder crashed nearby, crushing two soldiers and knocking a dozen others to the ground. "Are we under attack?"

"A power vat has cracked open," Kokabiel shouted, "and its energy escapes back into the Abyss."

"But there are no power vats there!" Ieropael replied.

"Yes," he said, "there are. There *were*." And while the soldiers watched the mountain erupt, he turned out his pocket and let the stone powder blow away in the wind.

CHAPTER TWENTY

THE FEW SURVIVING FRAGMENTS OF THE SHATTERED VAT flashed with remnant energy, rainbow sparks that leaped from the rubble into to the sky. Mashit stood on the shattered cliff surrounded by her Shield, pondering the disaster. Yesterday, she would have been standing in a dark tunnel underneath tons of dense stone. Now it had been blasted away to reveal an insects' nest of tunnels and passages, and the huge bowl that had housed the vat. A sky of plump red stars shone down onto the catastrophe, her secret project laid bare.

"WHO?" SHE SNARLED. "WHO DID THIS?"

Kokabiel had been deep into the Dissipation when the mountain exploded, and he had rushed back to the palace as soon as he had seen it. He was still covered in powdered gray dust. "Definitely sabotage," he said, pointing into the rubble. "There were three carefully placed explosions that severed the vat's concentric shells. Sheol's stone is dense, so the perpetrator had to know the structural weak points. The explosions themselves used powerful and ancient magic. This is no amateur, my queen."

Mashit frowned as a page ran up to her. His green carp-like lips quivered as he said, "My queen, I have the tally you requested. Four hundred and fifty two dead in the mines. Counting the human slaves, that number rises to two thousand and seventy four. In the city, a hundred and fifty two demons were killed by falling stone or escaping energy. More demons may be alive or dead in the rubble."

"And where is Thelus, Chief of Mines?"

The page hung his head. "Crushed, my queen. No more will the world know her clockwork masterpieces."

A team of sorcerers, wraith-like in dark robes, stood on the rubble below, arms raised. As they waved their hands, boulders rose from the rubble to fly off into the sky. The sorcerers removed tons of debris per minute, but it would take days to clear it all.

Mashit stared at Kokabiel, and the rat-faced demon stared back stolidly. "Curious, Kokabiel," she said, "that you and the Legion were deep into the Dissipation when the vat exploded. Explain this."

"My queen," he said. "First General Talman who ordered us to Bocker's Crack to perform drills. I thought it was an asinine plan and made it known to him, but he insisted."

"Bocker's Crack?" she said, incredulous. Her voice echoed back from the rubble below, broken, disjointed, and a few of the sorcerers looked up at her. "Why did he take the Legion so far from the city?"

"He didn't *take* us, my queen. He gave the order, but remained in the palace."

"To do what?"

Kokabiel paused. "I'm not quite sure."

Mashit howled and threw a bolt of energy at a rising stone. It shattered to pieces and came raining down onto the sorcerer who had been lifting it. "And where's Talman now?"

"No idea."

Mashit turned to the Shield commander. "Go, find General Talman! He has a lot to answer for!"

"Yes, my queen," said the Shield commander, and he and five others sped away.

"So," she said to Kokabiel, "Talman sends the Legion deep into the Dissipation and vanishes into the palace, perhaps the most well-protected building in all of Sheol, at the same time my vats are destroyed?"

"The barracks are underground," Kokabiel said, "he might have sent the Legion away to protect them, in case the tunnels collapsed."

"You're quick to accuse him, Kokabiel. I know how much you covet his job."

"I'll not lie. You know I want to be First General again. But I want the other thing we spoke of quite a bit more. And you must admit the coincidences are hard to ignore."

"That thing we spoke of..." She stared up at him. "You've failed me, Koko."

"*Failed*, my queen?" He seemed genuinely shocked.

"You were supposed to keep this a secret. Now all of Sheol knows."

"A job this massive, it was inevitable that word got out."

"Was it? We've kept bigger secrets than this." She shook her head; she'd been foolish to trust him, this one with loyalties as fickle as the stars. Perhaps he had cooked up this plan with Ashmedai, when he had visited him. This might even be the first stage in a coup. "You can forget about our deal. That's over."

He stared at her, and though his expression was unchanged, she had known him long enough to feel him stew underneath this cold exterior.

"These vats will be Great Abbadon's promise fulfilled," she said, testing him. "And this saboteur has thrown away our chance at abundance. It was a stupid, selfish act. Don't you think, General?"

Kokabiel took a deep breath. "Selfish? The saboteur may believe they acted for the greater good. And whoever did this is far from stupid."

Was it you, Koko? she thought, staring at him. But she dared not accuse him in front of the others, for that would only add to their growing doubts. But she wondered, was he plotting something? Either way, she needed him. For now. "Cast a wide net, Kokabiel. Use every method at your disposal to find this saboteur. I want him in my hands – with evidence – by sunset tomorrow or I'll have your pin. Do you understand me?"

"Perfectly, my queen."

"Well?" she said. "Go!"

But he lingered. "My queen, there's something you need to know."

"What?"

"It's the Legion's principal task to protect the kingdom, therefore, it's my duty to tell you that Maya Dorje is a danger to it. Her poisonous ideas are spreading across the Shards. Her forbidden book is still being printed and distributed. And, my queen, I submit I wasn't fully honest with you a moment ago. I do know where Talman was during the blast."

"Oh? And where was he, Koko?"

"With Maya."

"Maya?" She felt her bile rise. "And why didn't you tell me this before?"

"The First General of the Legion learning how to be kind! In the interest of the kingdom, I thought it best to keep it secret. It would only stir more doubt of your rule, my queen. But in light of these events, I won't protect Talman any longer. He's a danger to the kingdom. And, my queen, so is Maya."

"You are full of surprises today, Kokabiel. I assume you have proof of these visits?"

"Ask him yourself, if you doubt me."

"You can be certain I'll be asking him much."

"Well? What are my orders, my queen?"

How clever he was, to challenge her before witnesses, the leader of demonkind, faltering before all. She felt the Shield's eyes upon her, the sorcerers ears. She needed to show them she was still in full control. "Here are my orders," she shouted. "Slaughter anyone found with Maya's book on sight. Seek out and destroy every copy in existence. Post banners throughout Sheol decreeing Maya's pamphlet illegal under punishment of death."

Kokabiel nodded. "And Maya? Kill her too?"

"No."

"So will you abide her poison?"

"I will deal with the Pillar myself."

"How, my queen? She'll only continue—"

"I will deal with her *myself!*" she snapped.

"Yes, of course. My queen."

"We will finish building these vats, saboteurs be damned. You will have the Legion guard the new construction day and night. This is only a minor setback. Everything will proceed as I have ordained."

A pause. "Yes, my queen."

"Now, do as I command."

Kokabiel bowed and departed.

The stars burned down upon her. The stones flew up from below. She felt as if she were being pressed in a vise. A stone rose, revealing several crushed bodies, palettes of blood, viscera, and bone. A spark escaped from some subterranean pocket and leaped into the sky, flashing spectral rainbows as it fled. Energy that could have brought new life to Sheol would never touch this world again.

—

The hallway outside the Lamed Vav's inner chambers was blessedly empty as Mashit and her Shield made their way toward it. Russet starlight shone through the columned portico onto the marbled floor, dimly lighting the twelve Legion soldiers guarding the door. They bowed as she approached.

"Step aside."

The iron door opened with a groan, and here, squatting on the floor before Maya, was General Talman. He was laughing as she entered.

"My queen!" he said, his smile vanishing from his face. He leaped to his feet. "I was just..." He coughed. "I was seeing to the Pillar's security."

"I wanted to believe General Kokabiel was lying," Mashit said. "But here you are, giggling, while our city is under siege."

"*Siege*, my queen?"

"Great Abbadon, are you serious?" Was he playing stupid?

Talman blinked at her. "I heard a blast, but I thought it was the Legion, practicing battle drills. Was it not?"

She wanted to pop his squished little head, but she couldn't. Not here, in front of Maya. "Talman, give me your pin."

"But, my queen..."

She held out her palm.

He swallowed and said, "So be it." He unclasped the iron cracked egg pin from his chest. It was adorned with a ruby pentagon, designating him as First General. He looked as if he might cry as he dropped it in her palm. He glanced once more at Maya. "I'm ill-suited for war anyway."

"Take him," she said to her Shields. "Put him someplace cold and dark. I'll decide his punishment later."

Four Shields seized Talman and dragged him away. He did not resist.

"Why do you punish him?" Maya said. "He's come here only seeking peace." Her eyes were full of compassion and understanding, and her voice was unexpectedly kind.

"He was the First General of the army!" Mashit said, trying and failing to hold onto her anger. "There is no room in a soldier's heart for peace."

"Then that is exactly where we must make room for it," Maya said.

Mashit looked around at the others. Sunil sat in a padded seat beneath the window, arms clasped around his knees, watching her, something sinister in his gaze. The curtains fluttered behind him in the chill night air. Baaba and Paula sat across from each other at a small table. It was empty, but it was obvious they had been discussing something. Paula stared and Baaba snickered.

"Why do you laugh?" Mashit said.

"Because," Baaba said, "you think you're so powerful, but your strongest soldier was fawning at Maya's feet. You're like the men that came to my village and told us we were not as pious as they, just before they drank themselves into a fury, killed all the men, raped all the women, and cut the clitorises off of the girls. I laugh at your fucking hypocrisy."

Mashit turned to her Shield. "Wait outside. And close the door."

"My queen?" the commander said.

"These are my orders."

He nodded, and her Shield left the room. The door closed with a metallic groan.

"You're right," Mashit said to Baaba, who was adjusting her eye-patch. "About Talman, at least. While the First General of our army was sitting at Maya's feet, someone blew up one of our new power vats. More than two thousand were killed."

The smirk left Baaba's face. "Dear God," she said. "Talman said the sounds were just your armies playing games."

"Someone is playing a game," Mashit said. "A deadly one."

"You were attacked?" Paula said. "By whom?"

"An unknown saboteur. Talman is a suspect."

"He was here the whole time," Maya said.

"And not with our army," Mashit said. "Where he should have been."

"He is reforming his violent ways," Maya said. "He didn't do this. That I promise you. He's a new man."

"He's a *demon*. He's killed thousands. Do you think words can change him?"

"Not words alone," Maya said, "but action. He's planning to do much good."

"And much good he did, sitting here, neglecting his duties, while thousands died."

"So what will you do?" Maya said. "Shed more blood? Torture him and others to see who destroyed your vats? In the end, you only perpetuate the cycles of violence."

"Why do you waste your time lecturing these demons?" Paula said. "They don't negotiate or see logic. They operate from a narcissistic pathology. They lack empathy. They have no kindness, generosity, or mercy. They only know how to accuse, how to destroy. If you get in their way, they'll destroy you too. They're like terrorists. "

"I don't believe anyone is beyond redemption," Maya said. "Talman, a killer of thousands, cried with remorse. What do you call that?"

"Self-deception," Paula said. "He weeps today. Tomorrow, he slaughters again."

"Talman won't be slaughtering anyone, anymore," Mashit said.

"No," Paula said. "Because you'll kill him, right?"

"I can't let him live."

"Why not?" Maya said.

"Because it would send a terrible message."

"What message?" Maya said. "That you have mercy?"

"I cannot spare a coward's life."

"Talman's no coward," Maya said. "It takes courage to confront one's limitations. He's trying very hard to change himself."

"Into what?" Mashit said. "You?"

Maya glared at her, and her eyes seemed to glow. "Why the hell are we here, Mashit? You say you want to change this world, but you defend against change at every turn. If you really wanted abundance for Sheol, you'd let me help your people. But you refuse to see that they want this, they need this. They need *me*."

Baaba laughed uproariously. "Your head has grown as large as a mountain, Maya. You need them more than they need you."

Mashit sighed and sat in a chair. "She's right," she said. Sunil's eyebrows rose. "They do need her. Despite my orders, Maya's book has been spreading throughout the Shards."

"That's wonderful!" Maya said.

Mashit shook her head. "I can't understand why they love you so much. I've given all of myself to Sheol, and here you teach demons to bathe and say 'please' and 'thank you', and they flock to you as if you were a god."

"Is that what you want?" Maya said. "To be worshipped like a god?"

"I want to be loved for what I bring them. For what I do. Like you are."

"I don't counsel them because I want their love," Maya said. "I'm only an ear for their despair. When they realize they're not alone in their suffering, their despair lessens. And I use my teachings to show them ways out of their pain."

"Then show me," Mashit said.

Baaba and Paula exchanged glances. Sunil smiled.

"Gladly!" Maya said. "It would be my pleasure. Tell me, what hurts?"

"Everything," Mashit said. "I'm working as hard as I can to better this world, but every time I take a step forward, the universe shoves me two steps back."

"Perhaps this is because you're not stepping in the right direction."

"No, this is life on a Shard. Entropy always wins. Everything crumbles." She reached over to the hookah pipe. It lay cold and idle beside Sunil. With a wave of her hand she ignited the bowl and took a long gurgling puff, then exhaled blue smoke into the room. As the effects hit her, she leaned back into the warming haze.

"Does that ease your pain?" Maya said. "Or just dull it?"

"It makes the worst moments bearable." She shook her head and laughed. "Here I am, lamenting my troubles to a human."

"And you find this repugnant?"

"You're a feeble race," Mashit said.

"Feeble?" said Maya. "You're in the same room with four people who once held up the Earth. Each one of us has fought adversity in more ways than you can imagine. Our very presence brings life to this world. No one here is feeble. Few humans really are. That's just lie you've told yourself so you might come to terms with your ruinous world."

Mashit sighed and leaned deeper into her chair. "It's not fair."

"No," Maya said. "It isn't."

The room fell quiet. Sunil held out his hand for the hookah pipe. Mashit handed it to him, and he took a pull. Baaba frowned and shook her head.

"You said a power vat has been destroyed?" Sunil said. It was odd to hear his voice after he'd been silent for so long.

"Yes," she said. "A new vat, under construction."

"These are power generators?"

"Power collectors. They catch the power spilling down from Earth."

"To do what? I've seen no electricity here."

"It's a different kind of power. This is the life-force itself. Without the vats, Sheol would be a barren husk. Nothing would survive for long."

"So you want to collect more power falling from Earth?" he said.

"Yes."

"To increase the life-force here?"

"Yes."

"Presumably," Sunil said, "you've had vats before, otherwise this city and its infrastructure would not exist. Yes?"

"Yes, that's right."

"So why haven't you built more vats before now? Why are you building new ones? Will more power soon be spilling from Earth?"

Mashit paused. "It will."

"How? What's changed?"

She nodded and leaned back. This Sunil was more clever than she had presumed. She decided she would say no more about it and took another pull from the hookah.

"I see," Sunil said, nodding, and he stole a glance at Paula.

"So they're not just words," Maya said. "You are acting to bring change too."

"Of course I act!" Mashit said. "With my every breath."

"With every puff of the hookah," said Baaba snidely.

"I *will* bring abundance to Sheol," Mashit said, "but it will take time. People have to be patient with me. Including the four of you."

"I need to send a message to my children," Paula said.

"I told you before, I can't allow that. Not yet."

Paula slammed her fists on the table and abruptly stood; Mashit sat up. "You come here and pretend to be our friend," Paula said. "But we're just prisoners in your gilded cage. You make dull us with food and drugs. But we're not real people to you. We're tools. I've had enough of you! Get the fuck out!" Paula pointed to the door.

"Paula!" Maya said. "Please, don't –"

"Either set us free," Paula shouted, "or get the fuck out! We don't want to hear your poor self-pity. You're a monster. GET THE FUCK OUT!"

At this, her Shield burst into the room, eight soldiers, weapons drawn. "My queen?" the commander said.

Mashit rose from her seat. "Sheath your weapons. I was just leaving."

"At last!" Paula said.

Maya stared solemnly at Mashit, as if sad to see her go.

"I know you think me evil," Mashit said to them. "But you don't understand me at all. I was abandoned by my creator and tossed screaming into the Abyss, but instead of succumbing to despair, I helped my people build this city, this civilization. We literally rose from the ashes, and I'll do everything in my power to keep us from falling again. If that means I have to keep you locked in this room for a while, I will! Nothing – nothing will stop me from doing what I must for my people. They always come first!"

"*You* always come first," Paula said. "And you always will."

Mashit gazed at her soldiers, who awaited orders.

"Give your people a chance to make their own choices," Maya said, "And you'll be surprised at how often they choose a better path over their daily hell."

Mashit headed for the door. "This is Sheol. Hell has been chosen for us." At the door, she glanced back at Maya. The monk stared at her, silently mouthing a single word: *Alone.*

CHAPTER TWENTY-ONE

AS IT TURNED OUT, FRIX, DUILE AND KHEIN, WERE QUITE flammable, and if Daphna hadn't cast a spell to extinguish the flames they would have burned to death. She had almost let them, but at the last moment decided it was better to keep them alive than go on alone. Their human shapes were mostly glamours anyway, costumes they wore. Those were easy enough to change. But the burns underneath were another matter. For days after Caracas, Duile and Khein complained of unseen wounds, while Frix was unusually sullen and quiet.

They'd sent a message back home describing the encounter with Daniel, but they had not yet gotten a reply. In fact, they hadn't heard from Sheol in over a week, and Duile said this was unusual. Something was happening there, and it wasn't good. The three talked often of seeking revenge against Daniel, but they had their standing orders: the Carina project came first of all, and so a little more than a week after Venezuela Daphna found herself in this London studio dressing room, preparing for a film shoot.

The room smelled of synthetic fabrics and new plastic, smells she had only recently begun to recognize and loathe. On the long counter beneath the wall-length mirror, a tabloid magazine lay open to a short article about Moda by Carina, her product line, with several runway photographs from a Milan fashion week she'd been too busy to attend.

Everything was happening so fast. She wished Richard were here. She missed his self-deprecating humor. His goofy smile. He knew how to take her anxiety away with a bad joke. But no one had seen him since the fire. Duile had said Richard probably got spooked and ran – he had seen a lot these last few weeks – but Daphna doubted that. She tried his cell for the thousandth time, but his voicemail was full, and she wondered if Daniel was right: they'd killed Richard and would soon try to kill her too.

A glamorous dark-skinned woman helped Daphna into a burgundy skirt and a black corset top. Frix entered holding a metal briefcase and propped it open beneath the wall-length mirror to reveal an arsenal of accessories that gleamed in the lights. The woman fastened pyramidal earrings in Daphna's ears, helped her slip a metal cuff onto her right wrist, a large watch on her left. She clasped a plated necklace around her neck and secured a wide belt around her waist. She helped her into a leather jacket, and slung a quilted black handbag on a chain over her shoulder. All was golden, mirror-bright. Frix sat in the corner, arms crossed, a faint grimace on her face as Daphna dressed.

The make-up artist came next, a young woman with stunning eyes and a soft-spoken voice that made Daphna sleepy. Thirty minutes later, Daphna had transformed into a different creature. The woman before her in the mirror was from an alternate universe. She was stunning. She gleamed. The make-up artist deserved to have her effigy made in stone and hung in Abbadon's palace. When people saw Carina on the giant film screens, they would need no magic to fall in love with her. She was perfection.

"Carina?" Frix said. "It's time."

Frix led her out of the dressing room into the vaulted warehouse of the film studio. "You're fucking radiant," Frix said, hooking her arm. "You literally glow."

"It's not overdone?" Daphna said. "It feels like too much."

"There's no such thing. You blaze, my dear, and your brilliance will blast away their dull human minds, filling them with a new purpose. You're a goddess."

I am, she thought, smiling, and her heart warmed.

The film crew froze and fixed their gazes upon her. Mouths fell open. Eyes went wide. The hairs on the back of her neck rose as they passed an enclosed room just behind the set marked with many 'Danger' signs. Something powerfully magical lay in there.

Her stomach shifted, as if Earth's gravity had decreased. And the closer she came to the set, the lighter she felt, so that when she finally stepped onto the brightly lit scene, she was floating on a cloud. The magic here was intense; she'd never felt anything quite like it.

The set was a Manhattan coffee shop, not quite Starbucks. Twenty-somethings in hipster attire spread about the tables, soft chairs, and couches. They stared at her, mouths frozen in gasps of surprise. A green screen hung outside the windows; the bustling city would be digitally added later.

Spotlights shone onto the hot young baristas behind the counter: a dark-skinned woman with high cheekbones and a narrow waist; a brown-skinned man with a chiseled jaw and a day of stubble; a light-skinned blonde of ambiguous gender and doll-blue eyes.

High-watt spotlights beamed through the front windows, simulating the sun. Parallelograms of light fell across the tables and floor. The faux sunlight light gave the set a warm and cozy feel, a sanctuary den in an urban jungle.

She took it in, the set, their faces, and as she turned, the light spun with her, reflecting off her accessories. Frix was right. She was radiant. Light on her feet, she stepped up to the counter and said, "Double espresso! And Skittles please!"

The baristas blinked, then all laughed uproariously, as if Daphna had told the funniest joke in history, and the force of it startled her. As their laughs faded they stared at her, waiting.

Frix tapped her on the shoulder. "You know your lines?"

"I do," Daphna said. She'd memorized them in an hour. The lines were inane, the script basic. She'd nervously order a coffee, flirt with the stubbled boy behind the counter, then sit at the table beside the window. She'd sigh and put her head in her hands. Part of her dramatic reenactment of her arrival in America, her stay in a roach-filled apartment in a shady Brooklyn neighborhood, her struggle to find work, until this young manager, sees her sullen figure beside the window and comes over offering her a coffee and a job.

She'll work double shifts for months, investing all her money into making a demo tape. She'll go through hell to get it in front of a studio exec, who will turn her down because she isn't "commercial" enough. But then at an open-mike night at a bar in Williamsburg, when she's about to give up, she'll take the mike and sing a cappella, and a record producer in the crowd will notice her. The rest was history.

And it was all complete bullshit. The place names were fictional, and if reporters asked, she'd tell them it was a dramatized version of events. If they pressed for specifics, she'd say she preferred not to linger on the past. And anyway, the target audience, teens and twenty somethings, didn't care about the historicity of the film, but only for the myth: former Ukrainian sex slave makes it big in America as a pop-star. What was there not to love about that? Because if Carina could rise so high from such inauspicious beginnings, then they too could achieve greatness. And if they couldn't quite reach the same rarefied heights, then at least they could buy her products.

An orange-haired woman approached, and her voice cracked as she pointed to little Xs marked on the floor with colored tape. This X was where Daphna should pause after she walks in. That X was where she should stand before approaching the counter. At this X, she should turn left, toss her hair, and sigh dramatically. At this X, she should try not to blink for ten seconds. There were a lot of Xs and even more movements, and Daphna realized this shoot was going to be much harder than she'd imagined.

Khein appeared beside one of the cameras. She could barely see his pale face beyond all the lights. He nodded to Frix, and she gave a thumbs-up to the director. Someone shouted a command and everyone but the actors fled the scene. Then:

"Sound?"

"Set!"

"Camera?"

"Set!"

"Roll sound!"

"Rolling!"

"Roll camera!"

"Rolling!"

"Marker!"

"Scene 3b, Roll 1, Take 1." *Clap.*

"Action!"

She walked in, paused at the X, turned.

"Cut!"

"What?" she said. "What did I do wrong?"

The orange-haired woman returned. "You were too fast. Slow down. He wants the lens flare."

"The what?"

"The glare from your belt. It makes a flash in the camera. The director wants the audience to notice your accessories. But you have to stand exactly as I tell you, okay?"

How could you miss them? Daphna thought, but she just said, "Okay."

They started the scene again.

"Cut!"

"What happened?" Daphna said. "I was in the right spot!"

"You were perfect, Carina," the director said. "But the beam angle is off! Where's the fucking light tech?"

The entire film, she realized, was one long spell, designed to sway and seduce. Every frame was planned, every angle had to be perfect. They shot the scene again, and she got as far as the counter before they had to adjust another light, this time to glint off her watch. At the table by the window, it was her necklace. It took them the better part of the day to shoot a forty-five second scene. And when they finally wrapped she was hungry and exhausted and wanted to go straight to bed.

She walked with Frix past the sealed room marked 'Danger', and the hairs on the back of her neck rose again. A powerful magic leaked from this room. But something was off about it. Very off. She paused.

"Carina," Frix said, "Come on! We need to get you out of these clothes."

"What's in there?"

"Where?"

"That sealed room?"

"What do you think? Spells. Come on."

"I need to go in there."

"Forget it." Frix tugged her arm, but Daphna yanked away. She stepped up to the door. Whatever lay inside pulled her closer.

"Carina!" Frix said. "We need to go."

She tried the door, but it was locked. "Open it!"

"I can't."

"I know you can!"

"It's dangerous, you could–"

"Fuck it," Daphna said; she didn't care if the humans were watching. She melted the lock with magic – it was sealed with several spells – then kicked it in.

"Carina!"

The room was small and dim. On the floor, drawn in wax and ash, was a magic demonic seal covered in ancient sigils of power and surrounded by thirteen guttering black candles. In the center of all, a thousand spells carved into his pulpy flesh, was a naked human body.

"We needed a sacrifice," Frix said, shutting the door. "To power the spells for the shoot. He was too close to you, Carina. He knew too much. You know as well as I do that sooner or later this was going to happen. You just denied it."

She approached the body on the floor, dreading what she would see. She squatted down to gaze at his face, barely recognizable with all the bloody signs carved into to.

"Richard," she said. "Oh, no, no, Richard."

From his lips came a soft moan.

"He's alive?" she said.

"You know that's how it works. That's how it always works."

"C...Carina," he said, blood drooling from his lips. "What's hap...pening?"

"Shhh," she said, kneeling beside him. "It's all right, Richard." She gave Frix a hateful stare. "I'm here now."

Tears and blood leaked from his eyes. "They...did...horrible things."

"A nightmare," she said. "Just a bad dream. Now close your eyes. I'm here now. Everything will be all right."

She put a hand over his forehead, pushing sleep into his mind, and Richard's eyes fluttered and shut. Then with a quick wave of her hand she snapped his neck. He gave one last sigh and went still. She stood and fixed her eyes on Frix.

"Carina, you have to understand that–"

In an instant, Daphna had Frix pinned to the wall, her hand

around her neck. In her other hand was a knife, a charmed weapon that could kill a demon with a single strike; she'd carried it ever since Daniel had told her of Duile and Khein's plan. "I warned you!" she snapped. "I said if you harmed Richard I'd kill you all."

"But – it wasn't my wish!" Frix gasped. "I swear!"

"Don't blame Duile and Khein for this, you coward! I know you conspired in this!"

"No!" Frix said, gasping. "Not them! It was the queen! Mashit, your mother! I swear by Great Abbadon, she ordered his death!"

"Don't lie to me, Frix!"

"Check my right pocket! I saved the missive just for this!"

Daphna held the knife to Frix's neck while she reached into her pocket with her other hand. Out came a folded slip of parchment, laden with magic – Mashit's magic. Daphna unfolded it slowly. On the top was Mashit's royal seal. And at the bottom was her mother's unmistakable signature.

CHAPTER TWENTY-TWO

IT HAPPENED LIKE THIS:

He fled Daphna's villa, afraid the demons might come after him, and arrived at his motel room just before dawn. He didn't sleep, but waited till 7:00 a.m. to call Gram collect. God, how he missed her. Her phone rang, and rang, and the knot in his stomach twisted tighter with each pause. She didn't drive, so maybe she was asleep, or out with Maureen, who helped Gram with her errands.

So he tried Maureen. She picked up on the third ring and paused before she accepted the charges.

"Collect, Daniel? Really?"

"I'm sorry, Maureen. I – my wallet was stolen."

"Where are you? I couldn't understand the operator. Did she say Venezuela?"

"I'm in Caracas."

"What the hell are you doing there? Never mind – Danny, you need to come home."

"Why?"

"Eve is at LIJ. I'm heading over there in a few minutes."

It had been so long since he'd heard Gram's first name that for a moment he didn't know who she had meant. "Gram's in the hospital?"

"Long Island Jewish, room 646."

"What? What's happened?"

"I found her unconscious on the kitchen floor. The doctors said she had a brain hemorrhage, maybe a side effect from her meds.

Anyway, it won't be long. You need to get on the next flight home. Come as soon as you can if you want to say goodbye."

Gram's laugh that could shake universes. Gram leaping into his bedroom, saving him. Gram holding his hand as they walked in the park, his parents, alive, laughing and walking ahead of them. Gram lighting the shabes candles, the glow on her face. Gram reading a book in her favorite chair.

"Daniel?"

"I'll be there as soon as I can."

"Room 646 at LIJ. See you there."

He stood frozen for a moment, phone in his hand, before hanging up. He had no idea how he would he get home.

—

But he did. Through some arcane combination of unused airline miles and desperate phone calls to three of his credit cards, he scrounged up enough credit to book an evening flight to JFK. Six hours, the itinerary said, which would have him arrive well before dawn. But the flight was delayed for obscure "mechanical" reasons, and when they finally took off he knew he'd be in the air when the sun crested the horizon.

Hang on, Gram. Just a little longer.

Rays of sunlight crossed the cabin, but most people had closed their window shades to sleep, giving him reprieve from a fiery death. But there was one kid who kept opening the shade to peer out at the rolls of clouds. So Daniel fled to the bathroom, and remained there for hours.

A steward knocked, "Sir, are you all right?"

Gram. I'm coming.

"A little air sick," he said, even though the flight had been smooth. When it came time to land, the steward forced him out. He sat in the rearmost seat and prayed the sleeping man beside him wouldn't wake and want to glimpse the brightening world.

Just hang on, Gram.

Morning at JFK was like traversing the circles of hell. First came customs, where he was questioned for thirty long minutes. "And why have you been visiting all these countries, Mr. Fisher?"

"A walkabout," he said. "Just trying to find myself, you know?"

But the border guard did not seem convinced, especially since Daniel had only a small carry on. They searched him thoroughly, but finding nothing but dirty clothes they had to let him go.

In the terminal, he hopped from shadow to shadow, avoiding girders of light. A cigarette would have helped, but he had no U.S. currency, no money in the bank, and he was in too much of a hurry to exchange what little Venezuelan cash he had in his pocket.

He begged some woman for a metro card swipe and entered the subway, but it was its usual slog, the MTA's "customer service" consisting of garbled announcements and arcane track changes. The rush hour crowds pressed him tightly against the doors. People smelled of shampoo, cologne, shaving cream, and cigarettes. He wished he had one. A homeless man pushed through the car, asking for change, but Daniel had nothing to give.

Almost there, Gram.

At Jamaica, Queens, he maneuvered in the shadows to hail a cab. A hundred bucks to Long Island, but he didn't care. He'd figure out the payment later.

The drive wasn't far, but as they got closer each slowdown felt as if the universe resisted his arrival with every method at its disposal. At last, they pulled up to the hospital.

"Look," Daniel said, waiting until the very last moment to spill the bad news. "My grandmother's dying in there, and I'm going in to get some money from a friend. Just wait here, and I'll be back in ten minutes. I swear."

The driver said, "Wait, no, pay now!" But Daniel was already out the door.

"Room 646?" he panted when he reached the info desk.

"Sixth floor, south end," said the woman behind the counter. "The elevators are around the corner."

But elevators were too slow. He darted off toward the stairs as the cab driver cursed and shouted behind him. Up he went, each story more difficult than the last.

Almost there, Gram.

Sixth floor, he burst through the doors, looked for signs, oriented himself. He ran down the hall. And there it was, room 646, its door open. The air smelled of antiseptic, sweat, urine, and something else he couldn't quite describe but made his stomach lurch. IV units beeped and chimed.

Gram.

Maureen sat next to the bed. When she saw him, she said, "Oh, Danny." Her eyes were bloodshot.

Gram lay on the bed, pale as winter's snow, lips parted. Maureen came to hug him, but he shoved past her. There was a strange smell in the room that lingered in his nose and made him want to know it intimately.

"Gram. I'm here. It's Danny."

"She's gone, Daniel."

"No," he said, shaking his head. "No, I'm here. I've come, Gram. I'm here." He took her hand. It was already cold.

"She passed twenty minutes ago, Daniel. I'm sorry."

"It's not possible." Gram was always here and always would be. She was here when he nearly died in the fire, and she was here to raise him when his parents died. He had come all the way from Venezuela, risking death. It was not possible that he missed her because of twenty goddamned minutes.

Her hand, like most of her body, was scarred from her burns like a car-tire print in mud. He squeezed it. And all he wanted was for her to squeeze him back, even just a little. Then he would've known everything was all right. But her hand hung limp in his.

"Gram," he said. "Gram, no."

Maureen put a hand on his shoulder. "She was sleeping for most of the last few hours. But she awoke before the end and asked for you." Maureen wiped her cheeks. "She left you this. She said, 'Tell Daniel, this may open some doors for you.'"

Maureen held up the hamsa pendant, the Hand-of-God charm Gram wore to ward off the evil eye. He had once thought it was yet one more of her silly superstitions. But everything she had ever told him was true.

There was something else lingering here, under the pain. Something more awful than her impending eternal absence. It churned in his belly, this desire. It had been here, he realized, since he'd first entered the room, triggered by the smell of death. But he would not – *could never* – acknowledge it. No, not for her, not for Gram.

"I'm an abomination," he said.

Maureen put a hand on his shoulder. "I'll give you a moment alone."

He didn't want to be alone, but he couldn't find the words to stop Maureen. He crouched beside Gram, staring at her unmoving face. "I should never have left. I should have been there for you."

His hunger flared. "No," he said. "Fuck you! Not here. Not now!" He reached into his pockets searching for cigarettes he knew he didn't have. He rocked. "No, no, no..."

A nurse entered, perhaps drawn by his moaning. "Can I get you anything?" he said.

"A cigarette," Daniel said. "Please." He knew he sounded desperate.

The nurse frowned. "I don't smoke. And you can't smoke in here."

Down the hall, an IV unit was beeping. "I'll be back in a few minutes," the nurse said. "You're the grandson? We have some papers for you to sign."

The nurse left. Daniel looked at Gram's fingers and found himself salivating.

"No, no, no. Let me mourn her! Please, please, just leave me alone this once."

He grit his teeth and turned from her body. He wanted to hold her, to kiss her forehead and hug her one last time, but the hunger would not allow him. He might do vile things. He had to leave, now. He walked outside the room and sat in a chair against the wall, trying to catch his breath.

He signed some papers in a daze.

Eventually, they came to take her to the mortuary. He wanted to chase after her, but he wasn't sure what was driving this need, love or hunger. They wheeled her down the hall and vanished into the elevator. He hadn't realized Maureen had been sitting beside him.

"I paid your driver," she said. "A hundred and fifty dollars."

"He told me a hundred."

"Well that's what happens when you skip out on a fare," she said. "He was pissed. I expect to be repaid, Daniel."

He was fumbling unconsciously with Gram's hamsa pendant, when the top suddenly flipped open. There was a small button on it, and sandwiched between the two halves was an inch-long flat metal key.

This may open some doors for you.

Maureen was staring at it. "What's that open?"

"I think I have an idea."

She sighed and rubbed her eyes. "I skipped breakfast. Are you hungry, Daniel?"

"No," he said. And it was the greatest lie he had ever told.

—

He told Maureen he had a skin condition that made him extremely sun-sensitive, so it was imperative that she buy him the long-sleeved hoodie with the LIJ logo from the gift shop. Plus a pack of Marlboros. He noted the irony of selling cigarettes in a hospital, but he supposed if there were any place people needed a smoke, this was it. She shook her head and scowled, but she paid for it all without a word.

He hastily smoked in a shadowed nook under an awning before squeezing into Maureen's old Buick, wrapped in his hoodie, hoping he wouldn't catch fire the moment she drove into the sun. She said nothing as they sped onto Wantagh Parkway and headed south.

"Thank you, Maureen. For looking after her."

Both hands on the wheel, she drove in silence, clenching her jaw. After a time, she said, "Where the hell were you?"

"Venezuela."

"I mean," she said, turning her intense green eyes toward him, "what have you been doing all this time?"

He swallowed. "I've been looking for something."

"A door?" she said.

A ray of sun pierced the trees and landed on his hand. He yelped and dropped the cigarette on the vinyl seat between his legs. He quickly snatched it and flicked it out the window, but not before the cherry had burned a neat little black hole in the vinyl.

"Fuck, Daniel. Really?"

"I'm sorry." He turned his back to the sun, hoping the cotton hoodie was dense enough to protect him. But he felt an uncomfortable heat rising from the back of his head.

"What's happened to you?" she said. "You used to be so well

kept. Gram couldn't sing your praises enough. Are you on drugs?"

"No, it's not drugs."

"Did you get into some kind of trouble?"

"You could say that."

"Are you running from something?"

"Not from, but to."

"*What*, Daniel? What's so important that you couldn't be there for Eve?"

Past tense. Gram was gone. This was no dream. She would never smile again. He would never hear her voice again. "It's complicated."

"That's a coward's response," she said. "Eve's told me things about you. I'm not as naive as you think."

He took a deep breath and lit another cigarette. "You want the truth?"

"I do."

"I'm trying to prevent a group of demons from taking control of the Cosmos."

She laughed.

"I'm dead serious."

Her smile faded. "You *are* on drugs."

They pulled up to Gram's house as the afternoon light sent long shadows across her yard. The grass was wild and natty. The flower beds that had been Gram's pride were overgrown and weedy. Letters overflowed from the mailbox. Three copies of *Newsday* lay in the driveway.

"So," Maureen said, "will you come to the funeral, or is this where you vanish again, looking for more *doors*?"

"I'll be there," he said.

She sighed. "Do you need me to come in, make you something to eat?" She sounded as if it were the last thing in the world she wanted to do.

"No. Thank you, Maureen. For everything. I'll pay you back for the cab and for the cigarettes and for your seat."

"Forget it," she said, flaring her nostrils. The look in her eye said, *I know you never will anyway.* "Eve was the strongest woman I've ever met," Maureen said, and her eyes glistened. "Most people, if they'd been hurt like her, disfigured for life, in chronic pain, would succumb to helplessness and self-pity. But Eve, she pressed on with a smile. It made me realize how good we all really have it. God, I miss her already."

"Me too."

"You should have been here, Daniel. She did so much for you. The least you could have done was been there for her too. Seriously... demons?" She shook her head. "Get out of my car."

"Maureen..."

"Get out of my car, Daniel."

He pulled the handle and stepped outside into the bright sun. He quickly pulled his hoodie in close and stuffed his hands in his pockets. She drove away. Maureen lived only a few houses down the street, but she passed her house and kept on driving.

Gram's house loomed behind him. He ran into the shade, collected the mail from her mailbox. The door was open, as it always was. He stepped inside, and for a moment, he waited for Gram to remind him to take off his shoes.

Instead, silence. In the living room her reading glasses lay on a table next to a mystery novel. The place smelled strongly of her. In the kitchen there was a spot of blood on the linoleum floor where she'd fallen.

He bent down to examine the dried red splotch. He touched it, sniffed his fingers. He could smell her life force, lingering in the blood. And with it came the hunger, a storm rolling in from the sea. He had to quell it now. He smoked a cigarette in the backyard, then he got a sponge and cleaning fluid and scrubbed the floor.

He walked around the house. Here was the couch where they used to watch TV. Here was his old bedroom, posters of the Yankees, the Sombrero Galaxy and Saturn on the walls. Here was where Gram had read books to him, had told him Yiddish folk tales of golems and dybbuks, and tucked him in.

Here was her bedroom, a mess. Drawers, open and unkempt. Shoes and slippers scattered about. Her dresser, covered with sundry items. She had once been fastidious.

He remembered discovering her safe a decade ago, when he'd been rummaging through the house looking for something he'd lost. It had seemed the most important thing in the world at the time, but now he could not remember what it was. The old safe rested at the bottom of her closet.

The small key from her hamsa pendant fit the lock. It clicked and squeaked open on rusty hinges, and out came the smell of old paper and dust. He pulled out two books with hardbound covers, one green, one red, along with a yellowed copy of her will and the title for the house and a car that she'd sold a decade ago. The book opened from right to left, and there was a Hebrew word on the cover whose meaning he didn't know. But as he flipped through its many hand-written pages, the cigarette's curse-taming effect rapidly dwindled, and the words began to make sense. The word on the cover wasn't Hebrew. It was Yiddish. It said *Heft*. Notebook.

The first few pages were written in a child-like Yiddish script and were full of multiplication tables, grammar exercises, and a brief story about finding a mother and her ducklings in the weeds behind the house. But these soon gave way to diary entries signed with "Evele." Little Eve.

An entry dated 25 Sept, 1938, explained how Evele was angry with her mother for not letting her play with her friends, because Mame needed Evele's help preparing the Rosh Hashanah meals. Another, dated 12 March, 1939, told the story of a boy she encountered walking home from school one afternoon who tried to kiss her, but she kicked him and ran away. The entries grew sporadic. The last one, dated 2 Sept, 1941, was hastily scrawled.

"I write by candlelight and must be careful so the blankets will not burn. Mame and Tatu were arguing today. Mame says we need to flee, because the war is coming here. But Tatu says we must not worry. G-d will protect the righteous, as he does in every generation. They argued for hours. They tried to whisper, so we wouldn't hear, but Freya and I heard every word. I told Freya that Mame and Tatu were only practicing a play. Then I rubbed her head until she fell asleep. I believe Tatu. HaShem will protect us. But I am very scared and cannot sleep. Tatu is learned but Mame is wise."

Freya? Gram had never mentioned her name. She had never spoken of any of this.

There was a gap in the dates. The next entry was 18 June, 1946. The Yiddish script was more confident and serious. This wasn't a child's hand any more.

"I thought long on whether I should write in this notebook again after all that has come and gone or if I should let the past lie. But I thought, no, I'll not let those monsters make an end-point in my life, like a period at the end of a sentence. That hell is over, and my life goes on. Besides, this notebook is the only thing I have on this ship to write on. Paper is in short supply.

"They are all dead. Mame, Tatu, Freya, may their memories be blessings. They took us to Chelmno. They shaved Tatu's sidelocks and hair and made us reveal our shame before the soldiers, who laughed and mocked us, while the dogs growled and barked.

"Mame forbade me to use the wonders, because she said it would bring the wrath of an avenging angel. But I did not listen to her. I used magic to keep us alive. I charmed the mice to bring us bits of food from the barracks that had fallen from soldiers' mouths. I made thick dew form on the walls, which we drank. I gave Freya my food and water first. But in the third week, she fell sick with a fever, and nothing I did would help. One morning, she did not wake, and I wondered if this were the work of Mame's avenging angel.

"After her death, Tatu lost all hope. He openly cursed G-d and said the Lord had abandoned his people. One morning, after watching a guard strike an elderly man, Tatu leaped forward to attack the guard and was shot.

"Mame and I were kept in different parts of the camp, but I saw her from time to time. Each time, she was thinner, the glint of life removed from her eyes.

"The last thing she said to me was, 'Take care of Freya.' I hadn't the heart to tell her my sister was already dead.

"When the British soldiers liberated the camp, their eyes were stuck in wide-eyed shock. And I thought, 'How did you not know what was happening here?' I looked for Mame, but could not find her. The bastards had burned all their records to prevent the world from learning the extent of what they'd done. I hoped beyond hope that Mame had fled home. So when I gained back my strength in the military hospital, I took a train to Lviv, even though people said the Russians were killing Ukrainians as collaborators. And when they stopped our train in a quiet field, I feared the worst and ran into the woods. A few minutes later I heard gunfire. I did not look back.

"I traveled by moonlight. I stole food from farms and begged when my hunger was great. There wasn't much to eat, but I was used to starving. After four days I reached Pidhaitsi. Many Jewish buildings had been razed. More were boarded up or labeled 'Juden.'

"Our house still stood, because gentiles lived on the first floor. I ran upstairs to our apartment, hoping Mame would be waiting. But I found only mice, scurrying away. All our things had been ransacked or stolen, but my diary was here, behind the baseboard where I had left it. I waited for the Jewish residents of our shtetl to return. But no one came. So after a month I packed up my things and headed for the closest displaced persons' camp. I waited three months to get passage to America.

"Now, here I sit, in this crowded berth of this cargo ship with a thousand hollowed-eyed refugees. But I see in their eyes a spark of hope. We're going to start a new life in America. I'm going to build up what those bastards tried to take away. They tried to eradicate the Jewish people from the face of the earth, but in the end, it is we Jews who remain and they who have been erased.

"I had to stop writing for a moment. Sometimes the tears come, and I cannot stop them. I have moved outside. The ship heaves, and the ocean sprays upon me, but I welcome the salty air. I must stop writing soon. It's shabes eve, and the sun is going down. I wish Freya were here with me, to see this beautiful sunset. I wish I could sing shabes songs with Mame, Tatu and her. But tonight I'll sing with strangers, and it is bittersweet. The voices change but the songs go on."

The entry ended. Gram had never told him she'd been in a concentration camp. She'd never spoken of having a sister. There were more entries, and he flipped ahead.

"In a thousand sleepless nights, I've wondered why I survived when so many more deserving souls have died. But then I see Danny. He's lost his family at nearly the same age where I lost mine. The boy mourns for the ants in a rainstorm and weeps when he watches the news. His heart is as big as the world, and in these moments I know I have survived so I can raise him. His is a uniquely righteous soul – a tzaddik – but it would invite the evil eye – kaynahoreh – to say more."

"I may have been that person once, Gram," he said to the empty room. "But now I'm a monster."

He picked up the second book. It was bound in thick red canvas. The cover read "Roots of Names" in a sweeping Hebrew font. He flipped to the title page, and here, in bold Yiddish letters, a warning proclaimed: "You hold in your hands a book of great holiness, but also of terrible power. One must take the greatest precautions with this text, lest this book fall into the hands of an unholy creature, who might use it for darkness. Before reading this book one must conduct a thorough interrogation of one's heart and the hearts of those to whom this information might be transmitted. For as it is said, "Thou shalt not see my face and live." Prepare and purify yourself like the Cohain Gadol before he enters the Holy of Holies on the Day of Atonement. This book reveals the Divine Countenance and, read by the unprepared, can destroy the mind and spirit of a person. I have seen this firsthand. This book, used maliciously, can cause irreparable harm to the world, delaying the arrival of Moshiach by generations. May G-d protect he who reads these words."

Then Daniel, sitting on the floor, papers scattered all about him, opened to page one.

CHAPTER
TWENTY-THREE

THE THRONG ROILED BELOW KOKABIEL LIKE A STORMY SEA. HE stood on a high balcony near the palace apex as the wind blew sharply against his fur. The crowds poured into Abbadon's crooked streets, and he could not fathom how the city could fit them all. Yet they kept coming, pressing all the way to the lake's shore, even though sea creatures periodically crept from the waters to snatch whomever might be near.

He took a steadying breath and began his ascent of the Outer Stair. Its precipitous wrought-iron frame was a late addendum to the palace, added centuries ago. This far down, it was poorly maintained. Rust from the railings flaked off in his hands as he climbed. The twin suns hung low in the sky, spreading scarlet light and casting copper shadows over the crowds. The throng undulated like a turbulent sea, and their expectant voices rose and fell in tumultuous waves. There would be a slaughter today.

The stair's appearance improved as he climbed, so that when he spotted the parapet from where the queen would address the crowd, the stair and its metal arabesques had become a gleaming ornamental masterpiece. The crowd spotted him and ferociously cheered. He would deliver the prisoners to the queen – a symbolic exchange – and she would declare them guilty and order their execution for all to see.

Far below, in the center of Abbadon's Peace, on a raised platform, fifty-five prisoners squirmed in their cages, each a different size, compact enough so they all had to crouch. None would stand before the queen again.

Generals Ieropel, Ghoful, Nefthada, Abezethibou, and several other lieutenants surrounded the prisoners, waiting for the queen's word.

Ubesk the Shadow, growled and tore at his iron bars. Three centuries ago, Ubesk had cheated at a game of Break Bones he and Kokabiel had played together, and Kokabiel had never forgotten Ubesk's supercilious laugh as he had collected the night's winnings.

Thume, a sculptor of stone, sat slumped in the corner of his cage, puddles of gray sweat spilling from his pores. At one of the feasts for the Swap of Suns, Thume had drunkenly declared in front of all the guests that Kokabiel had cuckolded the king.

And there was Regolus, and Ablisum, and Hefachel and fifty more, and the only thing uniting them was Kokabiel's hate of them all. They, more than any, would stand in the way of his ascendancy to the throne. Thus they had to be destroyed. The fact that he was the one who had sabotaged the power vats made their deaths that much more satisfying.

He stopped beneath Mashit's parapet at the penultimate landing. Far below, Ghoful lifted a ram's horn and blew one long, sustained blast. The crowd fell silent, anticipating her arrival. But the queen would come when the queen would come.

Eventually, after a dramatic pause, Mashit emerged in a flowing white gown bedecked with jewels that flashed in the suns. The crowd cheered uproariously. She lifted her hand, and they fell silent again.

She weaved magic into the air to project her face and voice, so that down below it would seem as if she spoke to each of them personally, intimately.

"General Kokabiel, what news do you bring of the accused?" she said. This close, her voice thundered through him, shaking his body to the bone. Such beauty. Such power. And all of Sheol under her thrall. He lusted for her more than he'd ever had. They should have ruled side by side, queen and king, uniting the generations, old and new, but she had always kept him like this, one landing beneath her, looking up, just as the First Ones had kept all the children of the Fulcrum generation one level beneath them.

"These prisoners laid out before you, my queen," he said, his voice projecting over the crowd with hers, "are traitors of demonkind. Their excuses ring hollow. Their pleas for mercy fall on deaf ears."

"I am innocent!" screamed Hefachel, his voice amplified by magic that slipped past his guards. Ieropael silenced him with a crystal shard through his tongue, and the pink meat fell to the floor of his cage in a quivering lump. The crowd laughed and cheered.

Kokabiel swept his gaze across the city toward the base of the palace. Crowds were often dense for executions, especially on Stoning Day, but it seemed as if all of demonkind were here today. Those who could not squeeze into the streets hung from bridges and balconies and slanted roofs. And – he had never seen this before – some even braved the sharp cliffs beside the lake to catch a view. Even the humans had come to watch. Several stories below, the four Pillars had stepped out from behind a curtain onto a high balcony.

"Does anyone," the queen said, "wish to vouch for the accused, to defend them against the charges?"

But for the sound of banners snapping in the wind, there was total silence. Even the gloom vultures did not stir. Any fool knew to vouch for the accused meant they would die with them.

"Then by the laws of Great Abbadon and his Ancient Seal, which marks this ground as the place of judgment against those who would destroy us, I sentence these fifty-five traitors to death by torture, in methods unique to their essence. Commence the sentence."

A roar went up in the crowd like none he'd ever heard. The moment they had come for was at hand. The fifty-five demons squirmed and screamed, but the noise was too great for anyone to hear their pleas.

"Come, Koko," Mashit said; her voice spoke now for him and him alone. She held out her hand. "Come witness their deaths beside me."

What was this? A moment of magnanimity? He took a deep breath and ascended the last stair to stand beside her. "I'm honored, my queen," he said, surprised. To be seen beside her was no small gesture. All would see that he was on equal footing with her.

"The crowds are overflowing today," she said.

"You draw the largest crowds I've ever seen, my queen."

"Do you think so?" she said, beaming. "Then they do love me after all."

"Or fear you," he said, and then immediately regretted it.

She stared daggers at him, but the smile would not leave her face, not in front of so many people. Down below, General Ghoful was readying a sword to much cheer from the raucous crowd. "Perhaps I was hasty inviting you up here, Koko. I wanted to share this moment with you."

"And tomorrow," Kokabiel said, "will I'll be on the lower landing again?"

"Are you angry with me because I didn't make you my consort?"

"Yes!" he growled. "We can do glorious things together!"

The smile held firm on her face "You are a great soldier and an even greater lover. But you don't have the heart to rule Sheol. None of your generation ever did."

He burned with rage; he wanted to throw her off the ledge. Instead he remained the stolid, faithful general before all. "There should be fifty-*six* down there," he said.

"Talman was derelict in his duties," she said, "but I'm not convinced, Koko, that you had nothing to do with the explosions. I know these fifty-five are your enemies. Some of them are mine too. Talman will die only after he tells me everything he knows."

"Is that the reason you keep Talman alive?" he said. He looked down at the four Pillars on the their balcony. "Or is it because of Maya?"

"Don't be ridiculous," she said. But there was a quiver, however slight, in her smile.

"I'm utterly serious. She's affecting your behavior. I can see it."

"You see what you want to see, Koko."

"No. Some things cannot be doubted. For example, here I stand beside you with all Sheol watching and Talman in your dungeons, yet still I'm the Second General."

"Be patient. I'll choose a new First General soon enough."

"You're considering another?"

"I'm considering many things. I've just given you a boon, Koko, by killing these fifty-five. Should I give you another by giving you full command of the Legion? Then, who would stand in your way, should you try to usurp the throne?"

"That's not what I want," he said, and in the moment, it was true.

"Then what? What do you want?"

"What I want, Mashit, is to be your equal."

"Oh, poor Koko, my dear, have you been listening? You're not my equal. You never can be."

He inhaled sharply. He wished to grab her by the neck and choke her until blood spilled from her mouth. He wanted to knock her off the ledge and listen to her screams as she fell. But it took all his strength to remain still, the faithful general.

Down below, on the raised platform, General Ghoful was taunting the caged prisoners with a flaming sword. The weapon had been forged in the fires beneath Sheol and tempered with ancient magic, and it was said Great Abbadon himself had slain thousands with it. It could kill these middling demons with a single blow. Instead, Ghoful poked and prodded them as if they were animals, and the crowd adored it.

"If you don't consider me an equal," Kokabiel said, shaking with rage, "Then why have you asked me up here to stand beside you?"

She eyed the crowd. "Because the people need symbols. They need to believe we have things under control, that there is unity, even when chaos knocks on our door."

"Chaos that you have brought upon us, my queen."

"No," she said. "Chaos has always been here. But I am the one who will stop it."

Down below, Ghoful swiped off one of Thume's many fingers. The demon wailed, and the crowd erupted in another monstrous cheer.

Mashit raised her hands, and the crowd silenced. Ghoful turned his eyes up to her, awaiting her command. She projected her voice over the crowd again, saying, "Show no mercy upon the traitors, General Ghoful."

"NO MERCY!" the crowd shouted.

Ghoful bowed, then approached Hefachel's cage to slice off his six feet. Hefachel wept as his orange fluid poured from his ankles. Ghoful laughed as he poked out one of Hefachel's eyes.

Mashit turned to Kokabiel again. "Help me rebuild the new vats," she said to him alone. "Help me expand the city. Tell your soldiers I work for the benefit of all demonkind. Do this, and it will help me rebuild my trust in you."

It is always something, he thought, *which prevents you from fully committing to me. But in the end, nothing I do is ever enough.*

On the balcony below, three of the Pillars turned away from the bloody scene and returned to their chambers behind the curtain. But Maya remained to watch.

Hefachel's ichor flooded his cage. He spat up yellow foam. Ghoful cut him as if he were a beast for eating, but expertly, to prolong his last breaths.

Mashit turned to Kokabiel and the smile departed from her face. "I've given you a gift, Koko. I've silenced your enemies. Now, give me a gift in return. Help me make Sheol great, and I just might return to you that shining ruby pin."

Down below on the balcony, Maya was staring up at them.

CHAPTER TWENTY-FOUR

It was late afternoon, and Adar was throwing rose-colored light across the cliffs. Mashit and the Pillars walked a lofty, snaking pass through the mountains beside the city. Her Shield kept their distance, but she had ordered them to keep a close eye on the Pillars, because parts of the path were steep and treacherous. One slip and they might plunge to their deaths on the rocks below. But the views were stupendous, so it was worth the risk. From this height one could see the entire lake, the sprawling city and palace, even the Dissipation beyond. She hoped this walk would make the Pillars feel less confined, but she had a second reason for taking them this far from the palace. Every time she and Maya met eyes, her heart filled with warmth and delight. Here, they might speak alone.

Baaba and Sunil treaded carefully over the well-worn path, while Maya and Paula, perhaps more accustomed to mountain walks, walked assuredly over the uneven terrain. These branching ancient trails led to small hamlets and crumbling enclaves deep in the mountains, where some reclusive demons still lived. Why they might want to live away from food and warmth, she would never understand. As they walked, the Pillars were mostly silent, taking in the glorious views.

It had been a week since the executions, and her spies had told her that though they could find no evidence linking Kokabiel to the blasts, it was still possible he was the saboteur. If that were true, she had none left to trust. She had not chosen a new First General

227

yet, but she would have too soon. The people needed to see a show of strength.

The wind picked up as Adar touched the western peaks, and the black lake below rippled, its surface scintillating – a remarkable sight, since the lake had forever been black and reflectionless. Mashit smiled as her white robe fluttered in the wind.

After walking around a sharp outcrop of stone they finally reached their destination. A patch of young grass clung to the steep slope above them, an opulence of aqua and jade, colors new to this world. Mashit leaned over and tore a few blades from the ground. She inhaled their verdant, sage-like scent before letting them fly off in the wind. "These grasses were not here a month ago."

Thistled spikes grew among the grasses, and their peaks bloomed with mangled gray flowers. Maya reached for one when Mashit screamed, "Don't!"

Maya froze, her fingers outstretched.

"Careful!" Mashit said, striding over. "That one will bite off your finger."

Maya slowly withdrew herself. "And this is what we four have brought here? Carnivorous plants?"

"This species was here long before you arrived, but grew only in inaccessible places, rarely seen by demon eyes. Now they're as common as Earth's dandelions. But these grasses" – she gestured at the steep hill – "are quite new. Aren't they lovely? If we walk far enough today I can show you a grove of young apple trees."

"All because of us?" Sunil said.

"Yes, because of you! Do you smell that?" She inhaled deeply. "There's life in the air. Sheol has always reeked of ash and decay. Now, if you close your eyes and smell the air, this could be a spring day on Earth."

"All but for our chains," Baaba said.

"I see no chains," Mashit said.

"And if I were to walk ahead alone," said Baaba, "would you'll let me go?"

"You'll all be free to roam on your own soon enough."

"When?" Baaba said. "Fifty years?"

"When we establish mutual trust."

Baaba shook her head. "I can't listen to her bullshit any more.

I'm tired. I'd rather be locked in the palace. At least I don't have to listen to nonsense there."

Baaba was a large-bodied woman, but she bounded tirelessly on ahead, and Paula and Sunil followed close behind. But Maya remained near Mashit, taking in the mountains and sky. They walked in silence for a time, then turned a bend, and the palace spiked up from the city beneath, its claw reaching even higher than they stood. Its peak glimmered in the sun, and its base was a labyrinth of shadows. The city's titanic layers of stone encircled it, and dust clouds rose from the new construction sites. Just that morning she'd heard reports of demons taking up sculpture and painting, like the early days, when Great Abbadon's inspiration filled all hearts. She delighted at the sight now. She, Mashit alone, would fulfill the ancient promise, the dream of demons since the beginning.

"It's beautiful," Mashit said. "Isn't it?"

"Beautiful to some," said Maya. "Hideous to others."

"And what is it to you?"

"A little of both, perhaps."

Mashit nodded. "You've been quiet, Maya. Is something wrong?"

Maya laughed. "Are you serious?"

"Humans are so different from demons. I find it hard to read you."

"We're different in some ways. Same in others."

"Have I done something to offend you? Hurt you?"

"I'm your prisoner, Mashit. Are you really so naive?"

"When I last saw you, you mouthed a word to me. 'Alone.' Well, here we are."

"Alone, yes. With all your soldiers, and the three other Lamed Vav."

"Who are out of earshot. It's just you and me now. So what do you want to tell me?"

"That day you came to visit us, you revealed a hidden part to us. A vulnerable part. And I wanted to help you. But now, after what I saw the other day, I don't know."

"Are you referring to the executions?"

"Among other things."

"I saw you," Mashit said. "You remained on the balcony. You

watched."

"I wanted to see what you were capable of."

"And now that you've seen, do you loathe me?"

"Does it matter what I think?"

"To me, yes, it does. Very much."

"Then I pity you. All of you."

"Pity?"

"Yes."

"We don't need your pity, Maya. I don't need your pity."

"But you do, and you most of all. You are blind, stumbling in the dark, thrashing at whatever stands in your way, while ignoring the teacher who offers her hand to bring you into the light. Over and over you refuse her aid!"

"And you are this teacher."

"I could be, if you'd allow me."

Adar dropped behind the mountain, but the larger and dimmer Ora sent a cascade of orange beams down the cliffs. The air still held on to the heat of the day, but when Ora set, the night would become frigid and unforgiving. But there was still a little bit of time.

"I've lived for millennia," Mashit said. "You're but a few decades old. What could you possibly teach me that I don't already know?"

"Compassion," Maya said. "Empathy. Most of all, mercy."

"Why are you so obsessed with mercy? You speak as if it's the solution to all problems! How does mercy defeat our many enemies? How does mercy lift us up from the ashes? Even the one whom humans call the Creator showed us no mercy. She smashed our world and countless others because, in her deluded eyes, we were all flawed."

"A great injustice."

"Do you really believe that?"

"I do. You and your people were never given a chance."

"Yes!" Mashit said, nodding. "So you do see. And therefore you understand that the choices we make, which seem vile to you, are the only ones that make sense for us. The alternative is annihilation."

"Before, perhaps," Maya said. "But now we're here, the Pillars. Things are changing." Slowly, she reached over and plucked a blade of grass from Mashit's cheek. Mashit surprised herself that she didn't flinch, that she did not wince or turn away. Maya lifted her palm and blew, and the blade floated off in the wind. "New life grows on Sheol."

Mashit shivered, and then sighed, and wondered if Maya could be right. Was there room in her heart for mercy?

Maya stared at the second setting sun. "They might kill themselves."

It took Mashit a moment to process her words. "What? Who?"

"The others. Sunil suggested it after the executions. He said that our deaths might be the best way to stop you."

"When? How?" She glanced ahead. The three Pillars walked perilously close to the cliff's edge.

"It was just talk, I think. I'm not sure if they have the heart to go through with it."

"And you?"

"Suicide is a grave sin. This human life is a precious gift."

"Yes," Mashit nodded, shivering. She'd never considered this possibility. She would post guards around the Pillars day and night, and she'd have their chambers checked for anything that might be used for self harm. "Maya, thank you for telling me."

"I've seen enough death," Maya said. "I can't fathom any more."

"They mustn't die," Mashit said. "This world has only just begun to grow."

"I know. I know." She turned her face into the breeze. "It feels good to stretch my legs, to breathe in the fresh air. These mountains remind me of the Himalayas. Have you ever been?"

"No," she said. "I haven't. Tell me about it."

"There are monasteries so high in the cliffs that only experienced monks can go because the air is so thin. It's so quiet you can hear your own heartbeat, or the sound of snow falling on a mountain a dozen miles away. I miss it. I miss my people." She looked at Mashit, and water glistened in her sun-flecked eyes. Mashit met her gaze only for a moment before she had to look away.

The air had already grown a chill. They would need to return soon. The other Pillars had become tiny specks surrounded by soldiers as they walked down the winding switchbacks to the city. Ora touched the cliffs across the lake, and a brisk wind swirled down the slopes, carrying new and strange smells.

"I'm sorry," Mashit said. "For everything. I truly am."

"I know," said Maya. Then, to Mashit's immense surprise, she took her hand. "I know." Her hand was warm, and it was welcome, and Mashit sighed. And as they walked down the mountain together Mashit held on as if Maya's hand were the last fragment of life in all the myriad worlds. Perhaps it was.

CHAPTER TWENTY-FIVE

THE LINE OF FANS WAITING FOR CARINA'S SIGNATURE SEEMED to stretch all the way back to Sheol and beyond. The queue began at Daphna's small table inside Berlin's bright and opulent Galeries Lafayette department store, then snaked out one of the large exits, turned right, and wound past several vine-choked windows. Frix had estimated there were six hundred fans waiting along Friedrichstraße and Französische Straße. The polizei had said the queue was disrupting traffic and they would prevent it from growing any longer, which was not good, since some fans had come from as far as Hungary, and there were fights when people were turned away.

Daphna's hand began to cramp from signing, and the acrid smell of marker pens was giving her a headache. Still, she smiled and shook hands and hugged quivering young fans, some of whom had waited twelve hours just for this ten-second encounter. How could she refuse them?

A young woman stepped up to Daphna and in brisk German said, "Krisztina! With a zed!" Her hand shook as she handed over a post-it note with her name written on it. Her eyes sparkled behind gold-rimmed glasses, and a large gold watch flashed on her wrist. Both Moda by Carina. Daphna smiled and signed her headshot in German, "To Krisztina, stay golden! XOXO, Carina." Krisztina took the paper with both hands, as if afraid it might vanish, staring at it, tears streaming down her face, as Duile shoved her toward the exit. Hundreds more waited their turn.

Stuffed into the Moda by Carina purse hanging on Daphna's chair was a folded copy of the *Berliner Zeitung*, which had published a review of her film, *The Carina Story*, that morning. She had read the review a dozen times, its words echoing in her mind as she signed her photo in a Dutch tabloid for a young man.

"Produced on a rush schedule that baffles the mind, *The Carina Story* is a rags to riches tale we've seen a thousand times before. It's a formulaic hodgepodge, full of trite plots and clichéd lines. Still, the film had enough visual beauty to make it morbidly entertaining. I found myself awed more by the obscure camera angles and curious lighting choices than the story itself. And more than once I lost the narrative thread and drifted into a kind of waking dream, imagining myself inhabiting the film's luscious sets. When the dialog grew laughable – which was often – I sat back to enjoy the view. Forget the plot: if you see this movie, go for the color and the light."

Not quite heaping praise, but the reviewer had clearly been affected by the magic. The results were similar around the world: critics generally panned the film, yet despite this people were seeing it in droves. In fact, *The Carina Story* was the highest grossing film of the week, and it was on course, if the numbers held, to be the highest grossing film of the year. Mostly teens and twenty-somethings were seeing the film. But it was a bell curve, and one Swiss news site reported a group of elderly alphorn musicians had sold out their local theater for four straight days. Frix said that, considering they had shot, edited, and distributed the film in just a few weeks, this was utterly spectacular.

A young woman with bright blue eyes and amber hair said in German "You're so talented!" A Moda by Carina belt at her waist reflected the department store lights. "You're my role model."

"Aw," Daphna said. "That's so sweet." Her hand moved automatically as she signed a headshot. Almost everyone waiting wore Moda by Carina. And though her accessory line was not expensive – it was designed to be affordable – it was clear there were fans of lesser means among them: those who had tried but not quite succeeded in making themselves appear affluent. Perhaps, she thought, the money they'd used for Moda by Carina might best be spent on more important things, like food, rent, and health.

Most of them looked frazzled, overworked, worn out. She'd seen this look before in a thousand demons throughout Sheol. But to see it here, on human faces? It made no sense! They had so much more on Earth than she had ever had. How could it be that they suffered too? They stared at her, desperate, as if she would fill the gaping hole in their lives.

But I can't save you, she thought. *I'm only giving you another dream.*

She had hoped to bask in their adoration. But they didn't love *her.* They loved "Carina," an idol crafted by her mother. And their love was fickle. That morning a fan on Twitter had noticed that a young Turkish performer named Yasmeen had an act almost identical to Carina's, and some were commenting that Yasmeen's was actually the better performer. Of course, an argument erupted; it was the Internet after all.

Yasmeen's video was sung in Turkish, with English subtitles, and she bounced around a flashing set in a clear rip-off of Carina's act, even down to the angle of the lights. Yasmeen was similarly bedecked in gold and joined by two dancers, who hopped and twirled in golden outfits beside her. And Daphna knew her. She recognized the pale face, her round cheeks, and bright blue eyes. Her name wasn't Yasmeen. This was Neta, her sister. Mother, it seemed, had sent another.

A sudden crash startled her, and Daphna looked up. At the exit where the people queued out the door, a tall window had just shattered, and the sound was echoing through the vaulted department store. Scared shoppers and employees turned to look, and Daphna looked too. A thick vine growing from a giant pot outside was still leaning store-ward as it had before. But where there had just been a window, now there was only air. Glass shards lay scattered everywhere, inside and out, and cool air tumbled into the store. A security guard ran over, shouting into a radio.

She didn't like this. Her heart pounded as she prepared a powerful protection spell and reached for a charmed knife that she kept in the rear of her belt, just in case Duile and Khein were actually plotting to kill her. Her fans were staring at her, and it was only as she stared back into their eager eyes that she realized that none had turned. Every last one had kept their eyes fixed on her, as if they hadn't heard a crash at all.

Frix, Duile, and Khein ran up to her, and she stood. "What's going on?"

"It seems," Duile said, "that the vine was growing against the window and the pressure shattered it." A polizei and two security guards were putting caution tape around the scene.

"The *vine* broke the window?" Daphna said, and she remembered what Richard had said in Rio about the wild plants. She felt suddenly sick and dizzy. Perhaps she had stood up too fast. Perhaps she had inhaled too much marker. Perhaps she missed Richard. She put her hands on the table to steady herself, when the world went black.

She reached for her chair, but there was no chair. She no longer had hands to grasp with. She was adrift in a black and silent and frigid space. She would have screamed, but she had no mouth.

"Save your energy," said a thunderous voice, and the universe shook with it. "You'll need it." When she'd calmed enough to make sense of the words, she recognized the voice.

A pressure lifted, and she could speak. "Who are you?" Her voice came from a tiny point, spreading out into the black infinity.

"We met in Caracas," he said, and the universe shook again.

"Daniel," she said, gasping. The air, if it were real air, was cold and stale.

"Hello again," he said.

"Where am I?"

"An empty universe. I could trap you in here forever. It would take you eons to die."

"You don't scare me," she lied. "What do you want, Daniel?"

"You know what I want."

"Passage to Sheol?"

"That's right."

"I told you, travel's not my department."

"But you know who might get me there."

"Maybe. And what will you do once you're there?"

"Right a great wrong. Now, tell me how to get to Sheol, and I'll release you. If not, I'll leave you here to rot for an eternity."

The thought filled her with such fear that it took her a moment to speak. "You were once a Pillar, and now you use black magic?

You've fallen far, Daniel."

"And I'm willing to fall much further. Will you help me, or not?"

"Yes," she said. "This would be an awful place to retire. There are no books. Please, Daniel, get me out of here."

"First, tell me some things. I've traced your Moda by Carina line to a manufacturing plant in China. What exactly happens there? What are you doing to the accessories?"

"I really don't know."

"Eternity is a long time, Daphna."

"It's the truth, Daniel! I've no idea how the accessories are made. I never been privy to that part. Mashit doesn't seem to think I'm trustworthy enough."

"But you must know they are charmed, right? What they do to people? I bought one of your rings the other day."

"Did you, now."

"I put it on and then I watched one of your videos. After, I felt so drained. I couldn't think straight. I had trouble remembering things for the rest of that day. The accessories and the music are synergistic, weakening people as part of a larger plan to gain control of Earth's people, right?"

"You have quite a vivid imagination, Daniel!"

"And this film, *The Carina Story*. I haven't seen it, and I don't plan to. But the people coming out of the theaters look like fucking zombies."

"What's a 'zombie?'"

"Enough with the games, Daphna! I swear I'll trap you here if you–"

The void vanished. She was back in Galeries Lafayette, in her body again. Dizzy, she blinked. And then – *flash!* – she was back in the void.

"Fuck!" Daniel shouted, and the universe thundered. "No!"

She flashed, back and forth, into and out of that empty hell, and Daniel's voice stuttered and stretched across time. Then, all at once, the thunder stopped. She was seated in the department store, before hundreds of eager fans.

"Are you all right, Carina?" Duile said. He offered her a bottle of water. She snatched it and drank half the bottle, shivering, and waited for Daniel to thrust her back into that frigid hell. But she remained whole.

Duile stared at her, his pallid skin bright in the store's gleaming lights.

"Duile, just now, I was..."

"Yes?" he said, and there was something sinister in his gaze, as if he were happy she'd fallen ill.

"I...I just fainted," she said. "I haven't eaten all day. Get me some Skittles and some coffee, would you please?"

"Are you sure you're all right?" Frix said. A cleaning crew had just arrived to sweep up the shattered glass.

"I'm fine," Daphna said, to the thousand golden reflections before her. "I can't disappoint my fans. They've come from all over the world to see me." She reached over and took up her marker, and a huge cheer arose in the crowd.

Duile was still staring at her.

CHAPTER TWENTY-SIX

Gram's bedroom air conditioner didn't work and maybe hadn't for years, but she had never mentioned it. Sweat dripped from Daniel's nose onto the linoleum floor, onto the four Hebrew letters of the Tetragrammaton written in calf's blood. But blood – *treyf*, forbidden in kosher foods – was the only way to open the doors of darkness.

Bouncing from one butcher shop to another, Daniel had felt a strange mixture of shame and surrealism as he sought a whole calf. He had drained it in the yard and carried the blood inside a bull-leather pouch hand-stitched with human hair into *her* house – Gram, the woman who had proudly been kosher her whole life. But he could think of no place better to perform the spell.

In oddly grammatical constructions of twelfth-century Yiddish and ancient Aramaic the *Roots of Names* declared that the spell had to be cast in a place of frequent peace. The living room was carpeted and so were the bedrooms, so the kitchen was the only place. Plus, the linoleum floor would make for easy cleanup.

And the seal was this: a Star of David surrounded the Tetragrammaton. Written around this were names of archangels, which were further surrounded by names of demons and lower angels. This within a seven-pointed star, on which was written more demonic names and alchemical symbols, all within another circle. Around this were ancient signs of the zodiac matching tonight's stars. And around this, seventy-two Hebrew letters spelling out one of the Divine Names of God. All of it written in blood.

Ash from a rooster he had cooked first in the oven and then charred on the grill marked the sign in twenty-five places. It was well after midnight, the kitchen shades were drawn, and a thick black candle, its flame steady, burned above a Hebrew name written in blood – דפנאי – Daphna.

And he had summoned and trapped her. The spell had worked. For a time.

"Fuck!" he screamed. He slammed his fist upon the seal, splattering blood. He'd been so close. Just as the book had promised, he'd captured Daphna in the void. What the book hinted at but never openly said, what he should have remembered from Marul Menacha on Gehinnom, was that a spell's power came not only from the ritual items but the spellcaster himself. No doubt this was the author's way of weeding out the weak. He was spent, as if he had been without sleep for three straight days. The book warned that those who toyed with the black arts risked life and sanity. But he had not expected to be stymied so soon. He wanted to try again, but he was so weak that if he tried, it might kill him. He reached for his pocket, for a cigarette, only to remember he had left them on the kitchen table. It was just a few feet from him, but the table seemed miles away.

He collapsed and rolled onto his back, smearing the sign. The calf's blood seeped into his shirt. He stared up at the ceiling. Dozens of dead insects lay inside the frosted glass of the light. Gram, so fastidious, had eaten in this room ten thousand times. Had she not seen this abomination above her? But then, as the insects shifted, he knew. These bugs had only just arrived, called forth from his dark spell only to leap for the light and die.

What the hell had he just done? This was Gram's house! Daphna was right. He had fallen far.

God, he missed Gram so much. The pain was less acute than it had been when his parents had died. It was as if, without her, he had lost a limb while on a high mountain, with many cliffs yet to climb. Gram had always been his guide, even when he was across the world. Without her, he was lost.

Maureen, his old colleague Christopher, and a few distant cousins had attended Gram's funeral. And he'd stood graveside covered under gloves, sunglasses, and a hood even though it was a beautiful spring afternoon. The rabbi had asked him to speak.

"Everyone knows she saved my life," he said, "and paid a heavy price because of it. But not everyone knows she saved my life a thousand other times too. I can't believe she's gone. I'll miss her very, very much."

He shoveled a scoop of dirt onto her pine box coffin, and relatives he barely knew hugged him, shook his hand, patted his shoulder. Christopher said, "Hey Danny, I'm so, so sorry 'bout Eve. She was a real firecracker. Huge heart. One of a kind." They hugged.

It hurt so much to see his old friend and colleague, his former best man. He knew Christopher had a lot of questions, but was too much of a gentleman to ask. And so they departed, with Daniel promising to call even though he knew he never would. Everyone got back in their cars to carry on with their lives. The rabbi asked him if he would be sitting shiva, but Daniel declined.

The rabbi might have sighed in relief. Daniel knew he was a strange sight, wrapped up like a mummy, while the sun was bright and warm.

Daniel awoke from the memory on the floor of Gram's kitchen, his clothes and skin smeared in blood. He'd been sleeping. With great effort he rose, found his cigarettes, and went out to the backyard, leaving the kitchen door open. The sun had just set – damn, he had slept through the whole day! – and the sky was an orange ribbon fading to black. He sat on a rusted lawn chair, smoking and listening to the wind rustle through the densely leaved trees, as if the world was trying to tell him something he couldn't yet hear.

The phone rang inside the house, startling him. The phone might not have rung since Gram died. But he was too tired to get up, so he let it ring. On the fourth ring, something clicked, and he heard the voice he thought he'd never hear again.

"Hi! You've reached Eve." He sat up. "I'm likely out, dancing, frolicking, and painting the town red. Or probably just taking a nap. Are you jealous? At the beep, tell me all your troubles, nu?"

Gram.

A long beep, as the old answering-machine tape forwarded to the proper spot. Then, another short beep, and a different voice. "I'm in Beijing on Wednesday."

Daniel stood. It was Daphna's voice.

"There'll be a message waiting for you at the Fairmont Hotel. Let's chat, Danny. I think you and I can help each other."

The phone clicked. He shuddered. How had Daphna gotten Gram's number? How did she know he was here? Perhaps he should have paid more attention to all those stories of demon summonings gone wrong. *Beijing*? Her invitation was almost certainly a trap to lure him out and kill him. But as he picked the dried blood from under his long fingernails he knew he would go anyway.

CHAPTER TWENTY-SEVEN

KOKABIEL HEARD THE MOB LONG BEFORE HE SAW THEM. He and Ieropel rushed along Abbadon's crooked lanes, shadowed tunnels, and crumbling bridges, following the rising medley of voices. They climbed a steep and staggered lane and turned abruptly left. And here, beyond a low wall, the city spread beneath them. The chants and screams echoed from low-slung roofs, arching overpasses, and countless crooked folds of stone.

In a panoply of voices they shouted, "Better life for all! Better life now!" It was more cacophony than chorus, and their chants were growing louder.

"Their leader's name is Evora," said Ieropel, at Kokabiel's side. Though the twin suns had just risen, spilling wine-colored light over the buildings, most of the city lay in shadow. "Evora has been distributing treasonous material in the slums." Ieropel extended one of her crystal limbs, and a translucent projection of Evora's likeness appeared above it: Evora was an amorphous leathery black mass of mouths. Many smaller mouths, separate from her main body, clung to her glistening skin.

"I know her," Kokabiel said.

"You *know* her, sir?"

"I encountered her in the slums." On his way to visit Gedeon, she was one of the demon's he had lectured. "I thought she was just another slum dweller, mired in self-pity and learned helplessness. I clearly have misjudged her."

"It seems we've misjudged many," Ieropel said. "She has several hundred followers in the slums and the numbers are growing. We have to stop this."

The shouting crowd marched passed a row of squat homes. In little pots resting on windowsills, seedlings stretched their tiny green limbs toward the suns. Life, sprouting, here. He shook his head. Seedlings? This was not the Sheol he knew.

"Better life for all! Better life now!" they shouted.

"'Better life?'" Kokabiel said. "Can they be more vague? I want a better life too!"

"They seek better housing," said Ieropel, handing him a leaflet with their demands.

"'A right of trial by jury, if accused of crime,'" Kokabiel read. "'Healthcare for the sick.' Are they fucking serious?"

"If they become sick," Ieropel said, "instead of being tossed into the fires under the city, they want the palace sorcerers to heal them of their ailments."

Kokabiel grimaced and crushed the leaflet in his hands. "It's that human witch, Maya," he said. "Her toxin has spread into the blood of this city."

"And throughout Sheol and the Shards," Ieropel said. The throng turned a corner, passed behind a low-slung roof and out of sight. But their voices were growing ever louder. And though he and Ieropel stood many stories above the march, the street still shook from their footsteps.

"They're headed to the palace?" Kokabiel said.

"Yes," said Ieropel. "They plan a *sit in*."

"A what?"

"A human tactic. They will sit on the palace steps until their demands are met."

Kokabiel grimaced. "Do they forget where they are? Whose door it is that they knock upon? Do they think this is Earth, and we its feeble governments?"

"I admit, General, I'm baffled too. What shall we do?"

"Let them reach the palace steps."

"Sir?"

"The queen says the people need signs and symbols. Let us give them one. Let them sit and grow comfortable. And when they feel most confident, we'll rout them all. We'll close off all exits and destroy every soul. No prisoners, do you understand? And I want their bodies left in the streets. We'll leave them to rot until the gloom vultures descend. This will be *our* symbol. For this is what happens if you defy the throne."

"Yes, sir," Ieropel said, nodding, and her crystalline expression gave the hint of a smile. "An excellent plan. I shall take much joy in slaughtering them myself."

"Better life for all! Better life now!" they shouted.

Kokabiel and Ieropel followed the mob, keeping a comfortable distance. Ieropel called up a flying green worm, whispered orders to it, and the worm buzzed off to relay the message to the soldiers waiting throughout the city. With each chant from the crowd, Kokabiel felt his frustration grow. "They must know that we will kill them for this," he said. "And still they go marching to their deaths? I don't get it."

"It is a *unique* suicide, I'll give them that," Ieropel said.

"Make sure to wait for my word."

Ieropel eyed him curiously. "Yes, sir."

The marchers reached the giant palace steps, its marbled-granite tiers rising up to the iron gates. The palace guards stood at attention, but Kokabiel's orders had already reached them: their weapons were not drawn. The chanting slowed and stopped, and the protestors murmured nervously amongst themselves.

Kokabiel and Ieropel waited on a street that sloped down into the courtyard facing the palace. The protestors hesitated, too timid to climb, but Evora departed from the throng and defiantly climbed half the steps herself. The palace guards stiffened but did not draw their weapons. Evora's many mouths quivered, and her glistening black body turned brown in the morning suns.

"Sit, my friends!" she shouted from one of her mouths, and as she spoke several of the baby mouths, clinging to her breast, shifted positions. "Sit!"

Slowly, the protestors took their seats upon the palace stair and turned their eyes up to her. "My friends," Evora said. "We gather here not to destroy, but to lift! To demand a better life for ourselves and our fellow demons. Those in this palace above us eat feasts every night. Half their food gets discarded, uneaten, while nightly our lot scours the midden heaps for remnant scraps. We huddle around flickering fires to keep warm against the frigid nights, while they sleep in hearth-warmed beds. We when grow sick and old, they toss us into the fires. But those in the palace have sorcerers to heal their scratches! Queen Mashit, we do not ask for much, only that you share your wealth with us, the wretched of Sheol, especially now that this world is growing more abundant. The palace can spare a small amount for their brothers and sisters. Or are you, our queen, no better than the Creator, who cast us all into the Abyss and forced to live on scraps falling from above? We can do better. We will do better. This is just the beginning."

They truly hate her, Kokabiel thought. *In this we are kin, at least.*

"Such drivel," Ieropel spat.

"Yes," Kokabiel said. "Drivel."

"She won't shut up. Are *all* her mouths talking?"

"Only the largest," Kokabiel said. "The twelve other mouths are her children, suckling upon her breast."

"And if she thinks that will stop us from killing her, then she is twelve-times a fool. Well, they're upon the steps. Your orders, General? "

He stared at Evora, hesitating. "Not until I give my word." Because the truth was, in all his long military history, he had never killed an unarmed demon, nor a mother and her children. He might arrest them, or kill only a few and lock up the others. Or he could make Evora a martyr. None of these would be good for the queen.

"As we wait," Ieropel said, "Evora speaks more drivel. They have to die, General. All of them. You have to send a message that such actions will not be tolerated. You must be merciless with them."

"Yes, Ieropel," he said. "I know."

"So why do you wait? Show them our power. Show them *your* power. Or are you weak, like General Talman?"

"No!" he growled. "I'm nothing like that coward. Do it, Ieropel. Send them in. Kill them. Kill them all."

Ieropel nodded. "With pleasure, sir." She lifted one of her crystal limbs into the sunlight, and within her translucent flesh angles changed, refracting the light into crimson rainbows that flashed at precise angles into the courtyard. More lieutenant generals waited in the shadows and, seeing the bright flash, marched out toward the mob.

The protestors rose from their seats, alarmed.

"Stay seated!" Evora shouted. "Don't let them scare you! We are stronger together!"

But some got spooked and tried to run. They were slaughtered first. Spells tore them apart and their guts spilled into the courtyard. The others panicked. They tried to run, but General Ieropel charged them, slicing a dozen in half with her crystalline limbs in her first strike alone. Some protestors defended themselves with spells or weapons. But they fought the Legion of the First. There was no hope for any of them. Hundreds screamed and fell, and their ichor dribbled down the steps.

Evora ran up to the top the steps, but the gates were closed and four guards blocked her path. She could go no further. Rahab the sea dragon crawled up toward her. "Please," Evora said. "Spare my children. They have committed no crime against you."

Kokabiel thought, *Yes, we will spare them at least*, and was about to give the order when Rahab belched a column of fire. All of Evora's mouths screamed horribly for many excruciating seconds. Rahab burned Evora until all that was left was a pile of ash. The gloom vultures already circled above, and the walking fish from the lake were already creeping toward the remains.

Just like that, all the protestors were dead. The wind gusted, and Evora's ash blew into Kokabiel's face, his eyes, his mouth. His purging of the slums had once brought him such joy. But this? There was no thrill of victory against this defenseless foe. He felt sickened and hollow. He looked up at the palace, but his eyes were cloudy with ash.

"Great Abbadon," he said. "What have I done?"

CHAPTER
TWENTY-EIGHT

PLASTIC NO-SMOKING SIGNS WERE CROOKEDLY POSTED ON THE greasy walls beside each table, but that didn't stop the patrons from lighting up. Daphna sat in the rear of the narrow restaurant puffing on a hand-rolled cigarette under a crude oil painting of Beijing at night. An untouched plate of dumplings sat before her, already cold. The grizzled patrons had given her furtive glances before returning to their newspapers or the TV mounted near the ceiling, which was droning the late-night news in Mandarin. She feared at any moment one of them would look at her and shout, "It's Carina! The pop-star!" So she kept her head down and smoked and waited.

Daniel would come. He had to.

All it took was a smile at the hotel concierge for him to divulge his deepest secrets, like the location of this speakeasy, accessible only through a hard-to-find Beijing alleyway that stank of fish and garbage. Here, restaurant workers came to smoke, drink, and relax after late-night shifts, which, thanks to bribes, remained out of the watchful gaze of the government's anti-smoking squads. None here desired attention. They kept to themselves. But still, she kept a low profile.

Earlier that evening, in the hotel suite with Duile, Frix, and Khein, she played an old demon game of dice and got them drunk on a bottle of 18-year-old Macallan, spiking their glasses with an ancient spell her childhood warden had taught her to help her with her insomnia. They'd drift off for a pleasant eight-hours and feel great in the morning.

She left their snoring bodies, washed off her makeup, ruffled her hair, then donned a gray sweatshirt, cotton hat, cheap sunglasses, torn jeans, and black sneakers. Thus disguised, she snuck out of the hotel. On the street, no one paid her much mind. She knew enough Chinese to make it to this little place without fanfare. Now, she waited.

She smoked and waited more. An hour passed and another neared its end. Perhaps he'd never come. It started to rain, and she sighed. The water pattered against the cobblestones outside and splattered in through the door. A cool breeze blew around her ankles, and the cigarette smoke swirled in pirouettes.

She reloaded Yasmeen's Twitter feed on her phone. In the last hour, her sister had acquired a hundred and twenty seven new followers. At this rate, Yasmeen would surpass her numbers by the end of the month.

Yasmeen – Neta – had no natural artistic talent. She had once taken up painting, but an infant vomiting across a canvas could make better art than Neta ever had. Out of deference, the servants had hung Neta's pieces throughout the palace, and the first time Daphna had seen one, she thought someone had defaced it.

Has Mother lost faith in me? she thought. *Or is she hedging her bets? But I am the best artist among all my siblings. I always have been! Mother knows this. This is why she sent me here!* No other reason made sense. It couldn't be, for example, that she was just another one of Mashit's tools. No, Mashit knew Daphna was special. Unique. Didn't she?

A knot formed in her belly as she worried over these thoughts. She stamped her cigarette firmly into a napkin, until the paper caught fire. The weary-eyed waitress scowled as Daphna dropped the burning napkin into the ashtray. The flames leaped from it and the smoke was thick. It burned and became ash.

She looked up. A silhouetted figure stood outside the door, just beyond the reach of the neon light. Like her, he wore a hood over his head. She stared into the blackness of his face and wondered if she had made a mistake inviting him. He kept exceeding her expectations, and sometimes it was best to let angry dogs lie. She shuddered as the hooded figure stepped into the light.

He was soaked and dripping, gaunt, with dark circles under

his eyes and skin as pallid as the fluorescent lights. Daniel Fisher paused at the entrance. Hands at his sides, he squeezed them into fists. He threw back his hood and the other patrons took him in. The whole place seemed to hold its collective breath. They didn't have to be demons or sorcerers to sense his otherness. Daniel looked around at the glass-enclosed food case, the patrons, the cheap art on the walls, the narrow corridor leading to the bathroom, ready to leap away at any moment.

"Are you going to sit," she said in Mandarin, "or just stand there dripping water all over the floor?" With her foot she pushed out a chair.

He slowly walked over, and the patrons went back to their newspapers and TV. He looked frail, but she knew not to underestimate him after Caracas. He took the offered chair, this creature not quite demon, not quite human, not quite Pillar. An unknown, and unknowns were dangerous. The waitress came over, scowling intensely.

"Drink?" the woman said, a nub of a pencil in her hand and a cigarette dangling from her lips.

"Coffee, black." Daniel replied.

"They have tea and dumplings," Daphna said.

"I'll have water then."

Daphna gestured at his soaked clothes. "Haven't you had enough water?"

"You must buy something," the waitress said.

"He'll have tea," said Daphna. "On me."

"How generous of you," he said.

"Something wrong with the dumplings?" the waitress said, pointing to Daphna's uneaten plate.

"They're perfect," Daphna said. "I was waiting to share."

The waitress frowned, walked away, and came back a minute later with a small pot of tea and a porcelain cup. She dropped them on the table with a thump, before wandering back to her place behind the counter. Daphna stared at Daniel, and he stared back.

She rolled another cigarette. She was reaching for her matches, when he said, "Please, allow me." Then he whispered fire into the air. The tip of her cigarette glowed cherry red. She froze for a moment, then inhaled deeply and leaned back. She would not be intimidated by this dog-man. He had no idea what *she* was capable of. She smiled. "I was about to go back to my hotel. I wasn't sure you got my message."

"I took a red-eye to San Francisco," he said. "Then stowed away on a cargo plane to Hong Kong, and then spent a miserable day on a train to Beijing. I came straight here. I haven't eaten or slept since I left." From within the plastic of an orange Chunghwa cigarette pack he removed a folded slip of paper with Daphna's handwritten instructions on where to find this restaurant among the folds of Beijing's twisted streets. "It took me an hour to find this alley," he said. "It has no sign."

"This is where people come to not be found."

"And yet we've found each other." Water dripped from his face and he shivered.

"You're cold. Have some tea." She pushed the pot towards him.

He stared at the cup, then back up at her.

"Not thirsty?"

"Not for that, no."

She smiled. "Give me a break, Daniel. Do you think I called you across the world just so I could slip you a mickey?"

He tilted his head. "'Slip me a mickey?'"

"It means spike your drink."

"I know what it means. I just haven't heard it used in real life."

"It's something I wanted to say ever since I've read it in a book."

"Why are we here, Daphna?"

She took a drag. "My mother," she said, exhaling toward the ceiling.

"What about her?"

"Are you still in love with her?"

"That's not the question I was expecting."

"You nearly married her."

"I almost married a lie."

"So you don't love her?"

"Are we here to talk about my feelings?"

"Yes, Daniel. I need to know your loyalties."

He blinked at her. "I loved a fantasy. Its name was Rebekah." She watched the waves of emotion flicker over his otherwise stoic facade. "I don't love her, no. Your mother murdered thousands and nearly killed everyone on Earth and countless other Shards. I watched people die because of her. No, I could never love that."

"You're a good liar, Daniel. But your emotions radiate from you like heat. When you speak of her, your body language changes. It's obvious you still love her."

"No. That's just the afterglow from your doting fans. I don't – I cannot love her."

"Deep down, your heart still beats for what you had. You may not like what she truly is, yet you cannot help but love what she might have been. This gives you no end of torment. We have that in common."

"We have nothing in common."

"But we do. I love what my mother might have been. Not what she is."

"What the fuck do you want, Daphna?"

"To tear her from her lofty perch and humiliate her before all."

He squinted at her. "Why? What terrible thing has she done to you?"

"Like you, I've been used."

He laughed, and it was a deep and gravely. All the patrons turned, and in this moment, Daniel seemed more sinister than she had ever seen. "Oh, poor Daphna," he said. "She's had her feelings hurt."

She frowned as she took another drag. "I know why you want to get to Sheol, Daniel. You want to bring the Pillars back home. I'll help you."

His smiled faded. "And why should I trust you?"

"Because we are here, and you aren't dead."

"Maybe you want to hand me over to your mother."

She leaned back and looked him up and down. "You're clever, but no. That's not what I want. You're right about the gold, the film, my music. There's magic in them all. They drain human power and transmit it across the Great Deep to Sheol, where it's stored in vats and used for all sorts of little miracles, but mostly to help Sheol grow.

"But things aren't progressing as fast as Mother had hoped. So she thinks that if she brings more humans to Sheol, she can absorb their power more efficiently. And it just so happens that my fans will do anything I ask. Anything. You see, I've done all of the work for her, and she reaps all the benefits."

He stared at her. "You're going to send *your fans* to Sheol?"

She nodded. "At my concert in Singapore, sorcerers will open a portal on stage using the people as, well, batteries. They'll transport the entire audience to Sheol."

"That's insane."

"That's my mother."

"And you want to stop them?"

"No, I want you to go with them."

He blinked twice, then turned his head. "I don't understand what you get from this."

"Freedom. Mother has too much power over me. I want to sever her yoke and cut myself free from her."

"And your fans? Do you care that they'll be sent to – to hell?"

"Only a small fraction of them. And, besides, they don't love me. They love a ghost. I haven't written any of my music, Daniel."

"You'd sacrifice all these people for your own freedom?"

"Yes, just as you will sacrifice them to save the four Pillars."

"You don't know that."

"Yes, Daniel, I do. It's this, or nothing."

He stared at her for a long moment. Then he reached down, poured himself some tea, and drank it in one gulp. "And when I get to Sheol, I'll be a slave, just like them."

"Daniel, did you ever ask yourself why, even though you've worn my golden accessories, watched my videos, and listened to my music – why you're not fawning at my feet like all my other fans? It's because you're part Mikulal, a Cursed One. You are made of different stuff. You can't be fully my slave because a part of you belongs to another master."

"Azazel," Daniel said.

"And his brother Ashmedai, in his stead."

On the flickering TV was a news report of a forest, burning.

CHAPTER TWENTY-NINE

ON ABBADON'S STREETS, ONE MIGHT BE FOOLED BY A FEW seedlings into believing Mashit's promises, but down here in the sewers, the world reeked as foul as ever. And to Kokabiel, this was a comfort. Change had not reached Sheol's foundations, yet.

He weaved a twisting course through the sewers, following a map he had committed to memory. The parchment had been delivered to his bedroom window by a gloom vulture, which had turned to ash the moment Kokabiel untied the parchment from its leg. The cursive Demonsbreath script was written in a cypher, and it was only after Kokabiel spoke the right words did the letters swim to their rightful places. The letter read:

"My lord, at last, I have the news you seek. But the knowledge is too complex to outline in this brief letter. Let's meet, but not in the slums. Your killing of those protestors has done more harm than good. (And really, was it necessary to kill the children?) The slum-dwellers have banded together, fearing retribution for Evora's march. They've built encampments among the ruins and have been attacking anyone smelling of palace comforts who ventures too close. I'm surprised at how strong they've become, now that they've joined forces. Even I, Master of Sewers, reeking of dung, cannot safely walk there. I've already lost several workers who've taken shortcuts through the slums. I know it's risky, but let's meet under the palace, in the sewers. I have drawn a map for you on the opposite side of this letter. Memorize it, then meet me there in the hour before dawn. This note will turn to ash the moment it leaves your hands. –Your Librarian"

And now as Kokabiel walked toward the sewers deep below the palace, his heart beat ever faster. He'd soon find how to kill Mashit. The throne would soon be his. His nose told him he was close. There were no lights to guide his path, and only by the green flame he cast above his palm could see.

With the reek of shit came other smells – dust and newly hewn stone. He entered a large cavern, and the light from his palm was unable to touch the most distant corners. Four streams spilled down a sloping wall to splash thunderously into a great pool, which drained through a gated flue into many smaller channels, newly cut, that vanished into darkness. The sheer volume of liquid had always baffled him, and he had begun to think of these rivers not as flows of demon excrement but as the blood and viscera of Sheol itself. And – he wasn't sure if he imagined it – but the waters seemed a little clearer today.

"Impressive, my lord, isn't it?" Gedeon said, beside Kokabiel as if he'd been there all along. The crocodile-faced demon flared his huge nostrils.

"No one appreciates shit like you, Gedeon," he said over the noise of the waters.

"You should see what we've done in the Dissipation, my lord. The queen had us build a veritable labyrinth of sewers."

"Such is the outcome of her rule."

Gedeon inspected the pin on Kokabiel's breast. "Still only Second General, my lord? Talman's in the dungeons. Who leads Sheol's armies?"

"I do."

"Then why aren't you wearing the First General's pin?"

He grit his teeth. "A pin is a trinket. True command is the measure of how much power one wields. For all purposes, I am the First General."

"But not in name. So...the queen has lost her trust in you, my lord," Gedeon said. "And she waits for you to prove yourself worthy of holding the title again."

"How do you suss this, Gedeon?" Kokabiel snapped. "Has one of your little spiders been spying on me again?"

Gedeon smiled. "In this instance, a guess, my lord. But your reaction proves my hunch true. This is not good news. If the queen distrusts you, she might have you followed."

"I'm alone."

"Are you certain?" Gedeon looked around. "The way is long and dark."

"I took precautions. And used concealing spells. And anyway, Gedeon, you shouldn't always listen to your hunches."

"Not all are mine. In these tumultuous times, many voices speak. It's not easy knowing whom to listen to."

"If you listen to me, Gedeon, you'll go far."

"Perhaps." Gedeon said, looking askance at him. "Perhaps not. It all depends on what we do from here on, doesn't it, my lord?"

"Well, do you have it, or not?"

"I do!" Gedeon said, pleased with himself. "Thanks to your help, I was able to enter the palace library again in secret. I spent long nights there, pouring over ancient books, under the great stacks. I read by candlelight, smoking pipes of nightshade to keep me alert. I read two thousand four hundred and seventy one texts, start to finish – most speed-read, of course. And I began to see that the knowledge I sought had been carefully excised from these records. But hints remained, and I gleaned more from what was missing than what was found. I discerned an outline, a silhouette. I cross-referenced, interpolated, and cast all sorts of spells. Once I accidentally summoned a stymphalian bird."

"I didn't ask for a romance, Gedeon. Tell me how to kill a First One."

Gedeon took a deep breath. "When the first universes were shattered, fragments were left behind."

"The Shards."

"Those are the largest of them, yes. But when we blast a mountain to form a tunnel, we free large stones, yet we also make much fine dust. In the powder you will find miniscule fragments, some as sharp as knives. And just the same, fragments of shattered universes float in the Abyss. They are not formed of normal matter, like Sheol, but of the Cosmic mortar, which glued the early universes together – mortar that the Creator herself laid. And if we make one of these fragments into blade, and if we stab a First One with it – through her heart – all her energy will dissipate into the

Abyss. She will die. But there is a one problem. As far as I can tell, all such fragments were destroyed. I was unable to find any record of them in the texts. Trillions of such fragments float in the Abyss, but since the Abyss is infinitely large, it might take an eternity to find even one."

"No, it won't, Gedeon. Because I already know where we can find one."

"You do? Where, my lord?"

"Mashit keeps it close, on a strap attached to her leg, under her robes. Its hilt is gleaming silver. Its crystal blade shines like a moon. Only those who have lain with her have seen it; only then does she take it off. When she and I first bedded, she would not take the knife off, even when we lay naked in each other's arms. She calls it the Shard Knife, and it's her defense against those who might harm her. I held it once and sensed its power. And I thought it a simple charm. I'd no idea the weapon to destroy her sits strapped to her thigh every moment of every day. Gedeon, you've done excellent work."

Gedeon beamed. "Thank you, my lord. All I ask is that you return me to my station as Master Archivist when you are king. I can't tell you what a joy it was to be among my books again. In no place am I happier than within the stacks."

"Consider it done. And this knife, Gedeon, it will kill any First One?"

"And many other creatures besides. It is one of the deadliest weapons."

"Perfect."

"Then you plan to kill Ashmedai too, my lord?"

"Yes, Gedeon. I do."

Gedeon nodded. "And when can we expect your new reign to begin, my king?"

"On the eve before Stoning Day, Mashit will close her eyes for the last time, killed with the same knife she wears to protect herself."

"A poetic ending. And Ashmedai?"

"He'll declare his fealty to me before all, or I'll kill him too."

"It's a bold plan, my lord."

"*It is a bold plan!*" said a new voice from the shadows, and Kokabiel and Gedeon turned to face it. "Too bad you won't live to see it through." Like a walking boulder, Talman stepped out of the darkness, followed by twenty Legion soldiers. Talman had lost weight, and there were fresh wounds on his body. But his eyes were bright with fury.

Gedeon yelped and leaped back, and Kokabiel drew his sword.

"Throw down your weapons," Talman said. "I have twenty of the finest soldiers with me. You are done, Kokabiel."

Kokabiel backed into the wall. The only escape was into the surging river. He scanned the ranks of the soldiers, marking names and faces, surprised to see General Nefthada's wormy mass among them.

"I expected better of you, Nefthada," Kokabiel shouted. "I didn't think you would follow a coward."

"Nor did I think you a traitor." Nefthada spat yellow mucus onto the ground.

"I've chosen my friends carefully," Talman said. He gestured at Gedeon. "Have you?"

"Gedeon has opened more doors with his sharp mind than you could with a thousand keys," Kokabiel said.

"We all heard your treasonous plans, Kokabiel. We will take you to the dungeons to await your punishment, and Nefthada will tell Mashit of your plan to murder her and usurp the throne."

"And, Nefthada, will you also tell the queen how you freed Talman from his prison, defying her explicit orders?"

"When she learns of your coup attempt," Talman said, "and how you framed me–"

"*Framed* you?"

"Yes, *framed* me, then she will return me to my station. I've done a lot of thinking in my cell, and I've realized I'm a warrior after all."

"No, you've always been a coward, Talman. But you're an even greater fool. Mashit won't believe you. She found you prostrate before Maya when our city was attacked. You and all these traitors will be destroyed."

"*You* blew up the vats, Kokabiel." Talman stepped forward. "I know that now. I'm afraid it's you who must die."

"You have twenty soldiers," Kokabiel said, "and I have a librarian. Let's even the stakes. Let's fight, just you and me, without weapons or spells. Let he who survives return to Mashit victorious. The other shall be cast into this river of death." Kokabiel dropped his sword. "Fight me, Talman! Or are you too much of a coward?"

"You never know when to give up, Kokabiel," Talman said.

"A true soldier never surrenders. But you wouldn't know that."

Talman threw down his sword and screamed as he charged at Kokabiel. He readied for his blow, when the waterfalls shifted, as if the entire cavern had turned ninety degrees. The thundering waters crashed into Talman and the soldiers, knocking them over. They screamed as they were swept away in the current.

Gedeon stood paces away from the torrent, chanting a spell. Kokabiel saw the little librarian and laughed. "Gedeon, you little imp! You should be a soldier! That was glor–"

The rivers crashed upon him, knocking him over, and he plunged into the river. He gasped and swallowed mouthfuls of filth as he was thrust into a tunnel. He tried to grab onto the walls, but they slid from his fingers. He tumbled and choked and was flushed into darkness. He tried a spell, but he kept slamming into walls, breaking his concentration. No, he was not ready to die. Not like this! He was about to pass out when he saw light, a sky of bloody stars rippling above. He swam for it with all his strength.

But something was pulling him down. A flurry of many-toothed mouths tugged and nipped at his flesh. He swam for the pregnant stars, for the orange light he now saw in the east. For dawn. He swam for his life and for all of Sheol.

He gasped and pulled himself onto the rocks. A worm-like creature with a thousand teeth and huge black eyes hissed, and spat, then leaped for him. Kokabiel grabbed its head and screamed as he tore it apart with his hands. He threw the pieces into the water, toward other worms floating near. They eyed him briefly before diving back into the dark waters.

He panted. He was alive.

He'd come this close to death many times and knew that profound insights often came in moments like these if he were open to them. He looked across the lake, the faint reflection of the distant mountains rippling across the surface. So this was where Sheol's shit went, dumped here, to be feasted upon by these underwater beasts. No wonder they grew so repulsive, so numerous.

And we demons, he thought, *eat these beasts to survive. A perfect metaphor for what Sheol really is, recycled waste.*

His thoughts slowed. He was covered in slime, bloody from abrasions. His clothes were torn, and he could barely stand. Across the lake, the palace loomed over the city, stark against the pre-dawn sky

Gedeon had tried to kill him – the wretch! – and Kokabiel almost respected the librarian for his bravado. But he'd deal with Gedeon later, because if Talman or any of his soldiers had survived, they were right now rushing to the queen to tell her of his plan. The first sun was already rising. He had to get there first.

CHAPTER THIRTY

THE MORNING SUNS SHONE ONTO ABBADON'S DAPPLED STREETS below the bedchamber window. On the nightstand beside the bed was a folded letter Mashit had received – an unexpected letter – delivered to her chambers before she had retired for the night. It read:

"I should have written you sooner, Mother. But I believed that sooner or later you would write to me. Now, I know better. Now, I know all.

"I know about Neta. I know I'm not alone on Earth, that you've sent another here. And probably others too. I thought you had recognized my worth, that you saw me as I have always been – utterly astounding – but no, I am just another one of your servants in different clothes. In this case, golden. To think I believed you valued me! Richard was my friend, Mother. He was helping me. Helping us. And you had him killed, why? Was it really for the movie, or that you couldn't abide me being closer to that human than I ever was to you? I hate you for that.

"But despite my anger, I don't regret coming to Earth. Because here I've finally experienced abundance. And I adore it, Mother, these treasures I have always deserved. You don't see my value now. But you will. I'm far greater than you can imagine. I will do things on this Earth that will astound and terrify you. And one day, you'll look back and realize what a mistake you've made by not recognizing my value. But it will be too late, Mother, because if it's not clear, you've already lost me. This is goodbye."

Mashit reread the letter as a cool breeze spread the curtains, revealing Maya, naked and stunning in the orange light. The Pillar stared down at the waking city, a solemn expression on her face.

Of course Daphna wasn't alone on Earth. Mashit couldn't have entrusted such a large endeavor to her fickle daughter. There were four of her sons and daughters on Earth, and more on their way. Daphna had the privilege of being the first. Before Mashit had sent her, she was yet one more anonymous palace face. Now millions of people on Earth adored her. So why was Daphna so angry? Because of one dead human? Mashit sighed.

These children of the Fulcrum generation never understand real choice, she thought, *because they've never had to face the horror of the Shattering. Everything to them is theoretical and imaginary.* Still, the thought of never seeing Daphna again filled her with an indescribable despair.

"What do you see," Mashit said to Maya, "when you look out the window?"

"Delusion," Maya said. "Eons of unremitting suffering due to ignorance."

"But we're ignorant no longer," Mashit said, rising from the bed to approach her. "Look at those buildings below," Mashit said. "Those are radishes growing in boxes on window sills. Squint and we might be in a Medieval human city. The once barren cliffs are swathed in green. Life comes to Sheol."

"Yet you quell an honest desire for justice with murder. How many demons did you kill to quiet that unrest?"

"I told you that was not my order." She put her arm on Maya's shoulder, and the Pillar stared out the window. "General Kokabiel did that without speaking to me first."

"Yet you didn't punish him as you punished the others."

"Because I need him."

"For what? More murder?"

"Kokabiel is the only one in the Legion I trust."

"But you *can't* trust him, Mashit. He just showed you that."

"Things are complicated, Maya. Much more complicated than you can imagine. There are forces here that have been at play for millennia. I can't change them overnight."

"Why not? You say you want change, but you resist it at every turn."

Daphna had abandoned her, but she would not let Maya go too. "Perhaps I have," she said. "But I don't want to anymore. Show me, Maya. Show me how to heal this world."

Maya shook her head. "Are you saying this just to please me?"

"Does it matter? Don't you wish to be pleased?"

"What matters is what's in your heart. I'm not convinced that your heart has become soft and open. I have noticed a tendency among your kind to..."

"To what?"

"To obfuscate."

"You mean to lie. Yes, we demons are superb liars."

"Even to yourselves," Maya said.

"The truth, Maya, is that I'm not sure if I'm lying to myself about what I want. I'm only sure that I want the chaos to end. With you, I feel peace, and I've never felt that before. Not with other demons. Not with Daniel. Only with you."

"But do you want peace just for yourself, or for everyone?"

"What do you think?" Then she leaned in, their lips met, and Maya sighed deeply into Mashit's mouth. Her body was as warm as a burning hearth. Mashit closed her eyes and felt as if she were holding onto a spark in the Abyss, spinning around. But she was not afraid as long as Maya was with her. They fell onto the bed.

Later, when they lay exhausted in each other's arms, Mashit said, "New poetry is being created all across Sheol. We are in the midst of a demon renaissance. There are granite statues, newly carved in Zybath, by the southern gates. Painters have adorned the high walls along Cessation of Agony with colorful art from our history. Minstrels sing new songs. Our bards are writing new tales."

"It all sounds wonderful, Mashit. But I've seen none of it. You keep me locked up here, like a pet."

"And I think you secretly like it."

Maya frowned. "Don't be cruel."

"I'll show you," Mashit said. "I'll take you around the city. Without you, none of this would be possible."

Maya nodded. "I'd like that very much." She was shivering.

"Are you cold?" Mashit said. "I'll have them make us a fire."

"No," Maya said. "I'm just not used to...to *this*."

"You've never lain with a woman before?"

"I did, before I joined the monkhood. But we had to swear off sexual pleasure. It's seen as an obstacle on the path to enlightenment."

"And do *you* feel this way?"

"Some monks use their sexual energy to reach profound states of consciousness. I never understood that fully until now."

"You flatter me," Mashit said.

"I feel out of place," said Maya. "Like I'm drifting into a new mode of being. It seems we both are not ourselves when with the other."

"And in so doing we become a greater being."

"Yes, I'm terrified of who this new being will be."

"What do you fear? Her power?"

"Her weakness."

"Neither you nor I are weak. We are furthest from it."

"I suppose." Maya turned her gaze from the window, where the suns were quickly rising. The air was growing hot. Fiery light blazed across the room, sending scarlet ladders across the floor. "You know my fears," Maya said. "Now tell me yours."

Mashit smiled. "All right. I brought the Pillars here to help Sheol. And it has, but much more slowly than I'd hoped. At this rate, it'll take centuries to bring true abundance here. But the people will not be so patient with me. They accepted my rule because I promised abundance. If they were to learn it will take centuries for my promises to be fulfilled, my reign won't last very long."

"So what are you going to do?"

"Do you remember the explosions that destroyed the vats?"

"How could I forget."

"We've been rapidly building more. The vats capture the energy that drips from Earth. Normally, it's a trickle, like mist from a distant rain. But the flow has increased fifty-fold in the last few weeks."

"Because of us, the Pillars?"

"Partly. You are this world's foundation. But also, I've had gold mined from the mountains sent to Earth, where it was plated onto golden accessories. When humans wear these, some of their power is transmitted here, to fill the vats more quickly."

"Their *power*?"

"Their life-force, essentially."

Maya sat up. "How many?"

"How many accessories?"

"How many *people*?"

"As of last count, nearly ten million."

"And do these humans know that you're draining them?"

"No, not consciously. But they have plenty of energy. Earth literally overflows with it. We're just skimming a little off the top for ourselves."

"But you don't have their consent."

"Don't I? Humans *want* to give their power away."

"Of course they don't."

"Maya, don't be naive. Humans have been doing this for millennia, before demons ever came along. Think of all your leaders throughout history, the countless masses of people who freely gave their power over to demagogues and tyrants, even to their deaths. Look at how humans worship celebrities today. Every day, humans give their power away without the help of magic or coercion. They want to be subsumed into something larger. Subservience takes their pain away. Worshiping another gives them freedom. All I have done is facilitated the process."

Maya looked stricken. "And what happens to these humans, once they're drained? What becomes of them?"

"We don't kill them, Maya. They just become docile and obedient."

Maya leaped from the bed. "You're talking about slavery."

"Only for a few, and only for a short time. Once Sheol has enough power, I'll grant everyone their freedom. They will lead comfortable lives here."

"Lives that they haven't chosen for themselves!"

"On the contrary, they'll choose whatever we ask of them."

"Only because they've had their wills taken away."

"I don't understand why you're surprised. It happens all the time on Earth. Tell me, Maya, is what I do so different from the CEO of a corporation, who hires low-wage workers so he can make his fortunes?"

"It's completely different!"

"No, it's the same. From birth, humans are programmed to see work as a path to happiness. And yet the more they work, the more they struggle, only to sink deeper into debt slavery as they buy material possessions they've been programmed to need. I'm doing exactly the same thing, except I'll eventually give them the happiness they have always wanted. I'll give them a purpose. They will help right a great wrong in the Cosmos – they will heal Sheol and all its residents – and when the work is complete, they'll be heralded as heroes for all time."

Maya grabbed her monk's habit and quickly donned it.

"What are you doing, Maya?"

"I thought I could teach you compassion and mercy. But I see now this was a delusion of my ego. You'll never change. I can't believe I allowed myself to be defiled by you. You're a monster."

Mashit had been called worse, but these words from Maya hurt more than a stab from a knife. "Come now," Mashit said, forcing a smile, hoping levity would erase the disgusted look on Maya's face. "Enough with this silly tantrum. If I were a monster, would I be able to pleasure you so?"

"Even more so," Maya said.

There was a knock on the door, angering her. "What is it?" Mashit snapped.

A soldier from her Shield entered the room, and when he saw her naked body, his yellow serpent eyes looked down to the floor. "My queen, apologies for disturbing you. The palace guards have captured former general Talman at the gates."

"Talman? Out of his cell?"

"Yes, my queen. And he freely admits that the Legion had a hand in his escape. Also," the Shield went on, "Talman says that Kokabiel plans to–"

Just then the giraffe-necked demon burst into the room, soaking wet, reeking of sewage and knocked the Shield to the floor. "Leave!" Kokabiel shouted, "and wait for me in the corridor, Daimool, if you know what's best for your scaly hide!"

The Shield looked back and forth between Kokabiel and Mashit.

"Leave!" Kokabiel said again, "Before I slay you where you stand."

The soldier stood and fled.

"General Kokabiel," Mashit said. "What in Great Abbadon is

happening? Why is Talman free, and why do you stride into my room smelling of shit and smacking guards?"

"Apologies, my queen, for interrupting your..." He glared at Maya. "Your business."

Mashit rose from the bed and strapped the Shard Knife to her thigh. Kokabiel watched her intently as she dressed, as she slipped on a white gown and fastened a silver metal band around her waist. "Well?"

"Talman escaped into the tunnels under the palace with help from twenty Legion soldiers," Kokabiel said. "I went hunting for him and came upon them, and I overheard them plotting to overthrow you. But before I could hear their full plan, one of the soldiers spotted me in the shadows. He cast a spell that caused the sewers to overflow. It knocked me into the waters. But he underestimated its power. They were all knocked into the waters too. Talman is a deadly threat, my queen. We must kill him and all the soldiers who aided him. I know all their faces. I know all their names."

Beside the window, Maya was staring at her.

"Round them up, General," Mashit said. "But do not kill them."

"What? Why? If we don't kill them, there's no telling what they might do. They probably have allies. We have to send a message, now."

Mashit looked at Maya. "That is my order, Kokabiel. Do *not* kill them."

He tightened his jaw. "But my queen–"

"You heard me, Koko!" she snapped.

"Yes, my queen. I heard you, and I obey. But I've just thwarted a plot against you. There are those in the Legion who wish you dead, and the Legion itself has no master of the helm. Now, more than ever, you need to show the people you're in control. Mashit," he said, stepping forward, "make me First General again."

"So you may kill more protestors?" Mashit said, glancing at Maya.

Kokabiel stepped forward. "Don't you see? Your kingdom is collapsing, bit by bit. If you do nothing, you'll fade away, a footnote in Sheol's history. A failed experiment, never to be tried again. Unless, Mashit, you act with a firm hand."

Mashit looked back and forth between Kokabiel and Maya. Kokabiel was right. It was all falling apart. She just needed to hold the kingdom together long enough, and then they would see! She lifted her left hand, squeezed it into a fist, and chanted a spell in Demonsbreath. She opened her palm, and there lay the cracked-egg iron pin with the ruby center signifying the highest rank of Sheol's armies. She offered it to him.

Slowly, he came over, took the pin, and attached it to his breast. Unusual for Kokabiel, he smiled.

"Congratulations General," she said. "Make sure I don't regret this."

"I shall serve Sheol with all my heart," he said.

"That's what makes me nervous. Don't kill them, Koko. That's my order!"

"Yes, my queen."

Mashit kept her gaze on Maya. "Also, make it known that on the next Stoning Day, no one shall cast stones at Ashmedai, nor spit, nor throw their filth at him, nor make a sound at his passing. He is to be paraded by the crowds in total silence."

"Why, my queen?"

"Because, before the whole body of Sheol, I will show mercy," Mashit said. Maya's eyes were wide and expectant.

"Mercy, my queen?" Kokabiel said.

"I will free Ashmedai from his cramped cage, and I will feed him and give him warm clothes, and I will show the masses that demons are capable of change. We are entering a new age, Koko. We are experiencing its birth pangs. Our old ways aren't working anymore. It's time to make new ones."

"Do you really believe that?" Kokabiel said.

Maya stepped closer to her. "Yes, Mashit, do you really believe that?"

"I do," Mashit said. And for the first time it wasn't a lie.

CHAPTER THIRTY-ONE

Even from within her dressing room, five closed steel doors from the stage, Daphna heard their cheers.

"*Carina! Carina! Carina!*"

She sat before her mirror, alone. A woman had just applied her makeup and left. Duile, Khein, and Frix had come to inspect her accessories several times, making sure they were aligned with ancient equations, the positions of the stars, and hovered about her annoyingly until she demanded time alone before the show. She lit a hand-rolled cigarette and blew the smoke toward the stranger in the mirror.

"Who are you?" she said.

An alien face stared back at her.

"WHO ARE YOU?" she screamed.

She punched the mirror, and it shattered. Its spider web of cracks crossed her reflected face. Her fist bled, and she licked the blood. Is this how the Creator felt when she shattered the worlds, disgusted with what she had wrought? Had she seen her own distorted reflection and loathed what she saw?

"I'm not my mother's daughter," she said to the mirror. "I'm not Carina. I'm Daphna, princess of Sheol."

Outside, the chants grew louder, "*Carina! Carina! Carina!*"

"They know not whom they worship," she said. "They adore a ghost."

There was a knock on the door, and Frix entered without waiting for a response. She glanced at the broken mirror. "A problem?"

Daphna wrapped her wound with a small towel, and it quickly turned red.

"Here, let me," Frix said. She came over, hands raised to cast a spell.

"No!" Daphna said. "No spells. Let it bleed."

"You can't go out there with a wound."

"Yes I can."

"It will affect the spell! You can't be–"

But Daphna shoved past Frix into the hall, where roadies were speaking with Duile and Khein. The hall was filled with cigarette smoke and she made vortices as she bounded through it. Lights shone upon her, reflecting off her gold to make constellations on the walls. They gaped at her as she headed for the stage.

—

Daniel waited in the crowd, fifty rows from the stage, desperately wanting a cigarette. But Daphna had said it was his cursed nature which made him immune. Or so he hoped. There were at least twenty-thousand people here, and a lot of them kids. He wanted to scream, "Run, run! All of you! You're about to be made slaves in hell!" But that would mean the Lamed Vav would remain in Sheol, that Sheol would grow in power to consume the Earth, and he couldn't allow that.

The crowd was chanting "Carina! Carina! Carina!" as he looked down at a girl, no more than twelve, accompanied by her mom. The girl wore golden earrings and a gold bracelet. She looked up at Daniel and smiled.

—

Soon Daphna would drop this charade and let go of pretense. She wouldn't need her golden accessories after tonight. These were Mother's adornments, and all things Mashit would be discarded. She'd give mother thousands of slaves, but it was worth it knowing Daniel would be among them to ruin her. Chances were he wouldn't succeed. But then she'd continually underestimated his abilities. Maybe he would sneak into the palace and steal the Pillars from mother's arms. And that made Daphna pleased. She was not a mere accessory to be worn by anyone.

She stepped through the final door before the stage. She grabbed a mike from a tech and stood hidden behind the plywood frame. The crowd roared, chanting. She paused, taking deep breaths. Her heart pounded. She dropped the bloody hand towel to the floor. Her knuckles still bled. And maybe Frix was right. Blood might affect the spell.

An enormous amount of preparation had gone into tonight's show, and she was the most important part. There was no turning back now. She raised her left hand to signal the production team, blood dripping down her arm. The show began.

—

The lights dropped. The stadium went dark, and Daniel tensed. The audience roared. Purple spotlights beamed onto the glassy-eyed masses. So many eager faces. He squeezed his fists. He was ready.

A film projected onto the wall behind the stage, a movie screen for the crowd. A thousand images flashed upon it, scenes from Carina's film, hot young things wearing bright gold, a field of sunflowers, a blue sky, a setting sun, clouds, laughter. And Daniel knew that beneath these flashing images were signs and sigils meant to open long-closed gates, to draw power down from black stars, ancient spells that seeped into the concert air like a toxic mist. He tried not to watch, but it was impossible. The images drew him in, the most engrossing spectacle he'd ever seen.

The crowd's cheers faded as he was swept into a blissful dream. He fought it, but it was like fighting a shot of anesthesia. He walked across a field of flowers beneath a cloudless sky. The wind blew his hair. He felt unnaturally calm.

In the distance, a baseline throbbed and grew in volume. It rose to crescendo, and at its peak Carina broke through the wall, shining and brilliant.

He was back in the crowd again, his heart beating frantically. Purple lasers and white spotlights beamed onto her, as if she were an atom forced to fusion. The light reflected off her accessories into his eyes, into everyone's eyes, and it felt wonderful. The light was her attention, her love, and by shining upon him made him whole.

She spun, and a million stars swept across twenty thousand faces. Their cheers rose and fell with her every move, and he cheered too. She walked down the steps to the beat of the music, and when she reached the stage she sang the first word of "Goodbye to Day." Dancers leaped from the sides, men and women in lesser gold, like him, like all of them, diminutive echoes of the queen.

The dancers hoisted flaming staffs and ignited gas jets on the stage. The flames leaped skyward in bursts of green and red, and the audience roared. She sang, and her words were bliss. She danced, and his eyes followed her. He sang along with words that praised futility and shunned hope, her nihilism slipping deeply into his psyche and wrapping his thoughts so he would not question how weak and subservient he'd become.

Why change when all is meaningless? Better to dance until you're dead. Let the world burn, burn, burn. You only live once, baby.

He loved it all. He loved her.

The song ended, the lights winked out, and Daniel and the crowd stood in stunned silence. Moments later, he applauded – everyone did – and it was raucous, bordering on riotous. The stadium floor shook. He stared at Carina. Did she see him? Did she love him? He and the others shouted for her to continue. This silence was too long. He was in danger of glimpsing his own emptiness. That had to be avoided at all costs.

She began "I've Nothing Left," a love song. The crowd sang with her. "Why love, when all is transient? Why reach, when nothing's worth reaching for? Love ends, and so does life. Might as well enjoy life's pleasures before we're gone."

Something was leaving him, as if he were sliding into a dream, but it was also something else, an energy that he hadn't quite noticed before because it had always been there. But now that it flowed from him in rivers he felt it go. And it was horrible, a literal feeling of death. Part of him welcomed it, the peace.

—

Soon the portal would open. Behind Daphna, on the stage, a host of sorcerers were honing and directing the power, shaping the doorway across the Abyss. Earlier Daphna had seen the black coffins with breathing holes carted into the stadium. Humans, who would be sacrificed. There was more than enough power in the crowd, these singing masses, but these unlucky coffined souls were insurance.

She did not see Daniel among their adoring faces. Was he among them? Did they know they worshipped an illusion? She could be singing about the rivers of shit beneath Abbadon, and still they'd adore her. But soon they'd see who she really was, and they'd love her for her true self, not this facade.

A pause, a rainbow flash, an explosion of indoor fireworks to make a fireman blush. The third song began. She pressed the button behind her ear mike and dropped the handheld. Blood flowed down her arm, more than she thought possible. Was the spell affecting her too? Arms outspread, she sang, while behind her, the wall, three stories high, began to part. And there it was.

The door.

—

The door. Daniel drifted into a dream. The door of his bedroom burned as Gram came in, aflame, to save him. The door to Rana's house, an enormous stone that turned on a miniscule pivot. The door of Shyama's hut, a flap of fabric, before Daniel saw a version of hell. The door to Dvoyre's house, with the mezzuzah she made him kiss. The door to Gram's house, unlocked, always welcoming. "The quickest path to hell is through our own minds," Pandate, the monk, had said a long time ago.

A great vortex spun and flashed behind Carina. A storm, swirling. It was so beautiful. So terrible. Delightful and sickening. A work of art. An abomination.

This was what he had been searching for all along.

"Come!" Carina said, arms outstretched. "Join me! Join me onstage!"

Yes, Daniel thought. *I will!*

"Come," she said to someone in the front row, taking her hand

and hoisting her up on stage. "And you too," she said to another. "All of you, come up here. Come to me!"

The damn broke. They went forward, and Daniel went with them.

"Walk up the steps," Carina said, "and through the vortex. A great gift is waiting for you on the other side."

Yes! Daniel thought. *A gift!*

As the first person stepped through, there was a flash and a crack of thunder. Beautiful, Daniel thought. Wonderful!

"Go into the vortex and receive your gift," Carina said. "You deserve this!"

Ten at a time they went, and lightning flashed as each one went through. He climbed onto the stage with the others. Carina was here, his queen, his goddess, and his love for her was limitless.

"Daniel!" she said. She came for him. Her voice wasn't booming as before, but close and personal. Loving. "Daniel, wake up! Wake up, Daniel!"

But wake up from what? This was all he had ever wanted. To let go.

He turned from her, climbed the steps to the portal, and stepped through.

—

"No!" Daphna said. "No!" Daniel was entranced and might never wake up. Was it the blood from her hand? Did she alter the spell? *No!*

Hundreds more followed him, and there were thousands to go. A few stragglers lingered, watching in horror, dragged to this show by their children or offered a ticket from a friend, and, having only just encountered Carina's music, their wills hadn't been sufficiently drained. A few tried the exits, but the doors were chained. Those who fought for escape were tased and restrained.

They poured into the portal. And when nearly all had gone through, the portal shrunk. With a bright flash and a clap of thunder it vanished. Only a handful remained in the stadium now. Some lay supine by the doors, tased and unconscious, or bound by guards. Some sat shuddering in their seats, holding themselves. Some kneeled, weeping. Others wandered aimlessly, shellshocked.

"Go home," Daphna said, her voice booming across the emptied stadium. "Go the fuck home. Carina is done." She threw off her headset and stormed off the stage.

Her hand was still bleeding.

CHAPTER THIRTY-TWO

DANIEL, WAKE UP! WAKE UP, DANIEL!

The memory of Carina's voice swirled in the velvety blackness. A peaceful place. A horrible place. Daniel's heart beat more restfully than it had in years, and hot blood poured through his body, pushing him down into majestic dreams. Terrifying dreams.

Wake up, Daniel!

Whose voice was that? Gram's? Was he late for school? Visions floated up from the dark. Crowds, adorned in gold, chanting bleak words with a woman who shone like a sun.

Wake up, Daniel!

A horrid falling. A brutal shift in the world. The smell of sweat, of fear.

Wake up, Daniel!

Another smell. A delicious smell. A coppery smell.

Wake up, Daniel!

Blood. The vile hunger came like never before. He was *home*. He gasped and awoke. He was in a large cave, dimly lit by floating balls of flame, walking in single-file with the people from the concert. Almost all were adorned in Carina's gold; it flashed in the firelight. The air was so hot it hurt to breathe, and it stank of fungus and rot. Daphna's bloody handprint stained his right shoulder, and he was soaked with sweat.

A short distance ahead an entrance to a large cavern loomed. A creature stooped there, a corpse with skin pulled taut over his bony frame. Scattered wisps of white hair grew from a lesioned scalp. What few teeth he had were sharp and long, and he wore only a small strip of leather around his waist, held up with a belt that sheathed a sword.

A Cursed One. A Mikulal.

"Take off all your clothes," the creature said in perfect English. His voice was like rending flesh and crumbling stones. "Toss everything you wear into the pile. Become naked." He repeated himself in Malay, Mandarin, and Tamil as the queue moved forward.

Daniel moved with them into a larger cavern. A heaping pile of discarded clothes rose toward the lofty ceiling. The crowd obeyed their instructions. First came bracelets and watches, necklaces and earrings, then shirts and bras, pants and belts, undergarments and socks. The humans got naked without shame, their hairy, sweaty, flabby bodies here for all to see. Daniel hesitated until a second Mikulal caught sight of him, then he feigned the crowd's mindless expression and removed his clothing. It was too damn hot to wear a hoodie anyway.

More Mikulalim at the opposite end of the chamber ordered the humans into a tunnel, and Daniel walked with them. After a short distance, the tunnel opened into another cavern, larger than the first. Mikulalim were clasping heavy chains around the ankles of the arrivals and ushering them twenty at a time into one of many tunnels adjoining the chamber. All obeyed without question.

But Daniel slipped from the queue. The humans didn't notice. Their faces still held the beatific glow from the concert. He crept along the wall, trying to remain unseen, when he heard the voices.

What an ugly lot, said one. *So fat and indulgent. If only they knew what they had before they'd lost it.*

Get used to them, said another. *This is only the first of many.*

That's what I dread.

They spoke not words, but in thought pictures. This was the Silent Tongue. And since Daniel was half-Mikulal, he understood them too. This gave him an idea.

He turned back into the tunnel. People walked mindlessly past him as he scraped dust from the floor and rubbed it on his body. He ruffled his hair and stooped to imitate the Mikulalim's lumbering gait. Then he reentered the chamber where they were binding the humans, walking astride them, as if he were an escort.

A Mikulal came over.

What an ugly lot, Daniel said in the Silent Tongue.

The Mikulal grimaced as he looked Daniel up and down. *Who are you? Where's your skirt? Your belt and sword?*

I drank too much greyel, Daniel said, *and wandered off into the caves to sleep it off.*

Greyel? the man said. Two more Mikulalim were walking over. *The greyel fungus doesn't grow here, only in Gehinnom, by the city of Yarrow. How did you get some? Wait, I know your face. Aren't you–*

Daniel sped off, crossing the cavern, over tangles of iron chains.

"Hey!" the Mikulal shouted aloud. "Stop!"

Daniel ran into a dark tunnel and emerged into another cavern, hotter, and much larger than the others. Its walls shone with golden light. He stood on a high ledge. Below him, a titanic cauldron of molten gold steamed. On other ledges, Mikulalim were tossing the human clothes and golden accessories they had just collected into the cauldron. It burped flame with each new addition.

He ran down a ramp and approached a Mikulal.

Where's the exit? he said.

What exit? Who are–

How do I get to the surface?

I know you! the Mikulal said. *You're Daniel Fisher, the Pillar! I've seen your likeness. My brothers on Gehinnom speak of the one who promised–*

Three Mikulalim were running down the ramp toward him, and Daniel sped off.

"That's Daniel Fisher!" one shouted. "The long-promised one!"

He ran into a tunnel, broke left, then right, taking passages randomly. Mikulalim were fast creatures, but so was he. Getting to the surface didn't matter, only escape. He had not come all the way here just to go into chains. He passed bound human slaves, dutifully chipping away at stone in dim caverns. He darted past their surprised guards. He chanced a look back, and saw only shadows, yet he did not slow.

He sped into a tunnel, when suddenly he was surrounded. At least ten Mikulalim blocked his way forward. Even more blocked his retreat.

You can stop running, said a tall one, stepping forward.

Daniel panted, looking for escape. But there was none. But he had his power of fire. He was about to scrape the fabric of the universe when the tall one said, *Wait! There's no need for that! My brothers here will not hurt you. The others of my kin, however, I cannot vouch for. Not everyone in Sheol wants change. Please, hear us out.*

Who are you? Daniel said.

I am Raigul. I am a friend.

My friends usually don't point swords at me.

A precaution, Raigul said as he sheathed his blade. He was tall for a Mikulal. He had sharp cheekbones and long gray hair down to his waist that was tied with a leather strap behind his back. A large scar crossed his chest, and Daniel wondered if this is how he had died as a man.

We've heard much of you, Daniel Fisher. It's said that King Havig of Gehinnom has built a giant effigy of you in Yarrow, that his women have composed epic hymns about you. Stories of your promise, in the desert of Dudael, have calmed many despairing hearts.

Raigul stepped closer. "But on Sheol," he said aloud, in ancient Aramaic, "we're more skeptical of saviors. They praise you on Gehinnom as if you're a god. But here, some think you're a tale made up by our master, Azazel, to torment us, as is his wont.

"Just yesterday I found an image of your likeness under my daughter's sleeping stone, weaved into a fabric. When I asked her why she'd put it there, she said so her dreams might loft her from this hell. She's not alone. Mothers here whisper to their children of the day when our savior will come to free us from our wretched curse. And here you stand, naked before us. I would not have believed it had I not seen you with my own eyes."

Raigul lifted his chin. "So tell me, Daniel, is it true? Did you promise you'd help the Mikulalim, or is that a lie we tell our children?"

"It's not a lie," he said, shivering. "I did promise."

Raigul lurched forward, and Daniel thought for a moment Raigul might kill him. "Promises are hard to keep," Raigul sneered. "When I was human, I promised my wife I'd protect her. But when the king of Ephesus sent soldiers to our hamlet to take our livestock and land, they raped my wife to death and made me watch. She gave me a look of utter betrayal and disgust before she died. She could not speak, but her eyes said all. I had broken my promise to her. The soldiers tore a hole in my chest and left me to die. Later, the Mikulalim came to feast on the bodies and offered me a chance to live again. I vowed that night I would never break another promise. And I, Daniel Fisher, have promised my brothers I would one day free them of their curse."

"I want to help you, Raigul. I want to help *us*. But–"

"But not today," Raigul said.

"I'm sorry, but I've come here to bring the Lamed Vav back to Earth."

Raigul laughed, an ugly sound, like the cackle of a crow. He turned to his companions. "Even our savior has no time for us."

"I never said I was your savior."

"But you did promise to save us."

"I promised only to try. And still I plan on trying. But right now, Raigul, I have to rescue the Lamed Vav. The safety of Earth depends on me."

"On Gehinnom they think you're a god. But I see now you're just another man. You act only in your self-interest."

"No," Daniel said. "I'm acting on behalf of the billions of Earth, and all the creatures on the Shards. Sheol cannot rule the Cosmos. That would be a disaster." Daniel turned to take all of them in. "You each owe me nothing. We've only just met. And I'm not the savior you think I am. But I still need your help. I have to bring the Lamed Vav home."

"Home?" Raigul said. "Sheol is already starting to grow because of them. And you would take that away from us?"

"Sheol grows at the expense of Earth. Mashit won't free you. She only uses you as she uses everyone. She only wants more slaves. Look at all the humans that were just delivered here. This is only the beginning!"

"This, we know," Raigul said. "But what happens to us, the Mikulalim, when you go back to Earth?"

"After I bring the Lamed Vav home, I'll come back to help you all."

"Just as you promised our brethren in Gehinnom," Raigul said.

"I'm afraid, right now, a promise is all I have."

Raigul sighed deeply, like the sound of an ancient city crumbling into the sea. "Mashit has cast a powerful spell around the palace of Abbadon, so that our kind cannot get too close. It will be difficult getting you into the city."

It took Daniel a moment to reorient. Raigul was offering to help.

"It's impossible for us to enter there," Raigul said. "The closest we can go is deep beneath the city, where the rivers of lava flow under Lord Ashmedai's cage. He's quite keen on seeing Mashit destroyed. Perhaps you two can work together."

"Ashmedai is here?"

"Locked in a cage under the palace, yes."

Daniel shuddered. He remembered the wolf-gray eyes of the demon who had burst into his life and destroyed everything he had ever known. "No! I don't want his help. I've seen what Ashmedai can do."

"Then what do you propose?"

"This spell, it blocks Mikulalim from entering the city?"

"It does."

Daniel straightened. "Raigul, I'm only half-Mikulal. My curse hasn't quickened. Do you, by any chance, have a cigarette?"

CHAPTER
THIRTY-THREE

MASHIT HAD ORDERED KOKABIEL NOT TO KILL TALMAN, Nefthada, and the others, and he had obeyed. Instead of slaughtering them, Kokabiel hauled them out to the Dissipation, and trapped them in a giant oubliette deep within Bocker's Crack. He didn't kill them, no, but the elements or starvation would. And when he returned from the Dissipation, he discovered on his bed pillow a note from Gedeon, deeply apologetic, explaining how the librarian had lost control of his spell – he repeated a dozen times that he had no intention of harming Kokabiel – and the librarian detailed how glad he was that Kokabiel had survived. But of course Gedeon had tried to murder him, and Kokabiel would make that sniveling little demon pay soon enough. But he needed to see the queen first.

The suns had set hours ago, and the plump stars shone dimly through the arched windows in the hall outside Mashit's bedchamber. Kokabiel strode up to her door, and six Shields moved to block his path.

"Do you see this pin?" he said to them, pointing to his chest.

"A shiny gem," said one. "But we of the Queen's Shield do not obey your Legion. We obey only Mashit, queen of Sheol."

"Then ask the queen, you dolts, if I may enter."

For a moment, they considered, when one turned and knocked three times. Then he opened the door a crack, and its groan echoed down the long hall.

A faint voice from inside said, "What? What is it?"

"Kokabiel wishes to see you, my queen."

"Send him away!"

Kokabiel stiffened. "I need to see her, *now*."

"He's most insistent, my queen."

She sighed, and he hated the sound of it. "Very well. Send him in."

He entered, and the door's creak shuddered down the hallway. She lay on her couch in a silken evening robe, thin enough to reveal her milk-pale skin and the dark circles of her nipples. For a moment he lusted for her, but that era had ended. He looked under the silken folds for her Shard Knife, but did not see it anywhere.

A healthy fire burned in the hearth, spreading warmth and scarlet light deep into the room. Beside her was a hookah pipe, and a faint column of blue smoke drifted toward the ceiling, where it was caught in the draft from the window and blown apart.

Like this world, he thought, *as we are blasted to atoms.*

By the shape of her eyes he knew she had been at the pipe for hours. "It's late, Koko. I was about to go to bed. What is it?"

"My queen," he said, bowing, one last act of deference. He shut the door. "Can we talk for a moment?"

She smiled wanly. "Come," she said, patting the couch beside her. "Share some smoke with me, like the old days."

He stared at her, rage and lust battling in his heart until he wasn't sure which emerged victorious. "How can you addle your mind now, when so much is at stake?"

"Smoking brings me peace, and with peace comes clarity. I see through you Koko. You are as translucent to me as these curtains." She gestured toward the window. Outside, the lake shimmered under the light of the stars, and the sight of it made him gasp. "I know you wish me off this throne, so that you may sit upon it. But, Koko, that would be a grave mistake. Look at how the lake shimmers. Look at its stark beauty. I brought that here. I, Mashit, Queen of Sheol, made Lake Hali shimmer. That beautiful sight exists because of me." She sighed deeply. "Smoke a little with me, Koko, and let's enjoy the new beauty of the world together."

Her voice had a touch of tenderness in it, and a hint of the old love they had shared softened his heart. "Perhaps just one puff," he said.

He sat beside her. Her warmth was driving him mad. He wanted to tear off her gown and ravage her on the couch. Instead he took the tube and inhaled deeply. The water bubbled, and he let fly a stream of blue smoke from his lips.

The effects hit quickly. The bitter cloud that had been fogging his mind lifted, and a weight flew from his chest. His arousal grew with the throbbing of his heart.

"My queen," he said. "My queen..." Everything in the room shone, even in places where the firelight did not reach. Even the shadows seemed to cast light of their own. And there it was, her Shard Knife, sheathed in a thin strap slung over a chair beside the bed. His heart pounded at the sight of it. With one strike he could cut her down forever. But he didn't want that now, not in this moment. He stared out the window at the shimmering lake, and everything felt as if it were a blissful dream that would end at any moment.

"We used to do this often, you and I," he said.

"Smoke?" she slurred.

"Sit," he said. "And talk for hours."

She nodded. "Yes, how we used to talk."

"Do you miss those days?"

"Aren't we sitting and talking now?"

"It's not the same."

"No?" she said. "I say some words, and you say some in reply. Is that not talking?"

"Words leaves my lips like smoke. But the words are insubstantial. We are speaking to each other, but the feelings behind the words have evaporated."

"Don't mire yourself in the past, Koko. It will eat at you until you are nothing but a bitter husk."

"And isn't that what we are now? Stuck in the past, cursing the Creator? We mourn, we mourn – oh, how we mourn! – and what has this brought us? We've become, as you have said, a bitter husk."

"And this is why," Mashit said, "I do what I do. Why I try to free us from our past. To bring life into that which is not dead, but dormant, like the Vestigal Stem."

"And like the Stem, is there still life left in us?"

"Sheol has much life left to live, Koko."

"I mean, you and I."

"All things that are born die, Koko. Everything is transient." She stared out the window at the waters lapping on the shore. "It's so utterly beautiful..."

"Once," he said, "you looked at me the way you look at those waters. Now I am but a shadow that passes away."

"Don't be morbid, Koko. You're still here."

"Here, but not with you. You're somewhere else."

"And where am I if not here? By your words I'm a ghost, present but insubstantial."

"Our past feels like a ghost to me."

"Then at least you admit, Koko, that whatever we had is now dead."

"Is it?" He turned to her, and desire filled his every cell. His face flush, sex hard, he moved to kiss her, longing to feel one more brush of her soft lips against his.

But she pushed him away. "One puff for you is one too many, Koko." She got up from the couch. "The smoke has done me in. I'm tired and need sleep. You may leave."

"But, Mashit, I–"

"I've only just made you First General again. Was that a mistake?"

He lifted his chin. "No, my queen." He rose and moved toward the door. "By your leave, then, I shall go."

"Koko, wait."

She'd changed her mind. She desired him after all. He spun. In her hand was a small ring with an emerald signet. "You dropped this ring," she said.

He examined it. "It's not mine."

"No? Then whose is it?"

He looked into her eyes, brown whorls flecked with green, the corners veined with blood, pupils large and glowing. There was a wildness in her gaze, an unsettling disconnect from reality, beyond what the smoke had caused. Did she really forget who had entered her quarters today? "From one of your *other* lovers," he said.

She frowned. "Be gone, Koko, before I make you regret your visit."

"I already do," he said, then exited her chambers.

The door closed behind him with a thud that echoed down the hall. The six Shields glanced up at him, and he heard them chuckle.

He turned to face them.

"Something funny?"

"'twas a good try," one said. "Better luck next time, *General*."

They snickered, when all six Shields were suddenly silenced. With one quick spell he had crushed all of their throats, and, as they gasped for air, he stabbed them all in the heart with six quick swipes. They collapsed, and before too much of their blood seeped onto the marbled floor he cast a spell to whisk them away, deep into the slums, where no one would care about a few dead palace guards. All that was left of their presence was a few streaks of blood, which he wiped with his boot.

A cold wind blew through the hall as Kokabiel stared back at Mashit's door. If he could not have her, no one would.

CHAPTER THIRTY-FOUR

THE MIKULALIM GAVE DANIEL A LEATHER KILT TO COVER HIS groin, sandals for his feet, a belt with an attached pouch, and a sheathed short-sword. Besides having more hair and a great many more teeth, he looked identical to them. One of them had found a pack of Marlboros in some poor woman's purse, and Daniel slid it into his pouch.

"It will be harder for them to spot you dressed as you are," Raigul said. "Many of our brothers would help you, the savior. But some would rather turn you over to Mashit in the hopes of gaining her favor. I won't allow that. We have to keep moving."

They slipped into a new hiding place, a cave smelling of rot and death. Animal bones – he hoped they were animal – were scattered along one wall. A Mikulal held a torch, lit with fire magic, and all their eyes flickered in its light.

"You said you may have a way to get me home?" Daniel said.

"Yes," Raigul said. "We've been preparing a new shipment of gold for many weeks. It's not supposed to be sent to Earth for several more days, but I've sent a small detachment to try and expedite the shipment. We send the gold to Earth in large containers, and you and the four Pillars will be inside one. But you must be back by dawn, tomorrow."

"Why tomorrow?"

"Because that's when the gate will open."

"But that's not much time, Raigul."

"That's all the time I can give."

Daniel nodded. "Then it will have to be enough."

They shifted caves, avoiding Mikulalim search parties, who, Raigul said, had begun to suspect his arrival was a hoax, that the half-Mikulal, once-Pillar known as Daniel Fisher had not really come to Sheol, that the arrival of thousands of new humans had confused those who had supposedly spotted him. The lie, spread by Raigul's men, seemed to be working. The ones who had seen him had been detained and questioned, Raigul said. But sooner or later, news would reach the queen that he was here. "And we have to move long before then," Raigul said.

They waited until there were few bodies skulking about before they set off for the palace. The others wished him luck, then Raigul and two Mikulalim escorted Daniel away. They weaved through many twisted tunnels, backtracking when they heard other voices. They passed human slaves, their eyes vacant, chipping away at rock. In another tunnel, hundreds of slaves, chains around their ankles, slept fitfully on the rocky ground. He sickened at the sight of them.

"I'll come back for you," he whispered to them as he passed. "I promise too."

In a narrow tunnel, where the air was thick with the acrid reek of urine, a burning pressure rose in his chest. At first he thought it was the caustic smell, but Raigul grabbed his arm.

He looked stricken, as if someone were choking him. *Don't speak aloud*, Raigul said in the Silent Tongue. *We might be heard. The barrier begins just beyond that wall.*

I feel it, Daniel said. From his pocket, he removed a Marlboro cigarette and put it in his mouth.

Raigul winced. *If we inhaled fire*, Raigul said, *it would kill us.*

No offense, he said, *but that's kind of what I'm trying to do to my curse.* He weaved fire into the air with magic, and the tip ignited. He inhaled, and Raigul and his two companions grimaced. The corridor dimmed as his night-vision faded. The sharp smells of the animals lessened, and the barrier's repulsive effect waned in his chest.

Raigul spoke something in the Silent Tongue, but his words were far away, like a stray thought vanishing before it could form.

"I can't hear you anymore," Daniel whispered.

Raigul spoke Aramaic aloud – or so Daniel thought. He didn't understand it anymore either. "Can you speak English?" he said.

Raigul frowned and whispered, "It's painful for us to remain here. Do you see that door?" He pointed down the corridor, where Daniel made out the vague outline of a rusted metal door. "On the other side are the animal pens. Take the stairs at the far end. They lead up to the kitchens. Across the kitchen is a servant's stair. It will take you up into the palace. But first, put this on."

Raigul gestured to one of the men, who removed a jade blouse and a hooded black leather cloak from a satchel. "You can't walk through the palace looking like one of us," Raigul said. "With these habits you might pass for a palace dweller."

Daniel took one more drag, stomped out the cigarette, then slipped on the jade blouse. Its heavy fabric was unfit for these hot caves, and it was a few sizes too big. But the velvety black cloak fit him all too well, like the cloak he'd worn on Gehinnom.

"There," Raigul whispered. "There's nothing more I can do for you now."

"You've done enough." Daniel held out his hand, and Raigul hesitated for a moment before taking it. Raigul hand was leathery and warm. He nodded once, then he and his companions vanished back into the dark.

Daniel stepped up to the door and put his hand against the rusted metal. It was cool to the touch, and he felt a faint repulsive force, like two magnets pressing together. But the force was weak, and he overcame it with little effort.

He reached for the door's lever, a heavy iron bolt, and pulled. A sharp pain shot up his arm into his heart as he pulled the lever free from its clasp. The heavy door creaked and groaned as if it hadn't been moved in ages. On the other side was a dimly lit space. The acrid smell of feces and urine assaulted his nose, and he gagged.

He stepped over the threshold and another sharp pain flashed down his spine, as if someone was shunting electric current directly into his nerves. He pushed through the pain; he could not stop now. He closed the door as quietly as he could.

A flickering gas lamp on the far wall filled the space with a warm glow. The brick walls dripped moisture, and the floor was littered with straw and dung. Ahead, beyond an arched passageway, a perpendicular corridor crossed this one.

He crept toward it. With every step, electric needles pierced his spine. He heard a loud scrape and turned, only to remember he had a sword on his hip: he had been dragging it along the stone floor, and the sound still echoed through the space. Someone might have heard. He cursed under his breath. When he crept forward again, he kept the sword from touching the ground.

He walked under the archway into the adjoining tunnel. It extended into shadows in both directions. Oil lamps hung from the ceiling by chains, swinging gently, casting meek yellow light onto the walls. When Raigul had said to "take the stairs at the far end" he hadn't specified which end. Daniel turned right.

The corridor was lined with cages large enough to fit a rhino and enclosed with thick iron bars. Most were dark and empty, but he sensed movement in some. He peered between the bars into shadows. A creature with a mule's body and a putrid yellow human head sat in the far corner on piles of filth. Black drool fell from its mouth to the straw-covered floor. Its smell was powerfully bitter, and Daniel covered his nose. Its eyes, black and glistening, peered despairingly at Daniel as he passed.

Another cage held a group of featherless birds like oversized chickens. Their long orange beaks had many sharp teeth. When they spotted him they pressed up against the iron bars to snap and hiss at him, and he leaped back against the wall. Afraid their sounds might attract attention, he quickly moved on. But that was a mistake. To move fast invited the pain. And when he moved slowly, the pain abated.

A yellow fungus clung to the wall in another cage. He looked away, and when he looked back, the fungus had moved ten feet closer. He saw no discernable movement, but when he looked away and back again, the fungus had pressed itself against the bars, and a thousand little tendrils were reaching beyond the bars toward his face.

He walked on.

He passed dozens of bizarre, terrifying creatures, some threatening, some despairing, all locked in cages, when he finally reached the end of the hall. A narrow stair led up into a brighter space, and a distant murmur of voices drifted down from above.

Was this the kitchen?

He slowly climbed the steps, pausing before the top. The room beyond was brightly lit with many torches along the walls and a great flaming chandelier overhead. The air reeked of blood, meat, and charcoal. He saw only a little ways in – a stone wall blocked his view – but there were many counters and tables filling the large space. He heard muted voices close by and didn't understand the words anymore.

He climbed fully into the kitchen and crept past large cuts of strangely colored meat hanging from rusty metal hooks. The room reeked of dead flesh. He slipped into the next room, a scullery, with sharp knives hanging from the walls, then into the next room, where an enormous cauldron simmered over a coal fire, its steam vanishing into a wide flue above. He walked through the next room, a store house full of sundry jars and boxes. And beyond this room, at last, a stair.

He crept up slowly, listening carefully as he went. He drew his sword in case he met an unexpected guest – it was heavy and unwieldy – but he wasn't sure if he even knew how to use it. But no one would stop him now.

He climbed, two stories, three. Each floor was different from the last. One was for storage, crowded with containers. One was a long-abandoned hall covered in cobwebs and dust. The next, a labyrinth of shadowed rooms. He peered into each floor, to see if anyone was near, and kept climbing. Why was there no one here? Was it late? A terrifying thought struck him. He had no idea what time it was, nor how soon dawn would come.

The pain came and went as he climbed. Sometimes, he didn't feel it. Other times it was so sharp he doubled over. He thought about smoking a cigarette, but he worried someone might smell it.

He remembered the brief glimpse of the four Lamed Vav he'd had at Dvoyre's house. They were on a high balcony, somewhere in this palace. And as he climbed, he thought, *If I were Mashit, where would I keep my most precious possessions?*

I'd keep them close, he thought.

And if I were the queen, where would I live in this monstrous place? At the apex so no one would ever stand above me.

He nodded to himself. He had to go up. All the way.

But after eleven floors, the stairs ended. He stepped into an enormous hall more opulent than Versailles. Huge paintings in gilded frames adorned the walls, depicting demons tearing off human heads, stomping on corpses of the weak. On stone plinths, tall marble statues snarled and raised their fists to the sky, toward the Creator who spurned them all. Burgundy curtains draped over the walls, their bases tied with golden thread. The ceiling was a gilded masterpiece of concentric squares, carved into byzantine arabesques. At the far end a broad doorway led into another hall, more opulent than the first. As he approached, his footsteps echoed from all directions, fooling him into thinking he wasn't alone. But when he paused, nothing stirred.

The air was stale and murky; what little light there was didn't travel far. As he passed through one hall after another, the air grew steadily colder until he shivered with its chill. He'd reached the end of the hall, where a many-columned portico framed the city beyond. It was night, and its crooked buildings were in silhouette, their agglomerated forms from some best-forgotten nightmare. Daniel gasped, because it seemed as if some dread beast had taken an ancient human city, crushed it in its enormous hands, and dropped it back into place with all its angles broken, all its walls crumpled. This city was a festering wound that had never healed. And above these jagged shadows, huge red boils infected the sky. Sheol's stars. They wavered in the frigid air, and he shuddered with them.

Fuck, he was really in hell.

He stepped onto the terrace as a wave of pain doubled him over. He collapsed to the floor, unable to stifle a scream. The walls echoed his voice, and he shoved a hand over his mouth. He heard footsteps approaching. Another wave of pain, and there were stars in his vision. He bit his hand to stop from screaming, and blood spilled into his mouth.

The footfalls grew closer. Someone would see him. He had to move. He heard voices, but he didn't understand their words. Sword in hand, he pulled himself toward a column along the inner wall of the portico. He tried to stand, but the pain was too great. Hideous silhouettes approached from down the hall. He pulled himself behind the column as they stepped out onto the portico's brisk wind.

There were three demons. One was faun-like, with a man's slender body, a goat's head, and long pointed horns. Another was a huge black, many-legged scorpion, with a shivering pincer above its head. The third had a crocodile's face, moon-gray skin, nostrils as large and round as his eyes, and a long lock of fiery-red hair tucked into his belt. The demons spoke and Daniel did not understand a word.

The crocodile-faced one took out a small vial, uncorked it, and took a swill of its dark liquid. They passed the bottle around, and each took a sip.

"There," said the crocodile. "You should understand me now."

And Daniel, surprised, understood too, and this explained his renewed pain. His curse was coming back.

"We're speaking Quechuan," said the crocodile.

"What did you say?" said the faun. Then, surprised, he touched his lips as if unaccustomed to them.

"Quechuan, an uncommon human language," said the crocodile. "It's a precaution. You never know who might be listening."

"A *human* language?" said the faun. "No wonder that potion was so bitter. "

"Better a bitter potion than a bitter life."

The scorpion looked around. "Where is everyone?" she said. "I've never seen the palace this empty."

"In bed," said the crocodile, "so they might rise fresh for the spectacle, for tomorrow is the first Stoning Day when no stones will be thrown."

The faun shivered. "I don't like it. I haven't seen even a single guard."

"Neither have I," the crocodile said. "Kokabiel has obliterated the top ranks of the Legion. Amateurs now guard these halls, and they are few and the palace is large."

"Yesterday," said the faun, "I would have said this works in our favor, but now I'm not so sure. The Legion brings the only stability Sheol has ever had. Without them..." The Faun sighed. "So tell us, Gedeon, why have you dragged us out here at this late hour?"

"Because tomorrow Mashit plans to free our lord from his cage."

"I heard this rumor," said the scorpion dismissively. "And it's just that. A rumor. There's no truth in it. The queen would never do such a thing with all Sheol watching."

"No," said Gedeon. "You're wrong. She plans to release our lord."

"I've heard this too," said the faun. "Mashit wishes to show the Pillar Maya she's capable of mercy."

"And we will show Mashit," said Gedeon, "what a mistake that is. My friends, our time of plotting has come to an end. Tomorrow, we act."

"Tomorrow?" said the faun. "But we're not ready! General Kokabiel banished half of our allies to Bocker's Crack! Without them–"

"Without them," said Gedeon, "we go alone. We cannot wait. We'll not get another chance and we must take advantage of this. Tell your people to be ready, and wait for my sign. Tomorrow, our lord Ashmedai will rise again."

"Are you sure this is good for Sheol?" said the scorpion.

"You still have doubts," said Gedeon.

The scorpion nodded. "My sons grow herbs in window boxes. The other day as I walked down Suffering's End, I saw a violet flower growing between the cracks in the stone. My old bones used to ache with every step. Now, I don't feel the pain. When Mashit seized power, I wished for Lord Ashmedai's return. Now? I have my doubts. Gedeon, perhaps we should wait and see what Mashit will achieve."

"I thought you would say that," Gedeon said. "That's why I brought this." He reached into the folds of his shirt and removed a small scroll.

"What's that?" the scorpion said.

"Our future. *Your* future."

"I don't understand."

"Just read and you will."

The scorpion sighed and took the scroll from Gedeon. And as she read, a cone of scintillating light shone from the parchment onto her. She began to shrink, first slowly, then all at once. She shrieked as she and the cone of light were sucked into the parchment. With no one holding the scroll now, it fell to the ground and rolled itself back up. Gedeon leaned over, picked up the scroll, and returned it to his pocket.

"She would have betrayed us," he said. "Now, do you have doubts as well, Huum?"

The faun shook his head vigorously. "No! None at all! But…"

"But what?"

"We needed her, Gedeon. She has many allies!"

"She was redundant, and would have slowed us. I know who her friends are anyway, and I know yours. I have spiders everywhere, remember? I'll get word to her friends."

"Very well," said the faun. "Tomorrow, it is then."

Gedeon rubbed his hands together. "Tomorrow, Huum, you shall be a smith again and I shall be a librarian."

At this, the two fled the portico and vanished down the corridor. Daniel let out the cry he'd been stifling. He fished in his pocket for a cigarette, put one in his mouth, and lit it with magic. With each puff, his pain waned, and he climbed to his feet. Was this revolt, this freeing of Ashmedai, why Raigul told Daniel he had to be back by dawn? So he would come before the revolt began? He had no idea what time it was, only that the night was short and he had a long way to go.

He walked to the edge and peered out at the city as the frigid winds whipped at his hair. He looked up at the palace, its scalloped floors, precipitous walks, columned porticos, and treacherous balustrades, when he saw, some sixty stories up, leaning over a balcony ledge, a face he recognized even from this great distance, like a hawk seeing its prey, a face he'd seen once, a long time ago, in a vision. A face he had marked and remembered.

Sunil Pranadchandr.

As the Lamed Vavnik stared down at him, Daniel knew what he had to do. He tamped out his cigarette, got up onto the railing ledge, and began to climb.

CHAPTER THIRTY-FIVE

TIME PASSED, AND THE PLUMP STARS TURNED THEIR CROOKED orbits in the sky. Kokabiel stood in the chilly hall outside Mashit's chamber, when the ever-present wind suddenly ceased. He straightened. What dark portent was this? The nightwinds never ceased.

He had never heard Abbadon this quiet. He listened to the sounds of the city. Demons snoring. Gloom vultures tittering. Insects creeping up the walls. Several floors below, a drop of water plopped into a puddle, and its sound echoed through miles of marble and granite, up the twisting stairwells, to his ears. Someone howled. Another screamed. A third creature cursed at the shivering stars. He walked to the edge, but before he reached it, the wind picked up again, and all these sounds were lost.

The shift would change soon, and the new Shields would arrive to find him alone with blood on the floor and on his boots. They might sound an alarm and send a small army against him. And he could take a few, maybe all. But he had no quarrel with the Shield. They were only doing their duty, like all good soldiers. His quarrel was with her and her alone.

But the time wasn't right. No, he would wait for Algol, the shivering star, which just now hung above the peak where new orchards had sprung up – Algol, the first star Abbadon had named; Algol, the symbol of triumph over chaos – he would wait until its smouldering fire touched the cliffs before he would act.

"Abbadon," he whispered to the halls, to the palace, and to the sky, "progenitor of this world and all of its manifestations. If you wish me to change my course, send me a sign in the sky. If I see none, if the stars turn their blind courses unimpeded, then I will know that your promises to us have always been a lie. I will slip open Mashit's door, creep over to her canopied bed where she sleeps, and with her Shard Knife I will tear a hole in her heart. Abbadon, great or small, I await your sign."

He sat outside her quarters intensely watching the stars.

Time passed. The fierce winds blew. Algol dipped, and was about to touch the mountain peak, when a huge ball of screaming fire plunged right past the window, so bright, it left spots in his vision.

CHAPTER THIRTY-SIX

THE CHILL WIND TORE AT HIS BODY, AND HIS BLACK CLOAK whipped and cracked like a flag in a stiff breeze. And the higher Daniel climbed, the colder it got. He grabbed onto granite imps to hoist himself onto balconies, and he stepped on basalt hobgoblins to climb ever higher. Every few stories, he looked down to glimpse the bleak city below, a few rare fires flickering in small windows, here and there a fuzzy patch of mold.

He was so damn high. This was insane. He was no climber. All it would take was single slip and he'd be dead.

Above him the palace pointed toward the stars. From a distance, it had seemed like a gigantic talon. But this close, clinging to its walls, he felt as if he were riding on the back of a great worm. Most windows were heavily curtained, and he couldn't see inside. But some floors allowed him glimpses into strangely decorated parlors, opulent like the halls below, or covered in centuries of dust, or full of grotesque shapes of unknown provenance. He saw movement in many rooms, creatures with too many mouths, limbs, and eyes, bizarre agglomerations of form. They ate, they wrote, they fucked, but mostly, they slept. He climbed as quickly as he could.

The stones were slippery with dung and mold, and he grabbed each new ledge with the utmost care. But he was exhausted after only climbing fifteen stories, and there were at least three times that left to go. He hadn't the strength to climb all the way.

Or maybe he did. A sharp pain electrified his spine, and when the pain abated he found more strength to go on. His Mikulal nature

298

gave him energies his human side did not possess. But when the cursed side asserted itself, so did the pain.

The answer was compromise. He would allow himself minutes of pain, climbing as many stories as he could. Then, he would pause to smoke a cigarette and push the pain down to a dull ache. And after a cigarette, his legs weak and wobbly, he'd climb again. But the physical exertion quickly negated the cigarette's curse-killing effects, and his Mikulal strength returned with the pain. And so it went: climb until the pain was too much, then smoke and catch his breath, then climb again. All while trying not to die.

When his Mikulal nature asserted itself, he caught scent of odors on the wind. Fires and ash and dust and rotting flesh. And every now and then he caught wind of a different scent, human sweat. He followed it like a dog, knowing he was growing closer. He kept to the shadows, hoping his black cloak kept him hidden from any observers below.

Exhausted, freezing, he collapsed onto a ledge overlooking the sleeping city. He was about to light a cigarette, when the beast was upon him. The demon was huge, seven feet tall and nearly as wide, boar-like with long tusks. He growled at Daniel in some demon tongue, a flurry of words Daniel didn't comprehend. Daniel hopped to his feet and said, "Just getting some air! Sorry to disturb you! I'll be on my way now..."

The demon narrowed his eyes and stepped closer. "I know you," he said in Akkadian. "You're, Daniel Fisher, the Pillar. I was with the Legion's ninth regiment on Gehinnom when the sky cracked open."

"Beautiful, wasn't it? Nice to meet you...um?" He held out his hand.

The demon withdrew a glowing coil of rope that didn't exist a moment before. "The queen will be very pleased with me when she sees what gift I've brought her. I'll be promoted to lieutenant general!"

Daniel drew his sword and pointed it at the beast, but the boar just laughed, and knocked the sword from Daniel's hands. Daniel gasped and stepped back against the wall.

"Now," said the boar, breathing heavily. "I shall bind you or kill you, but either way you're coming with me."

As the demon lifted the rope, Daniel weaved fire into the fabric of the world. The boar burst into flames and screamed, twisting back and forth as he tried to pat out the fires. Then, with a running start, Daniel knocked him over the ledge. The demon wailed as he plunged to the ground like a fiery meteor. He thudded hard when he hit the courtyard far below, and the sound echoed through the twisted folds of the city.

Daniel was on the verge of panic. His whole body shook. With his power of fire he had killed again. And someone had heard that scream, he was sure. The pain surged; he had to get away from here. He leaped onto the ledge and climbed. After two stories, he glanced down at the body. Several figures surrounded it and were pointing up at him. He shivered and climbed on.

Up he went. Maybe ten stories left. It was hard to be sire. Sunil was no longer on the balcony. But the smell of humans was strong and growing stronger. He was reaching for a railing to hoist himself onto a ledge, when another wave of pain hit. He lost his footing and slipped, but caught the railing with one hand. He tried to swing around to grab it with his other hand, when his pack of Marlboros tumbled free from his pocket to the streets below.

"No!"

The pain intensified, and he ground his teeth so hard one cracked. Blood spilled down his chin and blew away with the night wind. He swung his other arm around again, and this time grabbed hold of the railing. He growled, summoning all his strength, and began to hoist himself up.

He heard a dull flutter, like the sound of a some dread flock, when suddenly they surrounded him, enormous black, vulture-like birds. There were hundreds, and they beat their wings slowly, watching him. They hovered in near-silence, all but for the throb of their slow wing beats. What were they doing? Were they waiting for him to fall?

One alighted on the ledge between his hands. As large as a man, the bird's gray talons were huge and sharp. It peered down its long gray beak at him, its eyes flickering with the bloody light of the stars. It squawked, then pecked his finger, drawing blood. Daniel yelped, and it pecked again.

"No," Daniel whimpered as his bloody hand slipped free. Only one hand now between life and death. The vulture pecked at his other hand.

"Stop!" he shouted. He tried to use his power of fire, but only the barest puff of smoke appeared on the bird's wing. "*Stop!*" he screamed again.

Then, behind the bird, a face. A human face. Sunil Pranadchandr.

"Help me!" Daniel said.

"I can't," said Sunil. "There's a invisible barrier."

The bird pecked, and Daniel struggled to hold on.

"But there might be a way," said Sunil.

"Tell me!"

"You have to bleed more."

"What?"

"Grab the railing with your other hand and spread your blood over the ledge. It will draw the gloom vultures."

"But I *don't* want to draw them!" Daniel shouted.

"Yes," Sunil said. "You do. I promise you, this is the only way. You have to trust me."

Daniel didn't know what to think, but it was this or death. He swung his other hand up and grabbed hold of the ledge again. The vulture was almost at his tendons, and he screamed. With his other hand he smeared his blood on the ledge as best he could.

A second vulture landed above him, cocked its head, and pecked at his bloody hand. Daniel screamed again.

"It's working!" Sunil said. "Spread some on your shoulders too!"

"You're trying to kill me!"

"I'm trying to save you."

This was madness. Daniel let go of one hand and spread blood onto his shoulders. It was only by his Mikulal strength that he hung on now. Another vulture swooped in, and another. They landed on his head and back, pecking at him, and his cloak offered little protection against their sharp beaks. Then more came, and more, and he wailed in terror. They swarmed him, hundreds of them, and he closed his eyes as they attacked. He heard electrical arcing and crashes, and smelled ozone, singed flesh, and blood.

This was it. There was no escape from this.

And then their hands were upon him, hoisting him up, past the ledge, over the railing, and onto the stone floor of a balcony. He looked up and there were four faces staring down at him. Four human faces. He didn't have to ask to know their names. They were Baaba, Maya, Paula, and Sunil, the Lamed Vav.

"Who is he?" said Baaba. She had a patch over one eye and was missing a hand.

"I think he's come for us," said Sunil. His eyes were bloodshot.

Something stirred beside them, and Daniel watched as Paula stepped over to a vulture, grabbed it by the neck, and snapped it. Another was trying to fly away but kept hitting some invisible barrier which, when the bird collided with it, flashed with sparks and rippled like a phosphorescent pool. The vulture fell stunned to the ground, its dark feathers singed, before trying again. Paula killed this one too. Beyond the barrier, under a sky of plump red stars, hundreds of vultures were circling. A few tried to punch through the invisible barrier to get at him, but they were forcefully repelled and fell from the sky screeching. Another bout of pain hit him, and he doubled over.

"What the hell just happened?" Baaba said.

"I noticed that the shield around our balcony weakens for an instant with every collision," Sunil said. "So I hypothesized that if it were to receive a great many collisions at once, it might weaken enough for us to grab him. It appears my hypothesis was correct."

"You weren't sure...," Daniel said, gasping, "if it would work?"

"You're alive, aren't you?" Sunil said.

"Barely," said Baaba. "Let's get him inside."

"Wait," said Paula. "Who is this man?" And the look in her eye made Daniel wonder if she might kill him too.

Maya, dressed in the crimson and gold habit of a Buddhist monk, stepped forward and said, "He's Daniel Fisher, and he's one of us, a Pillar."

"How do you know?" said Baaba.

"Because she's seen him before," Paula said.

"Just a photo," said Maya. "Mashit keeps it in a drawer beside her bed."

"Does she have one of you too?" Baaba said, shaking her head. "Come, help me bring him inside."

They carried him through a curtained doorway and onto a couch, where they set him gently down. He looked at their faces, so different, yet all the same: they looked upon him with pity and compassion. By their anonymous, righteous acts they had held up the world, but by looking at them you would never know it.

"I'm not one of you," Daniel said. "Not anymore."

"Shhh," Baaba said as she fetched him a glass of water. Paula tore up a shirt to use as bandages and with a bottle of some kind of alcohol tended to his wounds. "Be still for a while," Baaba said, handing him the water. He drank heartily, spilling some onto himself. "The birds did a number on you."

"It's not...just the birds," he said. "I'm cursed."

"Cursed?" Baaba said.

"Please....do you...have a cigarette?"

"We have the hookah," Sunil said. "It will help you with the pain."

"No!" Baaba snapped. "No more of that damned hookah!"

"I need a cigarette," Daniel said. "Tobacco. Please!"

"We don't have any tobacco, Daniel," Paula said. She put a cool hand on his forehead. "And a cigarette would be terrible for you. You're feverish."

"It's the curse," Daniel said. "I'm half-Mikulal. Mashit cast a spell around the city so no Mikulalim can enter." He paused as another wave of pain hit. "But since I am only half..."

"Then you *could*," Sunil said.

"Yes," said Daniel. "But the curse still affects me. A cigarette... stops the pain...and dulls the curse."

"But we have no cigarettes, Daniel," Baaba said. "I'm sorry."

Daniel shuddered as another wave crashed onto his nerves. These bouts were getting worse. He couldn't take much more of this.

"Why were you climbing up the walls?" Paula said.

"To rescue you."

"Rescue us?" Paula said. "You can barely stand."

"Admittedly," Daniel said, "this is a problem."

Baaba laughed. "This man is not right in the head."

"I've come all the way from Earth. There's a door...a portal... opening at dawn, in the mines. It will take us all home."

"A portal?" Paula said. "Home?" She looked at the three others. "Then this is it. This is the moment we've been waiting for."

"But we still don't have enough data," Sunil said. "We don't know the guard shifts on all the levels yet. And we haven't fully mapped the dark stair. If we go now, we'll just end up lost, or we'll walk right into the hands of guards."

"You're welcome to stay here and smoke your hookah, Sunil," Baaba said. "I'm going with Paula. I'm going home. We'll use what data we have."

"What are you talking about?" Daniel said.

"We've been plotting our escape for weeks," said Paula. She walked over to the far corner of the room and lifted the stuffed cushion of a chair. She reached into its side, stuck her fingers into a small incision, and pulled out several folded strips of paper. "These are the shift schedules for the guards," she said. "And this one is a partial map of the palace. And this one is a map of the Dark Stair, as much as we know."

"The Dark Stair?"

Paula glared at Maya. "It's how our friend here has been visiting Mashit, alone."

"I don't understand," said Daniel.

"They're lovers, you fool," said Baaba.

"We're not lovers," said Maya. "I tried to get closer to her so I might find ways to facilitate our escape. But I've spoken much with her over these past several weeks, and I've come to know her inner torment. She means well, but she lacks wisdom. She repeats the cycles of violence because that's the only tool she knows. I've been trying to teach her other tools, such as mercy and compassion."

"With your face between her legs," Baaba said.

"Does it matter how Maya *feels*?" Paula said. "You heard Daniel. There's a doorway to Earth opening at dawn, and I plan to go through it. Are you all with me or not?"

"It'll be dawn soon," Daniel said. "We have to go *right now*."

"Then let's go," said Sunil.

"I'm ready," said Paula.

"Lead the way," said Baaba.

But Maya said nothing. She crossed her arms and stared at her feet.

"You're not coming?" Baaba said.

"No," Maya said. "I can't."

"Because you love her?" Baaba said.

"Because there's still work to be done," said Maya. "Mashit's changing. I know you don't see it. How could you, locked in here? But when I'm alone with her, she shows me another side of herself. A vulnerable side. Yes, she's violent, often brutal. But there's a seed of compassion in her heart, and if I can water it, if I can teach her to grow her compassion to encompass her people, then to her world, then all of existence, then perhaps one day, demons will not be our enemy."

"She won't change," Daniel said. "It's her nature."

"But she's already changed, Daniel," Maya said. "Tomorrow morning, for the first time, they won't throw stones at Ashmedai, the Traitor King. She plans to free him. Before all of Sheol, she will show him mercy. And this whole world will be taught a great lesson: justice does not need to be cruel."

Baaba shook her head. "If this is your wish, if this is what your heart wants, Maya, then all I will say is *adhhab mae alllah*. Go with God."

"And may all of you," Maya said, "be free of the wheel of suffering."

"Goodbye, Maya," Sunil said, and without warning, he hugged her. Tears streamed down his face as he pulled away. Paula hugged her next, then Baaba, and soon it was a veritable waterfall of tears. Daniel felt embarrassed and looked away.

With much effort he sat up from the couch. "There won't be another chance, Maya," Daniel said. "This is it."

"I've made my choice, Daniel," she said. "Now, all of you, go!"

The others helped him stand and led him through a door into a narrow, windowless hallway that seemed to lead nowhere. At the far end was a marble bust of Medusa in the Greco-Roman style, sitting on a stone column. Maya approached the bust and stuck her finger in its mouth. There was a soft click, and a small panel on the wall behind the column slid open to reveal a blackness beyond.

"Mashit took away all our matches," Sunil said. "How will we light the candles?"

"I think I can handle that," Daniel said, shaking with the pain.

"Do as we discussed," said Maya. "Take the Dark Stair down as far as you can go. I'll distract Mashit as long as I can." Then she pressed her palms together, bowed slightly, and said, "Namaste."

"Namaste," they all replied. Then the four of them squeezed into the dark tunnel, while Maya remained.

"Wait!" Sunil said. "You're not taking the Dark Stair too? Don't you need to go up?"

"I will," said Maya. "But there's something I need to do first. Good luck." Then she slid the panel back into place. It was pitch dark, but Daniel could see perfectly.

"Daniel? Those matches?" Sunil said, holding up a small taper.

Daniel waited for a bout of pain to wane, then summoned his strength to whisper fire into the world. It was only a spark, but it was enough. The wick of the taper flashed and the flame grew. A sphere of warm light now lit their faces.

"I don't want to know how you did that," Baaba said.

"I do!" said Sunil.

"It's one of the...many benefits...of the curse," said Daniel.

"Sounds lovely," said Paula.

"We should whisper," said Sunil. Then, with candle in hand, he led them on as Paula gave them directions using her hand-drawn map.

"How did you find this place?" Daniel said.

"According to a legend here," Paula said, "the demons who constructed this palace built a series of secret passages for Abbadon, their first king, so he could move about unseen. A few weeks ago, Mashit showed it to Maya so she could visit her bedchamber whenever she wanted."

"And she trusted her?" Daniel said. "Mashit didn't think Maya would tell you three about it and try to escape?"

"At first, Maya *didn't* tell us," Paula said. "And I'm not sure if she was ever planning to. Sunil was up late smoking his hookah one night, when he saw Maya sneak from her bed and venture down the hall to vanish. He confronted her when she returned. I wanted to strangle her, when I found out. But I'll give Maya this much: Mashit is much less of a demon when Maya's around."

They reached a narrow stair and were about to descend, when a wave of pain hit, and he doubled over. He tumbled into the others, nearly knocking them down the stairs.

"His curse?" Paula said.

"I think so," said Sunil.

"We can't stay here," Paula said.

It hurt so much he could barely speak. "I...I can't...I can't stand."

Baaba squatted beside him and put her hand on his shoulder. "Yes, son, you can. I know it hurts like the father of all hurts. But you're going to stand, Daniel, and you're going to put one foot in front of the other, and goddamn it, son, you're going to take us all home."

A tear rolled down his cheek as pain shuddered through him. He turned over, pushed himself up, and slowly rose to his feet. He took a step.

"That's my boy," Baaba said. "That's it, now."

And in this way, step by slow step, Daniel and the Lamed Vav made their way down.

CHAPTER THIRTY-SEVEN

MASHIT SOARED ABOVE THE RENEWED CITY ON WINGS OF LIGHT. Beneath her, Abbadon's majestic walls glimmered with colorful gems, and the people, bedecked in bright fabrics, crowded the golden streets. They chanted her name, "Mashit! Mashit!" And her heart was full to bursting. From below came a small voice, difficult to hear above the crowd.

Like the others, this voice called her name, but not in praise. It was pleading with her. The voice grew louder, until the world thundered with its sound. Mashit's wings dissolved, and the shining world dimmed. She tumbled toward the ground as the voice pleaded to her over and over. A shadow rose, a human shape without features, only darkness. A snaking tendril from its head, a probing shadow tongue, grabbed onto her ankle and pulled her down, toward its mouth, a yawning chasm as wide as the Abyss.

She screamed and awoke, instinctively reaching for the Shard Knife on her thigh, but it lay draped over a chair and out of reach. She was in bed, and Maya stood beside her, shaking her arm. "Mashit, wake up."

It was still dark outside, and the fire had died in the hearth, but a faint rose light petaled the horizon. It would be dawn soon.

"How the seasons change," Mashit said, blinking sleep from her eyes. She sat up. "Winter becomes summer again. You've come back to me, Maya."

Maya sat in the chair where her Shard Knife lay draped. "This is not about us, Mashit. I've come to help Sheol. I want to bring spring to this world."

Mashit smiled. "You don't know how much hearing those words warms my heart." She took Maya's hand. "So do I, my dear. Honestly and truly, so do I."

The door to her chamber swung open on its heavy hinges, and the giraffe-necked Kokabiel stormed in.

"Kokabiel?" Mashit said. "What in Abbadon are you doing here?"

"Abbadon, my queen, is why I am here," he said as he stepped closer. "I asked the spirit of our progenitor to send me a sign in the sky to prove his promises were real. And I vowed that if I saw the sign, I would alter my course. And so I waited just here, outside your chamber, watching the stars turn."

"You were outside my chamber this whole time? Where are my Shields?"

"Algol was about to touch the cliffs," Kokabiel said, coming closer. "I readied myself to act. But just then a ball of fire streaked from above past the hall window, shrieking as it went. If ever there were a clearer sign, I do not know it."

"A ball of fire? Koko, what are you talking about?"

He stepped up to her, and his eyes were intense. "I said to myself, 'Abbadon has sent me an unequivocal sign that I must alter my course. I must *not* proceed.' And so I resigned myself to this fate, for a moment. But then I thought, what of Sheol, and the tatters it's become? I struggled with my decision for a long time, and then I smelled *her.*"

"*Her?* Koko, what are you on about?" There was something wicked in his eyes. "Shields!" she shouted to the open doorway. "Shields! Come at once!"

"They are gone," Kokabiel said as he approached her bed.

"Gone?" She slipped from underneath the covers and stood beside Maya, putting a hand on her shoulder. "Koko," she said, pointing to the door, "leave my bedchamber at once or I'll strip you of your command for good and have you sweeping up slop in the kitchens!"

He reached the bed. "This human creature has corrupted you beyond recognition. She has corrupted the kingdom. She has poisoned your mind, and the minds of millions. When you lay with her, you lay with vermin."

She stared into his eyes. "Have you looked in the mirror?" she spat. "You're a rat, Koko. Inside *and* out. You know nothing of what's good for me, or for this world."

"And *this* creature does?" he said, pointing a long finger at Maya.

"Yes, Koko. As a matter of fact, she does."

Kokabiel inhaled deeply and seemed to grow in size. He exhaled and said, "Then I vow that, after tonight, I shall not interfere with your affections ever again. Give me one last kiss, a farewell to settle my aching heart, and I will leave you alone for good."

"That will not happen, Koko."

He removed a knife from his belt and she stiffened. "I swear by Great Abbadon and the Fires of Sheol," he said, "that if you allow me to kiss you one last time, I will free you from my heart. I will never trouble you with my desires again." He raised the knife and sliced open his palm, and his blood dripped to the floor.

Maya winced and rose from the chair.

"You're serious, aren't you?" Mashit said.

"I've never been more serious in my life."

"One kiss, and you'll stop this foolishness forever?"

"I've vowed to Abbadon and my blood."

And she had seen how much those vows were worth to him. She moved toward her Shard Knife. "Then come, Koko. Kiss me, and let's put an end to this madness." *Yes*, she thought, sadly, *I must put an end to your tiresome, adolescent pining, your petty jealously, your sniveling face, for the health of the kingdom.*

Maya stepped aside as Kokabiel approached her.

"Please," Maya said, as if sensing what Mashit had planned. "Please, both of you. I beg you. *Stop.*"

Kokabiel had always been large, but he seemed especially tall now as he stood over her. He took Mashit in his arms. He could have crushed her easily, but he held her tenderly. Their lips met. He kissed her deeply, and her body stirred with memories from a thousand warm nights. His kiss was long and slow. But when he let go she knew all her passion had fled. All that was left was a fading cinder that would soon wink out forever.

"Goodbye, Koko," she said. She reached behind her for the Shard Knife. But it was missing from its sheath.

The knife was in his hand. He lunged at her, but Maya leaped to block the blow, and the Shard Knife plunged deep into Maya's heart. The Lamed Vavnik fell, gasping, staring at the gaping wound in her chest. Kokabiel stared at the bloody blade in his hands, in shock.

"No!" Mashit wailed. "Koko, what have you done?" She turned to Maya, who was gasping as she desperately tried to staunch the seeping wound in her chest. Kokabiel screamed as he lunged for Mashit again, then the whole world shook.

A great crack of thunder split the air, louder than the sound of the vats exploding, and the mountains blasted away. They both fell to the ground. The palace shook violently. Items crashed from shelves and tables. Paintings tumbled from the walls. Large cracks forked across the ceiling.

The palace rocked, back and forth, in long pendulous swings. Kokabiel and Mashit struggled to stand. The Shard Knife glowed brightly blue-white in his hand, the same color of light that was now spilling from Maya's wound into the air in illuminated, sparkling vortices. It twirled out the window into the sky. Mashit crawled over to Maya, who was breathing rapidly. "Maya! Maya, I'm here!"

The light, the peace, the bottomless compassion, had left Maya's eyes. She struggled to make eye contact with Mashit. Faintly, she whispered. "I still...believe...in you."

She stopped breathing.

"No!" Mashit screamed. Maya lay limp in her arms, surrounded in a pool of her own blood. The palace was still rocking when Kokabiel finally got to his feet. He howled as he lunged at Mashit, and she leaped away. The palace shook, knocking them down again, and while he was prone, she took a last look at Maya before fleeing into the entrance of the Dark Stair at the far end of her chamber, which Maya had left open.

She knew the way, but she had no light, and the darkness and the shaking made progress difficult. She bumped into walls and nearly tumbled down a stairway. Kokabiel was close on her heels. She heard his heavy breaths, his plodding footsteps in the dark.

He snatched her ankle, but she pulled away and leaped through a hidden door into an unused drawing room. He lunged at her with the Shard Knife, missing her by a finger. Centuries of dust that had slept like ash on everything in the room flew into the air as she crossed it, her presence turning this once-forgotten chamber into a foggy maelstrom. The pre-dawn light peeking through cracks in the heavy curtains sent bloody beams through the gray dust as she retreated into a corner.

He emerged panting from the passage, a sweaty beast. This room had no other doors but the one she came through, this room, used by Abbadon centuries ago when he wished to be alone with his thoughts. There was nowhere to run.

Kokabiel raised himself to his full height, and his horns brushed the chandelier's crystals, and they rang like chimes. He slowed, took several deep breaths, and with the Shard Knife in hand, he approached her, his eyes locked on hers.

She searched the wall behind her for panels, exits. An escape. But she knew there wasn't. She had explored every corner of this palace. The only way out was through him.

"No!" she shouted, punching the walls. "No, Koko, you mustn't!"

He stepped closer.

"Whatever sin I did, whatever wound I made in your heart, I can heal! This isn't the end of us, Koko. Don't make this the end!"

He raised the knife.

"Wait!" she said, putting her hands up. "I was cruel to you, Koko. Unimaginably cold. I was unfair. I used you. And, Koko, believe me...I'm sorry! Please, will you forgive me?"

"You want me to show you mercy?"

"Yes, Koko," she said as she fell to her knees. "A little mercy will help us all."

He lowered the knife. She let loose a shuddering sigh. "Oh, thank Abbadon."

He stared at her. "Abbadon is dead," he said. "And so are his promises. And when I am king, there will be no mercy left to give." Then he plunged the knife deep into her chest.

The force of it threw her backward into the wall. The pain was too much, an impossible thing. No, this wasn't happening, *couldn't* be happening. Her heart was aflame. Her limbs were great conflagrations. She crumbled to the ground as Kokabiel stood above her, the bloody Shard Knife dripping in his hand.

There was a dusty painting on the wall beyond his head, a

replica of the tapestry hanging in the Emerald Drawing Room, the one she had shown to Daphna that depicted the Shattering, where Great Abbadon stood atop Sheol, his waves of change rippling out across eternity. At the farthest edges of the painting, the ripples weren't visible at all.

CHAPTER THIRTY-EIGHT

IT WAS THE WORST PAIN HE HAD EVER FELT, AND IF IT NOT FOR Baaba's patient and continual encouragement, Daniel would have crumpled onto the floor and died. They were heading down, step after painful step into the darkness, guided by Paula's map and Sunil's candle, when the palace shook with an earthquake. They tumbled down the stairs and collapsed onto a wide landing. Sunil's candle went out. Cracks split the walls, and the metal stairs groaned as they violently twisted.

"What's happening?" Paula shouted.

The palace rocked, and Daniel feared that any moment the whole thing would come crumbling down, shattering them as the Creator had shattered all the worlds. He tried to speak, but could only groan. The rocking seemed to go on forever, and they all held each other, huddling there, in the dark, not sure if they'd live or die, and Daniel thought, *This is us. This is how it's always been. Humanity, huddling in the dark, afraid of what may come.*

Then, something snapped. A vessel under great pressure had shattered inside him, and all the agony floated out into the dark. He could not believe it. But for a few bruises on his body the pain had thoroughly fled. The rocking slowed, and they did not die.

He stood. "My pain. My pain is gone." He found Sunil's candle on the floor, and with a word ignited the wick. Sunil had a bleeding cut on his face, and Paula was holding her wrist. Baaba held her ribs. And all of them were covered in dust.

"Can you walk?" he said to them.

They all slowly climbed to their feet and nodded. The palace was still shaking, but it was slowing. "We have to keep moving."

They treaded carefully over sections of the stair that had snapped and left dangerously sharp metal edges. *Why?* he thought as they walked. *Why did my pain go away? If Mashit cast the spell, then did something happen to her?*

They were heading down as fast as they could, when something stirred below. A group of soldiers was ascending the Dark Stair several stories down. He quickly blew out Sunil's candle. "Shhh!" he whispered. "Hold onto each other. We're going back up."

"Back *up?*" said Baaba.

"Yes, come on!"

In the pitch dark, holding onto each other, Daniel led them up several flights, and now there were voices above, coming down. "Fuck," he whispered. "Fuck, fuck!"

"If I've counted the stairs right," Paula whispered, "we're on the forty-second floor. I can't see a thing, but there should be a corridor to the right of the stair. It leads to the hall of Gabriel's Tears."

Paula was right. There was a passage leading away from the stair. He led them down it, when they reached a wall.

"I need light," Paula whispered, and Daniel lit the candle.

Paula searched the wall with her hand, when there came a soft click. A square panel slide aside to reveal a bright space beyond. Bright scarlet light flooded in.

"Hurry!" Daniel said. "Go, before they see!"

The three leaped through, and he went last, and just as he stood it felt as if a hot brand had just burned his face. He winced and turned away from the light.

"What is it?" said Sunil. "Your curse again?"

Daniel saw the streaks of light across the floor. "A different part. I can't be in direct sunlight," he said. But the cloak Raigul had given him protected him from the light. He threw the hood over his head and squinted to take in the brilliant room.

It was enormous, like twenty grand ballrooms placed side-by-side. Hundreds of translucent emerald columns rose from a checkered floor toward the lofty ceiling, which was covered in frescoes and gold. Along the distant wall, huge curtains had been pushed aside, and the bright light of the twin suns, just risen over the shimmering lake, shone across the hall, refracting through the emerald columns to make a million scintillating stars. Daniel had never seen anything like it. It was astoundingly beautiful. And demons had made this. In hell.

He couldn't look for long, because even the refracted light hurt. Paula needed help sliding the panel back into place with her injured wrist. And in the light, Sunil's face wound seemed worse. They crossed the immense space, and as they went, images appeared inside the columns – colorful scenes brought to life by the sunlight: the twisted forms of demons in great battles, led by Abbadon, their first king; the foundation of a city being laid; the palace, growing skyward.

"What is this place?" Daniel said, careful not to face the suns.

"The hall Gabriel's Tears," said Sunil. "Mashit took us here once. They have their banquets here. The tiles are numbered, and if you walk them in order, you can view the entire history of Sheol inside the columns, like holograms."

"It's breathtaking," Daniel said. "I never thought demons could appreciate beauty."

"Admire this art later!" Paula said. "We have to keep going!"

"Why the rush?" Sunil said. "We're already too late. Daniel said the portal opens at dawn. The twin suns have already risen. It's dawn. We've missed it."

"No," Baaba said, shaking her head. "No, I won't accept that!"

"Oh my god," Paula said, stopping beside a column to stare at it. And they all paused to stare with her, because, floating inside the translucent emerald crystal, were the four hologram faces of Baaba, Sunil, Paula, and Maya. They'd become history too.

CHAPTER THIRTY-NINE

He had done it. He had killed her.

Kokabiel blinked. He could not believe his eyes. On the floor, her breath quick and waning, Mashit, a First One, one of the oldest creatures in the Cosmos, lay bleeding. Titanic bolts of lightning leaped from her wound, leaving behind black scorch marks where they pierced the walls. Dust fluttered down all around him like ash. Shivering, he stood over her as her labored breaths grew rapid and shallow.

She deserved this, didn't she? Death was her just reward for what she had done to Sheol, wasn't it?

He felt sick. The world shook. Or was it him? He turned and vomited. He wiped his mouth and looked down at her body. Her eyes were open, glassy, unblinking. Lightning bolts leaped from her wound, crackling as they zipped through the wall. The air reeked of blood – her blood – and fire, and dust. He waited for her to revert to her natural form, the four-headed creature he had seldom seen. But here she lay, human-shaped.

He collapsed to the ground, staring into her leaf green and cinnamon brown eyes. Did they still see? Great Abbadon, what had he done? The lightning waned. The bolts weakened to sparks that fluttered to the ground. Her body let slip a final sigh, and she stirred no more. Mashit, queen of Sheol, was dead.

"*Mashit.*"

He watched her for a long time. Slowly, he became aware of voices. The palace had stopped shaking, but dust was still falling from the cracks in the ceiling. He climbed to his feet and moved toward the voices. He pushed aside the heavy curtains, stirring up more clouds of dust, to reveal the brightening sky. He punched the frosted glass pane, and it shattered and fell away. A chill and biting wind smacked him in the face, and the room became a gray storm. He peered over the sill, looking down.

Cracks had split the streets below as they had split the palace, and gloom vultures were circling in great numbers, which meant there were many dead below. But still the denizens of Sheol had marched themselves up from lethargy and fear to assemble in the pre-dawn streets. It was Stoning Day, when Mashit had planned to show Ashmedai mercy.

He turned around. Dust snowed down onto her body, which lay crumpled in the corner, small, inconsequential. How had he ever let himself feel intimidated by her? He lifted her flaccid body and placed her on the couch, and a million motes of dust swirled in the light from the window like the myriad Shards. Her pallid face was as white as bone, her lips as gray as worms. He kneeled beside her and took her hand. "My queen," he said. He leaned over and softly kissed her forehead. "Goodbye."

He rose, charged through the Dark Stair, and reentered Mashit's bedchamber. Maya lay on the floor, her monk's robes soaked in blood. He'd have to clean this up before–

Gumwin, a Legion soldier, burst into the bedchamber through the open door. "My queen, sorry to disturb you but–" He spotted Kokabiel and his eyes went to the dead Pillar on the floor.

"Sir!" Gumwin said. "Apologies – I – is that Maya?"

Kokabiel approached him. "What is it, Gumwin?" His voice was hoarse and slow.

"The Pillars have escaped from their chambers, sir. But you must know that?" Gumwin looked down at Maya's body. "Is she dead, sir? Is that why the world shook?"

Kokabiel raised himself high. In Maya's corpse, and the Pillars' escape, he had exactly what he needed. "I have terrible news, Gumwin. The queen is dead."

"*Dead*, sir?" He looked at Kokabiel's hand, which still held the bloody knife.

"Maya killed her. With this." Kokabiel held up the blade. "This was Mashit's Shard Knife. She wore it on her hip. Maya snatched it from her when they lay together and killed her to aid the Pillars' escape. Mashit should never have trusted a human."

"You witnessed the queen's murder, sir?"

"No...no, I came here to...to speak with the queen, when I discovered the Shields were absent."

"'Absent,' sir?"

"Sent away, by Mashit, at Maya's behest, so she could be alone with the queen."

"And you heard this order, General?"

"I surmised it. Why else would Mashit send her Shields away? When I saw no soldiers present, I grew suspicious and entered her chamber. When Maya saw me she quickly stabbed Mashit. I rushed her and I killed her with the very same knife."

"*You* killed Maya?"

"Yes, Gumwin, to protect the queen. But I was too late."

Gumwin scanned the bedchamber. "But *where* is the queen, sir?"

"After Maya stabbed her, she fled into the Dark Stair. I found her in an old dusty chamber." He paused, overwhelmed with emotion, and there was no ruse in it. "There, I found her dead."

Gumwin seemed entirely overwhelmed too. "If the queen is dead, sir, then who rules Sheol? One of her children? Who's the eldest? Maavet? Resheph? Dever? The rites of succession state that the-"

"Until further notice, Gumwin, I am your king."

Gumwin swallowed, then snapped his heels. "Yes...yes, of course, sir! What are your orders, sir?"

"Find the escaped Pillars, and bring them here."

"Yes, sir. We already have search parties assembled."

"Send the whole damned Legion, Gumwin, for they will pay for the queen's death."

"Yes, sir."

Gumwin turned to leave, when Kokabiel said, "Wait, Gumwin. Don't tell anyone of the queen's death. Not a soul! With the Pillars loose, it will only cause chaos, and right now we need cohesion most of all. I will announce Mashit's death later this morning, from this balcony, when all Sheol is assembled."

"I understand, sir."

"And, Gumwin?"

"Yes, sir?"

"I'm trusting you. I don't deal kindly with those who disobey. If you keep the queen's death between us, I might have a high place for you in my kingdom."

"Your...*kingdom*," Gumwin said, as if adjusting to the new reality. He blinked for a moment, and then nodded. "Yes, sir. Yes, of course you can trust me."

"I know I can. Now go!"

Gumwin sped away. Alone, Kokabiel sat on the edge of the bed, and the canopy billowed above him. Mashit's impression was still indented upon the sheets. He ran his hands over them. He brought the fabric to his nose, closed his eyes, and inhaled. Her scent was thick upon them.

"What have I done?" he said, shuddering. He walked over to the window, where the first sun of Adar had just crested the mountain, spilling carmine light over the streets and the lake below. The lake sparkled, and the voices grew louder.

He looked at the empty bed, and the truth struck him like a sword to his heart. It had always been about her, his quest for power, his need for dominance. He had always tried to prove himself worthy of her, but in her eyes he had never been more than a tool. And now, with her dead, he had no one left to prove himself.

Gloom vultures darted across the buildings, settling on terraces and rooftops, awaiting morsels and crumbs that would invariably fall from the assembling masses. More pecked at bodies crushed in the earthquake.

Was that what he had become? A vulture, who picked from the dead? He wanted to rule in triumph and in glory, but who would look up at him in praise now? Those rabbling fools below? They quarreled in dust over scraps and worshipped whomever gave them their daily bread. Their praise meant nothing to him.

The only one whose praise had meant something was dead by his hand. No, he did not want to rule. Not like this. Why hadn't he seen what lay clear before him? He swallowed the sob rising in his throat, straightened his clothes, adjusted his belt, and wiped water from his eyes.

In the distance a horn bellowed, nine long notes. A pause, then nine more, the Legion's call to arms as the soldiers assembled to hunt the Pillars.

No, he did not want this. Why had it taken him so long to see everything he had ever done had been for her? The pain was too great. But there was a way out, and Kokabiel finally understood why Abbadon, the first king of Sheol, had chosen the same escape.

He would "forgive" Ashmedai before all, just as Mashit had planned. He would even invite the Traitor King to dine with him. He would ply the weak demon with food and wine and salves for his wounds. And when Ashmedai was sated and sleepy, he'd destroy him as he had destroyed Mashit, with the Shard Knife.

Ashmedai would choke on his own blood. And when the Traitor King was dead, Kokabiel would cut off the heads off the Pillars too. Then, finally, his knife soaked and warm with blood, he'd step onto the balcony, standing under Algol and the cinder stars, and drive the Shard Knife deep into his own heart.

Curse Mashit. Curse Ashmedai. Curse the Pillars. Curse Sheol, and all its wretched people. He would leave them with chaos and death, what they deserved. Nothing mattered anymore. He squeezed the hilt of the knife and returned to the canopied bed to wait.

CHAPTER FORTY

HE HAD A DREAM, AND IN THE DREAM MASHIT CAME TO HIM.

"Ashmedai," she said. "I'm sorry. I truly am sorry."

Her face floated in a sea of darkness, a Shard in the Abyss, and when he reached for her, to place his fingers on her cheek, she drifted away, shrinking until she was a glimmering star. The star winked out, and all was black and silent. He awoke gasping.

Something had changed. The world had suffered something from which it would never recover.

"Good," said the pig-faced Rethuel. "You're awake." Rethuel walked across the iron ramp toward Ashmedai's cage. He lifted his shimmering golden key toward the magic-sealed lock, smeared sigils and signs in leviathan blood on the lock's plate, and the bars ceased their incessant burning. "It's time to rise, again."

Something was different about him and the others. Ashmedai could barely muster the strength to speak. "Why so solemn today, Rethuel?"

"Today is your lucky day, Ashmedai. The queen has ordered that no one is to curse you nor throw stones at you today. You'll be paraded in absolute silence."

The dream of Mashit's receding face lingered in his mind, and he sensed something was dreadfully wrong. But he could not grasp its essence. "Why silence?" he said. He tried to rise, but hadn't the strength. "Why am I to be spared humiliation today?"

"How should I know?" said Rethuel. "The queen is as fickle as the twin suns. But I suspect it has something to do with the earthquake."

"What earthquake?" Ashmedai said.

"You did not feel it? Though I suppose your cage is always rocking. The whole world just shook not long ago. We had to take a different route here because of it. Many tunnels have collapsed."

They lifted him from the floor, and he tried not to groan as they dragged him across the iron ramp and locked him in a smaller cage. Then they wheeled his cage through a long and winding route they had never taken before, while flickering torches and bronze lamps threw scattered light down the many corridors. Dozens of tunnels were impassible due to fallen stone, and they turned often.

"Tell me," he said. "Are these the last moments of life? Am I going to be killed, Rethuel? Allow me to make my peace before I go to oblivion."

"Like I told you," said Rethuel, "I've no idea what the queen plans today."

Ashmedai swallowed, and the sense of dread lingered uncomfortably in his breast. Was this his final hour? He did not want to die, but neither could he endure this suffering much longer. Again, he thought of Mashit's face, receding.

One of the soldiers unlocked a heavy gate and pushed the doors open. The light of the twin suns pierced his eyes. It hurt to look at, but it was a glorious sight, the city at dawn.

This must be the end, he thought. *For I have never seen such a sight in this world.*

They wheeled him through an empty alley, and he inhaled deeply. The air was strangely sweet and – could it be? – *fertile*, like a spring day on Earth. He had doubted her, but had Mashit truly succeeded in bringing life here?

And then he saw: large patches of green and yellow mold, clinging to the alley walls; swarms of giant purple dragonflies hovering about a puddle; tall weeds growing between the gaps in the cobblestones.

She has, he thought. *By Abbadon, she has done it.*

His cage rattled painfully as they wheeled him over the cobbles, and he caught glimpses of the distant mountains, patches of verdure their steep cliffs. He had thought it impossible, but she had done it. She had brought life here.

They exited through a postern and moved onto the crowded street of Suffering's End. At the sight of the masses he winced, expecting stones and shit and buckets of urine to come hurling toward him. Instead, they all stared, solemnly, silently, as his captors wheeled his cage through the narrow street. In their eyes he expected to see malice and hate. Instead, he saw weariness. Like him, they had had enough.

They turned onto the wider street of Final Despair, and for a moment he did not register what his eyes were seeing. In stone and metal boxes, in ceramic pots and glass jars, set on window sills, ledges, bridges, and balconies were thousands of thriving plants. It was absurd to see them here, on Sheol, these herbs and colorful flowers and vines. He'd never thought it could be said of this place, but Sheol had become beautiful.

The crowds grew thicker as they wheeled him toward Abbadon's Peace, but none uttered a word. And here he noticed, underneath the glamour of the plant life, the cracked facades, crumbled ledges, and collapsed bridges. No doubt many had died. Yet, here they were, in silence, standing upon rubble and scree to watch him pass. Even the gloom vultures had gone still, solemnly watching from rooftops and ledges.

They turned onto Last Gasp of Desperation, then into Abbadon's Peace. He had never seen so many demons assembled at once. Tens of thousands filled the streets, stood on roofs and balconies, even watched from the cliffs beyond the city. And all but for their breathing, none uttered a sound.

They stopped his cage under the statue of Great Abbadon, where a group of Legion soldiers waited. His heart pounded as he looked up to the palace.

All of those torturous months spent in a cage, all of those horrid Stoning Days – those were mere run-ups to this moment. This, he knew, was his day of judgment.

If they had been quiet before, an impossible silence spread over the crowd as they looked up to the palace and held their breath. A soldier blew his horn, signaling that Ashmedai was in position.

A moment passed. Another. Mashit would tease and torment the crowds by drawing out this moment as long as possible. Then, movement. A curtain was swept aside from a room, not her usual parapet of the Emerald Drawing Room, where she addressed the crowds, but her bedchamber. A figure appeared. Not the queen.

Kokabiel.

What was this? The queen should have appeared first. The dream vision of her receding face came to him again. A portent. What had happened to her?

Kokabiel cast a spell to project his visage out over the city, so when all looked up at him, Kokabiel seemed to be standing an arm's-length away. The giraffe-necked demon took a deep breath and scanned the crowd for a moment before he spoke,.

"I..." he said, and his voice thundered over the streets. "The queen..."

What has he done to her? Ashmedai thought.

"Great changes have come to Sheol," Kokabiel said. "Plants grow in our streets and on our mountains. Change has even grown in our hearts. The Pillar, Maya Dorje, has taught many of you the concept of mercy and forgiveness. The queen..." He swallowed. "She has learned mercy too. She has ordered us today to show mercy to the Traitor King. Today, we free Ashmedai from his cage."

A murmur of shock spread through the crowd, echoing Ashmedai's. Many turned to gape at him, before turning back to Kokabiel.

"We will bring Ashmedai into the palace," Kokabiel said. "And he shall dine with the *merciful* queen. His sins against Sheol will be forgiven."

A shout rose in the crowd. "But Ashmedai betrayed us!" Others murmured their assent. "He abandoned us!"

"He tried to make a better world!" cried another.

Many more in the crowd shushed them, fearing retribution.

"These are her orders," Kokabiel said. "Release the traitor, and bring him to me."

What have you done to her? Ashmedai thought. He knew that whatever Kokabiel had waiting for him in the palace was the furthest from mercy. A nervous titter arose in the crowd and grew in volume. The Legion soldiers glanced at each other, incredulous.

"Did you not hear my order?" Kokabiel shouted, and his voice shook the city, stirring up dust and setting free loose stones.

The soldiers who had escorted Ashmedai from the dungeon

looked at each other. Rethuel stepped forward and used one of his many keys to unlock Ashmedai's cage. Then two Legion soldiers helped him climb out, while the crowd watched, stupefied.

He stood upright for the first time in months, and it felt wonderful and strange. He was so frail he had to lean onto a soldier to stand. The soldier whispered in Ashmedai's ear, "My lord, have no fear, for our redemption is at hand." Ashmedai turned to the soldier. His narrow face, oval eyes, and short horns were familiar. He was Fip, a Legion lieutenant general under his former command.

As Fip led Ashmedai toward the crowd, the Legion soldiers looked at him and up at Kokabiel, as if unsure if this were really happening. Ashmedai scanned their eyes, looking for answers. But no one knew who or what to believe, including him. He paused to catch his breath, and everyone stared, as if waiting for him to speak.

A hooded figure, his face in shadow, waited in the crowd, and ever so faintly, twin candleflame eyes peered back at him. The figure nodded, once. Elsewhere in the crowd another hooded figure nodded at him. And elsewhere, three more.

"Redemption, indeed," Ashmedai said, straightening as he recognized these glowing eyes. And if they were here, this meant that Mashit was....The dream came to him again, her face, receding. Was she dead? Kokabiel had been plotting to kill her for a long time, but Ashmedai never suspected he would go through with it. He loved her too much. Mashit, dead? Ashmedai couldn't fathom it. He looked up at Kokabiel and seethed.

"Kokabiel," Ashmedai shouted, and the crowd quieted. "I am thankful for this show of mercy. But where, may I ask, is the queen?"

"Kill the traitor!" A flying demon leaped from the crowd, his wings glowing from a powerful spell. Green lightning shot from his fingertips, but Fip raised his thick bracelets and parried the attack. The energy reflected into the crowd, incinerating several bystanders, and many screamed. A hooded figure leaped on the attacker and cut off his head with a sword, eliciting more shrieks from the crowd.

The hooded figure rose from the dead creature, turned to Ashmedai, took a knee, and bowed his head. "My lord," he said, his voice like grinding stones. A Mikulal.

Someone in the crowd shouted, "Hail King Ashmedai!"

The crowd was astonished, because under Queen Mashit such statements were punishable by death. But the soldiers seemed more confused than angry and did not move. Another cry rose from the crowd. "Lord Ashmedai, Sheol's true king!"

"He's a traitor!" another screamed.

"Kill him!"

"Show him mercy!"

"Hail our true king!"

"The betrayer must die!"

"Anger is destructive, we must forgive!"

A stone struck him in the head. The one who'd thrown it was tackled by another. Fights broke out. Soldiers fought their way into the masses to try and quell the violence, but there were so many people they struggled to reach them. Fights multiplied.

"Stay close, my lord," said Fip, raising his sword, its magic etchings glowing red.

In the distance, some were chanting, "Hail King Ashmedai!" Others countered with, "Death to the traitor!"

"Calm yourselves!" Kokabiel shouted from the high balcony. "Calm yourselves or I'll kill every last one of you!" But his thundering voice only agitated the crowds. The riots turned bloody, and screams rose up from the plaza. Knives and stones and other projectiles flew over the crowd. The Legion soldiers were slaying anyone in their path.

"My lord," Fip said, "we must go!"

A lizard with glittering scales charged Ashmedai with a glowing spear, but Fip sliced her in half with his sword. Her orange ichor splattered over the stones.

"I agree wholeheartedly, Fip, but I cannot walk," Ashmedai said as he stumbled to the ground. A creature with fanged mouths inside his palms lunged at Ashmedai, but two Mikulalim leaped in to slay the attacker with their swords. The two lifted Ashmedai and carried him in their arms. Fip led the charge, battling off attackers, as the Mikulalim, Ashmedai held high in their arms, followed close behind, while more hooded Mikulalim fought off their pursuers. And, to his great joy, so did four Legion soldiers.

More were headed their way.

"Go ahead! Fight!" Kokabiel wailed from the palace, but no one was listening. "Destroy yourselves! It is what you're best at!" He reentered the palace and was gone.

Ashmedai's two bearers fought off attackers with their free arms as if they were one body, and he dipped and ducked as they parried the blows. They carried him through the rioting streets, while civilians, when they spotted him barreling through, shouted praises and curses at him.

A winged blue beetle shouted, "Hail King Ashmedai!" before a large white worm swallowed her in one gulp. An axe-wielding hobgoblin sliced the worm in two, and her two halves squirmed away, leaving the winged beetle, covered in white bile, stunned on the ground. The beetle immediately got up and continued chanting, "Hail King Ashmedai!"

The Mikulalim carried Ashmedai, and he felt as if he were waking from a deep dream. Some cursed and some praised him, but all had something to say. "Not so different from my former rule," he shouted. "Wouldn't you say, Fip?"

"Indeed, sir!" said Fip, as he sliced off the legs of an attacking spider.

When they reached the courtyard before the palace steps, they all paused. Some fifty Legion soldiers waited here, weapons drawn, blocking the palace gates, while hundreds of civilians were rapidly fleeing the courtyard.

Ashmedai sighed. "Well, that was short-lived."

Their leader, face like an ox, eyes black and luminous, approached Ashmedai. The Mikulalim raised their weapons, but the ox held up a hand. Yurial was his name, if Ashmedai remembered correctly. Yurial sheathed his sword, took to a knee, and said, "All hail Lord Ashmedai, the true King of Sheol. May his reign be eternal."

The fifty other soldiers took to one knee and bowed with him.

Yurial lifted his chin and said, "We've missed you greatly, my lord."

Dozens of civilians watched from a safe distance, and when they saw Ashmedai's searching gaze, they quickly bowed too. Ashmedai smiled as he looked across the city and said, "And you've no idea, Yurial, how much I've missed all of you."

CHAPTER
FORTY-ONE

IT WAS JUST AS THEY HAD REACHED THE EXIT OF GABRIEL'S Tears, with its holographic history, when Daniel and the Lamed Vav were captured. The soldiers were upon them in an instant, throwing them to the floor, crushing their faces with boots, pointing sharp weapons and magical objects at their necks. Only by blind luck did Daniel's cloak fall to shield his face from the bright suns beaming through the windows.

The others struggled and cried, but it was no use resisting these soldiers who breathed war and death. Their pleas only made them angrier. "This is a watchman's cloak," said a soldier to Daniel, his foul breath hot in his face. "Who gave it to you?"

Daniel said nothing as the soldiers bound their hands using coils of rope made only of phosphorescent light, which tightened even after the guards had let go. Paula's wrist was broken, and she screamed, but they didn't care. And thus bound, the soldiers marched them through endless hallways, up many flights of stairs, threatening to disembowel them whenever they paused to catch their breath.

"We were so close," Paula said, panting. "So damned close!"

"Hush!" shouted a soldier as he struck Paula with his fist. She stumbled, and Baaba and Sunil paused to help her up. As she rose, Paula gave the soldier the same look she had given the gloom vulture on the balcony. At this, the soldier smiled.

As they walked, they passed open windows, and sounds from a great crowd floated up from the streets below. They shouted in some demon tongue – curses or praise, he couldn't tell – but it mostly sounded like they were rioting.

The soldiers shoved them through a tall iron doorway into a large bedroom, and here Daniel and the others collapsed to the floor, exhausted. Cinders from an enormous fireplace sent dying waves of heat into the room. Opposite the fire was a gigantic canopied bed, ruffled and unmade. Large paintings and colorful tapestries on the walls depicted demonic scenes, and fine works of art filled nearly every space in the room. But something was very wrong here, and that's when Daniel realized he was smelling human blood.

It assaulted his nose like smelling salts, jerking him to wakefulness. At the far side of the room the demon Kokabiel waited, the same monster who had led the Legion on Gehinnom to slaughter the Bedu people. His body was giraffe-shaped, covered in white fur. Atop his long neck was a giant, rat-shaped head with eyes the color of the deepest sea. He had huge, spiraling ram-like horns. Kokabiel rose to his full, frightening height, and the Pillars shuddered. He stepped forward, examining them as if they were animals.

"We found them outside Gabriel's Tears, sir," said a soldier.

At this, Kokabiel laughed. "The world falls asunder," he said, "and these lot go to the banquet hall."

Daniel spotted a trail of blood on the floor. It led toward the bed. He peered beneath it, beyond the posts, to see her crimson and gold robes stained in blood. Maya's blank eyes stared back at him. "Maya!" said Paula. "Oh my god, Maya!"

They all saw her now. Baaba burst into tears. Sunil grimaced and turned away. Daniel was shocked most of all, but more than this, he hated himself, because the smell of her blood made him hungry. Kokabiel seemed to notice this. He approached Daniel and said, "Who is this?"

"A Mikulal, aiding their escape, sir," said a soldier.

"No," Kokabiel said. "I know his face." He crouched before Daniel and used the tip of his knife, its blade glowing moon-white, to lift Daniel's chin so he could peer more closely at him. "He's no Mikulal. He's thinner than I remember, but this is Daniel Fisher, another Pillar." He paused to consider. "So, Daniel, you've come here to rescue them, have you? To bring them home?"

Daniel was about to weave fire into the air, when Kokabiel waved his hand, and suddenly Daniel couldn't speak. "Don't try your Mikulal magic here, Daniel. I think you'll find I'm a formidable adversary. Though I respect you more for trying."

"Murderer!" Baaba shouted. "Beast!"

"Hush!" Paula said.

Kokabiel smirked. "I'd never understood the use of epithets, until recently. I used to think, unless the curses are full of magic, what harm can words do? Now I know better. Words can be just as harmful as spells and swords. Maya poisoned this world with her words, but I won't let you lot poison it anymore."

"You can't kill us," Sunil said. "You *need* us."

"You overestimate your value," said Kokabiel.

"No," Paula said, staring into Kokabiel's eyes. "We're the Pillars. We uphold the world. Maya's death caused the earthquake, didn't it? Kill us, and the world will shake again. And all the progress you've made here will fall apart."

"I don't care about *progress.*"

"But your queen, Mashit, does," said Paula.

"Mashit is DEAD!" Kokabiel shouted, and his voice knocked them all over.

Dead? Daniel thought, struggling to rise. And then he knew: Daphna had been right all along. He still missed her smiling face and could not fathom a universe in which she was not in it. He lay there, thinking of Mashit, when he knew her once as Rebekah.

"Mashit is dead," Kokabiel said, "the kingdom teeters, the people riot, and Ashmedai has been freed from his cage. Do you think Sheol will be saved by the weeds growing between the stones? Flower boxes in our windows?" Kokabiel laughed bitterly, and at the corner of his eyes were the glimmer of tears. "Nothing will save us now," he said. "You are meaningless. All is meaningless." He approached Sunil with the glowing knife raised.

"No!" Baaba said. "Please don't!"

Two soldiers burst into the room through a dark panel in the corner. Another entrance to the Dark Stair, Daniel noticed. "My lord!" one said in some ancient tongue that might have been Druidic.

"What is it, Gumwin?" Kokabiel said in the same language.

"My lord, she's gone."

"Gone?"

"We searched but could not find her."

Kokabiel straightened. "You went to the dusty drawing room at the end of the passage, like I said?"

"And found blood, my lord, and much of it. And a thousand footprints in the dust. But no body, my lord."

"She died," Kokabiel said. "I saw her die."

"Perhaps someone took the body, my lord?"

"I saw the life fade from her eyes..."

"My lord, should we send out a search party?"

"She died in my arms..."

"My lord?"

"We must find her," Kokabiel said. "Whatever it takes! Send the whole Legion! Do you hear me, Gumwin? We can't let her go! We can't let her go."

Something metallic whizzed through the air. It collided with flesh, making wet thuds. There were gurgles and yelps. And in the next instant, there were dozens of Mikulalim in the room, slitting the throats of all the soldiers at once. Their bodies crumpled to the ground, heads shrieking and gurgling, as a colorful spectrum of blood pooled next to Maya. They slit Kokabiel's Achilles tendons and he cried out as he fell to his knees. The phosphorescent rope binding Daniel and the others suddenly turned to liquid, dripped to the floor, and evaporated. The Pillars looked at each other and at Daniel.

The Mikulalim surrounded Kokabiel and pointed their swords at his chest. One snatched the glowing blade from Kokabiel's hand. This Mikulal was taller than the rest, with sharper cheekbones, long gray hair tied with a strip of leather into a tail, and a wide scar across his chest. "Hello again," Raigul said to Daniel.

Kokabiel grimaced as he raised his hands, about to cast a spell, when Raigul, the glowing blade pressed to his throat, said, "Go ahead. Do it, General. I shall be happy to slay you where you kneel. You may be stronger, but I am faster."

Even sitting, Kokabiel was tall. He spat in Raigul's face and said, "Mashit was wise to keep you wretched creatures from the palace."

Raigul wiped the spittle from his face. "You killed five hundred of my kin when you blew up the vats. Women and children among them."

"A pity I did not kill more."

"I know this is no ordinary blade," Raigul said, pressing the knife against Kokabiel's neck. "With one prick, you would die in the most painful way."

"Then kill me, you coward," Kokabiel said. "What are you waiting for?"

"We've better plans for you. We'll bind you in chains that absorb your magic, then we'll send you down the mines, where you'll never see the suns again, and your days will be full of endless hard labors. Then, at the end of many long years, when your past life feels like a dream and you pine for death, I'll sentence you to life, more labor, and more despair."

Kokabiel shook his head. "Don't flatter yourself. My people will find me, and they'll kill all of you wretched half-dead vermin."

"*Who* will find you, Kokabiel? Mashit is gone. Your allies have fled or been killed. No one will know you're there."

"Who – *what* are these men?" Paula whispered to Daniel.

"The Mikulalim," Daniel said. "My half-bothers."

"The cursed men" Paula said?

"And women," said Raigul. Five female Mikulalim turned to Paula and nodded. But for the mild difference in their cheeks and hips, they were indistinguishable from the men.

Baaba crawled over to Maya's body. "Oh dear, oh dear." Sunil and Paula crept over too. Raigul said to Daniel, "Ashmedai is free. He has entered the palace. By our curse we are compelled to obey him. But as you are not fully possessed of our curse, he may not compel you. Either way, I suggest you leave before he arrives. I will send escorts with you to help you find your way to the mines. I want you to succeed, Daniel. I want you to get home, so one day you might save us too. I must wait here for Ashmedai, as he has commanded me."

"But we missed the portal," Daniel said. "Didn't we?"

"No," said Raigul. "I've heard there's been a delay. They have a shortage of power. If you hurry, you might make it in time."

"Then what are we waiting for?" Daniel said to the others. "Let's go!"

"What about Maya?" said Baaba.

"We'll dispose of her body honorably," said Raigul.

But Daniel, in the Silent Tongue, turned to Raigul and said, *You must not eat her!*

Why not? Raigul said. *Few of Maya's teachings reached us down in the mines. But I heard one that always stuck with me. In her tradition of Tibetan Buddhism it's their custom to lay their corpses in the mountains for vultures to devour. The body, she said, is a mere vessel, and once the vessel is emptied, its matter must return to the world. We Mikulalim do the same. We eat the dead, so their bodies become part of us. By eating her, then, we respect her tradition, and ours.*

"Why are you staring at each other like that?" Sunil said.

"I think they're communicating," said Paula.

Daniel looked down at Maya's crumpled body. Was Raigul right? Was her flesh just matter to be recycled?

Aloud, Raigul said, "Maya Dorje gave all of herself to benefit this world. And she will give one last time. We will revere her body with same respect we give to all of our fallen brothers and sisters."

Daniel sighed. What else was there to say? These Mikulalim lived brutal lives, and if this was they how they made sense of their horror, then it was not his place to judge.

"Raigul," he said, "I didn't lie to you back in the mines, and I didn't lie to your brothers on Gehinnom. One day, I promise I'll free you all from this curse."

"As I said, Daniel, promises are hard to keep." And then, in the Silent Tongue, he said, *I thought I had sent you into the palace to die, yet here you stand. I believe now that our hope in you is not misplaced. You are our Redeemer. Good luck, brother.*

Raigul held out his hand and Daniel took it. *Thank you, Raigul. For everything.*

Raigul nodded, then he turned his attention back to Kokabiel.

Each Lamed Vavnik said goodbye to Maya. Paula recited the Jewish Kaddish. Baaba said a Muslim dua. Sunil spoke a Hindu prayer. When they were done, and had said their farewells, a group of Raigul's soldiers led Daniel and the others into the hall.

"I am Fruun," one said, a sharp-nosed woman, dark-skinned, and completely bald. "We'll take you down to the mines. Stay behind us. Stay close. Prepare yourselves. It's a long way down."

Baaba shook her head. "And here we go again."

CHAPTER
FORTY-TWO

HOW GLORIOUS IT WAS TO FEEL THE COOL AIR AND NOT THE heat of flaming bars on his skin! How delicious it was to stand upright without the sway of his cage! The Mikulalim hoisted Ashmedai up the marble stairwells, past statues of ancient demons, all female now, and through the palace halls. When they met unexpected parties, those who were unarmed kneeled and pledged fealty to him or fled before he and his soldiers got too close. Dozens from the queen's Shield took to their knees and offered to join his assault. Those who fought back were slaughtered without mercy.

His party quickly grew to more than a hundred. They marched through the halls, boots, hooves, and claws heavy on the stone floors, so that their sounds scared away most. Those foolish enough to challenge them met furious swords and spellcraft. They left pools of blood and spattered flesh on the walls as they ascended.

How pent up they all must have been, because the Mikulalim and the demon soldiers let fly their wrath, obliterating their opponents when a mere strike would do. It was wonderful to behold this whirlwind army fighting for him. Though weak and unable to stand without help, he felt as if they were part of his body, each soldier one of a hundred deadly limbs clearing his path back to the throne.

But all this movement caused his old wounds to suppurate and bleed. His energy seeped out onto the marble floors and granite steps, and he grew faint.

"My lord!" Fip said, coming to him. "You're hurt!"

"Don't stop moving!" he commanded, half delirious. "Let my essence fill these halls again. Let my blood mark the trail back to victory."

At this Fip and the others fought even harder. They crossed the immense hall of Gabriel's Tears, where he had once presided over days-long bacchanals. And though on those nights he and Mashit would taste the pleasures of others, in the end they had always returned to each other's arms. As his blood spilled onto the checkered floor, he thought, *Tonight I come back to you again, my love, but my return is bittersweet. For I know in my heart that you are dead.*

The few now they met in the halls turned and ran when they saw his bloody visage and his raging army approach. A tall and unusually thick-haired Mikulal sped down the hall toward them, paused, and bowed. "I am Raigul, my lord," he said. "You know me as the spark from the fires of Sheol."

"So you weren't a dream after all," Ashmedai said.

"Only if we are still dreaming now, my lord." He rose. "Please come. We have Kokabiel bound and waiting. And we have healers who can tend to your wounds."

"And what of Mashit?" he said. "Is she dead?"

"My lord..."

"Tell me, Raigul."

"Kokabiel says the Pillar, Maya Dorje, killed the queen. Yet, we know he has been plotting her death for months."

"Raigul, I know all this. *Is she dead*?"

"My lord, we presume so. Otherwise, my kin would not be able to walk in this palace. But we cannot find her body. It is gone."

"Gone?"

"Vanished. Moved, or...or something else."

Ashmedai smiled. "Only Mashit could find a way to be absent for her own death."

"My lord, you're bleeding. Let our healers tend to your wounds."

"Later. Take me to Kokabiel. I need to speak with the queen killer."

"Yes, my lord."

Raigul led Ashmedai and his small army down the halls to Mashit's bedchamber. There were too many soldiers to fit inside, so

Ashmedai entered with only Raigul. There were twenty Mikulalim here, this chamber where he and Mashit had spent many long nights together, and they all bowed as he entered. There were bloodstains on the floor, yet there were no bodies. Disposed of, no doubt, by the flesh-eating Mikulalim.

This had once been his bedchamber, and to his surprise many familiar items remained. His golden hookah that he'd puff in the light of the setting suns. A bust of Ozbyouth given to him by their son, Calcyon, the day before he died in battle. The huge gilded mirror on the wall where he had gazed every morning before meeting his court. He didn't recognize the creature looking back at him now. He was as frail and emaciated as a Mikulal. His beard had grown long, his face was gaunt, his eyes were rheumy, and his body was leaking pus and blood.

In the corner, bound in heavy, magic-draining chains, Kokabiel kneeled. Blood dribbled from his calves. Ashmedai held onto the furniture as he maneuvered toward him.

"I never thought I'd see the day," Kokabiel said, "when Ashmedai bleeds."

A Mikulal struck Kokabiel in the face with the butt of his sword, and blood flew from his mouth.

"No," Ashmedai said, raising his hand. "Let him speak. I want to hear his words."

"There's nothing more I have to say," said Kokabiel. "All is said. All is done."

"Says the demon who once commanded the most powerful army in the Cosmos." Ashmedai stepped closer, and his hatred for this creature who once shared this very bed with him too grew with every step. "*Why* did you kill her, Koko? Did you think you would become king? You have the charisma of a fly. The people would never accept you."

"And you think they'll accept you, the Traitor King, to lord over them again? They'd no sooner accept you than one of your thousand bastard children. Already they vie for the throne like rats fighting over a morsel. Besides, I didn't kill her. Maya did."

"Enough, Koko. I know what you did." Without a word, Raigul walked over and handed Ashmedai the Shard Knife. "You stabbed her," Ashmedai said, "with this."

"I told you. That was Maya."

Ashmedai turned to a stack of old books piled on a small table. He thumbed through the *Ars Almadel*, one of Mashit's favorites, and his bloody fingers left stains on their pages. "When I was king, reading was one of my favorite pastimes. There was a time when I did nothing but read."

"How learned of you."

"Do you know that after the Library of Alexandria, the most extensive library of knowledge in the entire Cosmos resides here, in the palace? I'd head down to the Archives several times a week to fetch new books. I befriended a librarian there. He always had excellent recommendations and a new stack of books waiting for me. I was so happy with his selections I promoted him to Master Archivist."

Kokabiel stared at him.

"His name was Gedeon. Did you know he visited me in my cage almost every week? He couldn't give me books of course. They would have just burned from the fires. And there were times when he was just too busy to visit. But while there he would sit across the heated gap and read to me from my favorite texts. I think if it were not for his soothing words, I might have gone mad.

"He told me many stories. True stories, about how you came to him, Koko, seeking revenge against Mashit for neglecting your poor, bruised ego. He told me that you sought a way to kill her. To kill me. Gedeon planned to kill *you*, you know, before you could succeed."

"Then why did the fool tell me how to kill a First One?" Kokabiel said. "Unless Gedeon wanted you dead as well."

"I've considered that," Ashmedai said. "But perhaps like all bookworms, Gedeon couldn't resist a good mystery."

Kokabiel sighed. "I did everything I could to please her. It was never enough."

"No, Koko. Everything you have ever done was for yourself."

"She put you in a cage above a river of fire, had you humiliated and stoned and shat upon, and yet you loathe *me*? I did you a favor by killing her."

"A favor? How ignorant we've all become. In my cell, I've had a lot of time to think. I stole Daniel Fisher from the Earth to use as a Pillar in a new world I'd hoped to build, one without suffering or death. But when I came out from the dungeons this morning, the first thing I saw were flowers, growing between the cracks."

"And you think a few flowers will save Sheol?"

"Not the flowers themselves, no. But what they represent. *Life* has come to Sheol, and Mashit has brought it here. I once thought her plan absurd. She felt the same about mine. But now I see that we were both working toward the same thing. Her plan is working, Koko. The irony is that it took her death for me to see this."

"Is that it, then?" Kokabiel said. "You wish to just pick up where she left off? That will be difficult without your Pillars."

"How do you mean?"

Kokabiel straightened, then a smile crossed his face. "Then you don't know? Daniel Fisher was *just* here. He and the Pillars are already on their way back to Earth. And your friends – these vermin – they helped him."

Ashmedai turned to Raigul. "Tell me, Raigul, that Kokabiel speaks more lies."

In the Silent Tongue Raigul said, *My lord, it is true. I aided their escape. But do not punish my brothers and sisters, for they were only following the orders I gave them.* Raigul fell to his knees and hung his head.

"But *why*?" Ashmedai said, shaking, furious.

"Because, my lord," Raigul said, looking up into Ashmedai's eyes, "I believe in him."

Beside them Kokabiel began hysterically laughing.

CHAPTER
FORTY-THREE

THE RIOTS ON THE STREETS BELOW GREW LOUDER AS DANIEL, the Pillars, and the Mikulalim made their way down the palace. They had begun with two dozen, but as they descended, more Mikulalim joined them, so that as they sped across a giant parlor, their party had grown to fifty. "Your human feet are too slow!" Fruun said. "Now make like birds and fly!"

The sound of their feet pattering down the stairs was like a thousand fleeing rats. They passed an open window, and the rioting masses screeched and howled below. Baaba said, "It sounds as if they're killing each other. Do we really want to go down there?"

The morning suns had not yet reached the window, so Daniel chanced a look down. The crooked streets were mostly in shadow, but the suns were quickly rising. Piles of demons, dead and wounded, filled the avenues, littering the streets like rainbow confetti after a parade. The heady smell of blood and meat wafted up from below.

"Halt!" Seven soldiers waited for them on the next landing, blood smearing their faces and armor. But when they saw how many Mikulalim were descending, their faces grew fearful, and they readied weapons and spells. "More cursed ones!"

Fruun turned to Daniel and the others and said, "Stay back!"

The Mikulalim charged the soldiers, and the soldiers parried with swords and spellcraft. A soldier drew marks of yellow light in the air with his fingers, forming a strange-looking hovering symbol.

"Don't look!" a Mikulal shouted. He leaped for Daniel, threw him to the ground, and covered his eyes with his hands.

"Get off me!" Daniel said.

There were shouts and screams, and when the Mikulal finally let go, there were five screaming Mikulalim dissolving beside him into piles of steaming brown liquid. Baaba, and Sunil huddled in a corner, away from the fight, while Paula picked up a small sword from a dead Mikulal. Though it was unwieldy in her hands she held it high.

Weapons clashed and scraped. Spells flew. The Mikulalim weaved fire into the air, burning soldiers, who fought fiercely through the flames. A soldier slew the Mikulal who had saved Daniel with a broadsword through his chest. Fruun leaped back to Daniel and fought off several more attackers.

A demon was about to cut Fruun in half with a long scimitar, when Daniel whispered words of fire to burn the soldier's face. The soldier wailed, missed, and Fruun stabbed him in the heart. She looked at Daniel once and nodded.

A Mikulal threw a glowing chain around a soldier's neck and pulled. The soldier struggled to free himself as his face turned quickly green. He jerked backward and flipped the Mikulal onto his head. The Mikulal dropped the chain, and the soldier used it as a whip to strike the Mikulal across his face. Another Mikulal stabbed the soldier in the back, but the demon turned, and lopped off his head with a sword.

The battle raged. Baaba and Sunil stayed back, but Paula was in the melee. A soldier slapped away her sword, but with a swift round kick she knocked the soldier to the ground. Another Mikulal killed him. Bodies lay everywhere. The one who had written the deadly sign in the air was trying to scribe another, while three Mikulalim held him off.

"Come!" Fruun said to Daniel, grabbing him. "Let's get you out of here!" Three more took Paula, Baaba, and Sunil, and together they fled up the stairs, while the battle raged on behind them. Once fifty-strong, now they were eight.

"We have to find another way out," Fruun said as they crossed halls and chambers, and the sounds of the battle faded.

They walked into a large hall, its walls made of dark stone. It was heavily decorated with busts and statuettes. Paula said, "This room is familiar."

"I don't remember it," said Sunil.

"Did Mashit take us here?" said Baaba.

"No," Paula said. "I came down here one night, when I was exploring the Dark Stair. It was dark, but this was definitely the room."

"The Stair," Daniel said. "Where is it?"

"I don't remember!" Paula said. "And I dropped my maps!"

"Try to remember," said Daniel. "Hurry."

Paula closed her eyes for a moment, then suddenly opened them. "Over there," she said, pointing to the southeast corner. "Yes, over there!"

They ran to the corner, where several large busts rested atop tall pedestals. She felt around them, pressing fingers into giant eye sockets and fanged mouths and pointed ears and flaring nostrils. Everyone searched with her.

There was a click. "I got it!" Baaba said, her finger down the throat of a stone snakehead. A panel behind the bust slid open to reveal a square of blackness beyond.

"Come on!" Fruun said, and in they went to the Dark Stair. When the panel slid closed behind them, it was pitch dark, and there were no candles or lamps to ignite, so the others made a chain and held onto Daniel as the Mikulal led them down. They descended a dozen flights, when the stairs abruptly ended. They searched the walls for an exit and emerged into a dusty storage room, which looked as if it hadn't been touched in decades.

"I think I passed this room before," Daniel said. And he was right, because on the opposite side he found another stair which led down to the kitchens.

"What's that awful smell?" said Baaba, covering her nose as they went.

"It's the queen's dinner," Fruun said. "A meal she'll never eat."

They ran down several flights, then through a store room full of sundry jars and boxes, then into a space where an enormous cauldron simmered over a coal fire – its smell offensive even to Daniel – then a scullery, with sharp knives hanging from the walls, when finally they emerged into the kitchen proper.

Huge slabs of meat hung from hooks. Enormous black flies hovered around them in clouds, and he gagged. On a table, a long snake-like creature with a dozen legs was skinned and partially filleted. Whoever had been working here had fled, and recently too. The bowl of a long wooden pipe still smoked from the table, and bloody footprints led down the corridor to the exit. Fruun led them down the narrow stair down to the animal pens, past the menagerie of queer beasts trapped in cages.

"My God," Sunil said. "What are these creatures?"

"Dinner," said Fruun.

"People eat these poor animals?" said Baaba.

"Mostly the palace-dwellers. Everyone else starves."

"We have to free them," Paula said.

"There's no time," said Fruun.

"Then we make time!" said Sunil.

"Yes!" said Paula.

"Yes!" said Baaba. And all three of them stopped.

"This is nonsense!" said Fruun. "We have to go!"

Daniel paused too. "And if I had the keys to your freedom right here, Fruun, what would you think of me if I said there was no time for you? We passed the keys to their cages just at the top of the stair in the kitchen."

"The portal could open any minute!" Fruun said.

Baaba stepped forward, eyes glowing in the flickering lamplight. "And if we miss it, because of this, then it still would be worth it."

"Yes," said Sunil.

"Yes," said Paula.

And at this Daniel knew why these three had once held up the world.

Fruun sighed. "Krig, fetch those keys and free these animals." Then, as Krig retrieved the keys and began letting them loose one by one – most scurried away up the stairs – Fruun turned to Daniel and said to him silently, *Have the Pillars any idea of where we are about to go? Of what they will soon see?*

And Daniel realized that, no, they'd hadn't a damn clue. Animals were one thing, but on the other side of that rusty door were thousands of human slaves.

CHAPTER
FORTY-FOUR

SHE LAY ON THE FLOOR OF HER DRESSING ROOM, AN OPEN BAG of Skittles beside her, a cigarette burning down to a nub in her hand. Daphna had shed her stage costume and now wore blue jeans and a black t-shirt. She reached over and grabbed another candy, dropping it in her mouth. The cut on her hand had finally stopped bleeding. She was completely drained. She watched the smoke drift to the ceiling until the cigarette burned her fingers. Though it hurt like hell, she let it burn, and the air filled with the smell of charred skin.

Her phone lay on the counter by the mirror, madly buzzing, but she didn't care anymore. That was Carina's phone. She would never touch it again. During the concert, she'd seen the blue-white glow of a thousand lofted phones, which meant by now, word of the concert was spreading. Photos and videos were being shared all across the world. And soon people would panic when their sons and daughters, friends and lovers did not come home. Part of her desperately wanted to know what they made of this intrusion of absolute reality into their bubble of ignorance. The other part of just wanted sleep. The concert ended almost an hour ago. The doors had been unlocked and the stragglers let go. The police would be here soon.

She remembered their empty faces, how they walked blindly into their enslavement. They had loved and worshipped her. And what was their reward? Slavery in hell. She pushed down the rising shame. This would end.

Mother could have those doting fools. Daphna would build her own loyal army of fans, not through coercion or manipulation, but simply because her art was worthy of high praise. She knew this to be true and absolute.

There was a knock on the door, and Khein entered without waiting for a response. Duile followed him and closed the door. Their eyes were intense. It might have been from the spell. Everyone had been affected one way or another. But there was also Daniel's warning to consider. She sat up.

"Carina," Khein said. "You did wonderfully."

"Carina is dead," Daphna said.

Her stage outfit and golden accessories lay heaped in a pile on the floor. After the show, she could not have shed them fast enough. In the room's spotlights they glimmered, and the sight of them made her sick.

"Your mother will be proud," said Khein.

"Mother can rot in Sheol," she said.

"A pity you two were never close," Khein said, stepping closer. Duile remained by the door, hands clasped behind his back. And she knew it in his face, now. This was it. Her great work done, they would destroy her.

Shaking, she climbed to her feet.

"Sit, sit," he said. "The spell has tired you. It's tired us all."

"No, I think I'll stand, Duile."

He came closer, an arm's length from her. "I'm Khein," he said.

"Really?" she said. "I can never tell you two apart."

Khein looked back at Duile. "We have different color skin."

"Still," she said. "You seem the same to me."

At this, Khein smirked. "Look at what we've done for you, Daphna. When you came here, you were an unknown. But in just a few short months you have millions of adoring fans. They hang on your every word as if you are their goddess. We brought you this, Daphna. By *our* labors."

"They love a phantom," she said.

"A phantom with your face."

"But still a phantom." She slipped her hand into the rear pocket of her jeans.

Khein glanced at Duile. "It's a shame," Khein said. "If you had appreciated us more, if you really understood what we've done for you – what we *do* for you – we might not have had to do *this*." He swung at her, a metallic object flashing in his right hand, but she was ready for him. She dove from his swing and slashed at his arm with her knife.

She caught him just below the wrist. Khein yelped and dropped the object in his hand – a dark-metal claw. It sparked with powerful magic as it fell, while the tear in his arm quickly opened to reveal sinews and muscle underneath.

"Bitch!" he spat. "What have you done?"

The split tore into his flesh, unzipping him as if he wore a suit of skin. He screamed as it reached his head and all his skin dropped off. Then the magic unzipped his muscles and bones, unfurling him like a thousand blossoming carmine flowers. When it reached his demon essence, below the human fascia, Khein wailed. Under his efflorescing flesh his core glowed brightly green and spat out sharp yellow rays onto the walls. Khein's scream rose in pitch until all that remained of him was a spark of phosphorescent light and a pile of his unraveled flesh on the floor. The light winked out, like the last cinder of a dying fire.

Duile had been watching in stupefied awe, but now he charged her. Arms outstretched, he hurled a lightning-bright blue orb at her. She leapt out of the way, and the orb crashed into the wall, setting it aflame. She fell to the floor, tumbled, and raised her knife as he came for her. He formed another ball in his hands.

"Khein was my brother!" he screamed.

She grabbed her golden belt from the floor cast a spell to magnify the brightness of the lights. They reflected off her belt into Duile's face, blinding him. He winced and shielded his eyes, then cast a spell to shatter all the bulbs. The fire blazed up the far wall, and the room turned red in its flickering glow. She swung at him with her belt and cracked him in the skull. He fell, blood dripping from the back of his head.

"Here, Duile!" she screamed. "I've the perfect accessory for you!" She wrapped the strap around his neck, and tugged with all her strength. He resisted, but the blow to his head had stunned him. She tugged until he lost consciousness. He lay unmoving in the rippling firelight as she picked up her knife and stabbed him in the eye.

Duile split apart, flesh unfurling into bloody flowers, until his essence flashed and winked out. The fire tripped the alarm, and water burst from the sprinklers in the ceiling. She stood in the rain, panting, as the water doused the flames. The smoke grew acrid and thick as the alarm screeched and wailed.

The door burst open, and Frix paused in the doorway. Light from the hall spilled into the room, cutting through the smoke, and Daphna saw herself in the broken mirror, soaked, tired, and covered in blood. But underneath all this she saw her face, her real face, and she recognized herself. She smiled.

Smoke whirled into the hallway, and Frix coughed as she stepped into the room. "Carina, what's happened?"

"Carina is dead," she said. "She never lived." Daphna shoved past Frix into the hall. "I've let Duile and Khein go," she said as turned toward the exit, her legs wobbly.

The fire alarm wailed. When the crews saw her drenched, unadorned figure, they gaped and stared. "Yes!" she shouted. "This is the real me! My name is Daphna! Carina never existed! Go home! She's gone forever! You've all wasted your lives worshipping her!"

Frix came up behind her. "You're tired," she said. "You've had a long day. Come, I'll take you back to the bus." She took Daphna's arm, but Daphna shoved her off.

"I need no escort."

"No," said Frix. "But you need a friend. The police have arrived, and the fire department is on its way. We need to get you out of here. The bus is waiting for you outside one of the fire exits. I'll help you there. You can barely stand." This time when Frix took her arm, Daphna did not resist. "For the record," Frix said, "I never liked those two assholes."

Frix took her through the narrow halls to a fire exit, and they stepped through a steel door into a small parking lot, where the bus idled. The stars twinkled brightly overhead, and the cool night air seemed to blow right through her soaked body, chilling her to her core, waking her from her stupor. She was alive, renewed.

Frix helped her onto the bus, and Daphna pulled the curtain closed and collapsed on the small bed in the rear. "Duile and

Khein will not be joining us," Frix said to the driver. "Go! Get the fuck out of here!"

They sped away from the concert hall at a rapid clip. The blinds were closed, but she heard the wail of sirens as they fled. She found her stash of tobacco beside the bed. And with her shaking hands stained with blood, she rolled herself a cigarette. As the nicotine entered her body, she shivered. She took her laptop from the shelf and flipped it open. In the search box she typed, "carina concert singapore."

It was late, and the story hadn't quite found its way into the Asian news sites yet, and the sites in Europe and the U.S. were slow to pick up the story. But it was on social media where her concert was receiving the most attention.

Someone on Instagram captioned a photo of the portal with, "The back of the stage just opened like a hole in the world!"

Someone on Tumblr wrote, "... everyone was in a fucking trance! They just walked up the steps into this huge spinning whirlpool thing. It felt like I was in a movie. I couldn't believe what was happening. They locked the doors and no one could leave."

And on Twitter: "I was so scared! I thought I was going to die..."

And on Facebook: "This is the work of Satan, punishment for our sins of promiscuity and immodesty."

Exhaustion washed over her as her cigarette burned down. She felt as far away from their words as Earth was from Sheol. Did she really just send thousands of people to hell? She felt as if they were speaking about another person. Her eyes drooped as she scrolled through page after page of searches, when a headline caught her eye.

"Mass Disappearances Reported at Carina Simulcasts."

She sat up.

"Tonight at more than twenty simulcasts of Carina's concert in Singapore, multiple witnesses have reported concert attendees walking onto the stage and vanishing into what some describe as a 'giant whirlpool' or 'vortex.' According to several reports, some kind of 'doorway' opened up on stage in the middle of Carina's act. Witnesses at first assumed it was a video or lighting effect, but were surprised when Carina invited the audience up on stage with her. Those who did as Carina's asked 'vanished' into the whirlpool.

As many as ninety percent of the attendees vanished on stage, according to one witness.

"While users on social media are speculating this is part of a marketing hoax meant to stir up publicity for Carina's new album, ITN World News has confirmed more than eighty cases of people attending Carina's concerts who have gone missing. And our source at ITN says the numbers are still coming in, and they expect the actual number to be much higher. None have yet been able to say where all these missing people have gone, but Richard Tan of the Department of..."

She paused and reread the paragraph. It did not say "concert," singular, but "concerts." Plural. "Frix!" she shouted. A moment later Frix peeked her slender face through the curtain into Daphna's private nook. "*Simulcasts?*"

Frix sighed. "I never wanted to keep that from you. I had no choice."

"We always have choices, Frix. What the hell is a simulcast?"

"You, multiplied."

"How?"

"We sold tickets to a virtual concert at twenty-three locations around the world. Your performance tonight was recorded with special cameras, and your hologram was simultaneously projected at these twenty-three concerts around the world."

Daphna shook her head in disbelief. "Why didn't you tell me, Frix?"

"The queen ordered us not to."

"And why would she want to keep this from me?"

"I believe the queen feared you might not go through with it."

"How many?" Daphna said.

"There were twenty-three concerts, plus yours."

"No. How many people?"

"Twenty-four, times fifty thousand? About one point two million."

Daphna reached for her Skittles, for a cigarette, for something, because the world was spinning.

"We'll be at the airport in a few minutes," Frix said. "A lot of people are looking for you. We need to get you out of this country as soon as possible."

"So that's it then," Daphna said. "After this, there's no turning back."

Frix frowned and said, "Yes, and this phase is done, I'm afraid. It was a great run, Daphna, and you did a fantastic job. When the queen hears of our success, I'm sure we'll all be highly praised."

"Is this what we did all this for? Praise?"

"What else do you want?"

Daphna stared at her. "*Everything.*"

"Sometimes we have to compromise, Daphna."

"Yes," Daphna said. "But I'm not letting this go. Where are we flying to, Frix?"

"Sydney. We'll lay low for a while and await word from Sheol." Frix sighed. "Look, if it were up to me, Daphna, I would've told you everything from the start. But it wasn't, and I'm sorry. But from now on, I'll tell you everything. I promise. Because, like I said, I'm your friend." Then she closed the curtain to leave Daphna alone. The bus drove on.

Daphna sat in silence for a moment. Then she grabbed her laptop and searched for the phone number of the Australian Broadcasting Corporation in Sydney. She plugged in a headset into the laptop and dialed the number using Skype. After several rings, a tired-sounding man answered with, "News desk, Ben." She heard furious clacking on a keyboard.

"Hi," she said. "This is..."

"Hello?"

"Yes, Ben. I'm here."

"Who is this?"

"I'm...You know me as Carina."

The clacking stopped.

"My real name is Daphna, and I'll be landing in Sydney in a few hours."

"Is this a prank? Because I'm really fucking tired."

"No prank, Ben. I'm dead serious."

"Then prove it's really you."

"You have Skype?"

"Yes."

"Then give me your username and I'll call you back. With video."

He did, she hung up, and she reconnected with him. His glowing face stared back at her. He was young, with short hair and a well-trimmed beard. "Hello, Ben," she said.

He stared at her. "Um, okay. *Wow.*"

"I know I look different without my makeup. But I assure you, I'm no impostor."

"No...no I believe you. What can I do for you, Carina?"

"Carina was my stage name. Please call me Daphna. Now, Ben, I want a live, exclusive interview, on your network, unannounced until just before broadcast. I want to arrive safely in Australia without being mobbed by the press."

"What happened at your concerts, Carina? People are saying some really crazy stuff. Is any of this true?"

"Turn off your recording, Ben, if you know what's good for your career."

She waited for him to click the mouse a few times. "It's off."

"Now, listen carefully to everything I'm about to say. If you arrange this interview for me *exactly* as I specify, I'll answer every one of your questions and tell you a whole lot more besides. Ben, you better be ready for me, because I've got the fucking story of the millennium, and I'm giving it solely to you."

CHAPTER FORTY-FIVE

THE CAVERNS WERE HOT AND GROWING HOTTER AS THE Mikulalim led Daniel and the others deeper into the tunnels. Through dank caverns, lit dimly by torches, the four Mikulalim led them on. Daniel could not escape the dense reek of humanity blowing through these hot and breathing caves. So many, trapped here like animals. And the air reeked of more than sweat. He smelled deodorant and shampoo, perfume and cologne. How long would it be before all earthly traces faded from their newly arrived bodies? A day? A week?

They emerged from a narrow tunnel, where a steep downward ramp led into a large cavern. At the bottom, hundreds of naked figures were pouring in from a tunnel to quickly crowd the space. "That's a lot of cursed people," Paula whispered to him.

"No," he said, dreading their response. "Those aren't Mikulalim. They're human."

"What?" Paula said.

Baaba looked ill. "No," she said, shaking her head. "It can't be, can it?"

"It can," Daniel said. "It is."

"But I thought we were the only humans here?" Sunil said, almost pleading.

"They use human slaves in the mines."

"*Ya 'iilhi!*" Baaba cried. *Oh my God.*

"I guess I never accepted it until now," Paula said. "We really are in hell."

"Hush!" Fruun said. "Guards are coming!"

There wasn't enough time to retreat up the ramp. But where the path turned sharply, a large boulder shielded them from view, and Fruun had them shelter there.

"There are children down there," Baaba said. "Boys and girls!"

"Hush!" Fruun said.

"This whole time they've been here and we didn't know," Paula said.

"Did Maya know?" said Sunil.

Silently, Fruun said to Daniel, *If you don't silence them, I'll cut out their tongues!*

Daniel turned to them and said, "Shut the fuck up, or we're all dead!"

Finally, this silenced them. Now, Daniel heard Mikulal thoughts drifting up from below. *There's no room for them all!* a guard said. *What was the queen thinking bringing so many humans here at once?*

She wasn't, said another. *And as always, we're left to deal with the sovereign's mess.*

He peered around the edge of the rock. Hundreds of humans piled into the chamber, now rank with the smell of sweat and piss. There were so many – mostly children – and he had been complicit in bringing thousands here. He was ashamed.

What the hell have I done? he thought, much too loudly.

One of the Mikulal guards turned and began ascending the ramp.

Fruun scowled at Daniel. "A guard is coming!" she whispered. "Act as if your wills have been emptied! Your lives depend on it!"

The guard spotted them now and said, *What is this? Who are you, and why are these humans still clothed?* He scanned them all, his eyes lingering on Daniel. He stepped forward. *I know you! You're Daniel Fisher, the long-promised one! And you are Fruun, wife of Raigul!*

And you are Bhung, fifth-ring stonemaster, Fruun said. *So what will you do now, Bhung? Let us pass or stand in our way?*

Bhung considered for a moment, staring at Daniel. *Go,* he said, stepping aside, his eyes still on Daniel. *Take the far tunnel and go right, toward the fifty-fourth mine. There are fewer guards there today. Everyone is busy with the new arrivals.*

Fruun nodded and they began to descend, but Bhung snatched Daniel's arm. *Will you come back to save us, Daniel?* he said. *I have nine children!*

Did you forget? Daniel said, seething. *There are children down there too!* He yanked himself free from Bhung's grasp.

But they're only human children! Bhung shouted.

Did you also forget, Daniel shouted back, *that you were once human to?*

Bhung stared down at him as they went.

"The Mikulalim speak telepathically, don't they?" Sunil said as they walked down the long ramp, and Daniel nodded.

"What were you just speaking about?"

"I really don't want to talk about it."

They moved into the human crowd, when two more guards saw them and came rushing over. "Go, go!" Fruun said, and she pushed them into the press of bodies – all so damned young, all naked, their eyes dilated to caverns, their jaws slack, their shoulders drooping. Baaba screamed. Sunil looked like he might panic. Paula seemed horrified.

They pushed against the flow of bodies into a narrow tunnel, but it was hard going against the human wave. People marched relentlessly forward, pressing all of them against the wall. A guard shouted behind them, and Fruun said, "Keep going!"

They struggled against the human torrent, while Daniel kept looking back for the guards. But there were so many people he could not tell who was human and who was Mikulal. They kept coming, and their number seemed endless.

The tunnel widened into a yawning cavern, where thousands of naked, glassy-eyed humans slowly circled around a gigantic floor. Bodies were flowing in through a far tunnel and trickling out through the near. The people moved as if they were swirling around a great drain, and he knew that if left alone these poor souls would spin around and around without complaint until they fell dead.

Four more guards waited by the far tunnel, and Fruun told Daniel to cover his face. The guards spotted them, but they seemed more concerned with trying to direct the great number of humans pouring in, and paid them little heed.

There's so many! Daniel said to Fruun when they entered another tunnel. *There weren't this many people at Carina's concert!*

There wasn't just one concert, Fruun said. *There were twenty-three others.*

Others? Daniel said. *How many people have been teleported here?*

Over a million, Fruun said.

"Holy shit," Daniel said aloud, his head spinning. "Holy fucking shit."

"What is it?" Sunil said.

"I've done a terrible thing."

"And what is that?"

Daniel stiffened. "We have to get you home." It was the only way to redeem himself.

The press of bodies had begin to thin, when a blast of thunder shook the cavern. A great spray of dust and falling stones tumbled from the ceiling, and everyone ducked to cover their heads. A few poor humans were crushed and killed, and Daniel turned from their bodies in revulsion.

A Mikulal came running out of the smoke toward them. Fruun and her companions readied their swords, but they seemed to recognize this figure and lowered their weapons.

Sug! Fruun said.

It's the Legion! said Sug, panting to catch his breath. A wound on his forehead dripped a line of dark blood. *They know we've helped Daniel and the Pillars escape the palace. They're searching for them. It's a rout! They're killing everything in their–*"

There was another explosion in the tunnel where Sug had emerged from, and the cavern shook violently. Acrid smoke poured out, and more rocks and dust fell. Something huge cracked in the cavern ceiling, and Fruun shouted, "Run!"

They fled back into the tunnel as the roof collapsed, crushing Sug with an awful sound of smashed bones and flesh. *Sug!* Fruun cried. She shuddered once, then she stiffened. "I know another way to the portal chamber," she said. "But if that passage blocked, there's no way to get you home."

They ran into a large cavern filled with hundreds of disoriented humans – the guards had fled – and they ducked into a narrow side passage. Five Mikulalim came barreling down the tunnel toward them, shouting in the Silent Tongue, *Turn around! The Legion are here! They're slaughtering us all!*

The five shoved through them and vanished down another tunnel. Fruun paused, breathing heavily, distraught. "The Legion is ahead," she said. "The Legion is behind."

Baaba was covered in dust and was breathing heavily.

"I don't want to die," Sunil said.

"Then be strong," said Paula, but she was shivering. They all were.

Daniel turned to Fruun and said, "There has to be a way."

"We may have already missed the portal," Fruun said. "And even if we haven't, with the Legion attacking, I doubt we could even open it."

"All I know," Daniel said, "is that I've come here to bring these three home, and that's what I plan to do. Fruun, please. Find us a way to the portal."

Fruun furiously rubbed her bald head, when there was a bright green flash in the cavern behind them. It was followed by a huge boom and more falling rocks. Chunks of flesh splattered to the ground in heaps of steaming gore as a beast emerged from the green smoke. The demon was huge, ogre-like, with a single eye and three irregular horns sprouting from his forehead.

The ogre shouted something in the demon's tongue, when Fruun whispered fire into the air, and a pillar of flame swirled down from the ceiling like a tornado to set the ogre's vest on fire. He growled, and Fruun said, "Run!"

They fled into the tunnel, while the ogre's heavy footsteps shook the ground, but he couldn't fit into the narrow tunnel. There was a new crack in the tunnel wall wide enough to fit them if they squeezed, and Fruun said, "Here! Turn here!"

They climbed through the sharp crevice and over piles of rubble to emerge into a gargantuan cavern. They hid behind a row of granite boulders to peer around the edge. On the opposite end of the cavern, thousands of Mikulalim – men, women, and children – huddled together, grasping overstuffed bags, guarding giant containers. They shuffled nervously, and in the dim light, their candleflame eyes were like swarming fireflies. They were all staring at the large cavern mouth at the far end, where a fierce battle raged.

Dozens of Mikulalim soldiers were holding off several large demons. The Mikulalim were lightning-fast compared to the hulking demons, and they sent columns of fire in bright fusillades. But one demon blew dust from a pouch into many Mikulalim faces, and their heads melted away. As they fell, more Mikulalim ran from the crowd to take their place, like an assembly line of death.

A demon swung a long scythe, chopping off a leg here, an arm there. The Mikulalim fought on, even with missing limbs. A gray spider revealed a square mirror, and its reflections burned to dust anything it touched. Many in the crowd caught fire, and their screams echoed wildly through the cavern as others jumped in to douse the flames.

With the battle raging at the far end, it took him a moment to notice that just down the slope from where they hid, thirteen black-robed Mikulalim were standing in a circle on the cave floor, chanting in a demon tongue. Thirteen black candles on tall bronze poles surrounded them, candleflames spiking up like glinting swords. Inscribed in blood and ash on the floor, in overlapping circles and polygons, were strange sigils and signs, some of which Daniel recognized from the *Roots of Names.*

"Come!" said Fruun said. "Let's go down!"

They climbed down the steep and rocky slope to the cavern floor, and the sounds of the battle grew deafening. There was an explosion by the far cave mouth, killing at least fifty Mikulalim. More were joining the front to hold the demons off. There were thousands of Mikulalim waiting here, but at this rate they wouldn't last the hour.

A Mikulal approached Fruun. *How did you get in here?*

An explosion cracked the wall in the sixty-fifth segment, Fruun said.

Which means the Legion might come through that way too, said the other.

Fruun nodded. *We should set up a guard here at once. But tell me, why has everyone come here with their belongings?*

They want to escape with Daniel, to Earth. But we can't open the portal.

Why not?

We haven't the energy. We had a sacrifice ready, but the body was killed in the attack. We have no other power sources, except the sorcerers themselves. We are trying the old method of power stacking. When one grows tired, another steps in to take his place. But it's going much too slowly. At this rate it will take years to open the gate!

Then why are you still casting? Fruun said.

Because we hoped someone might arrive with more power. The Mikulal looked at Daniel. *Is that Daniel–*

Three demons suddenly emerged from the new entrance – giant green ticks with rapacious beaks – and one snatched the Mikulal who had just been speaking with Fruun in his mouth and crunched. The Mikulal screamed.

"Fruun said, "Run!" Then she pushed him off toward the crowd, while she and the other Mikulalim turned to fight the giant ticks. Daniel and the others sprinted across the cavern, while a new wave of Mikulalim left the crowd to join the fronts. They sped past each other, and Daniel and the others hid behind a group of large metal trunks to catch their breath. One trunk lay partially open, and plates of brilliant gold shone inside it.

"LOOK!" a demon shouted from the main front in Akkadian. "THE PILLARS ARE HERE! Lord Ashmedai said he will make First General of the one who brings them back alive! THAT ONE WILL BE ME!"

At his words, the demons grew even more aggressive, slaughtering two, three, five Mikulalim at once. The battled raged on the two fronts, while the bulk of the Mikulalim waited with their belongings. One screamed as a giant tick split him in half with his jaws. More Mikulalim leaped from the crowd to join the battle.

"Is this it?" Baaba said. "Is this where we die?"

"They going to open the portal," Paula said. "Right?"

"They're trying," Daniel said. "But they don't have enough power."

"But what does that mean?" Baaba said. "Can they get more?"

"I don't know," Daniel said. "It's not like you can just plug in to the wall. They need magical power."

At this, Sunil's eyes lit up. "What about us?"

"What about you?"

"Mashit told us that just our presence alone has brought life to Sheol. Aren't we, as Pillars, a source of power?"

"Holy shit," Daniel said. "I think you're right. Stay here!" He ran over to the circle of sorcerers just as one stepped out from the chanting circle and another took his place. The circle sparked and thrummed with energy, but he could tell it was not nearly enough. He pulled aside the weary-looking sorcerer and said, *I'm Daniel Fisher, and I have the Pillars with me. Can we use them as a source of energy to open the portal?*

The sorcerer's eyes lit up. *Yes! Yes, I think so! But they would have to step into the circle and cast the spell themselves.*

And how would they do that? Wait – tell them yourself!

He ran back to the others and said, "They don't have enough power to open the portal. But you three do!" He pointed to the sorcerer. "Follow me!"

They ran back with Daniel to the spell circle, while another explosion rocked the cavern, and dust rained down upon them all. The sorcerer stepped forward and said, "Do you hear the words they chant? You must take their place in the circle and say them too. Channel all your energies into a singular goal, opening the gate between worlds."

"But we're not magicians!" Paula said.

"You'll have to be," said the sorcerer.

"They speak gibberish," said Baaba. "How are we supposed to speak that?"

"They speak ancient Demonsbreath," said the sorcerer. "The syllables will be difficult to pronounce at first, but if you repeat them, they will soon slide off your tongue like oil. Such is the clinging way of demon tongues."

"It's black magic!" Baaba said. "I don't know..."

There was another explosion and more screams. Swords clashed and bodies were split in half. "It's this or death," said Paula.

"This is the only way we get home," said Daniel.

"Then *humma alllah lana*," Baaba said. *May God protect us.*

"Right now," the sorcerer said, "the only one who can save us is *you*. Now learn!"

They turned to listen the sorcerers' bizarre words as the battles raged. A hulking demon with a single curving horn broke through the front, killing many, when several Mikulalim rushed to slaughter him. But there were countless more demons queued behind him, pushing through the dense lines.

One of the thirteen sorcerers collapsed, and the tall spiking candleflames stuttered and shrunk. Another sorcerer rushed to take his place. He took up the chant, and the candleflames spiked up again.

Baaba, Sunil, and Paula began to mouth the demon words. *"Gur jinul vaf fubegrark, gur yutug vaf orag, gur faxel vaf pheirik, gur yavsur funi ov cabherk gab bacra. Gur jinul vaf fubegrark..."* The syllables were guttural and harsh, and they struggled to keep up.

Demons broke through the smaller front. Nine hideous monsters marched across the cavern floor as many dozens of Mikulalim charged to stop them.

"Do it now!" Daniel said. "Take their place!"

Baaba, Sunil, and Paula jumped in to replace three of the sorcerers. The candleflames guttered, but the other sorcerers kept chanting. And when the Pillars began to speak the words, the flames leaped up twice as high as before, bright and blinding. Daniel squinted and shielded his eyes.

Their words were off tempo, and their syllables wrong, but the spell forged its own path. The more they got the syllables right, the stronger the spell became, until they weren't casting the spell so much as the spell was casting them.

Their hair blew upward as a vicious wind tore at them from below, and where the sigils and signs had been marked in blood on the ground, there was now a perfect mirror reflecting their bodies, as if they stood above a placid sea of mercury. The three stared in horror at their reflections, as if they saw something the others did not. Their voices grew louder, and Daniel knew this was not by their own will.

It's working! the sorcerer said.

The mirror shattered, and a trillion little shards blasted skyward. Then the scintillating shards reversed course and fell. They plunged through the dark hole in the ground, and then there was light. On the other side of the portal were the antiseptic walls of a factory and its metal machines. Daniel saw a sign in Simplified Chinese, "Danger! Moving Belt! Watch for Loose Clothing!" The room was shifted by ninety degrees, so the floor had become vertical.

When the Mikulalim saw the opening, they made a mad rush for it. They shoved past him and dove into the portal. Now, without new soldiers to replace the fallen, the smaller front collapsed. An agglomeration of Daniel's worst nightmares surged into the cavern, a writhing, grotesque, hideous mass of tooth and limb.

They slaughtered everything in their path. A few Mikulalim still fought the approaching army, but only because it was this or death. The bodies of the dead and dying littered the ground three bodies high. A huge worm the size of a bus crawled toward Daniel, teeth glistening with green drool. Daniel leaped out of the way as the worm swallowed living and dead alike. Ten more monsters came up behind the worm.

He leaped around the press of bodies and ran around the sorcerers' circle. He stepped behind Paula and shoved her into the hole. The thirteen flames sparked and faded, and the column of light flickered. Baaba collapsed to the ground, convulsing. Sunil fell to his knees and vomited. Daniel shoved both of them into the fading portal.

He looked back once at all the Mikulalim still fighting for escape as a giant pink hydra tore a sorcerer in half. The portal wavered.

"I'm sorry," he said, then he leaped through.

—

The world shifted. Daniel tumbled to the ground. Behind him the portal flickered like an old film as the ogre snatched a Mikulal already come through. But the portal snapped closed, and the demon's hand was singed cleanly off. Both the hand and the Mikulal it held tumbled to the ground. The man pried himself free of it.

The first thing Daniel noticed was the lack of sound. It was quiet, but for a few vents near the ceiling blowing cold, antiseptic air into the room, and the muffled cries of the Mikulalim who had come through. The place reeked of electronics, metal, and plastic.

At least two hundred Mikulalim had come through, and the large room, crowded with conveyor belts and cutting machines, was nearly full with their bodies. But even so, the number here was a mere fraction of those who had wished escape. Exhausted, panting, smeared in blood and dirt, none wept. It wasn't their nature to cry, but he saw it in their eyes, their bottomless sadness no words could ever express.

Baaba lay unconscious on the floor. He felt for her pulse. It was weak, but she was alive. There was water cooler against the wall, and Sunil ran to fetch her a cup. Paula propped up Baaba's head, and Baaba slowly opened her eyes. "Did we make it?" she said.

Tears streaked Paula's cheeks. "Some of us."

Baaba stared up at Daniel, weeping as she said, "We left them, Daniel. All of those poor children. We left them in hell."

Daniel hung his head. "I know," he said. "I know."

The Mikulalim moved closer to them.

"Stay back!" Paula shouted, rising into a defensive posture. "All those souls, trapped in that hell! And you put them there!"

The Mikulalim stopped and gazed at each other. "Come," Daniel said, feeling all their eyes upon him, waiting for him to lead them to freedom. But he had no easy answers for anyone. "I think we should go."

"Where are we?" said Baaba.

"All the signs are in Simplified Chinese," said Sunil.

They rose and walked past conveyor belts and stamping machines. Stacked four high against the wall were the same large metal containers he had seen in the cavern filled with the golden metal plates. At the far end of the room strips of clear plastic hung before a large double door. They walked through it onto a crowded factory floor. It smelled of ozone, electronics, and faintly of sweat. Vast arrays of machines hummed, rattled, and choked as they cut sections of the golden plates into numerous shapes. One line was cutting them into bracelets, another into belts, a third into tabs and epaulettes. The golden scraps were all funneled into a large bin at the end of the line.

The process was automated. Robot arms cut, torched, flipped, bent and polished. But a few workers sat by computer consoles at the end of each line, watching displays. They wore headsets over their ears, and they hadn't noticed Daniel or the others yet.

Did these workers know where these golden plates came from, that they worked for demons? Or was this just another job for them? The Mikulalim had begun emerging from the room, five at a time, following Daniel and the others. Sooner or later they would be seen, and he didn't want to be around for that.

"Come on," he whispered, leading them toward an exit. They left the factory floor through a side door and entered a cafeteria that smelled thickly of coffee and cigarettes, even though there was a large Chinese "No Smoking!" sign on the wall. The many tables were empty but for three smoking men, who were mesmerized by the TV mounted on the wall. At the far end of the cafeteria a door led outside, and it was light out. The sun – Earth's solitary, beautiful yellow sun – shone bright beams onto the floor. A clock on the wall said it was 11:13 a.m.

He put his finger to his mouth to quiet the others as they crept past the workers. The men were engrossed in the television and did not notice them. And as they passed, Daniel read the ticker scrolling across the bottom of the screen.

"Strange lights seen in skies all over the world. Otherworldly beings claim they're angels here to save humanity."

A reporter spoke hurriedly in Mandarin, while an inset window labeled "Wengen, Switzerland," showed a mysterious glowing figure walking along a steep moraine encased in thick fog. Wherever this glowing figure stepped, the ground blossomed with colorful flowers. The fog evaporated to reveal the bright sun. The reporter's eyes went wide, then he smiled and said, "This is a special effect! A silly hoax!"

The inset window zoomed into the glowing figure's face, which expanded to fill the screen. His countenance was as stately as a Roman Emperor, as wise as Socrates, as intelligent as Einstein, and as peaceful as the Dalai Lama. Daniel gasped because he hadn't thought these things himself. They had been projected into his mind.

In English, the figure said, "We are the Malachim, what you have called the Angels. We have come to save you from yourselves. Do not fear us. The time of your redemption has come. These are the End of Days your religions have spoken of. Demons have been manipulating your world for millennia, while we have watched from above, bound by our doctrine never to interfere in the affairs of humanity. But demons have upset the Cosmic order, and we have come to set things right."

The figure repeated the same message in Chinese, Spanish, French, German, Italian, and many other languages. The ticker along the bottom read, "Mysterious 'Malachim' appearing all over the globe, repeating the same message."

Finally! Daniel thought, *We have help!* And he welcomed their arrival, because he was so damn tired of fighting them alone. Let them take some responsibility. He was done.

"It never really ends," Paula said, shaking her head. "Does it?"

The three factory workers finally noticed them. They rose from their seats and gaped at Daniel, at his curious clothes and bloody visage. Mikulalim were filtering in from the factory floor, and the men grabbed each other and withdrew to the wall.

The TV spoke again, and all eyes turned to it. A malach stood on the ledge of a skyscraper in Dubai, filmed by someone's shaky phone.

"For too long," the angel said, "humans and demons have abused this world. We alone are the only beings capable of honoring this precious Earth. Humanity will be relocated to a place where your happiness is eternal. Do not fear us. We are here to give you what you have always sought, true peace, while we claim our divine and ancient birthright. From this moment on, *the Earth is ours.*"

Sunil shook his head. He turned to Daniel and said, "From one hell to another."

"What do we do?" Baaba said. "What the hell do we do now?"

Daniel glanced at the TV, the frightened factory workers, the Mikulalim pouring into the room, the terrified Lamed Vav. "We've been to hell and back," he said. "What's a few angels standing in our way? We do what we've always done. We go on."

CHAPTER FORTY-SIX

"ALL RIGHT, THANK YOU, MARY," SAID THE SOLEMN-FACED
reporter from the huge TV mounted on the ABC's makeup room
wall. A sheen of sweat beaded his brows. "We'll keep you informed
as further updates on these Malakim come in." He pressed his
finger to his ear. "Now we go live to Hillary Jensin, in Perth, who
says she's spoken to a local farmer present when a Malak first
appeared."

Daphna cringed. "It's *Malach*, you ignoramus!" she shouted,
twisting back and forth in her swivel chair. She waited in the
makeup room of the Australian Broadcasting Corporation, facing
her reflection and a dozen bright bulbs, while a cigarette burned
down between her fingers. "Not *me-lock,* like a Liverpudlian drunk
whose lost his keys! It's Mala-*kh*! A pharyngeal fricative! At least
get that right!"

So far, ABC had honored her request. They'd snuck her into
the studio without telling other agencies, and she would have her
live exclusive, they'd promised. A half-dozen reporters tried to
pry information from her so they could prepare on-air questions,
but she had said she would not speak a word until she was sitting
before the live cameras. Fine, they'd said. She'd go on soon, they'd
said. If she'd just wait here, in this makeup room, for them to get
ready, then all would be well. Several times she was asked if she
wanted to change out of her jeans and black t-shirt, which were
stained with Duile and Khein's blood, or if she wanted one of their
professionals to apply makeup.

"No!" she replied, getting more angry each time. "They will see me as I am."

But it had been more than three hours since she'd arrived, and her story, which had seemed to excite them beyond compare when she had first come, had been pushed aside as news of the Malachim's arrival spread over the globe. She vaguely understood why the appearance of angels all over the globe trumped the disappearance of a million people from thirty-three concerts, at first blush. But sooner or later they'd connect the two events. And she would not disguise herself anymore. She would tell them all.

On the TV, a parade of newscasters were interviewing endless witnesses and supposed "experts" about the Malachim. Their absurd assumptions and total ignorance made her laugh. A blonde-haired, blue-eyed makeup girl had been leaning against the wall, watching the news, growing increasingly worried with every report. She walked over to Daphna, makeup brush in hand.

"For the hundredth time," Daphna said, "I don't want any fucking makeup!"

The woman froze and seemed about to cry. "But...I was told I had to...that you should..." Her voice cracked.

Daphna stared at the young woman. "What's your name?"

"Li" – her voice cracked again – "Linda." Her answer sounded like a question, as if she were hopeful this was all a dream.

"Linda, you're frightened." She took Linda's cold and sweaty hand.

Linda stared back into Daphna's eyes, her gaze full of desperation. "What's happening to the world, Carina? Is any of this real?"

"Carina was my stage name. But I don't use that anymore. My real name is Daphna. Please call me that."

"Okay, Daphna," Linda said, and she let slip a nervous smile. She glanced at the TV. "This is so fucking crazy. It's hard to believe any of it." She looked back at Daphna. "Your concert.... People are saying the audience vanished into a big hole."

"A portal. And they didn't vanish. They've gone to Sheol."

"Where's that?"

"A long way from here. It's where I was born."

Linda shook her head. "I've never heard of Sheol. What country is that in?"

"It's not in any country."

"I don't understand."

"You will," she said. "Soon, everyone will."

Frix burst into the room with a solemn expression on her face. "Leave us," she said to Linda.

"No," Daphna said. "Linda stays."

"This is not for her ears. It concerns home."

"I told you. I'll have no more secrets and neither will you. What you tell me, Linda hears too."

"Very well," Frix said. "We just received a report, probably the last one from Sheol for a long time. The people, they've been rioting. There's chaos back home. A revolt. And Daphna, I'm sorry, but the report says your mother is dead."

Daphna froze. It felt as if someone had shoved an ice pick through her heart. "Dead?" She shook her head. "No, no, Mother is just having another game with me."

"Daphna, I'm sorry," Frix said. "I truly am."

"Oh, dear God," Linda said. "That's terrible. I'm so, so sorry, Daphna."

Daphna was shaking now. Mother couldn't be gone.

"You probably want to be alone," Linda said, heading for the door.

"No," Daphna said, grabbing Linda by the arm. "Please, will you stay?"

"Yes." Linda straightened. "Yes, of course."

Daphna scanned herself and found, underneath the shock and sadness, a growing rage. "For all my life it's been as if I had no mother. Nothing's changed now that she's dead. I'm still alone. And I always will be." For a time, no one said a thing, and the TV droned on.

Linda came over and put her hand, much warmer now, on Daphna's arm. Tears streaked down Linda's cheeks as she said, "I'm so sorry, Daphna."

"Why do you comfort me?"

Linda seemed shocked at the question.

"Is it because I'm famous? Because you adore Carina?"

"No! Do you know how many famous people I've met? Most are total pricks. But you're kind, Daphna. And you just lost your mother, for chrissakes! I'd be inhuman not to feel sympathy for you! And anyway I just think with all this craziness going on right now, we really need to come together." She gently squeezed Daphna's arm.

Daphna smiled, put her hand on top of Linda's, and let slip a single sob. "I was wrong. I was wrong about this world."

The woman on the TV was reporting about more Malachim sightings in Iceland and Yemen. "This is all so strange," Linda said. "The things you say, everything that's happening. I feel like I'm in a dream."

"No, Linda. Your life before today was a dream. Now you and everyone else are waking up."

A young woman with short-cropped brown hair wearing a dark business suit, a headset, and a pout, entered the room. She set her eyes on Daphna and scowled.

"Why isn't Carina made up yet?" the woman snapped. "She'll be going on in..." She checked her watch. "Six minutes!"

"My name is Daphna," she said. "And I refused Linda's makeup. I want the world to see me as I am."

The woman sighed. "I'm sorry you feel that way, but Mitch needs you to–"

"*Mitch?*"

"Our EP. You'll have four minutes."

"I'll need more than that."

"You're lucky we're giving you that," the woman said, and her contempt for Carina oozed from her every pore, so different from the blind adoration from her fans. It was, Daphna knew, because she wore no costume. She had laid herself bare, and doing so was an affront to all who put on their daily costumes to face the world. She made them see that it all was one enormous facade.

The woman pressed a finger to her headset. "Copy that. Yeah, fine with me. Segment eighty-sixed. Got it." She let slip a mild smirk and said, "I'm *real* sorry to say, Carina, but your segment's been canceled."

"What?" Daphna said. "I have to go on!"

"There's nothing I can do for you, honey."

"I'll go to another studio. You'll lose the exclusive."

"Whatever you have to do. It's out of my hands. But with these

Malokim popping up everywhere, you'll be lucky to–"

Daphna leaped from her chair. "It's *Malach*!" she spat. "The plural is *Malachim*! It's a pharyngeal fricative like Bach and Loch. You're all supposed to be professionals, so why is that so fucking hard for you to pronounce?" She shoved past the woman and darted into the hall. The woman said, "Bitch!"

Daphna stormed toward the studio floor, which was crowded with cameras and crew. Spotlights shone onto an oversized desk, where a reporter was speaking to a woman on location. Large screens along one wall showed Malachim sightings all over the world. The other wall was made of glass, and on its far side were news desks, where reporters were busy typing or speaking into a phone or running back and forth.

She ran past the cameramen and crew. Someone tried to grab her, but she slipped from his grasp and strode right up to the reporter at his huge desk. The spotlights smacked her in the face, just like they had on the concert stage.

"Idiots, every last one of you!" she said, interrupting the reporter.

"Excuse me," he said. "Hang on–"

"These aren't the singing angels of your myths!" Daphna said, turning to the camera. "Everyone on Earth will die if you don't resist them. These *Malachim* will kill you all. If you think demons are violent, wait until you face the wrath of an angel!"

A security guard grabbed her arm, and she shouted, "Get the fuck off me!" With magic she threw him ten feet across the room, where he slammed into several people. Everyone gasped.

"Stay on her!" she heard someone say. "Keep the live feed going!"

She took a deep breath and scanned all their faces. This was a show of a different kind. "Do you recognize my face without makeup? Do you recognize this body without all its flashing gold? Yes, you called me Carina. But I have cast off that name. She was a ruse, engineered to make you love me. A plan designed by..." She swallowed. "By my mother. But she is dead now, and that plan has ended. My name is Daphna, and I am a demon."

Gasps in the room. Whispers.

"Yes, a demon." As a demonstration of her powers she held up her palm to reveal a wide lick of blue flame. The reporter beside her flinched and slid his chair away. The flame burned in her palm as she spoke. "I was born in the Shard known as Sheol. For eons you have been told stories of demonkind. You have been taught to fear us, that we lurk by the thousands in every square yard of Earth!

"But the only thing you should truly fear is your own ignorance. We are angry beings, yes. And much of that anger is justified. For eons we have been denied what you humans take for granted. Your Earth is fertile and abundant. But Sheol and a billion other Shards are words of endless suffering and torment. The cards, as you say, were stacked against us."

She paused, squinting in the bright lights. All the cameras were focused on her. How many millions were watching? She closed her fist, dousing the flame. "Many of my kind have come to Earth to pillage and seek revenge. They see your kind as undeserving of abundance and wish to take back what they see as their birthright. And I fully admit to helping them. But I will help them no longer.

"I have freed myself of Sheol's yoke. These Malachim – and you can pronounce it correctly, it's not that hard – they are not your angels of folklore. Malachim are identical to demons in every degree, but where demons have an overabundance of judgment, the Malachim have an overabundance of mercy.

"And so you must ask, where is the fault in having too much mercy? But consider the angel who stands idle while millions die, though by a whisper could save every last soul. These beings have always possessed the power to guide humanity away from your wars and plagues and your millennia of torments, but they have stood idle, choosing not to interfere, while you all suffer and die.

"And now, after all this time, they wish to intercede? I implore you, humanity, do not trust them! And neither should you trust my kin, the demons, who over the same epoch have only tried to usurp your abundance and drain your power."

She paused to let her words sink in, and not a soul stirred.

"Something happened a moment ago. Something small, which opened my eyes. A realization that has been building in me for a long time. I have just learned my mother has died, and a woman, whom I've only just met, comforted me. 'Why did you comfort me?' I asked her. 'Because I'm famous?' She said, 'No, because it would be inhuman not to. Because with all this craziness going on right now, we really need to come together."

"As this woman felt my pain, I feel yours." She pointed at the camera. "Yes, *you*, who watch me on your TV, and *you* on your computer screen. You, humanity. The Malachim wish to change your world. And when they're done, your Earth will be unrecognizable. I'm offering you a chance to come together, to help each other, with me as your guide. I promise, there will be no subterfuge this time. No magical coercions. I wear no make-up. I bear myself naked before you. I speak the truth that's in my heart, which beats like yours and hungers only to be known.

"Let me lead you in rebellion against these Malachim. I can't promise we will succeed in removing them from this Earth. But I can promise you that, with your help, we will give them what they deserve. We will give them fucking *hell*."

Silence filled the studio, but for the faint whir of ventilation fans. Across the room, in the doorway leading into the hall, Linda watched. She was staring at Daphna, and when Daphna met her eyes, Linda smiled.

ACKNOWLEDGEMENTS

This book wouldn't be possible without the generous help from many people. Specifically, my thanks go to Paul M. Berger, Richard Bowes, Mercurio David Rivera, Lilah Wild, and Danielle Friedman for their insightful feedback on early drafts of *Queen of Static*. Thanks to Darin Bradley for his edits of *King of Shards* and *Queen of Static*. To Mark Teppo for publishing the first version of *King of Shards* at Resurrection House. To all my Patrons for their enduring support, especially David Rheingold, Sondra Barrison, and Greer Woodward. And to all the reviewers, bloggers, podcasters, and fans who kept interest in *King of Shards* alive, keeping the the fire lit long enough for me to produce this sequel. And most especially, thanks to my wife, Christine, for her invaluable advice, support, and love in this epic, crazy adventure we call life.

MATTHEW KRESSEL is a writer and a software developer. He is a three-time Nebula Award Finalist, a World Fantasy Award Finalist, and a Eugie Award Finalist. *NPR Books* called his first novel *King of Shards*, "Majestic, resonant reality-twisting madness." His many works of short fiction have appeared in such publications as *Lightspeed, Clarkesworld, Analog, Tor.com, Nightmare, Beneath Ceaseless Skies,* and multiple *Year's Best* anthologies, as well as many other anthologies and magazines. His work has been translated into French, Spanish, Russian, Chinese, Czech, Romanian, Polish, and Japanese. As a software developer, he created the Moksha submissions system (moksha.io), in use by many of the largest fiction publishers today. And he is the co-host of Fantastic Fiction at KGB reading series in New York beside Ellen Datlow.

Find him at @mattkressel or at *www.matthewkressel.net.*